TRIP ME UP

AN OPPOSITES-ATTRACT STANDALONE
WORKPLACE ROMANCE

SYNERGY WORKPLACE ROMANCE
BOOK 3

MICHELLE MCCRAW

Cover by Qamber Designs

ISBN: 978-1-7368294-2-4
BN ISBN: 979-83692366-4-2
D2D ISBN: 979-82238547-3-9

BOOKS BY MICHELLE MCCRAW

40 and Fabulous

Fashion and Passion

Frenemies and Lovers

Books and Hookups

Conspiracies and Chemistry

Synergy Series

Work with Me

Friend Me

Trip Me Up

Boss Me

Forget Me

Tempt Me

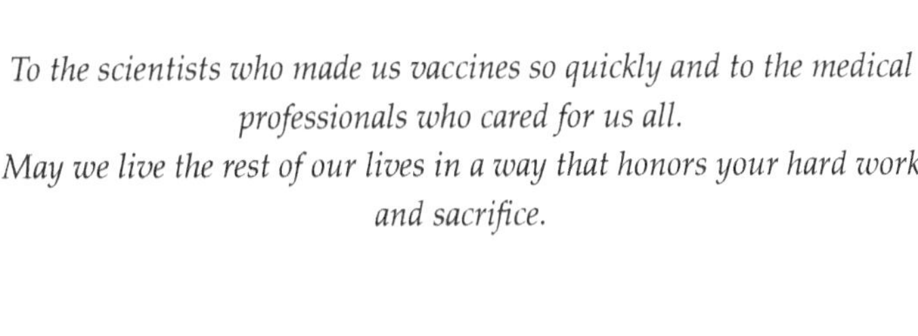

To the scientists who made us vaccines so quickly and to the medical
professionals who cared for us all.
May we live the rest of our lives in a way that honors your hard work
and sacrifice.

1

SAM

NOT EVERYONE WOULD SNEAK her dog into a fundraising luncheon. Her adorable, hardly-ever-barks, absolutely—well, mostly—nonshedding dog.

But, to my mother's never-ending disappointment, I'm not everyone.

Everyone wishes they had your advantages.

Everyone should marry someone who fits into their social circle. By that, she meant wealthy.

Everyone wants to be a Jones.

But at some point over the past twenty-five years, she should've realized that I'm a little…different.

"Bilbo Baggins," I hissed, lifting the white tablecloth of a large round table.

"Sam!"

Grimacing, I dropped the tablecloth and whirled toward my younger sister. She looked down at me from her sky-high heels, one hand on her hip and the other holding a pink cocktail that matched the baby pink of her silk dress. She always looked so effortless at these things. "What are you doing?" she whispered.

"Um, looking for an earring?"

Natalie squinted at me. "You're not wearing earrings."

"Oh. Then I guess I'm looking for two of them."

"Pearls. You should be wearing pearls." She scanned me from head to toe, and I nudged my huge black tote bag behind my back. "That suit is so two seasons ago. Didn't Mother send you a new one?"

I stared at the round toe of my low-heeled shoes, remembering how I'd dropped the lurid pink monstrosity at the donation box. This suit wasn't so bad. I'd bought it back when I still had new-clothes money, and it was my favorite color, black.

Natalie's voice was gentler than I'd heard it in a while. "Next time, tell her what you want."

"What I want is not to be here," I muttered.

"Oh, really? How would Dad have felt about that?" Her eyes went uncharacteristically shiny before she spun on her sparkly sandal and stalked off.

Dad? I made the mistake of glancing at his picture on the banner at the museum's entrance. He'd have been too busy working to come to an event like this, even though it was named after him. I rubbed the spot on my chest that ached, still, after fourteen years.

I wasn't there for him. Although I'd have rather been doing research or cuddling with Bilbo Baggins on my couch or having my appendix removed again, I was there for my mother. She demanded that her family show up picture-perfect at the foundation's events.

And that reminded me I needed to find Bilbo Baggins before she did. Where could he have gone? He wasn't usually shy. He wouldn't hide under a table. Unlike me, he'd be out in the center of the action, making friends. I turned in a circle, scanning the room.

A long buffet table took up one side of the high-ceilinged museum space. Mother usually hated the idea of people holding food, but dining tables wouldn't have fit with the large sculptures.

The other side of the room was scattered with smaller tables serving hors d'oeuvres. Maybe he'd gone to beg for a chicken wing. Not that Mother would ever serve messy chicken wings, but Bilbo Baggins didn't know that.

I'd taken one step in that direction when a silky-soft but steely hand clamped around my wrist. "Samantha, *what* is that?"

Frantic, I surveyed the area nearby. Had she seen him?

Pale, French-tipped fingers plucked at the strap of my tote bag. "Why didn't you leave your school bag at the coat check?"

I turned slowly to face her. "Mother, that's where I've got my wallet and keys." And my dog, too, before he'd made his grand escape.

Her red lips turned down. "What happened to the bag I gave you for your birthday?"

"It didn't match my suit." I waved my hand at my black pantsuit and white shirt. I didn't mention that when I'd sold the flowered fuchsia purse on eBay, it'd covered Bilbo Baggins' annual vet visit plus his heartworm preventative and allergy medications.

"Don't get me started on that suit," she muttered, brushing a speck off my shoulder. "Now, where is your date?"

"My date?"

"Yes, remember, I told you William Winford wanted to meet you."

"You didn't mention it was a date."

Her blue eyes, paler than mine, shifted to my collar, which she straightened. "He's very well respected. And brilliant. From what I hear, he's tripled his trust fund."

Don't let her get started on trust funds. "What's his line of business, drug kingpin? Weapons runner?"

Her mouth formed a shocked, red *O*. "Samantha Renée Jones, you know we don't associate with people like that."

"Mother, it was just a jo—"

"You can trust your family not to let you fall victim to people like that."

My lips parted. She wouldn't actually bring up my horrifying mistake here, would she? My heart raced.

"Samantha." She laid a hand on my sleeve. "You need to trust the people who love you. We'll help you find a partner who can support you."

"I can support myself." Maybe I made shitty decisions about men, but I didn't need her to match me up with a partner. I had a plan for my life. I crossed my arms. "The last thing I need is a partner."

"You need security. I've seen that hovel you live in. That's not—"

"Mother." My oldest brother's big hand settled on the shoulder of her jacket.

"Ah. Jackson." Her voice went all soft at my brother's name, the way it never did when she said mine.

He bent to kiss her cheek, but his crooked smile was all for me. "I need Sam for a minute."

"But I was going to introduce her to William Winford. You know, the *investment banker.*" She pursed her lips at me.

"She can meet your guy later. I have someone else in mind."

I narrowed my eyes at him. My brother didn't pimp me out or try to use me like some pawn in his business game. But he betrayed nothing under Mother's gaze.

"All right. I'll find you later, Samantha. With William." She stalked off, her heels clacking on the wood floor.

"What the hell, Jacks—"

"You didn't happen to bring that oversized rat you call a dog here, did you?" He flicked my tote bag.

I sucked in a breath. "Did you see him?"

"Over by the charcuterie table."

"Oh, no." With Jackson right behind, I scurried toward the table filled with platters of meats and cheeses. I squatted and pulled up the cloth draping it, but the space under the table was empty. "He's not here."

"Sam, why would you bring your dog to Mother's party?"

I stood and patted my tote like Bilbo Baggins could've magically reappeared where he belonged. With my dog against my side, my hands had stopped trembling, and my heart rate had eased from hummingbird speed down to frightened rabbit. "I don't know." But I couldn't help glancing at the giant banner of my larger-than-life dad's face.

His smile drooped. "I hate it, too, Samwise. But people pay big bucks to come here and eat fancy cheese, and the money goes to a good cause."

Dad's favorite cause, he didn't have to say.

"I know, but—" The Jones Foundation events were the worst. People wanted to talk about books, which I didn't read anymore, or Dad, which made my heart ache like he'd been gone only a year and not more than half my life. "Why can't they just write checks and leave me out of it?"

He shrugged. "Like it or not, you're a Jones."

I couldn't escape my name, not here in San Francisco. But someday—a year from now, if I could turn around my dissertation project—I'd be able to break out. I'd find a research professorship somewhere far away in the middle of the country where Mother wouldn't go. South Dakota or Iowa or even Arkansas. It didn't matter to me where, as long as it didn't have any designer boutiques or donors. All I needed was a computer lab and an apartment big enough for me and—

"Bilbo Baggins," I hissed again, low. With his giant ears, he should've been able to hear me even under the noisy luncheoneers.

"Look, we'll divide up and search. You cover this half of the room, and I'll check over by the buffet table."

"What if he ran outside?" There were foxes and hawks, maybe even coyotes, in the surrounding park.

"That dog would never leave you, Samwise. He just went looking for a snack. We'll find him."

The inside of my nose burned a little as I reached out and squeezed Jackson's arm. "Thanks."

"Don't worry about it. This is much more entertaining than talking to stuffy literary types. Hey, remember how we used to hunt for gnomes in that game we made together?"

"Gnome Dome? That was years ago." Ancient history. "And Bilbo Baggins is a lot trickier than the gnomes we programmed."

"He's pretty predictable around snacks." He winked before heading across to the buffet.

I turned back toward the hors d'oeuvres tables. He had to be over there, begging for a treat. I scanned the floor. No sign of his black fur.

A laugh, rich and deep, caught my attention. It wasn't the polite chuckle people used to signal their usually-false amusement at these things. It was pure and unrestrained. And loud. I glanced over to see who'd violated the social contract.

He was big and...and glowing, like he was on fire on the inside. His hair was the same color the sky had been during the wildfires last summer, a deep russet. Golden freckles coated his skin. He had the physique of someone who played one of those sports where you carry a ball on a field, broad across the shoulders and tapered below. Someone who'd look more natural in a fur-lined cloak and gripping an ax than wearing a charcoal-gray suit and holding a—

"Bilbo Baggins!" I skidded to a stop in front of the Viking.

"Excuse me?" With one oversized, freckled hand, he cuddled Bilbo Baggins closer against his chest. He walloped me with a pair of blue eyes. No. They were green. Flecks of gold lit them like sparks. His lashes were red. Was there a Norse god of flame? Because this guy was a bonfire, toasty warm but also popping with danger.

I checked right and left before I edged closer. More softly, I said, "That's my dog. Bilbo Baggins."

"This guy, here?" He looked down into Bilbo Baggins' bulging brown eyes. Bilbo Baggins flicked out his pink tongue to lick the man's clean-shaven chin, then squirmed in his grip. "He looks more like Toto than a Hobbit."

I couldn't arch an eyebrow like Natalie could, but I raised both of mine. "And does that make you the Wicked Witch of the West, kidnapping my dog?" Movie references, I could do. This guy looked more like a linebacker than a librarian; if we stayed in the shallow water, I wouldn't have to betray my literary ignorance.

A smile spread like honey across his face. "Kidnapping? More like safekeeping. It appears that Bilbo Baggins was ready for a quest. Bringing the excitement to his humdrum life."

"Excitement is overrated." My stomach hollowed. I couldn't even meet Bilbo Baggins' eyes. "I know I shouldn't have brought him. It's just that—" I pressed my lips together. I couldn't tell this stranger I needed my tiny dog to fend off the emotions that threatened me here.

"Hey, hey." He waited until I looked up again. "It's okay. He's safe now. See? I've got him." Bilbo Baggins sighed and pressed into his chest.

I wished I could've snuggled up to him, too.

The man chuckled. "Sure, there's plenty of room for you both."

"Shit, I said that out loud, didn't I?"

"'No legacy is so rich as honesty.'" He glanced around the room. "Though you couldn't tell that from this crowd."

I tilted my head to the side. "That sounds like Benjamin Franklin."

"Shakespeare, actually."

"Oh." Despite his appearance, despite his assessment of the fundraiser attendees, he was one of the literary types. "I'll take Bilbo Baggins back now."

His red eyebrows crunched together, but he extended Bilbo Baggins toward me, and my dog swam his tiny, fluffy feet right into my arms. I snuggled him close against my chest. Too close, I discovered when he let out a belch.

"You didn't happen to feed him cheese, did you?"

The Viking uncurled his other hand and showed me a crumpled napkin holding a single orange cube. "Just one or two pieces."

I grimaced. "I'm going to get him out of here before he sh— before he has gastric distress, I mean." I wrinkled my nose. "He doesn't tolerate dairy."

"Sorry about that. He seemed to like it." His voice, like his laugh, was low and rich. I didn't blame Bilbo Baggins for running to him. Hell, I'd snuggle up against this man while he fed me snacks.

A hint of stinky cheese smell wafted into my nose. I scooped Bilbo Baggins into my tote.

"He does like cheese, right up to the moment his little intestines let loose." Was that too much information? Probably. When I was nervous, my mouth was more unrestrained than Bilbo Baggins' bowels after eating Muenster.

He winced. "I really am sorry."

"It's okay. It'll give me an excuse to leave early." But my feet stayed right there in front of the friendly giant who'd rescued my dog.

"I'm Niall Flynn." He stuck out his right hand.

"Samantha." My hand disappeared into his much larger one, his fingers so long that they brushed the sensitive skin at my wrist. My heartbeat quickened, and I sucked in a breath.

He grimaced. "Sorry. Rough hands."

It was true. Calluses roughened his palm and each of the fingers that covered the back of my hand. Most of the men at these things did nothing more strenuous than click a mouse, and their hands were smoother than mine. Niall had to be an athlete. The foundation partnered with a few pro sportsballers.

"It's okay. I—I like it." I eyed the way his suit coat sleeves stretched over his biceps. My friend Marlee would tell me to go for it. Flirt. Have a drink with him. But I was no Marlee. I must've been in the computer lab when they gave the lessons on hair-tossing and small talk. On the conversational scale of light banter to deadly serious, I generally came off as an eleven—intense.

Realizing he was still gripping my hand, I tugged it out of his grasp. "Well, thanks for saving Bilbo Baggins from being spiked by someone's heel."

"Wait." He was studying me, a slow perusal of my face, like some people looked at art, not like the mental math most people did when they looked at a Jones.

I blinked. "Do I have something on my face?"

He shook his head. "Sorry, I—I guess I was just surprised to find someone like you here."

"Someone like me?" I wrinkled my nose. "What's that supposed to mean?" What had he figured out about me in our ten minutes together?

"Someone…real. And yet not. It's like you're going to turn into a woodland creature when the sun goes down." His face went red, even the freckles.

"Like in *Ladyhawke?*"

"Yeah, like—"

"Niall! There you are." A woman about my height, with curly dark hair and tawny skin, gripped Niall's sleeve. A volley of clicks behind her told me she'd brought a photographer. I cringed and turned my back to the sound. "What are you doing hiding over here? We need to get you out and circulating."

"I was talking to Samantha." He held out his hand toward me. No way was I getting pulled into his photo op. Each click of the shutter added to the cold weight in my belly. How could I have been so wrong again? He was no gentle giant. He was some minor celebrity here to dump cash for publicity.

Or worse, he was like Stephen, luring me into his trap, waiting to spring it. Somehow, he'd connected me to the Jones family even though I hadn't given him my last name. Blast that ridiculous family portrait they stuck on an easel for these events. I'd been ten with my straight dark hair in a zigzag part, a closed-mouth smile hiding my braces, and eyes too big for my face. Now my hair was back in a low ponytail and the braces were gone, but I still looked like that prepubescent kid too clueless to know she was about to lose her dad.

The woman's gaze turned on me, even more penetrating than Niall's had been. "What's your last name, Samantha?"

"Gabi," Niall said, "I need another minute with Samantha." I didn't usually like my full name, but the way it rolled out in his low voice made me shiver. Or maybe that was a warning tremor from Bilbo Baggins. What could Niall need another minute to do? Brush the dog hair off my suit for a photo? Once, I'd been willing to be a decoration on a man's arm, smiling for pictures I didn't want. Never again.

I raised my palms in front of my chest like I could push them both away. "It's cool. We're done. Nice meeting you, Niall." I strode toward the exit, leaving Niall and his entourage in front of the charcuterie.

When we reached a grassy patch outside the museum, Bilbo Baggins leaped from my tote bag to rid himself of the evil cheese, staring at me like I'd betrayed him. "That was your new friend, Niall, who poisoned you," I said as I cleaned up the mess. "And he totally wasn't worth it. He's just like Winford Whatsit. Wants to use me like an ID badge for getting into shitty parties like that." I shook the plastic bag of dog shit. "I'm no one's golden ticket. I'm getting my doctorate and getting out of here. Understand?"

Bilbo Baggins cocked his head.

"I know. You get it." I tossed the bag into the trash and spread sanitizer gel over my hands.

As I clipped the leash to his collar, my phone buzzed from the outside pocket of my tote. Dr. Martell's pattern. He usually respected my weekends. Maybe he'd forgotten about some tests he needed graded.

"Hi, Dr. Martell."

"Samantha. I thought I'd get your voice mail. Didn't you have some party this afternoon?"

"I—I'm all done." I led Bilbo Baggins to a bench and sat down, easing off my heels.

"Good. Good." I could practically hear his brain switching back to research mode. I'd always liked my adviser's focus on what was important.

"We need to talk about your research. Monday morning at nine, my office."

My stomach gurgled like I'd eaten the bad cheese, too. "I know it hasn't been going that well, but—"

"Don't worry, Samantha. It's an opportunity."

The last opportunity he'd given me had taken me down a rabbit hole, and I was still trying to steer the project back in the right direction. "An opportunity."

"You'll love it. See you Monday."

There was no question in his voice. He oversaw not only my stipend but also my doctorate. Without his signature on my dissertation, I'd be the Ph.D.-free version of Samantha Jones, unable to get the research position I needed to escape. "Okay," I said.

He'd already hung up.

I dropped the phone into my pocket. "Let's go home, Bilbo Baggins." I toed back into my shoes and stood. Passing the row of black Mercedes and Bentleys and Jackson's garish yellow Lamborghini, I trudged toward the nearest bus stop.

2

NIALL

I COULDN'T DENY it as I walked into my hotel suite and tossed the key card onto the counter in the kitchenette.

My fingers tingled.

Still, I didn't dare hope. It might've been the champagne I'd drunk or the choking formalwear.

As I tugged at the tie Gabi hadn't let me take off, even in the car, she tossed her purse next to the key card and tapped at her phone. "Still sulking?"

"Of course not." I fiddled with the buttons on my dress shirt and tried to smile at her, but she didn't look up from her device. She'd done so much for me: the book deal, the TV show. Sticking with me on this long promotional slog. I shouldn't have been mad at her. Until I remembered the way Samantha's big, beautiful eyes had turned to slate when that photographer started snapping pictures.

Big? Beautiful? I was a writer; I could do better than that. Or maybe I wasn't a writer anymore. Were you still a writer if you hadn't written a word in over a month? Was it a qualification you had to renew, like an organic farm certification? Or was it something that stuck for life, like Grandpa's veteran status? It felt like a muscle I'd allowed to atrophy from disuse, too weak to work the way it used to.

Except...my fingers tingled.

"Well, well, well." Gabi ran her gaze over me, finally distracted from her phone. "It's not like I haven't seen it before, but most of my clients prefer to keep their clothes on in front of their agent."

Without even thinking about it, I'd stripped out of my jacket, shirt, and shoes, and I stood in the middle of the hotel room wearing only my suit pants.

"Shit. Sorry." I scooped up the discarded clothes and strode into the suite's smaller bedroom. When I was dressed in jeans, a soft T-shirt, and a flannel shirt unbuttoned over it like a jacket, I walked out into the living room.

Gabi sat on the couch, still wearing her cayenne-red dress. She tapped on her phone. "We got some good pictures today. Qiana will be ecstatic. You and Audrey and Natalie Jones, you with that sci-fi writer—" She snapped her fingers.

"Tamarah Starr."

"That's the one. Though I wish you could've gotten one with that Samantha woman. I think she's a Jones, too. She had that look."

"A Jones?"

She rolled her eyes. "The family in charge of the literacy foundation? The dad, Jasper, died young before his company really took off, but now they're rolling in cash. They say the dad was into books, and that's why they created the foundation. Or maybe it's just a tax write-off. Who knows? Anyway, the mom, Audrey, runs the foundation. The daughters are socialites, and the sons are in tech like their dad."

Samantha hadn't looked like a socialite. She'd looked as uncomfortable as I'd felt. That minuscule dog of hers trotting up to me and scrabbling at my ankles had been the highlight of my afternoon—until Samantha herself skidded up.

She hadn't talked like a socialite, either. She'd been unguarded, open. Unlike every one of those plastic, wind-up-doll people there. Including me.

Until Gabi and her photographer had walked up, and she'd frozen stiff like a startled deer. What would've happened if Gabi hadn't interrupted us? Would we have dug a little deeper, exposed a sliver of ourselves, made a real connection that wasn't about what I could do for her and what she could do for me? *Synergy.* That was the word they tossed around here like my friends and I used to chuck pinecones out in the woods.

Speaking of plastic people… "No email from—from him?"

Gabi stopped tapping her phone and looked up, pity softening her brown eyes. "No, sorry, honey. But I got the shipping notice that the copy of your book was delivered to his office."

I shook my head like Sally, our goat, shook off flies. "Doesn't matter. I'm sure he's busy."

"I'm sure he is." She pressed her lips together for a second and then burst out, "But he's your dad. He could have texted."

Ironic, that. My dad was the CEO of one of the most successful phone technology companies in the world, and he couldn't be bothered to text his son. Rather, he hadn't texted my agent, since the remnants of the last phone he'd given me were at the bottom of our farm's pond.

Next to Gabi, on the end table under a copy of *Publisher's Weekly* and the mystery novel she was reading, the too-new, too-stiff red cover of my writing notebook poked out. My fingers tingled.

I walked to the table, tentatively, like I'd have approached a frightened calf or a wounded dog. Something that might lash out at me and injure me if I wasn't careful. I put a hand on the book and the magazine and slowly slid out the notebook.

Gabi watched me do it. Maybe she held her breath, too.

"You going to write tonight?"

"I dunno." Better not jinx it, tingling fingers be damned. They'd tricked me before.

She slid forward and picked up one of my favorite pens from the coffee table, the kind with the fast-drying ink that didn't smear as I dragged my hand over the words. "Here." Then she wavered for a second, like she didn't want to break the bubble of magic around me. "Want me to go somewhere else?"

"No, I—" I hadn't thought about where I'd take the notebook. But a whiff of eucalyptus, real or imagined, resolved me. "I'm going to the park."

She glanced out the window. "Just a few hours of daylight left."

"It'll be enough." I wouldn't presume that my muse would stick with me for more than a few seconds, certainly not hours.

"Still, better take a flashlight." She hopped up, went into her bedroom, and came out with a pocket-sized flashlight. She held it out to me. "Just in case."

I nodded like she'd given me the detonator for the bomb that was going to blow up the evil mastermind's lair. Although we'd blamed it on the TV deal and the consulting I'd done on the scripts, we both knew how serious my writer's block had been. Already a month late with my pages, I'd asked her to negotiate an extension with my book editor. Unfortunately, that meant a delay in our advance. Mom and Grandpa needed that money to buy organic fertilizer. Gabi would need her cut for rent and groceries when we finally got off this tour. And she wouldn't say it, not now when I'd reached for my notebook for the first time in a month, but the TV people were getting nervous. Without a second book, they couldn't make plans for a second season of the show. And we both knew what Heidi would say if we asked for another extension.

I tucked the flashlight into my jeans pocket and slid the pen inside the spiral binding. Picking up the key card from the counter, I slipped out, creeping down the hall and out the door as if any sounds would startle my muse.

Outside, the sun perched a couple handwidths from the tops

of the trees in the park across the street. I caught another whiff of eucalyptus. The trees called me.

Dodging cars, I crossed the street. I didn't bother with finding an entrance; instead, I climbed the berm directly into the forest. The trees welcomed me with caresses from their leafy branches. Less than a minute's walk into the park, the sounds of the city muted.

Sparrows called to each other. Squirrels chittered. I meandered among prickly live oak and fragrant eucalyptus, picking my way through ferns, filling my nostrils with the sharp scent of pine and humus.

A butterfly glided by my shoulder and I could almost imagine it was a sprite coming to whisper in my ear. It swooped away into the dimness, leaving me alone.

The deeply fissured trunk of a Monterey pine, not so different from the white pines at home, begged to be stroked. My hands had softened, the farming calluses still there but smoother after months without farm chores. Only the callus on the side of my left middle finger remained, and even it had shrunk.

I leaned back against the trunk and slid down to sit at its base. I pressed my back into the ridges of bark. Damp earth seeped into my jeans, and if I ignored the eucalyptus, it smelled just like summer in the woods on the farm. When I was a kid, every chance I got, I'd race off into the woods to lie on the forest floor and dream of wood elves and sprites and trolls.

If only one of those wood elves would pop out and tell me how to finish the story.

Tilting my head, I peered up into the canopy. A city person like Gabi might've taken the dappled patch for sunlight coming through the trees, but that was a spotted owl. She sat perfectly still on the branch.

So far, I hadn't written any owls into the story. One of them could fly in to rescue Nieven, who, in the last scene I'd written, had fallen with his horse, Winter, through a hole into a giant spider's lair. Ugh, no. I could hear the critics' words: uninspired, predictable, derivative. Lazy. Plus, there was the horse. Suspension of disbelief was one thing, but no way would readers buy an owl pulling a horse out of a hole.

The owl's spots, white on brown, stirred something in my brain. Not white on brown, but brown on white. Freckles. A constellation of them, no makeup to conceal them, across Samantha's nose. That nose she'd wrinkled at me when I'd compared her dog to Toto.

And her eyes.

No one who'd met Samantha could forget her eyes. Dark blue. No, dammit, I was a writer, a wordsmith. I didn't need a freaking membership card or certification. Indigo. Violet. The distant mountains. Night sky above the farm. Lobelia spilling from the pots Mom planted every spring.

Lobelia. A proper name for an elf. No, a fairy. Samantha could've been one, with her spare frame and delicate features. The black suit she wore like armor. A little more leather, and perhaps a cloak, and she'd have fit right into one of my stories. A faerie? A pixie? Warmer.

A sprite. A wood sprite. That was it. And if I gave the wood sprite wings, she could fly down into the spider's lair.

What would Lobelia say to Nieven? Samantha and I had talked about cheese. Her dog. And, briefly, *Ladyhawke.* Only the greatest fantasy movie ever. Maybe, if Gabi hadn't found me so soon, we could've talked about books. Or why she was at the fundraiser, seemingly unwillingly. Our hopes and dreams. Something real. If the photographer hadn't chased her away, I could've gotten her number.

But that horse had left the barn, and, shit, I'd forgotten—again —about Winter. How would a tiny wood sprite get a full-grown elf and his steed out of the trap?

I stared at the owl gripping the branch with her talons. A wood sprite would have some sort of tree magic, perhaps. Sprites helped the trees bud in the spring and turned the leaves colors in the fall. She could cause a tree root to grow down inside the hole and create a ladder—no, a staircase—for Nieven and Winter to use to escape. Add the big, hairy spider right on their heels, and—

I opened my notebook, flipped it over so the metal spiral wouldn't dig into my writing hand, and set the pen to the top of the page. *Chapter 17,* I wrote, *The Escape.* But not even my ritual could get me to focus on Nieven and his predicament, could dispel the image of her blue eyes laughing up at me. So I began to write about them. About her.

My hands tingling, the words flowed.

Like the burbling stream on the farm, like the salty wind off the Pacific Ocean that curled between the trees in the park, the words poured out of my pen into the notebook. Maybe Lobelia was there in the forest, whispering them into my ear. Right then, I didn't give a flying fuck whose words they were.

They were words.

When I scratched a word into a page that resisted my pen, I squinted to focus my burning, bleary eyes on the notebook. I'd hit the stiff cover. The end of the thick notebook. I flipped back through pages of scrawled words I couldn't read. The sky had gone purple in the gaps of the leafy canopy overhead, and thick shadows concealed the forest floor. The spotted owl was gone.

When I stood, cool air hit my jeans, damp from the dirt. The chill had penetrated my muscles, and I stretched to uncramp them, shaking out my left hand. But the cold, the aches, the subsiding tingle in my fingers were all the best kind of discomfort. The well-earned kind.

But I wasn't done. I needed more pages. As I jogged back toward the hotel, my brain remained in the mythical forest with Nieven, who now owed Lobelia his life and was about to lose his heart to her, too.

3

SAM

I SHOVED the hanger with the black suit into the far side of the closet, the one with the silly, girly dresses Mother made me wear to Sunday brunch and the shiny black evening gown I never wanted to have to wear again. From the center of the closet, I pulled out a pair of cargo pants, bought second-hand and already worn to softness, in a black so faded you might call it gray.

I already wore a long-sleeved black T-shirt, similarly washed and faded. After pulling on the pants, I laced up my combat boots.

Bilbo Baggins danced by the door of my apartment. He knew what the boots meant.

"We have to be quick today, okay, Bilbo Baggins? I've got to get to campus." For the meeting with Martell. About the *opportunity*. The heaviness in my empty stomach told me I wasn't going to like this opportunity.

Bilbo Baggins quivered as I hooked his tiny harness around him. He pranced along the hallway, his short legs churning so quickly I trotted to keep up. He led me down the stairs and out onto the street, where people smiled and waved at him. They mostly ignored me. I was only the leash holder to the charming dog with the outsized personality.

I hurried him along, and fifteen minutes later, I locked him inside my apartment with fresh water and his dog bed placed where it'd be warmed by the sun. Then I trudged the few blocks to campus.

What could Martell want to talk about? He probably wanted a status update on my project since I'd been avoiding him. My A.I., CASE, was supposed to take research results and turn them into a scholarly paper. I'd envisioned academics everywhere uploading their data into CASE, which would output a ready-for-submission paper in seconds. No more writing for weeks or months, taking valuable time away from their research. How much more efficient could CASE make researchers? How much more quickly would science advance? I'd boggled my own mind with the possibilities.

But CASE had a mind of its own. Instead of acceptable output like, *The hollow spherical structure of C60 with 30 conjugated carbon–carbon double bonds and unoccupied lowest molecular orbital enables it to remove excess free radicals*, it wrote, *C60's strangely beautiful structure could only have been designed by creatures of myth.*

Loading up the A.I. with works of fiction to give it a more solid grasp of language might've been a mistake.

Then, late one night, I'd forgotten to upload the dummy data. I woke up the next morning to a full-fledged novel that CASE had titled *Magician in the Machine*. When CASE had read it aloud to me, I'd laughed at the nonsensical story, which centered on a magician who lived inside the landscape of a computer's CPU and fought an evil necromancer and his zombie army. The Magician had died at the end of the story, though not before heroically defeating The Necromancer. The zombies had survived and taken over the silicon kingdom.

I'd sent it to Martell as a joke. But the next day, he'd found me in my tiny office and asked if CASE could produce more stories like that. I'd shrugged. What was the point? The only way *Magician in the Machine* could help researchers was if it helped them get to sleep at night so they'd be clearer-headed when they resumed their work.

Martell couldn't be about to cancel my stipend, could he? My belly clenched. But, like Dad used to tell me about challenges at school, the only way out was through. And I had to get through this meeting with my adviser to escape the Jones name's reach.

I flashed my badge at the entrance to the comfortingly bland computer science building and climbed the stairs to the third floor. As I stomped down the hall in my boots, Kyle leaned out the doorway of our shared office.

"Hey, Sam, a bunch of us are going out later. Want to come with?"

"I don't think so." My response had become automatic. The second I'd rolled off him last month, I'd realized that adding benefits to my friendship with my officemate was a terrible idea. Sure, I preferred orgasms that didn't require batteries, but sleeping with Kyle wasn't like my one-night stands on the other side of campus.

Regret had washed through me as soon as the endorphin rush faded. I'd felt something when I'd gazed into Kyle's kind eyes. Fondness, maybe. But fondness was a feeling, and I didn't do those anymore. I'd never again let myself be vulnerable. The inevitable pain wasn't worth it.

Stephen had knocked me so far off track that I almost hadn't graduated. It was why I was still in California for grad school and not on the East Coast like I'd planned. How could I know Kyle didn't want something from me, something he'd use my sex-lowered barriers to get? Nothing, not Kyle or anyone else, was going to keep me from finishing my dissertation and getting my first post-doc research position hundreds of miles from the nearest direct flight from SFO.

"Okay, maybe next time." With a wry smile, he retreated to his desk, and I trudged to the end of the hall and Martell's door.

I knocked, and at his gruff, "Come in," I turned the handle and walked in.

Dr. Martell had pushed aside the four large computer monitors for an unobstructed view of the guest chairs on the other side of his desk. The one on the right was empty. But someone sat in the one on the left.

She stood when I entered, her salt-and-pepper bob swinging as she turned. She was shorter than me, petite, but energy hovered around her like a halo.

"Samantha." Martell also stood. "Meet my friend, Heidi Lentz. Heidi and I went to undergraduate together—"

"Let's not talk about how many years ago that was." Heidi's smile was sharp. "We'll just say that John and I have known each other for a long time."

I shook her icy hand. "Do you also work in computer science?" My adviser had mentioned an opportunity. Was Heidi a venture capitalist who wanted to give us cash for CASE?

"No." She tinkled out a laugh that would've belonged at one of Mother's events. "I went into publishing when John went off to grad school. I worked my way up through a number of larger publishers until I started my own press a few years ago."

"Oh?" My attention had already started to drift to the rubber band–bound stack of papers on Martell's otherwise clean desk. I would have struggled to read it anyway, but upside-down, there was no hope.

Martell pointed at the empty chair, and as I sat, he said, "Samantha, Heidi runs Happy Troll, a small but growing science fiction and fantasy publisher."

"We're avant-garde. Innovative. Boundary-pushing," Heidi added, raising her eyebrows at me like I'd understand why she was here, talking to me.

I didn't. "That's nice."

Heidi's nostrils flared. "John shared a very interesting manuscript with me. *Magician in the Machine.*"

My breath whooshed out like she'd punched me in the stomach. "What?"

"I understand it was generated by artificial intelligence. It came out of the computer like that? You didn't edit it, or get a friend to do it?"

"No, I—" What was happening here? "CASE produced it, just like I sent it to Dr. Martell."

"And CASE is your A.I.?"

"It's an acronym for Computer Analysis and Synthesis Engine. For producing scholarly papers."

"But it produced *Magician.*"

"Yes." I scrunched up my nose. We were going in circles.

"I understand"—Heidi tapped her chin—"most programmers use source material to teach the A.I. how to write. Is that how you programmed CASE?"

"Um, yeah. I mean yes." Heidi was awfully smart for someone who didn't study computer science.

"Are the authors of this source material"—she raised her dark eyebrows—"dead?"

"Yes." Dad's favorites had been the classics, J.R.R. Tolkien, C.S. Lewis, Octavia Butler, Madeleine L'Engle, so I'd loaded those. "Except—" The last one I'd input, the one the university librarian had recommended, had been a recent title. The letters on the cover swirled in my memory. "Something about elves. By Nail Flying."

Her lips curved into a smile. *"Secrets of the Wood Elves* by Niall Flynn, you mean?"

My face heated while I wrestled with the letters in my memory. I knew that name. The image of a burly, redheaded man cradling Bilbo Baggins at the fundraiser last weekend stalled my brain. "Niall Flynn the…athlete?"

"No, he's a writer."

A writer? We'd talked about movies. *Ladyhawke.*

Heidi's sharp voice pulled me back to Martell's office. "He's the only living author you used?"

"That's right."

"Not a problem, then. I'd like to publish *Magician in the Machine.* Having the world's first fully A.I.-generated novel would be perfectly on-brand for Happy Troll."

"Publish it? You mean an article about it in an academic journal?"

Her nostrils flared again. "No, Samantha. I mean, put it on bookstore fiction shelves. Sell the ebook online. Produce an audiobook in a computer-generated voice if I can swing it."

Dr. Martell said, "Because CASE runs on university servers, *Magician in the Machine* technically belongs to the university. I've already agreed to let Happy Troll publish it."

"Oh. Okay." I could almost feel the vibration of the basement server room through the floors. Thousands of servers hummed down there, and one of them ran CASE's code. So I was here as an FYI?

"You're probably wondering why we called you here," Heidi said, her voice gentling in a way I knew meant the ask was coming.

I nodded. Did they want CASE to write another book? A sequel? It would be an interesting problem to solve since *Magician in the Machine* had come out as a fluke, and the main characters were all dead. What if I—

"I'm not yet ready to reveal the novel's provenance. I want to ensure it's successful before we do that. So I need an author." She leaned back in her chair.

I blinked away thoughts of setting up the sequel's parameters. "You're a publisher. Don't you have a ton of authors?"

"My authors are all writing more books. I need you."

Everything, from the tip of my nose to my toes, went numb like she'd plunged me into ice water. "Me?"

"I need an author's name to put on the cover."

"Why does it need to be my name?"

She exchanged a glance with Martell. "Because of your connection with the book. It's simpler that way."

I narrowed my eyes. "What's simpler?" Mother's simple things—like Saturday's fundraiser—always had a complication, like Winford Whosit.

"As an incentive"—Martell leaned forward—"I'd be willing to

fast-track your dissertation approval. There would be no need to complete the original scope of your plan. You could start writing your dissertation now based on what you've done."

"Now?" I massaged sensation back into my fingers. I'd save myself months of work on CASE, finding and fixing the bugs that made it write such flowery words. There'd be no question about walking across the stage next spring, taking my diploma from the university president's hand, then hopping on a plane with Bilbo Baggins—two or three planes would be even better—to some remote university, where I could start again. Without the dark history and mistrust, I'd be free to make a difference in the world on my own terms. If I could work the bugs out of CASE, maybe it would help researchers.

Bonus: I'd escape Mother's machinations forever.

The happy thought must've shown on my face because Heidi leaned back. "There's one condition to our deal."

"A condition?" I leaned forward.

"You will say you wrote the novel. You will not make any connections between *Magician in the Machine* and CASE or artificial intelligence until I announce it."

I hated lying. Besides, no one who knew me would believe it. I pictured my mother's face across the table at Sunday brunch saying, "Samantha, how did *you* write a novel?"

But in the end, the lie would get me out of a lot of Sunday brunches. And setups with guys like Winford. Like Stephen.

"Can we use a fake name?"

"Of course we can use a pen name. All I need is for you to be the person behind the name." Heidi steepled her fingers under her chin.

It was for science. For CASE. I could take my original idea to a different lab, far, far away, and make it into what I'd envisioned: a timesaver for scientists. It would fast-track so many investigations. Like heart disease prevention. To keep other little girls from losing their daddies.

"Okay. I'll do it."

Heidi's lips curled up into the approximation of a smile. "Excellent. I'll send the papers to John for your signature."

That sounded like dismissal to me. "Can I go now?" I asked Martell. My skin felt tight the way it had when I'd run out of Kyle's apartment while he stood in his boxers in the doorway with his eyebrows scrunched.

"Of course, Samantha. I'm sure you agree this will be an excellent opportunity for the department and the university."

"Sure." At that point, I didn't care about the department or the university. I ignored the heaviness in my gut. For science.

But I should've cared. I should've cared about the papers I was about to sign without reading them and about the lies that were already starting to wrap me up like prey in a spider's web.

4

NIALL

I FOLLOWED Gabi through the maze of white tablecloths in the bayside restaurant toward where Heidi sat, waving, at a table by the window. The bubbly notes of the '90s song "Breakfast at Tiffany's" played counterpoint to the tinkle of flatware on china.

Speeding up to catch Gabi, I whispered in her ear, "Don't mention I was blocked, okay? It's all good now." It was only partly a lie. My fingers had tingled for a few days after that fundraiser. But my muse was fickle, prone to abandoning me when I needed her most.

"You fucking better be good now. I need my fifteen percent in October. My nieces and nephews want Christmas presents from tía Gabi."

My chest tightened. Gabi was making light of it, but both my family and my best-friend-slash-agent needed cash. I'd lock myself in a closet for a week with a case of Red Bull before I'd accept another extension that'd push payday out again.

"Niall!" Heidi stood when we reached her table and beckoned me down for a hug. I bent and gently patted her delicate shoulders. She was strong, though, and her wiry little arms banded around my chest. After she hugged Gabi, I took the chair closest to the window where I could steal glances at the lowering clouds outside. Their undersides were dark, promising rain. Was the farm getting rain? I needed to call home soon.

In the potted tree on the other side of the glass, a song sparrow perched and opened its beak. Too bad I couldn't hear its call over the loud restaurant music, which transitioned to A-Ha's "Take On Me." Gabi swept into the chair beside me, across from Heidi.

"Thanks for meeting me before I have to go back to New York," Heidi said, checking her phone. "Where are you off to next?"

Gabi tapped on her phone. "We leave for Comic-Con on Saturday."

"Better you than me. I need to be in my office to get any work done." Heidi looked up from her own phone. "How's the book going, Niall?"

I choked on the water I'd dared to sip, and Gabi slapped my back. Finally, I spluttered, "Fine."

"Good, good. On track to meet your deadline?"

"I'll make it."

Heidi tore her gaze from her phone at my growl.

"Of course he will." Gabi glared at me before she turned a sparkling smile on Heidi. "You'll love the new character he's introduced. He's just adding those last, magical touches."

"Oh?" Heidi speared me with her shrewdest stare. "A love interest for Nieven?" She'd been pushing for a romantic subplot since she'd bought my first book.

"Maybe." I wasn't sure yet. After Lobelia freed Nieven and Winter from the spider's lair, she'd gone cold and silent. Nieven bumbled along the way he usually did, but so far, Lobelia hadn't had anything to say to either the wood elf or me.

"I thought Nieven might end up with Greva." Heidi's phone buzzed, and she glanced at it.

I didn't look at Gabi. Instead, I picked up my menu. She knew I'd modeled Nieven and Greva's friendship after ours. And although we'd dated in college—briefly, until that ill-fated visit to the wifi-free farm—we worked better as friends. And business partners. Like Nieven and Greva. "Who says there has to be a love interest at all?"

The *Friends* theme song started to play. The music was going to put me off my lunch.

"No one," Heidi said, her tone bland. "I can't wait to read this new character."

"Are we still planning to release next summer?" Gabi asked.

"Actually..." Heidi's smile hid a secret. "We're moving you up."

"Up?" Gabi dropped her menu onto the table and picked up her phone. "Send me the new schedule?"

"How much up?" My heart lodged in my throat, cutting off my breath.

"We have an opportunity for a one-two punch." Heidi stabbed at her phone. I wished I could hurl it out the window. "I can't say anything until it's officially announced, but I've signed a Very Exciting Book." Heidi had a way of capitalizing her speech like that. "It's an urban-fantasy-slash-sci-fi crossover, and it'll have Synergy with your fanbase. It comes out in a few months, and I'm expecting a lot of Buzz for it. Maybe even a Movie Contract. Your studio is reading it now, and they've agreed to cofund a Joint Tour. I've asked Qiana to set it up. In February. It's an excellent opportunity for you."

I couldn't swallow. I was going to pass out if I didn't get air soon.

"February?" Gabi repeated.

"We're already promoting *Treachery of the Wood Elves*. We'll have to fast-track it, but I don't want to miss this Opportunity."

"Of course not." Gabi beamed, but under the table, she kicked my shin. Hard. I gasped, and that restarted my breathing.

I gulped down the last of my water and set down the glass with a thunk. February was nine months away. I couldn't miss a single deadline, not even by a day. I stood. "I'm going to wash up."

"Torn" played as I passed the hostess stand. I looked longingly at the street outside, the green leaves on the stunted trees growing from the sidewalk. But I wouldn't run away. I couldn't. Grandpa, Mom, and the farm depended on me to finish the damned book on time.

Plus, I owed Gabi too much to fail. She'd believed in me. Even after we'd broken up, she'd come to my table in the library where I scribbled out my stories. She read them. Some, she liked; others, she made me toss in the shredder.

After we graduated, she wrote to me—actually wrote me letters because she knew I hated email—and pushed me to finish my novel. When I'd wanted to toss it in the compost pile, she'd made me mail it to her, and she'd edited it and mailed it back. Then she'd talked to some people she knew. Before I knew it, I had a three-book deal with Happy Troll and interest from Hollywood. I owed her for so much.

Including the heart attack I was about to have. "February," I wheezed in the hallway outside the men's room.

"Don't freak out, Niall." Gabi's small hand squeezed mine. I could always count on her to check on me. "You've got this."

"I—I don't know."

"You do. You just need inspiration. We're going to get you back outside and rolling around in nature and shit. Whatever it takes, okay?"

"I don't think I actually have to roll around in shit to be inspired."

She smiled. "Whatever you need, you tell me, okay?"

Can you find me Samantha and her violet eyes? No, I couldn't ask that. Because she would, and that'd be all kinds of awkward. She was right. I'd spend the afternoon in the park and try to channel my muse.

I had to. For Gabi. And Grandpa. And Mom. And, dammit, for myself, too. I was no one-hit wonder like Natalie Imbruglia. I had a three-book deal and a TV series that wanted a second season. I wiped my sweaty palms on my pants.

"I'll be fine. I promise."

Gabi's raised eyebrow told me she didn't believe me, either.

5

SAM

I STAMPED my boots on the mat just inside the café and ran my hands over my sleeves to sluice off some of the water. I peeked inside my tote bag, which I'd shoved under my jacket.

"You okay, Bilbo Baggins?" I whispered.

The bag shook with the force of his waggly butt.

"Good. Me, too." *So far.*

I scanned the café but didn't see Heidi or Dr. Martell yet. My stomach unclenched a little as I chose a table far away from the group of laughing teenagers and close to a window and the white noise of the pattering rain. Maybe they wouldn't show. What could we have to talk about, anyway? I'd signed the papers, just like they'd told me to do.

The door opened, and I looked up, but it was only a couple, their hands in each other's back pockets. They took seats in the opposite corner, near the teenagers. I'd give Martell and Heidi fifteen minutes. Wasn't that the rule for professors? He was always on time, so it'd never mattered. I checked my watch and tossed a dog treat into my tote bag. Bilbo Baggins crunched it with his tiny teeth.

Ten minutes later, Heidi walked in, shaking out a black umbrella. When she spotted me, she smiled, sharp, and strode to the table.

"Samantha!" She held her arms wide.

I stilled for her hug and let her make loud air-kisses near both cheeks. Where I was going with my Ph.D., there'd be no air kisses. No cafés. Just my quiet lab and Bilbo Baggins waiting for me at home.

She waved over the server before taking a seat on the other side of the round table. After we placed our orders, I blurted out, "Where's Dr. Martell?"

"He doesn't need to be here for this. Our discussion today involves only you and me."

I swallowed. "Do you have everything you need? Do I need to send you the manuscript in a different format? Or, um, spellcheck it?" Not that CASE ever made spelling errors. But I didn't know anything about book publishing. The few academic papers I'd worked on with Dr. Martell had involved a lot of fussiness around format and grammar, which was one of the things we were—had been—trying to ease with CASE.

"No, no." She tinkled out a laugh and waved away my questions like she'd shoo away a fly. "We need to talk about promotion."

"Promotion?" My brain churned to find context for the word but came up empty.

She pressed her lips together as if she were trying to hold back words and a smile at the same time. Her eyes sparkled. "We're sending you on a book tour next spring."

My brain scrambled again for purchase but slipped on the nonsensical words. "A…a book tour? And you need *me* to go?"

"The book can't go on tour by itself." Her laugh tinkled again like breaking glass. "Readers want to meet the author."

"But I'm not—" Dr. Martell knew my reading struggles, so he'd pointed out the clauses in the contract that had specified the consequences for breaking the confidentiality agreement. And since I'd donated my trust fund when I'd turned twenty-five, I didn't have the cash to fight anyone in court. Nerves clawed up from my stomach into my throat, making me whisper. "I'm not the author."

Heidi's glittering eyes turned lethal. "Of course you are, Samantha. Your pen name will be printed on the cover. You are Sam Case."

The server returned with our mugs of coffee, and I cradled mine in my hands to hide how they trembled. "What do I have to do?"

She turned down the flame in her eyes. "We're still working out the schedule. I'd estimate a dozen cities over three weeks. Most of the events will take place in bookstores. You'll do a book talk, then a signing."

"A book talk?" I didn't have anything to say about books. My lungs had forgotten how to work. I was drowning right there in the café.

Her eyes widened. "I almost forgot to tell you the best part! You'll have a tour partner, Niall Flynn."

That shocked my lungs back into action. "What? But I—"

"Niall happens to be a Happy Troll author, and he's coming out with a new book this spring." She slipped a hand into her designer tote and pulled out a thick hardcover. The cover did look familiar, an illustration of a pointy-eared person wearing a deep green cloak and sitting astride a snow-white horse. A long sword gleamed at his side. I took a few seconds to decipher the title at the top. *Secrets of the Wood Elves.* "You read this one, right?"

"Oh. Shit." Of course I hadn't read it. I'd never try to read anything that thick. Not anymore. I'd just loaded the file into CASE. Was she trying to punish me for it? How awkward was it going to be when I showed up on tour and said, *So, hey, your book helped create this novel I totally didn't write, but let's pretend I did?*

As if she could read the thoughts on my face, she said, "Don't worry about Niall. I'll take care of him. Just remember the NDA. It'd be better if you didn't talk with him about"—her gaze darted around the coffee shop before she whispered the end of the sentence—"A.I. His father's Paul Swift, the creator of the Swift-phone, you know."

I'd met Paul Swift a few times at the events Mother dragged me to. Tech people orbited him like planets trapped in the sun's gravitational field. No wonder Niall was so vibrant. His father was, too.

She smiled again. "So, like I was saying, you and Niall will ask each other questions and talk about your books. Qiana, our publicist, will send you a list of topics. And then you'll take questions from the audience. Oh, but first you'll read a brief excerpt from the book."

"Read? Aloud?" The thinking part of my brain switched off, leaving only the heart-racing, palm-sweating, body-shivering part functioning. The part that remembered reading in front of the class in school. The sneers. The snickers. The teacher's impatient glare.

"Of course, aloud. Just a short section. You can memorize it if you like. We're hoping to draw a couple hundred people at each event. Niall is wonderful at these things. You have nothing to worry about."

Nothing to worry about? Every part of this tour was something I had to worry about. To hide the tremble in my fingers, I opened the book to the end. On the back flap was a paragraph or two of text, and above that was a black-and-white photo. A man crouched in a field next to a dog. If I hadn't seen him in real life, I'd have assumed he was a brown-haired man with a regular-sized dog. But I knew that face and the flaming-red hair that crowned it. And considering how tall Niall was, that dog had to be some kind of hellbeast because it was as tall as the crouching man beside it.

I squeezed my eyes shut. Niall was a celebrity author who'd draw most of the attention away from me, which was a good thing. But there'd be attention, and I'd be expected to speak—to read—in public. Two terrifying things.

"Bilbo Baggins comes on tour with me." It was the only way I'd survive.

"Who?" At last, I'd managed to put Heidi at a disadvantage.

I reached down and pulled my tote into my lap. Bilbo Baggins' fluffy ears popped up first, and then his grinning face. "Bilbo Baggins."

Her lip curled. "It's not a rodent, is it?"

"He's a Chihuahua mix. And he goes where I go." My voice was stronger than I'd expected it to be.

"I don't think that's possible." When she frowned at Bilbo Baggins, he ducked back into the bag, trembling.

"You need an author. Either he comes or I don't." I didn't have a legal leg to stand on, and Martell would be furious with me if I backed out. Still, I jutted out my chin and held my head high, the same way I'd done when our family lawyer had tried to talk me out of donating my trust fund.

"Fine. Though not all of the venues will be dog-friendly. He'll need to stay in your hotel room."

"Okay. And also, no photos."

"What do you mean, no photos? Do you mean no publicity shots, or do you also mean—"

"No selfies. No photos with the readers. No social media. No image of me will be published in connection with the tour."

She blinked. "I don't know if that's—"

"Make it happen, or I'm not going." I'd sworn never to take another photo after what had happened with Stephen. It didn't matter that I'd be smart and have my clothes on this time. Any photo could be doctored. I knew exactly what A.I. could do.

She pursed her lips. "Fine. But no more conditions. If you so much as ask for an extra bed pillow, we'll sue you for breach of contract."

Damn. Now I really wished I'd read the contract. Mother would've killed me if she'd known I'd signed papers her legal team hadn't reviewed. But I'd focused on only one thing—my Ph.D.—and the shortest path between myself and freedom.

Next to getting out of the tour altogether, taking Bilbo Baggins with me and avoiding photos would give me my best chance at survival.

I nodded. I'd used up all my courage. I hugged Bilbo Baggins inside the tote. I was smart. I could find some way out of the mess I'd somehow gotten myself into.

6

NIALL

FRAUD.

That was the word on the sign I imagined hanging around my neck. Each time I answered one of the students' questions, it gained another pound, weighing down my shoulders. How could I talk to these kids about writing? After that glorious day last weekend, my muse had abandoned me.

The day before, I'd roamed, restless, through the park. The forest. The beach. The prairie. None of them inspired me. None of them whispered Lobelia's words to me. I'd scrawled some ideas on a page of my notebook, but in the end I'd ripped it out and thrown it away. They were all terrible.

Yet, these university students expected me to tell them how to write.

How could I if I didn't know how to do it myself?

When my talk ended and the students dispersed, I strode out of the auditorium and through the library until I reached the outside, where I gasped in the fresh air like it was a cure for my fraudulence.

I caught a flash of black in my peripheral vision, and my left index finger twitched. I scanned the library's portico. A couple of students trudged up the steps. A gray squirrel clung to a nearby tree trunk. I shook my head. I was imagining things. I'd find a different park. Maybe Lobelia would speak to me there.

But before I could step out from under the library's portico, a small barrier with a bounty of dark hair stepped in front of me.

"Hi, Niall, I'm Kari Singh, and I write a celebrity blog here on campus."

I wrinkled my forehead. "I can't tell you much about blogging, but I guess writing is writing. What are you struggling with?"

Her lip curled. "I'm good. But I have some questions for you."

"For me?" I narrowed my eyes. "I'm no celebrity."

"Look, you're the closest thing we've had in months since one of Mark Zuckerberg's sisters got lost and wound up on campus. This is a school for nerds. They know who you are."

"Oh. Okay." The Venn diagram of nerds and fantasy readers had a healthy intersection. Plus, Qiana and Gabi had prepped me for this. I was supposed to be positive but vague: *Yes, the book is almost done. Yes, you'll see all your favorite characters again. Yes, there will be some new characters and surprises. Yes, the show producers will get a copy as soon as it's finished.*

As an author, I should've been thrilled to be asked about a TV series based on my books. I should've been ecstatic to get this chance that so many other writers didn't. But the fear that coiled inside my chest strangled my excitement. What if I couldn't finish?

"Have you seen your father lately?"

"My…what?" I took a half-step back. No one asked me about him. Not for a long time.

She smiled, predatory. "You're in San Francisco, and he's just down the road in Silicon Valley. Have you seen him?"

"No." My voice cracked like it did the last time I'd seen him at the farm, when I was twelve or so. I cleared my throat. "No, I haven't. We aren't close." An understatement. He'd walked out of our lives and built a new family, a legitimate one, to go with his multibillion-dollar tech business.

Movement behind her caught my eye, but when I glanced toward it, nothing but the squirrel was there.

"And why is that, Niall?" She held out her phone to me to record my answer. It was one of his. I could tell from the silver icon of a bird in flight on the back. "Why aren't you and Paul Swift close?"

I wasn't about to explain to this total stranger how he'd faded out of our lives so slowly I almost hadn't noticed. How his business trips stretched longer and longer. How, instead of showing up at Christmas like he'd promised, he'd sent a box. Inside were three brand-new, top-of-the-line Swiftphones.

One of my friends had put mine up in an online auction for me, and I'd eventually convinced Grandpa to take the money for that season's seed. Even at twelve, I'd appreciated the irony of making my father pay for the rural life he hated.

I'd been angrier and more selfish when he'd sent the second one when I was fifteen. I'd smashed it, used my friend's phone to snap a photo, and texted it to my father. He hadn't sent another.

But none of that was this blogger's business. I shrugged. "People grow apart. He's got his life, and I've got mine."

Her mouth tightened, but a gleam came into her eyes. "Are you dating Lulu Bridges?"

I took another half-step back and bumped into one of the library's columns. It had been Gabi's idea to be seen at a restaurant with an actress when I was down in L.A. last month. Lulu's people had been agreeable—Qiana, Happy Troll's publicist, had set it up—so we'd sat at an outdoor café and let the paparazzi snap pictures.

"No, I'm not seeing anyone, and Lulu is a friend." That was a stretch. It'd been a dull two hours. She'd wanted to talk about my exercise routine, my diet, my favorite designers. And, of course, the show and whether I could get her an audition. I told her I'd put in a word for her the next time I saw the producers, and she gave me the name of her meditation guru.

Gabi had tried to hide it from me, but a magazine had printed a photo of us next to an even bigger picture of my dad onstage in one of his black button-downs embroidered with the SwifTech logo, a wireless microphone curving along his jaw.

That time, I caught the flash of black as it swept out into the open across the quad. And although I'd seen her only once, I'd replayed our interaction so often in my imagination that I knew that slender frame. That long, dark hair caught up in a drooping bun. If she'd turned around, I'd have seen a constellation of freckles and the most stunning eyes I'd ever encountered.

Lobelia. No, Samantha.

"Excuse me, Kari."

"Wait, I have—"

But I was already flying down the library steps and down the path that bordered the quad. I couldn't let her disappear into one of the badge-access-only buildings. Fortunately, her strides were no match for my long legs, and I caught up just as she turned off the quad onto a narrow sidewalk. "Samantha."

She stopped, her shoulders slumped. I jogged two more steps to stand in front of her. "Hello again."

"I-I'm not stalking you."

I felt my lips curl up. "You're not?"

"No. I go to school here. I saw you as I was passing by."

"Passing by, huh?" I didn't believe her, not really. But the small chance she hadn't sought me out made my belly twinge.

She hitched her backpack onto her shoulder. "You didn't tell me you were a writer."

I shrugged. "I am."

She glared at me. "A famous writer. With a TV series based on your novel."

I crossed my arms. "I don't know how famous I am. You didn't know who I was."

She mirrored my stance. "You also didn't mention that you're the son of Paul Swift. Or that you date actresses."

I spread my arms wide. "We talked for less than half an hour. I didn't have time to give you my life story. And I don't date actresses. It was a PR thing, nothing more." I didn't know why I needed to say that. I hardly knew Samantha. I didn't have to explain myself to her.

It was the way she'd drawn herself up. She was a tiny thing, compared to me, but she managed to look taller, like she stood on a dais above me and I was a serf requesting a boon from milady. My fingers tingled.

"Who are you?" I muttered, more to myself than to her. She was no socialite, no matter what Gabi had said.

"I'm a graduate student. I was on my way to my office when I saw you." She lifted her chin.

"You were?" She looked like a graduate student. Black cargo pants, a black T-shirt, combat boots. It didn't fit with the socialite picture Gabi had drawn me.

"Computer science." She flapped her hand, and the grace in that gesture took my breath.

"Huh." My fingers tingled again. I glanced back at the squat, beige brick building with too few windows. It was no fairy palace.

An analytical mind. Was she addicted to technology, too, like Gabi? I tried to superimpose Samantha's image today—wary, terse, guarded—with the engaging, funny woman I'd spoken with at the event. And then I tried to layer on what Gabi had told me about her socialite family. I failed. So far, Samantha Jones was an enigma.

"How's your dog?"

"Bilbo Baggins?" A slow smile spread across her face. "He recovered from the cheese incident. He's fine now."

"Good." I rocked on my heels. She was a puzzle, and I couldn't get all the pieces to fit together. Maybe I could shake them up and see them differently.

"I know your secret."

Her cheeks went pale, and the spatter of freckles across her nose seemed to darken. "What secret?"

"Your secret identity."

"How did you—"

"Gabi told me. You're Samantha Jones, of the Jasper Jones Literacy Foundation family."

She deflated. "Jasper Jones was my father."

I winced. In my desire to be Hercule Poirot, I'd forgotten she might miss him. "I'm sorry for your loss." It came out wooden. Jasper Jones had probably been a better father than mine. It wouldn't have taken much.

"Thank you." But she didn't look at me. Her gaze was unfocused, like she saw something other humans—I—couldn't.

My fingers tingled again. *Later,* I told them. Samantha was more than an inspiration. She was someone I wanted to get to know.

"Hey, can I buy you lunch? Or coffee?" If I could spend a little more time with her, I could unlock her secrets.

She blinked and glanced at the building again before she met my gaze. I'd never seen eyes that color. If I were a painter, which tints would I blend to replicate it? And how would I make them seem so clear and intelligent and alert, like they judged me and found me lacking?

"I—ah. I don't suppose—" She grimaced. "Of course not. Or you'd… I wish I could. But I really have to get to work. I have a stack of tests that aren't going to grade themselves." She flashed me a smile. One corner lifted higher than the other, like secrets weighed down the other side.

I wanted to discover them all.

"Tomorrow, then. Shit, no, we're leaving tomorrow." When would I be back in San Francisco? Not for a while, not until—"Next spring. I know it's a while from now, but I'll be on tour for my next book, and I'm sure we'll stop here."

The shades snapped shut over those opaque eyes just before

she looked down at the toe of her boot. "I—I might have an obligation then. I'm trying to get out of it, but…"

My chest tightened. "I didn't even tell you the dates."

"I know, but it's that kind of conflict, you know, that'll for sure overlap. But if I can, I'll come see you when you're back in San Francisco. I promise."

"If you give me your number or your—your email"—I could remember how to log into my email by then, couldn't I?—"I'll send you the schedule. We can arrange to meet up."

"I'll just come find you. It's more exciting that way, right?"

"Excitement is overrated." When we'd met, she'd said she wanted to snuggle up to me. Where had this new aloofness come from?

She wrinkled her nose, eclipsing a few of her freckles. "I think the mystery appeals to you, Niall Flynn. Let's keep it that way." And without even a California kiss on the cheek or a handshake, she strode away from me toward the beige building.

My brain took a few seconds to catch up. At last, I blinked and watched her walk up to the entrance, flash her ID at the sensor, tug open the door, and disappear through it, all without a glance back at me.

I waited half a minute, expecting her to—*do what, exactly, Niall?* Pop back out and shout her phone number at me? Slide through the doors in her superhero costume after shedding her mild-mannered graduate student disguise?

My fingers tingled again, the sensation sharp this time. Spotting a bench under a tree a few dozen yards away, I headed toward it, already pulling my notebook from my satchel. She was right. It wasn't understanding Samantha that inspired me; it was the mystery. With my imagination, I could solve the enigma myself.

I flipped the notebook to the next empty page, and before I'd even set my pen on it, an image formed. A princess in disguise, seeking adventure. Protecting not only her identity but her heart.

I filled page after page of the notebook until my hand cramped. Shaking it out, I continued through the pain until Lobelia revealed her secrets to Nieven—and to me, her creator.

7

SAM

I TUGGED my coat tighter against the damp January chill and trudged up the sloped driveway to Mother and Charles's house. It seemed like a different Sam who'd spent her middle- and high-school years in the upstairs bedroom Mother still called mine.

The one time Mother had visited my studio apartment near the university, she'd asked me why I insisted on living in a hovel. Despite the cracks in the ceiling, the leaky bathroom faucet, and the occasional ghostly clang of the pipes, I loved it because it was mine, paid for by my stipend and not the company that had finally succeeded only after Dad worked himself to death over it.

I climbed the steps to the front door and gave myself a moment to suck it up. Blaming my work, I'd ditched brunch for months. But my dissertation was in Dr. Martell's hands now, had been since right after the New Year. That'd been weeks ago. When I asked him about it, he said it was a fine first draft, but he wanted to see if we could get more "real-world results." The sales had been good, according to Heidi, since *Magician in the Machine* had released three months ago, but Heidi expected a "pop" from the tour.

As hard as I'd begged, Martell wouldn't get me out of it. He saw the tour as a key part of the experiment, wanting to measure how people reacted to a book they thought had been written by a human and how that response changed when they found out it had been written by a machine. It was a valid point.

But he'd ignored the personal aspect for me. How awkward was the tour going to be after I'd failed to mention my pen name to Niall Flynn that time I'd stalked him at the campus library last summer? By now, Heidi or the publicist, Qiana, must have told him I was Sam Case. I hadn't given him my number, so at least I didn't have a string of accusatory texts from him. But meeting him at our first stop in Ohio in a couple of weeks was going to be a shitshow. Especially when I tried to read.

But before I could get to that nightmare, I had to get past this one: telling my family I was leaving town without breaking the NDA.

The door opened, and my friend Marlee stepped out.

"What are you doing here?" My mother didn't consider Marlee, who worked for Jackson, part of the Sunday-brunch circle.

"Hello to you, too." Marlee clutched her pink coat to her neck.

"Sorry, I—" I winced. "I was thinking about something else, and you surprised me."

She grinned. "Don't worry about it. Remember, I work for your brother. I know how you geniuses operate. I had to drop off some papers. From Weston." She frowned.

"Nothing terrible, I hope?" Jackson had told me stories about his nemesis, the CEO of his company.

"No idea. It's above my pay grade. Hey, I've missed you since your internship ended. We should get together for lunch. Maybe next week? No, not next week. Big deadline at work. The week after?"

The tour started that week. My stomach clenched tight every time I thought about it. "Sorry, I can't. I'm going on a trip." *Please don't ask about it.*

"A trip? Tell me it's somewhere warm and sunny so I can live vicariously through you. Well, until our honeymoon next summer. Did I tell you? We're going to Hawaii!" She fluttered her hand, and her engagement ring sparkled.

"That sounds like fun. How's Tyler?" If I could get her talking about her fiancé, I'd be safe from her questions.

"Fantastic." She glanced behind me and waved. "He drove me here. And, actually, I should get going. We have, um…plans." Her cheeks went red.

Normally, I'd have asked about their plans, but the easy escape from having to hide the book tour was too tempting.

She hugged me. "Call me after your trip?"

"Sure." Maybe by then Heidi would have made the announcement and I could tell her about it. Marlee loved both books and computer science. She'd be interested in what CASE had done.

With a wave, she trotted down the walk to the driveway, where a blue Mustang idled.

When I turned back toward the door, Jackson grinned down at me. "You coming in, or are you going to stand out there all day?"

"B. Definitely the standing."

He glanced over his shoulder. "Wish I could've stayed outside, too, but Mother has grandchild radar these days. She can sense Alicia coming."

I reached out and squeezed his hand. He had that wild look in his eyes again. "You're going to be a great father, Jackson. Just like Dad."

"Let's hope I can stick around longer." He tried to smile, but his lips wobbled.

"You've got a much better work-life balance than he did. And you and Alicia take care of each other." Since he'd gotten together with Alicia, I'd seen the little checking-in touches they gave each other, the way Alicia tilted her head at him when he reached for that one-too-many drink, the way he rubbed away the tension in her shoulders. I almost envied him.

"We do." He squeezed my hand and released it. "I just hope I don't—"

"You won't." He was well known for his outrageous behavior when he was stressed. "And if you're tempted, call me. Remember, I'm the sensible one." Though, considering what had happened with Stephen, and now this fake book tour, was that really true?

His long arms came around me, and I inhaled the scent of leather as he hugged the breath out of me. "Thanks, Samwise."

He took my damp coat and shoved it onto a hanger and into the closet off the foyer. "You ready for this?"

I gave him a wry smile. Years ago, we'd been partners, Mother's two black sheep who always did the wrong thing. Jackson had taken the brunt of her attention, one-upping my screw-ups with another more outrageous one. But now he was golden, too. Not only had he founded an up-and-coming software company, but he'd been the first to marry and produce Mother's first grandchild-to-be. I was the only Jones disappointment now.

"I'll never be ready for brunch with the family," I said. "But I guess it's too late to back out now."

"I'll provide as much cover as I can."

"Don't dump coffee on the floor this time, okay?"

"You have to admit it was effective."

"I was wearing those silly ballet flats she bought me, and it burned my feet."

"But she stopped yelling at you about donating your trust fund."

"Temporarily." She'd never let that go. "And was it worth having to buy her a new rug?"

"Samwise." He pulled me to a stop right before we rounded the corner to the dining room. "Whatever I do for you is worth it."

I punched him in the shoulder the way he'd taught me, knuckles flat, my thumb outside my fist.

"Ow!" He rubbed his shoulder. "What was that for?"

"For trying to make me have"—I wrinkled my nose—"feelings."

He picked up my hand and squeezed it once. "It's okay to have feelings. You don't have to pretend them away."

It was a lie. This house was proof. The emotions I'd squashed—sadness about Dad, humiliation and betrayal over what Stephen had done, loneliness—practically oozed from the walls with their ghostly fingers, beckoning me back in.

No more. Those emotions had never done me any good, and I was just as done with them as I was with this house. With this family. Most of it, anyway.

I squeezed Jackson's hand and then dropped it. "Let's do this."

Everyone else was already gathered in the dining room when we entered. "Jackson, where did you—Samantha." Mother's face did something strange when she saw me. Maybe she'd gotten Botox again.

"Mother." I walked to the head of the table and kissed her soft, smooth cheek. It held a slight golden tone from their Christmas trip to Hawaii. She smelled like freshly ironed cotton and lavender, just like always.

Charles didn't wait for me to make it to the other end of the table. By the time I stepped away from Mother, he was there, his palm a warm weight between my shoulder blades. He smiled, his dark skin settling into its familiar lines. When I'd come two months ago at Thanksgiving, I'd noticed a few more gray hairs among his black curls. It made him look distinguished, like a stock photo for a successful executive. Which was exactly what he was. "Good to see you, Samantha."

"Hey, Charles. How's the, uh, golf game?" Charles had been a friendly presence in my life since he'd married Mother a year after we'd lost Dad. I'd tried to hate him—I'd been twelve—but no one could hate Charles. He was too nice. Still, we never talked about anything more substantial than golf or his business.

"I haven't played since we got back from Lanai. I wish you'd gone with us."

"It would've done you good, Samantha. You're looking so…
peaky." Mother reached a hand toward my cheek, but I pulled
away and headed toward my chair at the other end of the table.

"Hey, Nat," I said as I passed her chair.

"Sam." She kept her hands in her lap, exactly where they
should be, and her slim shoulders pressed into the back of her
chair like she had a steel rod for a spine. Her silky blond hair
cascaded over one shoulder of her rose-pink sheath dress. Mother
would never dream of calling her peaky.

"Sam!" Andrew stood and held out a fist for me to bump.
After I touched my knuckles to his, he pulled out my chair and
helped me scoot the heavy thing back under the table.

I waved at Noah, who sat between Alicia and Jackson on the
other side of the table. He was twelve, so he tried out one of those
chin-raises at me and then glanced back into his lap. He must've
had a phone or a gaming device down there. I wished I could've
gotten away with that.

Surprising everyone, Mother had welcomed Alicia's
nephew into the family like a flesh-and-blood grandchild.
And she was so ecstatic about the baby Alicia carried that
Alicia had moved to the seat of honor on Mother's right.
Jackson took his place across from me at Charles's end of the
table.

He elbowed Noah. "Remember what we said about books at
the table."

"What are you reading, Noah?" Charles asked. Charles often
had a book in his hand, especially after dinner in the library with
his reading glasses perched on his nose and a glass of something
brown in his other hand.

"This new book, *Magician in the Machine.*" He held up the
familiar green cover, and my heart jumped into my throat.

"Is it about computers?" Charles squinted at the cover, taking
in the circuit-board pattern under the title.

"Sort of. It's fiction. It's a little hard to understand, but everybody's reading it."

"Everybody?" My voice came out as a croak, and I reached for the closest cup of coffee, which happened to be Andrew's.

"Let me pour you a fresh cup." Andrew scowled and walked to the urn on the buffet.

"Yeah, mostly the kids in the upper grades."

Jackson ruffled his hair. "Noah reads at a tenth-grade level."

"I read it, too." Natalie's voice rang out over the table. "He's right. Everyone's reading it."

"What did you think of it?" Why, why, *why* was I calling attention to myself like this? I'd blurt out the secret, and then Mother would do something ridiculous like go to Heidi and demand that I, not the university, receive the royalties.

Natalie faced me over Andrew's empty chair. "Why do you care? You don't read."

I picked up my fork and poked at the eggs on my plate to keep from showing the hurt. "Just making conversation."

"I agree with Noah," she announced. "The writing style is dense. But it raises some interesting questions about our obsession with technology."

It did? I'd thought it was just about The Magician and The Necromancer. And zombies.

"Yeah," Noah said. "And whether artificial intelligence can be smarter than humans."

Natalie leaned forward. "The Magician seems to say no, but The Necromancer believes it. I think the message is that they're both—" She stopped as if she'd just become aware of the eyes focused on her. I'd never heard Natalie talk about books, unless it was some celebrity memoir. She picked up her coffee. "We should get this Sam Case person to come to the next foundation benefit."

"I suppose we should, if everyone is reading their book," Mother said.

Andrew set a steaming cup of coffee in front of me and set a second cup out of my reach. "How's grad school?"

I closed my eyes and breathed in through my nose. I knew this was coming. Might as well meet it head-on.

"It's going well." I wasn't about to mention the delay in my dissertation approval. "I'm on track to graduate this spring."

"Thank goodness you can finish this chapter and move on with your life." Mother sipped from her china cup. "The pittance you're earning is shameful. I tried to talk to John about it, but he said that's what everyone earns."

"You talked to my *adviser* about my stipend?" I could feel my nostrils flaring to suck in the air that had evacuated the room.

"Of course I did. I worry about you."

"What do you plan to do after graduation?" Charles's voice rumbled on my other side.

"I'm looking for research positions." I sucked my lips between my teeth to avoid telling them I'd gotten an offer for a postdoc at a university in Idaho the week before. I had months to build up to that.

"Well, I'm sure Charles or Jackson would be thrilled to have you." Mother pronounced it like the answer to a math problem.

"Research, Mother. Not programming."

"Research doesn't sound very…lucrative." Her mouth turned down like she'd tasted something bad.

"There are other rewards worth having. Besides money."

Silence dropped over the table like a blanket. A wet one.

"Like family." Jackson draped his arm around Noah's shoulders.

I winced.

Sure enough, Mother said, "Are you seeing anyone, Samantha?"

"No, Mother." I hadn't had even a one-night stand in months. Not since Kyle. All the stress over CASE had zapped my libido.

"What about Jackson's friend Cooper? I saw you talking with him at the foundation holiday party."

"Coop?" Jackson's laugh was loud. "Not a chance."

"He's like another older brother, Mother."

"He's very eligible. Maybe a better match for Natalie, though."

While she and Natalie argued about whether Cooper Fallon

was too old for Nat, I finally had a chance to eat my cooling eggs and pancakes. But the respite didn't last long.

"Samantha, I found the perfect dress for you for the Valentine's Day ball. I ordered the black one because I know it's the only color you'll wear. But it also comes in rose gold, which would be much more festive."

And now my news had to come out. "Mother, I'm not going to make it to the ball this year. I'm going on a trip."

"A…trip?" She blinked. "Another academic conference?"

So she had been paying attention over the past four years. "No, this is different." I had to pick my way carefully. Heidi's confidentiality clause didn't make exceptions for family. "It's a road trip of sorts. With a…friend."

"A friend?" Her eyebrows arched toward her hairline.

"Or a colleague?" I wished I knew the right words to use that wouldn't set her off.

"Which is it: a friend or a colleague?"

I hesitated. "A colleague who's also a friend."

"A male friend?"

I winced. "Yes."

"Samantha." Her mouth curved down. "This isn't another Stephen situation, is it? He's not angling for a position in Jackson's company? Or Charles's? He has to know you don't have any money of your own."

My chest heated. "No, Mother. It's not like that. We're friends. And colleagues. Nothing more. We're traveling together for a few weeks to do some school-related things." It was sort of true. The book tour was school-related for me.

Her forehead didn't crease anymore, but her eyebrows twitched. "School-related things."

"It's highly technical. Want me to explain it?" That usually got her off my case. Mother had a head for finance, not computers.

"How long is this trip?"

"About three weeks. You can text me if you need to check in."

"Be careful, Samantha. You don't want to get into another unfortunate situation."

She'd never let me forget it. Not that I could. "I won't."

With one last hawk's glare at me, she turned to Alicia and asked her something about the nursery she and Jackson were setting up.

I slumped in my chair. My appetite was gone, and even my coffee was too cold to drink.

Not looking up from his own pancakes, Andrew muttered, "This guy tries anything, Jackson and I are coming for him."

I rolled my eyes. "I'm a big girl, Andrew. I can handle myself."

He looked up at that. His gaze was full of the same pity it'd held that night six years ago when I'd sat at the dining table in front of my family, sobbing about how I needed early access to my trust fund so I could pay off Stephen or he'd release the nudes I'd been an idiot to let him take. "Are you?"

I pushed the cold eggs around on my plate. "That was years ago."

"You have such a soft heart, Sam. I don't want you to get hurt again."

He'd been right, once. I'd spent the past six years building layer upon layer over that soft part of me. Now my heart was like one of Mother's pearls, strong on the outside and hiding the flaw within. Nothing was getting through.

Maybe after I had my Ph.D. and I'd moved far away from anywhere the Joneses were a household name, I'd let someone get close enough to chip away at it. But until then, I had to focus on my goals.

Goal number one: get through the tour without making a fool of myself.

8

NIALL

I PUSHED through the back door into my mother's kitchen, dropping my snow-crusted boots on the mat next to her smaller pair. Thorin bounded past me, his wet paws skidding on the scratched wood floors until he gained purchase and slowed just short of smashing into the kitchen cabinets. He trotted to sit at Mom's feet in front of the stove. The aroma of frying bacon and buttery biscuits welcomed us.

So did Mom's smile when she turned. "Niall. Were you up early writing?"

I clenched my jaw. "Trying." I shrugged out of my coat and hung it on the hook next to the back door. I set my mostly empty notebook on the counter and put the jug of fresh milk in the refrigerator.

"Don't worry about it." She slid my notebook out of range of the popping grease. "You just finished your book. You should enjoy your downtime before you have to go back out on tour."

"Sure, Mom." I kissed her cheek, lined and winter-rough. I'd turned in *Treachery* months ago. It was past time to have at least an outline for the third book, *Battle of the Wood Elves.* I'd jotted down a few ideas for it. Not one of them was good. Certainly not momentous enough for the possibly-final book of the series.

I'd thought coming home to the farm would inspire me. But my brain was as fallow as the snow-covered fields outside. Even the brook that ran next to my favorite writing spot was opaque and sluggish. I needed something else. A pair of violet eyes swooped through my imagination like a swallow. I'd see her again when the tour stopped in San Francisco. Surely my muse would spark my imagination then.

"Did you see your grandfather out there?"

I blinked away the image of those eyes and the strands of dark hair that had fallen over them when I'd seen her on campus last summer. "He'll be in soon. He was having a talk with Sally about her milk production."

"Dad and those goats." Her face creased in a fond smile.

"It worked last time. He's got some kind of goat magic."

She turned off the stove and faced me. "That's one of the things I love about you, Niall. You've always seen magic everywhere you look."

Not these days. The shadows of the forest didn't look like claws or swords or trolls. They looked like naked branches on dry, fallen leaves.

"Frank Turner came by a little while ago. He brought a package for you from the post office." She nodded at the kitchen table.

"A package?" It was a small brown box, about the size of an unabridged dictionary. The return address was New York. Qiana, probably. I pulled out my pocketknife and cut through the tape.

A note lay on top in Qiana's loopy handwriting. Below that was a stapled sheaf of papers. And at the bottom lay two books, one paperback and one hardcover. The hardcover, about twice as thick as the other, had the now-familiar, red-tinted cover illustration, my name, and *Treachery of the Wood Elves* at the top. My first author copy. Warmth spread up from my center all the way to my fingertips as I caressed the embossed words.

"What is it?" Mom asked, setting down the plate of bacon.

"My author copy." I picked up the book and handed it to her.

She held up her hands. "Let me wash up first. I don't want to get grease on the cover."

Moving to the sink, she ran the water. "What else did they send?"

"The schedule for the tour. And my tour partner's book." I lifted it from the box. The paperback's cover was green. Not forest green like *Secrets* but a poisonous, acidic green. Like the tree python I'd seen at the Columbus Zoo on a long-ago field trip. The title, *Magician in the Machine*, stretched across a picture of something angular and technical-looking. The author's name, in white at the bottom, was Sam Case. I turned it over. No author photo, just the descriptive blurb and publisher information. I scanned it. *A fantastical techno-thriller?* Did Heidi really think our audiences would cross over?

Mom returned to the table, wiping her hands. I passed her my book. That first crackle of the spine when she opened it made the warmth surge again inside me. *My book.* I'd done it again. My words filled the pages. Soon, people would read those words. Nervousness punched through the warmth, like bubbles in a pot of boiling water.

"It's beautiful, Niall. I can't wait to read it." She took the other one from me. "This looks…interesting. Pretty different from yours."

"Heidi said something about synergy. I guess we'll have to read it to figure out what she meant."

I picked up the schedule and scanned it. We were starting in Columbus, just as Qiana had said. I'd wanted to launch the book at the Enchanted Forest library like we'd done for my first novel, but Qiana said the venue wasn't big enough. The library's function room could hold twenty-five people. How many readers did she think would come to my launch? For *Secrets of the Wood Elves*, there had been four: Mom, Grandpa, Gabi, and my high-school

English teacher. Maybe she expected Sam Case to pull a bigger crowd with his debut novel.

I flipped the pages. Chicago, East Coast, Southwest, California. We didn't hit San Francisco until the end of the tour. Bad luck, that. I'd have to wait for my hit of inspiration. If Samantha came at all. Had she been able to get out of her obligation? Would she be waiting for me at the bookstore in San Francisco?

Mom's voice pulled me out of my reflection on the smattering of freckles below those enchanting eyes. "That's some talk your grandfather is having with Sally. Would you mind going to check on him?"

"You know how ornery she is. She's probably talking back." I set the papers in the box and returned to the back door. No sign of Grandpa outside. I twisted my scarf around my neck, tugged on my coat, and shoved my feet into my cold boots. "Be back in a few."

Closing the door tightly behind me to keep the warmth inside, I strode across the snowy fields, following my footprints back to the barn. Sliding open the door, I stepped inside and let my vision adjust from the too-bright outside to the darkness within.

"Grandpa?"

Sally and Susie bleated back at me. I rubbed their soft ears with my gloved hand. Grandpa wasn't in their stall. I walked to the alpacas' pens and found them empty. We'd let them out into the pasture earlier that morning. I spun around, scanning the barn. "Grandpa!"

A moan came from the corner, next to the ladder that hadn't been there when I'd left.

"Grandpa!" I raced over to the ladder. Beneath it, Grandpa lay on his stomach, one arm under him and the other flung out to the side, his fingers covering the handle of an old broom. "Grandpa!" I gripped his shoulder.

"I slipped," he rasped. His back rose, twitched, and fell.

I touched his neck, gently. The angle seemed right. "Does this hurt?"

"No. My arm."

The arm I could see looked all right. I palpated it.

"Other arm." It came out as a grunt.

I gripped his shoulder and hip and pulled him toward me, cradling his body with mine. He wasn't frail by any stretch, and he was heavier than he looked. He whuffed when he landed on his back.

I grimaced. The arm tucked over his chest was bent wrong. The wrist dangled like a marionette's. "Grandpa." The word squeezed out of me like one of Thorin's squeaky toys just before he ripped it open.

I levered to my feet. "You know the cobwebs are my job." The job I'd forgotten to do that morning, too focused on how my story wasn't coming together. I fetched the first-aid kit from the cabinet by the barn door and picked up a foot-long scrap of wood from the bin.

"Can you sit up?"

His eyes flashed at me. "I broke my arm, not my back."

"There you are, old man." From behind, I pushed him upright, mindful of his wounded arm. Then, as gently as possible, I splinted his wrist.

"I haven't heard you swear like that since you caught your foot in the combine." I wrapped the mesh bandage one last time and secured the end with a piece of tape.

"I haven't broken a bone in years. Forgot how much it hurts. You got an aspirin in that kit?"

I found a bottle and palmed it. "You sure you don't want to wait for something stronger at the hospital?"

"Hospital? I'm good as new."

"Your wrist is broken. This is just to keep you from doing more damage to it until they can set the bone and put it in a cast."

"A cast?" His eyes were wide and unfocused. Maybe he'd hit his head, too.

I ran my hand over his thick, white hair. I couldn't feel any bumps, but that didn't mean he didn't have a concussion. "What's today's date?"

"January 31. Tuesday."

"What were you doing when you fell?"

"Taking down cobwebs. Gotta do it, especially near the lights. They're flammable. Danger to the animals."

Okay, so he hadn't lost his short-term memory. "How long have I lived at the farm?"

"Since you were just an anklebiter. Since your dad—"

"Your brain is fine. Let's get you in the truck." I gripped his good hand and elbow and tugged him to standing.

Much later, after the hospital, after dinner and evening chores, after Grandpa had gone to sleep thanks to the good painkillers, Mom and I sat on the old sofa in front of the fire. We each had a book—*Treachery* for Mom and Sam's book for me—but they lay abandoned on our laps as we stared into the flames. Thorin slept at my mother's feet, twitching his giant paws.

I broke the silence first. "I don't think I should go on the tour. I'll call Qiana tomorrow and cancel."

She shook herself and turned her wide eyes on me. "No, Niall. You can't."

"I can't leave you and Grandpa here. Not while his arm's healing. He'll try to do too much. You both will."

"We've got some money saved. We can hire one of Frank Turner's boys to come help with the chores."

"That money's for the spring seed. And Grandpa's hospital bill."

She traced the embossed title of my book. "The best way to help is to go on your tour. Sell books. You're always so generous with—"

"It's not generosity to make sure my family has a place to live, food to eat. To want to help. I'm not like—not like him." Not in the way he'd abandoned his family nor in his success. It'd take more than a couple of books and a TV show to become a name everyone knew as well as my father's.

She smiled, but pain shadowed her eyes. "You're more like him than you know." She stroked my shoulder. "Handsome. Talented. Full of fire and determination. Everyone who meets either of you falls in love."

I snorted. "If that were true, I wouldn't be—" I'd almost said *alone.* But I wasn't alone. I had Mom and Grandpa. My friend Gabi. *Alone* made me sound ungrateful for the people who loved and supported me.

"You can be surrounded by people—people who love you—and still be lonely, Niall."

"Are you lonely, Mom?"

She tucked her leg under her and rotated to face me. "Sometimes. But I have friends. Your grandpa. My son, when he's not off being a famous writer." She grinned and squeezed my shoulder, but then her smile faded. "I'm never as lonely as I was when I was with your father. Even when he was with me, he held a piece of himself back. He was always thinking of his work, of the future."

When he used to come visit, he'd seemed enormous—though I knew I was taller now—and full of life. Speaking his foreign technology language, he was so alien to the quiet of the farm, where we didn't have a television or a computer. The only time I missed technology was when Dad came and spent most of his time huddled over his laptop. Maybe if I'd had one, too, we could've sat side-by-side. Maybe he wouldn't have decided I wasn't worth staying for.

I'd been so naïve I hadn't thought, even as his trips to the farm became as infrequent as once a year, that he'd stop coming, so I'd never considered each time I saw Dad might be the last. If I had, would I have tried to save up the memories? To make the last one special?

Mom's warm palm cradled my cheek the way she'd done when she broke the news that Dad wasn't coming back. He'd married a Hungarian model ten years younger than my mother, and they'd bought a mansion in Monterey. "He loved you in his way. I know it wasn't the way you wanted to be loved. And that's made you hesitant to give your love away. Someday you'll find your person. The person you can trust with your heart. And I hope you'll let yourself be open. That you'll risk the pain. Because love is worth it."

"Is it, Mom?" It was a cruel question to ask, but I couldn't stop it from bursting out of me.

A light shone in her eyes. "Those early years, when we first met, when he was so charismatic, so full of passion and grand ideas? Those were the most exciting years of my life. And then we had you. I saw him every time I looked into your face. Felt him every time I held your little fingers in mine. You grew up and became your own person, one I love with all my heart. I wouldn't have missed any of it. Not the love, not even the hurt. The hurt is part of it, you see. Without it, I wouldn't appreciate the happy times."

I stared into the fire. Did I believe that? Finding someone who wouldn't hurt me seemed like a more sensible strategy. Someone who'd be happy to live a quiet life here on the farm. Who didn't need the fame—my fame—or even her own.

"Right now, I'm happy to be here." My smile was almost genuine.

"But you're still going on tour? You won't cancel?"

She was right about a lot of things. Promoting my book was the best thing I could do for her and Grandpa. That, and writing the next book. "I'm not canceling. As long as I know you two will be all right."

"We will. I'll talk to Frank tomorrow about an extra pair of hands around here. Don't you worry about us. Just enjoy the tour. Do you know much about your tour partner? Have you met him?"

"No. And his book..." I'd brought it with me to the hospital. Maybe it was the anxiety and distraction there that kept me from sinking fully into the story. The language seemed disjointed, each sentence open to multiple interpretations, more like a work of literary fiction than genre fantasy. "His book is unusual."

"Should be an unusual tour, then."

Probably not. Cities and tours were all the same. Bookstore after bookstore, reading the same tired words until they lost their meaning. I couldn't wait to leave it behind me and return to the farm where I belonged.

Only this time, I had something to look forward to: seeing Samantha in San Francisco. And getting my muse back.

9

SAM

I'D EXPECTED the bored-looking white man just outside the Columbus airport security checkpoint holding a sign that said, "S. CASE." I hadn't expected the Black woman standing next to him, jumping on her toes, her red-tipped braids flipping up into a halo around her face, which was lit by a delighted grin.

When I tentatively raised my hand, the one that wasn't clutching Bilbo Baggins' carrier, she flung out her arms. "Sam!" she squealed.

She didn't wait for me to take the last few steps toward them. She ran at me and squeezed me into a rib-crushing hug. I held on. How long had it been since I'd had a hug as soothing as hers? Too long.

She released me and stepped back. "I'm Qiana. We've emailed, like, a hundred times. And I couldn't wait to meet you, so… surprise!" She framed her face with jazz hands. "You prefer Sam or Samantha?"

"Sam, please."

"Your flight all right? No problems? They didn't make a stink over Mr. Baggins, did they?" She bent at the waist and peered through the mesh at Bilbo Baggins. His wagging tail rocked the bag. "Oh, you precious little guy! We'll get you out of there soon. There's a spot for pets just outside, and then we'll shoot over to Niall's book launch."

Since it was Niall's event, I wouldn't have to do anything except sign a few copies of *Magician* in the back room. I was glad about that. Still, I wasn't excited about meeting Niall for the first time as Sam Case. Especially not in public in front of dozens of smartphones. I'd said no photos, but Happy Troll couldn't control everything.

When Niall and I came face to face again, would he be angry that I'd used his work for CASE? Would he make a scene? He'd seemed pretty easygoing at the fundraiser. But so had Stephen, right up to the moment he'd broken my trust. It'd be much better to meet Niall for the first time at the hotel, preferably in some quiet corner of the lobby.

"Do you really need me at the launch?" I faked a jaw-cracking yawn. "I'm pretty tired after the flight. Bilbo Baggins is, too."

Hearing his name, Bilbo Baggins let out a series of high-pitched barks and scrabbled at the mesh door of the carrier. *Traitor.*

Qiana's dark eyes went wide. "Of course we need you! This is your joint tour. You guys are a team now, and you support each other. You can take a power nap on the way over. I promise I'll be quiet. Well, maybe not quiet—that's not really my style—but I'll try to let you sleep. 'Kay?"

"Okay." I could hide behind Qiana and her wall of words. Niall wouldn't have a chance to yell at me if she kept talking.

After I told the driver what my bag looked like, Qiana led me to a grassy patch outside, and I let Bilbo Baggins out of his carrier. He took care of business, then scrabbled at Qiana's ankles until she picked him up.

He licked her chin. "Whoa, little guy. Watch the lipstick. I didn't wear the smudge-proof today. I didn't expect to be doing any kissing." She held him a little farther from her body, and he strained toward her. "Okay, fine. I'll fix it before we go in." She snuggled him close.

My stony little heart grew three sizes. Maybe the tour wouldn't be so bad. Not if everyone was as nice as Qiana.

A black car pulled up at the curb. "Shawn's here," she said. "Let's do this!"

She sat in the back with me, still stroking Bilbo Baggins, who'd curled up on her lap. "Now. I know I sent you a lot of information. What questions do you have about the tour?"

I'd skimmed through the packet, still hoping I wouldn't have to go. Jackson's best friend, Cooper, was always saying hope wasn't a strategy. I'd learned that the hard way. "Are you coming with us?"

Her red lips turned down into a pout. "I wish! That'd be so fun. Niall is a dynamo, and I know you and I are going to be besties. I'm only here for the launch. I'll see you in New York, though. I'll be at all the events there."

Seeing my expression, she said, "Don't you worry! Niall is fabulous. Ah-mazing. I've never seen anyone perform for the cameras—I mean the readers—like he does. Of course there won't be any cameras at the events, per your requirements." Her grin went even wider. "You writers tend to be a shy bunch. Not Niall. He rolls with it. And he'll take care of you. He's the nicest guy—"

The buzzing in my ears had gotten too loud to hear her. *You writers.* So Heidi hadn't told her about me. She hadn't told her I was only there to prove CASE could write a novel people wanted to read. That I wasn't a writer at all, and not much of a reader, either. If Qiana knew who I really was, would she still like me? Probably not. If we didn't have books in common, what was left? I scooted an inch or two away from her and faced the front of the car.

"Hey, Sam, you all right? I'm sorry. You said you were tired, and here I am, babbling away."

"It's okay." I flapped my hand half-heartedly. "Don't worry about me."

She pursed her lips. "That's kind of my job. To worry about you. To take care of you. You need anything, you let me know, okay? I won't always be with you, but you'll have a handler in every city. I'm responsible for you while you're on this tour, and if anything happens, I'll take care of it."

I was used to having people trying to take care of me. When Mother did it, I hated it. But having Qiana in my corner felt better.

"Speaking of which…" She dug into her purse and pulled out a tiny red harness with the words SERVICE DOG embroidered in white on black patches on each side. "This way, Bilbo can go to the events with you."

"But he's not really—"

"Ah-ah. He's your emotional support dog. You need him, don't you?" Her brown eyes bored into me like she could see the part of my brain that Bilbo Baggins calmed.

I let my gaze rest on his silky black fur. Even that slowed my racing heartbeat. "I do. But I feel bad pretending he's a trained service animal."

"He's a good dog." Qiana scratched under his chin. "And it's only to get you through this tour." She pulled the vest over his head and buckled it around his middle. "Looking sharp, Bilbo." She ran her fingers over his oversized ears, smoothing the long hair.

"Thank you." The words came out as a whisper past the lump in my throat.

"I got you, girl."

If that was true, she'd be the only person besides Jackson and Dr. Martell who did.

10

NIALL

I STARED through the truck's windshield at the two-story, suburban Columbus bookstore. Fat snowflakes floated down, melting when they landed on the glass. My hands shook, and I gripped the steering wheel harder to hide it.

"We getting out, or you launching the book from the truck?" Grandpa leaned forward between the front seats. "Might be a touch chilly out, but I s'pose you could stand in the bed, do your talk from there."

"Dad, give him a minute. He just needs to put his game face on. Right, honey?" Mom's forehead creased, but her eyes shone with pride.

Game face. I drew myself up in the seat. Squared my shoulders. Nodded. "I'm ready." If I said it, it might be true.

I jumped out and opened the truck's small rear door for Grandpa, hovering nearby in case he stumbled. He was still a little off-balance with his arm in the sling.

His temper was unbalanced, too. "Step back, son. I'm not some frail old codger."

"Sure, sure. Just need to get my bag." When he stood steady beside the truck, I grabbed my battered satchel from the back seat and slung it across my chest.

Mom met us at the front of the truck, and we crossed the expansive parking lot. It was full of cars, but a couple of restaurants and a Tractor Supply shared it. The bookstore loomed larger until it filled my field of vision, brightly lit and crowded with shoppers on a Tuesday night. Why, why, *why* hadn't they scheduled the launch at the Enchanted Forest library? There was no way I'd fill any amount of space in this monstrosity. Maybe they had a small function room off to the side that wouldn't dwarf my small crew of supporters.

I held the door for Mom and Grandpa and followed them inside.

"Niall, look." Mom pointed at a sign. My larger-than-life-size face grinned back at us. Did I really have that many freckles? I winced. Maybe we shouldn't have done the cover in red tones. The poster looked like Enchanted Forest in autumn, all reds and oranges and gold. It made my eyes burn to look at it.

"Someday you'll be white-haired like me," Grandpa said. "You'll miss all that red."

"Today is not that day, Grandpa."

"It says we're upstairs," Mom said. Up the wide staircase, voices buzzed like that hornet's nest we'd found in the hayloft a few summers ago.

Taking a deep breath, I ascended the stairs with the same trepidation I'd climbed the ladder to take down the nest. I hoped I'd get fewer stings.

"Niall!" Qiana hit me like a cannonball to the chest, her arms banding around mine. "It's so exciting! Isn't it exciting? Look at all the people! Look at my hair!" She shook her head, waving the red tips. "I matched your cover! Wait, where's Gabi?" She peered around me like my agent would ever hide behind me.

My chest constricted at the reminder. "Can't make it. A situation with another client."

"Aw. I know you like having her here with you. Elaine! And Jerry! You're here! I'm saving seats for you up front. Let me introduce you to Sam first."

Sam. It was another Jenga block on the tower of nerves inside me. When I'd finished his book, I was an envious, irrational mess. How the hell had he done it? Written a literary masterpiece that was also a mind-blowing work of fantasy? I couldn't have produced anything like it, not if I'd toiled for twenty years. Not with a roomful of assistants and typists. I'd looked forward to this day—okay, and dreaded it a little—so I could put a face, a person behind the astounding literary talent.

But when Qiana pulled the person into our circle, my brain stopped. This wasn't Sam Case. This was someone I knew. Someone whose beautiful eyes had haunted my dreams, my imagination, my damned manuscript, for months. Lobelia. But she had another name. Samantha. Samantha Jones. Was she here representing the foundation?

"Niall!"

I blinked.

"Niall, are you all right?" Qiana clutched my arm. "You wobbled there for a minute. Need a chair? Some water? Essential oils? I think I've got some lavender in my bag."

I blinked again, hard. Samantha was still there. "I'm good. What's going on? Where's—"

"Hi, Niall." She extended her hand to me, pale and trembling. "Remember me, Samantha Jones? But I'm Sam Case on this tour."

Now I did need a chair. "You're Sam Case." She was a grad student, not a writer. She wasn't even a lit major. She'd said computer science. She couldn't be older than twenty-five. When had she had time, or training, to write a masterpiece like *Magician in the Machine?* My brain was stuck in neutral, unable to process the new information. I gaped at her, trying to rearrange what I thought I'd known before I stepped inside the bookstore.

"Sam." Mom elbowed me in the side as she pushed forward and shook Samantha's still-outstretched hand, the one I hadn't touched. "So nice to meet you. I read your novel. It's so interesting. I'd love to hear more about how you came up with the idea for it."

If it was possible, Samantha went even paler. "Thank you. But tonight is about Niall and his book."

"It is, isn't it?" Mom released Samantha's hand and tucked her arm around my waist. To Samantha and Qiana, it probably looked like a mother-son cuddle. It felt like a straighten-up-right-now-you-miscreant crush. Nearby, one of those fake shutter sounds clicked from someone's phone. Qiana turned away to murmur to the person.

I put on my publicity smile, the same one I'd used in my author close-up downstairs. I held out my hand, and Samantha's small, soft palm settled into it. I pumped it once and released it. "Nice to see you again. Sorry, I wasn't expecting—You didn't say you'd—You caught me a little off-guard."

"Wait, you guys know each other?" Qiana's sharp gaze didn't miss a thing. Not the drop of sweat that trickled down my hairline. Not my right hand I'd fisted because it still pulsed like I'd touched a hot wire in the tractor's engine. Not my breath that rasped in my throat. Not Samantha's wild eyes, staring at me like I was a copperhead, coiled and ready to strike.

"We met in San Francisco. At a fundraiser," Samantha said.

"And again at Samantha's university. She didn't mention she'd written a book. Isn't that something you'd think you'd mention when you're speaking to someone you know is a writer?"

"Niall." Mom pinched me under my jacket like she could snap me out of my boorish behavior.

"I'm just trying to understand." Samantha had seemed open, honest. And I'd written Lobelia that way, too. Was that my problem? I'd pictured her one way, and when she acted another, I got angry? I'd been looking forward to seeing her in San Francisco and—wait. She'd said she was trying to get out of an obligation. Did she mean this tour?

I'd ask her about it later. When she wasn't giving me the same expression she'd shown when all those photographers came up to us at the fundraiser last year. I had a fence to mend.

"Sorry." I grimaced and pointed at myself. "Pre-launch nerves. Let me try this again. Hello, Samantha. I'm delighted to see you again."

Warily, she scanned my face. Then she opened her bag, and a fluffy, black head poked out. "When I'm nervous, Bilbo Baggins helps." She scooped him out and passed him to me.

I cuddled him against my chest while my mother stroked his oversized ear. My heart rate slowed. This, *this* was my Lobelia. Or Samantha. Offering help when it was needed. I smiled. "Thank you."

"No problem."

"Niall, it's go time." Qiana held out her hands for the dog and passed him back to Samantha. "Why don't you all grab your seats —they're the ones up front with a *Reserved* card on them—while I get Niall mic'd up?" Qiana clutched my wrist. Her long nails matched my book cover, too.

"Come on, Sam. Or is it Samantha?" Mom asked.

"Sam. Please."

"We had a rooster once, name of Sam…" Grandpa's voice faded away as they made their way through the crowd to the front of the room.

Qiana tugged me down by my wrist until my ear was next to her red lips. "What the hell's going on? I've never seen you act like that with anyone, certainly not a fellow author. A *newbie* author on her first tour."

She glared at me for a second, waiting.

"I guess I was just surprised. That I knew her. That she—"

"Have you considered, Niall, that she might've been a little intimidated by a bestselling author with a TV deal? Especially by one with as much"—she paused to look me up and down—"presence as you have?"

Cold washed through me like the brook in January. I felt about a foot tall. Qiana could've stomped me with her shiny black stilettos.

"I'm sor—"

"Don't apologize to me. Apologize to Sam. Later. Now you have to pull yourself together."

For the first time, I glanced around me as she pulled me toward the podium. A sea of chairs lined up facing one wall of the upper floor. There had to be two hundred of them. And they were almost all occupied. Where had all these people come from?

Qiana released me when we reached the podium. She handed me the battery pack, which I clipped onto my belt. She fisted the mic. "You sure you don't need something to help you chill out?"

I shook my head. Samantha's dog—and her willingness to share him with me—had settled me.

Pursing her lips again, she tapped the mic to check that it was off before she clipped it to my collar. "You know what you're reading, right?"

I pulled my author's copy from my satchel. A red tape flag poked out of it.

Her expression relaxed the tiniest bit. "You're a pro, Niall. Now act like it." She kept her face frozen in a smile and gritted out the next few sentences between her teeth. "There are, like, ten book bloggers in the audience. And two local TV crews. Don't turn around. Their coverage could be picked up by the national book blogs and lifestyle websites. Don't let whatever's going on between you and Sam screw this up. You feel me? This is a big night for you."

I nodded, glad my back was to the audience and the TV cameras. She was right: it was a big night for me. Not only was I launching my book, but I was back in the presence of the woman who'd inspired Lobelia, who'd inspired me to finish the book.

I stared down at the red-toned painting on the cover. In the corner, flitting up by Nieven's ear, was the diminutive form of a wood sprite. The firm set of her tiny mouth reassured me. *Courage, Niall.*

I could do this. And now, with the source of my inspiration traveling with me for the next three weeks, I could do even more. As I stroked Lobelia's tiny wingtips, my fingers tingled.

I could write.

11

SAM

YESTERDAY, in Columbus, had been about Niall. Today was for both of us. Well, Niall and Sam Case, whoever she was.

From the car, the Chicago bookstore looked perfectly friendly. In the window to the right of the door, a stuffed bear sat in a rocking chair, a picture book propped between his paws, and stacks of other children's books flanking it. Because it was February, the window to the left of the door displayed romance novels, some with bright covers, others showing women with silk skirts pooling around them, their gowns' necklines drooping around their shoulders.

I tugged up the lapels of my jacket. The button at the top was missing. I hadn't needed it at home. But I was going to need more than a better coat to survive a tour with Niall Flynn. Like, a full suit of armor and a sword. And maybe a chastity belt.

Last night, after his book launch in Columbus, he'd looked like he'd wanted to talk. But, like a coward, I'd ducked out with Qiana, saying I was tired. And I was. But really, I'd been shocked by the blaze in his eyes and the spark of our touch. I'd fucked up by not telling him about the book and the tour when I'd met him on campus. At first, he'd seemed angry. But then, his gaze had burned with an intensity that didn't seem to be anger.

And my missing libido? Boom, found it. But so had every woman in that room who wasn't Niall's mother. A woman behind me had tried to ask a question but had lost it, giggling too hard to speak. And the crowd of women around the table after his signing? I couldn't have approached him if I'd wanted to.

I wished I'd told him about the tour back on campus. Or that I'd tried to reach him since. But right up to the moment Bilbo Baggins and I had stepped onto the plane in San Francisco, I'd hoped I could get out of the tour and all the lies.

Like the one about passing off the book as one I'd written. Especially after I'd used Niall's book as an input to CASE. Heidi had said she'd take care of it and that I shouldn't talk to Niall about the A.I. And now Heidi had control over whether or not I walked across the stage in June to get my doctoral hood and scroll, I had to do what she said.

A paper cartwheeled in front of the bookstore. I tucked Bilbo Baggins under one arm and braced myself for the dash from the car to the bookstore.

A sound like far-away fireworks, popping and crackling, began. I ducked. "What's that?"

"Just a little sleet. If you go fast, you'll hardly feel it." Kathy, our escort, nodded at the windshield, where tiny flecks of white hit the glass and bounced away.

But outside the protection of the car, the sleet was like tiny daggers on my exposed skin. I put a hand over Bilbo Baggins' eyes and ran for the door.

Long-legged Niall was there first, not even breathing fast. Fighting the gust of wind that wanted to blow it shut, he ripped open the door and held it for me as I darted through with Bilbo Baggins. I tugged open the inside door and gaped.

The bookstore had looked small from the outside, but inside, the center had been cleared of tables and bookshelves to make room for rows and rows of chairs. At the far end of the room, a raised platform supported two armchairs and a couple of potted ferns. Just in front of it was a long table with two chairs and two sets of stacked books, one with green covers and the other with red.

Almost every chair in the place was full. My eyes skimmed over the dozens of heads straight to the pair of stand microphones on the platform, one in front of each chair.

I was going to have to speak into one of those.

I squeezed my eyes shut and tried to forget the snickers of my elementary school reading group. The eye-rolls of my high-school classmates whenever we had to read—ugh—Shakespeare. The way the words swam on the page and I scrambled to pin them down and recite them.

"I don't feel so good." I clutched Bilbo Baggins so tightly he squirmed.

"It'll be fine. You'll be fine." Niall's slow, low voice was almost soothing. "Qiana sent you the list of questions, right?"

"Questions?"

"They were at the back of my itinerary. Didn't you get them?"

I'd hoped I'd never have to board the plane, much less answer questions.

He opened his satchel and pulled out a sheaf of papers. He flipped a few pages and held it out to me. "Read through these. They're nothing out of the ordinary. And if there are any you don't want to answer, just mark through them." He held out a pen.

Could I mark through them all? Read the passage I'd memorized and then skip to the signing part? I'd practiced signing my pen name, Sam Case. Big *S*, big *C*, with squiggly letters after the capitals. Fast. Efficient.

Carefully not touching his fingers, I took the list and scanned it. A few words jumped out at me. *Inspiration*—that was what Niall's mother had asked me last night. *Writing process. Next book.* How was I going to answer any of them? It was ludicrous, considering a mistake had prompted CASE to output *Magician in the*

Machine and that my plans involved hiding out in a research lab for the rest of my life.

A thin white man, his gray hair pulled back into a bun at the nape of his neck, tidier than my windblown one, scurried up to meet us. "Welcome, welcome. Mr. Flynn, I'd know you anywhere. And Ms. Case." He pumped our hands. "I'm Peter Pettingill, the store manager. We'll do a couple of photos first, and then—"

"No photos," I said, my voice flat and automatic. "It's in the agreement."

"No photos?" He shook his head. "We always do photos." He gestured behind the cash register, where dozens of pictures were tacked to the wall.

My stomach twisted. It seemed harmless to pose for a picture next to Niall. It probably wouldn't leave the bookstore. Peter Pettingill didn't look like he knew how to use Photoshop to put my head onto someone else's naked body.

"Do you want to?" Niall's voice was low in my ear, his breath tickling my neck. "You don't have to."

"Okay." My voice was a breathy whisper. I cleared my throat. "Okay."

Pettingill held up his phone. "Ready?"

The way the phone hid half his face rocketed me back. Not to a crowded, well-lit bookstore but to the bedroom in Stephen's swanky, off-campus apartment. I was a lowly freshman, still trying to figure out what the confident senior, someone even Mother liked, saw in me. So when he'd begged, I'd done a clumsy striptease. The memories were sharp snatches like the looping videos in Natalie's social media. The too-bright lamp shining on the white sheets and my naked skin. Stephen's dark hair and one eye behind his phone, snapping picture after picture. His pleas for me to touch myself and my embarrassed head-shake.

But it hadn't mattered. After, when Jackson had hacked into Stephen's computer, he hadn't deleted the photos fast enough. I'd watched over his shoulder and seen them all. And below the row of real nudes, Stephen had Photoshopped my head onto an actress's body in a still from a porn. Next to the ones I'd let him take, they didn't have to be realistic to be damning.

"No. No." I shook my head and backed away until my back hit a display table. "No."

"Hey." Niall was there, in front of me, blocking the man's camera. "Are you okay?"

I stared at the white button on his plaid shirt, gray crossing over darker gray, overlaid with pairs of thin red lines. "I can't."

"You can't take the pictures? Or you can't do the book talk? I can do it alone if you need to go to the hotel."

For a second, I fantasized about skipping the reading. About not having to stand up in front of all those people. About retreating to the hotel and hiding under the comforter with Bilbo Baggins. But what would Heidi say if I did? Would Martell side with her or with me? He hadn't been able to get me out of the tour. If he'd even tried.

"I'll do the talk. Just—just no photos."

"Are you sure?"

I dared to look at him then. His green eyes weren't the strident color of the cover of *Magician in the Machine* but soft and faded like a piece of sea glass. Maybe I'd screw it up. But I had to try. Not just because of what Heidi would do to me if I didn't but because Niall Flynn thought I could.

"I'll do it."

"Good." He reached toward my shoulder, like he'd caress it, but then he settled his big hand on Bilbo Baggins' head. "I'll take care of Pettingill. You take a minute. Breathe."

Niall smiled that camera-ready smile, threw an arm around Pettingill's shoulders, and led him off to the side. While they talked, the manager sneaked glances at me.

"Can I pat your dog?" The words came at the same time as a tug on the bottom of my jacket. I looked down into a child's face topped by curly black hair.

"Sure. His name is Bilbo Baggins." I eased my grip to expose more of Bilbo Baggins' fur. He wriggled in anticipation.

The kid buried a small hand in Bilbo Baggins' silky fur. "Like the Hobbit? He's so soft."

"He is. When I'm nervous, it always makes me feel better to touch him."

"You're nervous?" Round, dark eyes looked up at me.

"Yeah. I have to stand up there"—I tipped my chin toward the platform—"and read."

"Me and my dad came to see the authors talk. We read *Secrets of the Wood Elves* together. You're not that author, are you?"

"No, that's him." I let my gaze settle on Niall, who bent like a tree over the shorter bookstore manager, and the kid's eyes followed. "I didn't think that was a kids' book."

"Daddy helped with the hard words. He says we don't have to read only kids' books. We can read whatever books we want."

"My dad used to read to me, too. I hope you and your dad keep reading together for a long time." I tried to remember the happy times, when I'd snuggled up against my own dad, and for a few minutes every night, his time wasn't for his work or even my brothers and sister, but just for me. I tried not to think about how, without him, reading wasn't worth the trouble.

"If you get nervous, just be like Nieven and think about home. That'll make you feel better."

Who the hell was Nieven? And thinking about home would make me more nervous, not less. What would Mother say if she knew I had to read, to speak extemporaneously, in front of all these people today?

Still, I said, "Thanks."

Niall loomed between us. "Ready to head up there?" He must've talked Pettingill down because the manager had put away his phone.

"I met one of your fans." I extended a hand toward the kid.

He squatted to get closer to the kid's height. "Hey. What's your name?"

"Hero."

"Ah, your parents must be fans of Shakespeare. *Much Ado About Nothing*, right?"

The kid nodded.

"'If it proves so, then loving goes by haps: Some Cupid kills with arrows, some with traps.'" Niall's green-eyed gaze landed on me and then flitted away so fast I wasn't sure he'd done it on purpose. Shakespeare sounded knee-quiveringly resonant in Niall's deep voice, nothing like when my English teacher read it.

"I like *Secrets of the Wood Elves* better than Shakespeare. They talk like regular people."

Niall beamed at the kid. "And who's your favorite character?"

"Greva. She always rides up just in time to save Nieven."

"I like that about her, too. It was nice meeting you, Hero. I'll see you again when I sign your book, okay?"

"Okay." Hero's adoring gaze shone up at Niall.

I adored him a little, too, for his serious talk with that little kid. And the Shakespeare. And the way he'd fought off the store manager and his phone like a knight of old.

"Showtime." Niall held my gaze. "You ready?"

I shuddered. Once upon a time, before I'd made that awful mistake with Stephen, I'd hoped kids would look up to me. I'd wanted to be a programmer and entrepreneur like Jackson. I hadn't wanted the notoriety he'd created as a defense mechanism, but I'd wanted little girls to see what I'd done and think, *I could do that, too.*

But all that was in the past. Fame wasn't for me. After I did this tour and the truth was revealed, Dr. Martell and the university could take credit for CASE and leave me out of it. I never wanted to have to stand up in front of an auditorium full of scholars and explain what I'd done.

And that brought me crashing back to reality. I didn't want to be at this bookstore, talking about a book I hadn't written.

"No." I wasn't ready. All those people. Their stares. Their chuckles when I stumbled. My feet stuck to the floor.

"When we're up there, look at me. Listen to me. It'll be fine. Just like right now. Okay?"

"I don't know." I cast a longing look out the front door. Even subzero temperatures and sleet sounded better than having all those eyes and ears on me.

"We'll do it together. One." He paused. "Two." He gazed deep into my eyes. "Three."

And like they were powered by someone else, my feet started moving toward the platform. Niall's hand rested on my back, warm, steady, and sure. Maybe I could do this, after all.

12

NIALL

SAM'S FRECKLES—USUALLY such a subtle dusting, like grains of sand scattered on the page of a paperback at the beach—stood out stark against her too-pale skin. As she read the passage from her book, her voice trembled, and her gaze didn't leave the screen of her tablet. Yet I didn't see that she ever flipped a page. She squeezed the microphone, her knuckles white.

"I think she's about to lose her lunch," I muttered.

"No." Kathy put a restraining hand on my arm. "She's got that cute little dog up there with her. She'll do fine."

On the raised platform, Sam sat in the chair with her feet tucked up under her as if trying to make herself seem even smaller. The dog nestled beside her.

How the hell Sam had convinced Happy Troll to allow her to bring her dog on tour was beyond me. Though, given how superior *Magician in the Machine* was, they probably would've done anything to appease their star author. Even let her act like a diva.

She didn't look like a diva up there. When her voice had boomed out over the sound system, she'd jumped like a frightened mouse. She'd started out speaking so low, so hesitantly, that the audience members strained forward in their chairs. But as she read—slowly, carefully—her shoulders lowered. Soon she picked up speed, and while she'd never be an audiobook narrator or even a story-time librarian, her voice took on a more certain rhythm.

The audience loved it. We'd pulled a massive crowd at the bookstore near the Chicago lakefront. The people sat, silent and motionless, listening to her words. Perhaps it was the words themselves, or perhaps it was the contrast between the desolate, stripped-bare story full of hard edges and gritty dialogue and the elf-like beauty who'd written and performed it for them.

I was just as enchanted as they were.

Sooner than I'd expected, the audience applauded. *Good job, Qiana, coaching her to read a short excerpt her first time out.*

I strode to the front and turned on my own microphone. "Thanks, Sam. Don't forget, if you haven't already purchased your copy of *Magician in the Machine,* we'll have copies on the table for Sam to sign at the end. Now I'll read a passage from *Treachery of the Wood Elves.*"

The difference between my flowery descriptions and the starkness of Sam's prose couldn't have been more pronounced. The passage from *Treachery* was embroidered, rococo-style, with details: the scent of the horses' sweat, the thunder of their hooves, the sharp pain that arced from the stab wound in Nieven's side after the battle that ended the first book. Should I have cut it all to focus on the action as Sam had done?

Too late now. I wiped away the doubt and, taking a cue from Nieven, soldiered on.

During the question-and-answer period, Sam withered like a frost-bitten rose, her shoulders hunched and her voice low and monotone. Hadn't Qiana prepared her for it? She froze when an audience member asked, "Where did you get your inspiration?"

I knew for a fact that question was on Qiana's sheet. It was a softball. You could say literally anything: everyday life, dreams, the socio-political structure of the Ottoman Empire. I stared hard at her, willing her to say something, anything.

"Other books, I guess?" she said at last. "My dad used to read to me." She captured the gaze of a kid in one of the front rows. Hero, the one she'd been talking to before we ascended the platform.

"Any specifics?" I asked. I shouldn't have done it. I should have taken the next question and given her a break. But what a person reads says a lot about them. And I wanted to learn as much as I could about my tour partner, my muse.

She looked down, stroked the dog. "Tolkien. I remember we read *The Hobbit* together. In fact"—she picked up the dog and set him on her knees—"this guy's name is Bilbo Baggins. He's five years old, and I got him at the San Francisco SPCA. He likes long walks, unseasoned boneless chicken thighs, and being blow-dried after a warm bath. He hates beaches—the sand in his toes—and being alone."

The next two questions were about dogs, and Sam answered them with an ease she hadn't had when she was talking about her book.

Then the question came to me, the same one Sam had been asked a few minutes earlier. "Where do you get your inspiration, Niall?"

I had an answer, of course. I wasn't some newbie like Sam. But when I opened my mouth, I froze. When I'd prepared it, I hadn't expected the answer to the question to be sitting next to me. My throat went dry, and my tongue flopped uselessly in my mouth. I held up a finger and picked up the bottle of water next to my chair to take a long drink.

Sam's head cocked to the side. She had to be thinking about the dedication, too. Why hadn't we had it out last night in Columbus? Why hadn't she scolded me about it?

Why hadn't I taken her aside last night before she'd fled with Qiana to apologize for it?

I'd been acting like a coward, that's why. And I had to stop now. Today.

I set down the bottle of water. Still, I didn't have to do it in front of all these strangers. So I trotted out the answer I'd used on my first book tour. "There's a small forest on my family's farm, and a creek runs through it. When I was a kid, I used to run there after I'd finished my chores, and I'd lie on the forest floor and dream about the magical creatures who inhabited it."

Just like on my first tour, they ate it up. Everyone likes to hear about a farm boy with dreams who later finds success. Sometimes, I thought it was my backstory, and not my books, that had gotten me where I was today. And I hated that thought. I wanted to be valued for what I produced, not who I was. Especially considering who my father was.

I ended the Q and A after that, not wanting to field any follow-up questions, and we descended to the signing table.

Every time I signed the title page, the following page, the dedication, tried to burn its way through. Thank God for Kathy, who turned everyone's book to the correct page so I didn't inadvertently flip to it and spontaneously combust. Sweat beaded at my hairline and rolled down my back under my flannel shirt.

Finally, Sam's line dwindled, and she moved away from the table. *Almost done.* My hand hadn't cramped yet—it was in pretty good shape from writing my manuscripts longhand—but my muscles ached from sitting so long. I stretched and smiled at the next reader.

When the last person stepped up, electricity zapped through me. Sam stood over me, clutching a copy of my first book, *Secrets of the Wood Elves,* to her chest, the receipt tucked inside.

"You didn't have to buy a copy," I said. "Qiana would've gotten you one from the publisher."

One side of her mouth turned up. "I may be new, but I know how this works: you don't make money off free publisher copies."

"True."

"I thought I'd read this one first. Before I start on your new one."

A wave of relief gushed through me. She hadn't read the dedication. And I could explain before she did.

She handed me the book. As many as I'd signed, I hadn't yet gone nose-blind to the smell of fresh paper and glue, the heavenly scent of books. But this one had something extra, a woody, herbal scent layered over…rosemary.

"Look, I'm sorry," she said. "I should've said something to you that day at the university. But I was hoping I could get out of it. This." She waved her hand at the bookstore, that enchanting gesture that called to mind the flight of a sparrow. "That I didn't have to come out as Sam Case. That I could just be Sam Jones, and we could be…friends." She bit her lip, and I couldn't stop staring at it. Her lips were pink like rose petals. They looked petal-soft, too. Touchable. Kissable.

Nope. I squeezed my eyes shut. No creeping on my tour partner.

I cleared my throat. "Why wouldn't you—" Of course. The public speaking. She was one of those writers who wanted to stay in her cave and churn out words. Like Cormac McCarthy or Harper Lee. She didn't want to embody her brand, like Gabi was always pushing me to do. "I get it. I have to apologize, too."

"For what?" She crinkled her nose.

Lobelia's voice, low and melodic, whispered in my ear. *Courage.* She'd been brave. I could try it, too.

"Look." I pulled a copy of *Treachery* from the pile and flipped to the dedication page. "Read it. It's for you."

She took the book and studied the short inscription. She read it slowly, hesitating over the longer words. "'Dedicated to my violet-eyed muse, without whom this story wouldn't have found its soul.'" Her dark eyebrows slammed down the way I'd been afraid they would. "This is me? But my eyes are blue, not violet."

I spread my hands in front of me, palms up. "I'm a writer. A poet. I can get away with an excess of fancy." But she was wrong.

Her eyes were more than blue. They were the starry night. The deepest part of the ocean. Flowers with delicate petals that, if crushed, would stain your fingers purple.

"You dedicated the book to me?"

"Sort of." Confronted with the reality of Sam, I knew I'd embellished her, the same way I'd done with her eyes. I'd met someone new, and it had forged connections in my brain that'd made new words flow. I'd turned her into what I wanted her to be: my ethereal muse, hovering in that twilight space between a dream and consciousness.

But Sam didn't exist for my inspiration.

"I met an unexpected, intriguing woman in a museum, and again on a university campus. My idealized version of her inspired me. But you're a real person. With talent and your own creativity. I'm sorry."

She cocked her head, birdlike. "Sorry for...?"

"For turning you into something you're not. For making our interactions in San Francisco all about me." For feeling a little too much for Lobelia. "Normally, I'm better at distinguishing between fantasy and reality. But I was under deadline." I shrugged like it was no big deal she'd lifted me out of my creative slump, inspired a completely new character, literally saved the farm. I forced a smile even while my stomach shriveled. I hadn't told her all the truth. Maybe she wouldn't start *Treachery* while we were still on tour. Maybe she wouldn't see herself in Lobelia. Maybe Sally the goat would sprout wings and learn to fly, too.

Her lips tightened. "Maybe we inspired each other." She set the book on the table. "Sign it for me, please? Make it out to just Sam."

Above the dedication, I scrawled *To Sam* and signed below. I blew on the ink to dry it, then closed the book.

She took it, lightly brushing my fingertips. Her eyes really were the night sky in Ohio in summer, inky blue and spangled with stars.

I blinked and reached for the hand sanitizer. Holding the

bottle over Sam's hands, I drizzled liquid onto her flawless palm before I did the same with my own rough one. No, I didn't want to rub the gel into her hand and feel again how smooth it was.

"Come on, kids." Kathy's voice snapped the moment in two. "Niall's got an early interview, and Bilbo needs to stretch his legs."

I needed a stretch, too. And a slap upside the head for mixing up Samantha and Lobelia again.

I tugged on my coat. Chicago was colder than Ohio, and Sam's coat wasn't even Ohio-grade. It was made for cool, seasonless northern California, and certainly not for wind and sleet.

I picked up my wool scarf, the green one Mom had knitted for me for Christmas, and handed it to Sam. "Take this." My voice was as rough as my hands.

"But I can't—"

"It's cold out there. Can't have you catching something and being sick the rest of the tour."

"But that's not how—"

I took the scarf from her hands and wound it around her neck. The silky strands of her drooping bun caressed my fingers, and I shivered. "Humor me, okay? I'm just a Midwestern guy who knows it's important to keep warm."

"I think you're more than that." Those violet eyes twinkled.

"I think we're both more than we seem, Sam Jones."

Her smile faltered, and she turned to fuss with Bilbo. "Maybe."

13

NIALL

I DON'T KNOW who thought it was funny—Qiana, God, the universe—to put two people who'd been together all day—airport, airplane, car, book signing, car, an awkward dinner—in adjoining rooms at the Chicago hotel.

I sure didn't.

While I fumbled for my card key, Sam entered her room with Bilbo under her arm, dragging her suitcase behind her without a second look at me.

Maybe she was angrier than she'd let on about the dedication. Or maybe she was tired like me.

I shoved the card into the slot. Red. I pulled it out and thrust it back in. Red. Again. Flash of green, but I fumbled the card, and by the time I pressed the handle, it'd locked again. Slide. Red. Slide. Red. Slide. Green, and this time, I slammed down the handle and opened the door. I slipped through and kicked it shut. Fucking technology. Why couldn't I just have a goddamned key?

I dropped onto the bed, my eyelids drifting closed. It had to be a bad sign that I was already exhausted on day two of the tour. Give me a barn full of stalls to muck or a field to till, and I could go all day. Put me on an early-morning flight, drive me around in a car, and make me answer a question or two, and I felt like I'd been run through the combine.

My satchel lay beside me, its familiar old-leather smell a small comfort in the unfamiliar room. Gabi had loaded it with brand-new notebooks. It wasn't that late, and my fingers had been tingling all day. I hadn't had a moment to pick up a pen to capture the words Lobelia and Nieven had whispered, and now my hand was too heavy, my eyes too bleary to write.

An unexpected flash of glass caught my eye. The phone Gabi had insisted I bring on tour. Not a Swiftphone, but still a smartphone with the intimidating icons I'd refused to decipher.

I had promised I'd call Gabi that night to let her know how the tour was going so far. And tired or not, I kept my promises. I grabbed the phone and turned it on, pulling off the tape flag Gabi had placed on the power button. While I waited for it to power up, Sam murmured next door. Was she talking to her dog? It was a soothing cadence. My eyelids drooped.

Angry beeps startled me awake. Missed texts. Missed calls. Voice mail. The phone was just one more irritation.

Gabi's number was easy to find because it was the most recent missed call.

"It's about time you called me. Was your phone off?" Her voice was sharper than the soft Midwestern accents I'd heard today with their flat Os and two-syllable As.

"I have to turn it off when I'm at events."

"You know there's a vibrate feature, right?"

"The vibrations distract me, too."

She made a sound like a frustrated bobcat. "So how'd it go?"

"Fine. My part was fine. Sam was nervous, but she did okay."

"Fine. Okay. Where do your book-words come from? I have to read your manuscripts with a dictionary beside me, and you give me one-word descriptions of two days' worth of book events."

"The events were well-attended. The audience was supportive and enthusiastic. Happy now?"

"Better. What's Sam like?"

"You'll never believe it."

"Believe what?"

I turned away from the wall my room shared with Sam's. "Sam Case is actually Samantha Jones. I met her in—"

"Oh. My. God. Samantha Jones the socialite? The grad student? What the hell? Didn't you see her twice when you were in San Francisco? And the fact that she's a writer, too, with your *same publisher* never came up?" A keyboard clacked in the background.

"No, but—" At first, I'd felt the same way. But the anger had evaporated right about the time my fingers started to tingle. "She said she thought she could get out of the tour."

"Wait. Circle back. You liked her. You said she inspired you. You dedicated the fucking book to her, and now she's on tour with you?" If Gabi's voice went any higher, only Bilbo would be able to hear it. "Maybe that's why she wanted to get out of it. You're a total creep."

I flopped back onto the bed. "I know," I moaned. "I apologized. At the signing."

"For all of it?"

"For some of it. The dedication. She hasn't read the book yet. She's reading *Secrets* first. Maybe she'll stop reading before she gets to Lobelia."

Gabi's unusual silence told me exactly what she thought of that idea.

"I have to tell her, don't I?"

"You asked me before you turned me into an ax-wielding dwarf."

"That was different. We were already friends. When I wrote Lobelia, I didn't think I'd ever see Sam again."

"So you turned her into your manic pixie dreamgirl."

"Lobelia's not a manic pixie dreamgirl! She's got her own goals, separate from Nieven's. And I don't know that they're interested in each other. Romantically."

"She's not Nieven's dreamgirl, Niall. She's yours. Look at this picture."

"What picture?"

"I texted it to you. Take the phone away from your face and look at it. It's on Kari Singh's blog."

"Kari Singh? I met her. She's at Sam's university."

"Not anymore. She graduated, and now she's at *Gossip Grrlz*. An up-and-comer. She's built a bit of a specialty around you. And now some of the other gossip sites are following her. And you, too."

I tapped the text icon at the top of the screen and then opened the photo she'd sent. Sam—though she'd been Samantha then—and I stood in front of the beige building on her campus. That blogger, Kari Singh, must have snapped it. Sam's face was guarded like I'd remembered. But I grinned at her, completely gone.

Oh, shit.

"You like her, Niall."

"No, I don't." The words came too quickly to be believable. "She's a total techie. I don't think her phone has left her hand since I met her. She even read her passage on a tablet. She brought her purse dog on this tour like a diva. We have nothing in common."

"Wait, I've seen this movie before. They both say, 'No way,' in Act One, but by the middle of Act Two, they're in love."

"Fuck you." I rubbed my hand over my eyes.

"Love you, too, buddy."

14

NIALL

AS I PULLED Sam's suitcase from the trunk of the car, I gazed across the street at Centennial Park. It was warmer in Nashville than it'd been in Chicago, the afternoon sun lighting up the still-bare trees. I'd go for a run. Maybe the sap starting to stir in the trees would wake Lobelia and Nieven from their wintry sleep, and they'd speak to me.

I thanked the driver and heaved Sam's suitcase onto the curb. Clutching Bilbo's carrier, Sam stretched out a hand for the suitcase.

I waved her off. "I've got it."

She jutted out her jaw. "No, I—"

"Sam. You take care of your dog. And your"—I waved at the computer bag slung across her petite frame—"equipment. I've got this." She was rich. She had to be used to other people carrying her shit.

But she hesitated. Even with her bulging satchel weighing her down and that dog of hers whining in his bag, she glared at me. "I can take care of myself."

"I know you can." I tightened my grip on the handle of her

suitcase. "But let me carry this for you. My mother would have my head if I didn't."

A hint of a smile teased at the corners of her mouth. "I liked your mother."

I eased my grip. "She liked you, too. Now go on in. I'm right behind you."

She glanced again at the heavy suitcase but shifted the weight on her shoulders, turned, and walked into the hotel.

Focused on her regally straight back as I followed her inside, I didn't see him until he called my name.

No. There was no way *he* was there, in a Holiday Inn in Nashville. Not when I was lugging suitcases like a bellhop and rumpled and sweaty from our early-morning flight. The universe couldn't be that cruel.

"Niall." But that was his voice, stirring up long-ago memories of curling into his side on Grandpa's worn couch while he and my mother talked about grownup things.

I took a second to blank my expression, to roll back my shoulders, before I turned to him. "Paul." I used to call him Dad, but that had ended along with his visits to the farm. I held out my hand for a shake.

Irritation tightened his expression before he flashed me a tight smile. He gripped my hand, his palm smooth against my rough one. He wore one of his signature black dress shirts, the sleeves rolled up, with a stiffly pressed pair of black jeans. "Good to see you, son."

"What brings you to Nashville, Paul?" I'd seen him a few times in San Francisco and New York. Occasionally L.A. But never anywhere in the center of the country, not since he'd left Ohio for the last time when I was twelve. It couldn't be me he'd come to see, could it? Unless he'd finally read my book. I hadn't asked him before I'd inserted him as the villain.

His gaze flicked behind me. "Is that Samantha Jones?"

I turned, and she was at my elbow.

She stuck out her hand. "Good to see you again, Mr. Swift."

Again? Oh, right. Sam and my father traveled in the same circles of rich techies. I stepped to my left to give her more space.

He shook her hand. "What a surprise to find you here in Nashville with Niall."

"We're on a book tour together. She's Sam Case." I watched him carefully, and although his eyes widened theatrically, the surprise didn't extend to the rest of his face. He knew. Why was he there?

"I saw Audrey last week. She didn't mention your writing career."

"No, it's"—she looked down at her boot, her cheeks pink—"on the down-low."

"I see." And those sharp green eyes, harder than mine, saw everything. "Why don't we sit down and catch up?" He gestured behind him at a seating area screened by a gas fireplace and a few potted ficus trees.

"Sure, I'll just check in." Sam took a step back toward the hotel desk.

"Join us. Please." And he smiled, showing his teeth.

"Oh, um." Her gaze flicked to mine.

"It's fine," I muttered. Her presence gave me courage—and hope. Would he finally give me the approval I craved? I straightened my spine and wheeled the suitcases next to the ficus, then lowered myself to the stiff sofa. Sam unzipped Bilbo's carrier and sat on the other end, settling the dog on her lap.

"How's your mom?" My father arranged his lanky frame in one of the wing chairs opposite the sofa.

"She's fine." She was probably sitting down to a simple supper with Grandpa, her hands rough and chapped from hard work and her dark hair, threaded with gray, curling on her shoulders. My father's shoulder-length, sun-kissed auburn mane was pulled back into a bun. Were those highlights? I curled a fist onto my knee.

"What can I do for you, Paul?"

"Do for me? I'm just here to see my son." He wagged a finger at me. "If you'd texted me your tour schedule, I wouldn't have had to chase down your publicist."

My shoulders lowered. He'd come to see me. I'd finally done something right.

"I don't text." I flattened my hand and rubbed it on my thigh.

He smiled, tight. "I saw the news about the show starting filming. Congratulations. Do you think you'll be spending more time in L.A. now?"

I blinked. Did he actually want to meet more often? "Not really. I'm not involved with the show, other than consulting, which I can do by phone."

"No producer role?" His gaze was sharp.

"No." I held back a shudder. Living in L.A., working on the show, I'd never finish my book. Why was he asking about the series? We couldn't do a product placement of his phones on a fantasy show.

"You should negotiate for that next time. Just a little free advice from your dad." He chuckled.

I narrowed my eyes at him. What was his angle?

"Samantha." He twisted to face her. "Any Hollywood plans in the works for you?"

Her cheeks pinked. "No. The movie people said the effects would be too expensive. So it's just the book."

"Ah. Then you'll go home to San Francisco?"

"That's right." She eased back against the sofa. But the line between her eyebrows, the one that hadn't been there when I'd met her in San Francisco but had furrowed her forehead since Columbus, remained.

"So you'll be rejoining the family business."

She clutched the dog to her chest. "N-not really. I'm graduating this spring and planning on pursuing a career in research."

Research? Why wouldn't she write more books?

"But once a Jones, always a Jones, eh?" My father leaned forward.

She curled up like a hedgehog, and her words squeaked out. "I guess?"

Watching Sam's confidence collapse had turned my pride and excitement at seeing my father into simmering irritation. I tugged at the collar of my flannel shirt.

"Listen," he said, "I've been trying to get a meeting with your brother Jackson for a month. We've developed a handheld device to use in factories, and bundled with Synergy's software, it'd be a homerun pitch to auto manufacturers. You can call him, have his people connect with mine."

My eyes widened. *This* was why he'd chased me—us—to Nashville? To ask Sam to pitch her brother on a business deal?

I rocketed to my feet. "No."

"What?" My father leaned back and spread his palms. "It's a win-win. Jackson gets a new way to sell his software, I move more units. I'll even give Samantha a cut of the action. A finder's fee, we'll call it."

Did Sam want a finder's fee? Her wardrobe of faded pants and T-shirts on the tour was more starving artist than tech heiress. I'd assumed she was trying to blend in. But what if something had happened to her money? I'd certainly never seen a penny of my father's fortune. Not that I'd wanted it. All I'd craved was his notice.

Sam stood, clutching her dog to her chest. "No, thank you, Mr. Swift. I don't want to get in the middle. Jackson runs his business the way he wants it." She bestowed a tense smile on him. "Have a good evening." She shouldered her bags and reached for her suitcase.

"Wait, Sam. I'm coming with you." I turned to my father, who'd stood. He was tall, but I was taller. I pushed aside the little boy who'd sought his father's elusive approval. "I'm used to your treating me like shit. But don't ever try to leverage me to get to my friends again. Understand me?"

"You're making a mistake. She is, too." His emerald-green eyes glittered.

"I don't think so. I think you made a mistake by coming here." I grabbed both suitcases and strode to the hotel desk to check us in. My body vibrated like I'd been struck by lightning.

Sensing Sam at my elbow, I muttered, "Are you okay?"

"Yeah. You?"

"I guess so." I rubbed my chest, right over the spot that ached because I'd discovered—again—my dad didn't give a shit about me.

"You were great, standing up to him. That must've taken a lot of courage."

"I wish—" I stopped. Sam was into tech like he was. She wouldn't get it.

But she looked up at me with those otherworldly eyes, the same ones that had bewitched me all those months ago at that fundraiser where neither of us belonged, and set her hand on my forearm. Sparks traveled all the way up my arm to my chest and set my heart rabbiting. She asked, "What do you wish, Niall?"

It had to be a spell she'd cast on me because my mouth opened and I said, "That he'd come for me." The last time I'd said that, I'd been ten, crying into my mother's shoulder because Santa Claus hadn't brought my father home for Christmas. I'd never, ever said it to another adult. Not even Gabi.

Sam pushed up on the toes of her combat boots and stretched her arms around my shoulders. The tightness of her embrace made it hard to breathe. Or maybe that was the woodsy smell of her hair. When I ducked my head down to chase the scent, she whispered in my ear, "Paul Swift is an asshole who doesn't deserve you."

A surprised laugh bubbled out of my chest, and I hugged her back. "Thank you."

She didn't let go right away, and I let myself savor the moment of human connection. I had to bend a little, but we fit together, her head against my shoulder, her spine curved so her torso pressed to mine. The tingles spread from my heart out to my fingertips.

Could she feel them, too, where my hands prickled against her back?

Maybe she did because she gently wriggled out of my arms. She bent her head to fuss with Bilbo's carrier, but her chest heaved just like mine, like we'd been running and not standing in the hotel lobby.

A run. That was exactly what I needed to dispel the weird energy.

The desk clerk handed over the key cards, and I followed Sam toward the elevators, dragging our bags.

Who the hell was my tour partner? She was no flighty socialite like Gabi had tried to portray her. She wasn't a tech wheeler-dealer like my father thought she was. She was smart. Independent. And soft as a warm bed on a snowy night. If she hadn't been my tour partner, I'd have asked her to get a drink with me, and we'd have talked until I figured her out.

But she was my tour partner. And though my skin tingled again when she handed me my key card, I fumbled it into the door and entered my room alone.

15

SAM

I LET the hot water run over my skin, trying to warm myself from the outside in. Nashville wasn't as frigid as Chicago had been, but it was still colder and drier than I was used to. And then there was the stuff that made me cold on the inside: reading in front of strangers, fearing I'd stumble and they'd laugh. Not to mention Paul Swift's reminder that all I was good for was making tech connections. Like a router.

He'd treated his son the same way. He'd used him, too. I knew what it was like to be nothing more than a bargaining chip to a parent. He'd stood up to Paul the way I wished I could've stood up to my mother. To Heidi. And Dr. Martell. I'd hugged Niall out of admiration.

Bullshit. It wasn't admiration that made my nipples go hard against his chest.

I poured my rosemary shampoo into my hand and massaged it through my hair. The attraction I'd felt had caught me by surprise. If I hadn't been lying to him, Niall could've been a good friend. Kind. Supportive. *Look at me. It'll be fine.*

Fine? Hardly. Fourteen more days of being on display, of unfamiliar rooms, of airplane air and the jarring clicks of camera shutters. I scrubbed the shampoo out of my hair like I could wash it all away: the prickle of sleet on my cheeks, the strangers' stares, the brush of Niall's hand that made goosebumps erupt on my skin.

Bilbo Baggins' high-pitched barks startled me.

"Hey, Bilbo Baggins, it's okay. I'm almost done," I shouted through the open bathroom door. I couldn't let him bark too long. The hotel manager who'd checked us in had given Bilbo Baggins the stink-eye. He'd said they had a no-pets policy but would make an exception for my service animal as long as he behaved himself.

But Bilbo Baggins had forgotten that warning, and he was yapping his little head off. I shut off the water and wrapped a towel around myself before stepping out into the room.

Bilbo Baggins yipped again and scrabbled at the door. Shit, he'd scratch it, and then we'd be in trouble. I strode toward him. "It's okay, little buddy. It's not an intruder. It's just our dinner." When I'd placed the order, I'd typed into the comments that they should leave it outside my door without knocking for exactly this reason. But they didn't always read the comments.

I scooped up Bilbo Baggins and opened the door to grab the food. The food wasn't there on the hall carpet. Only a pair of sneakers. Low-cut socks. A muscled set of calves, sweat trickling through the forest of auburn hair. A pair of nylon workout shorts, on the longer side but short enough to show off the lower edge of a shapely pair of quadriceps.

A T-shirt, damp and sticking to his torso. And were those—my gaze stalled out there—ab muscles? The shirt wasn't tight enough for me to count, but there was definition. For sure.

And holy shit, those pecs. Squared-off, the nipples pointed. To either side, the sleeves could barely contain the biceps that bulged under them. Were all Nashville delivery guys this cut? My skin tingled. If so, I might stay awhile. And order lots of Thai food.

A throat cleared, reminding me that there was a person

standing in the hall, not just a sexy fitness mannequin. I looked up into his face.

"I—ah—didn't know if you knew—ah—your towel—I mean, your food. Your food is here." Niall's face had gone as red as his hair. When he held the plastic bag toward me, his forearm muscles bulged. My mouth watered, and not because of the aroma of my drunken noodles.

I took it from him, but I was still staring at his naked forearm. I'd only seen his arms covered by those plaid shirts he always wore. I had no idea he was hiding all…this. He'd been handsome in his suit at that fundraiser when I'd first met him, but now? Delicious. My fingers accidentally brushed his, and I felt a zing right down to my core.

His chest expanded sharply. "You always answer the door in a towel?" His voice was rough.

"I thought—never mind. Bilbo Baggins was barking."

"You should be careful." He jerked his gaze from my torso— had he been staring at Bilbo Baggins or my towel-covered chest? —to my face. "That dog isn't going to protect you from someone with nefarious purposes."

I clutched Bilbo Baggins to my chest, pinning the towel in place. "It's only you at my door. Do you have nefarious purposes?"

He licked his lower lip. "No." His freckles had disappeared against his flushed skin.

I leaned against the doorframe, letting the bag of food dangle from my fingers. It'd been a while since my last one-night stand. With Kyle. Okay, that'd been a bad idea. But in general, hookups were great. All the pleasure, none of the vulnerability. "Are you sure?"

"No. I mean yes! I'm sure. I'd never. Not with—" He mumbled something that sounded like *inappropriate.*

"Really?" I didn't see anything so inappropriate. Aside from my being mostly naked in the open doorway. The towel, soaked at the top by my wet hair, loosened at my chest. I set down the food to have one hand free to hold it closed.

His gaze followed my hand for an instant and then shot back up to my eyes. "Sam, I respect you. You're my colleague. I know there have been some instances of sexual harassment in the publishing industry, but I'm not one of those guys."

I wrinkled my nose. "I'm not talking about sexual harassment. I'm talking about two consenting adults scratching an itch." The Niall-sized itch I'd had since I'd hugged him earlier. He'd been decent to me. Who cared about the silly dedication?

He wouldn't hurt me. Couldn't. I wouldn't let him. A book tour with benefits wasn't like screwing my officemate. Just a little casual hotel sex and then, bam, two weeks later, done, and I'd never see him again. No messy feelings. In fact, the more I thought about it, the more I liked the idea. Did the gift shop stock condoms?

"But you're my tour partner. I wouldn't—"

"What, you're some kind of monk? Or a no-sex-outside-marriage person? Your body is a temple and all that?" The temple thing was working for him. I wanted to saunter in and splay myself across his altar. I squeezed my thighs together.

"No, that's not what I—I think we need to maintain our boundaries." He rubbed his hand over his chest, making the nipples stand at attention. The tease. Mine did the same in sympathy.

"Boundaries. Okay." I shrugged, gripping the towel tightly. His body might say yes, but he'd said no, and I had to respect that. I'd brought my vibrator and plenty of batteries. I perused his sweaty post-workout body one last time, storing it in my spank bank. Respecting those boundaries, you know. "You could moonlight as a fitness instructor. People pay a lot to look like"—I briefly released the towel to wave at his body—"all that. Have you thought about doing videos on TikTok?"

"On what?"

"TikTok." Funny, he didn't look that old. "You know, the short video sharing platform?"

The slack expression on his face told me he didn't know. "I don't do workouts, really, except running when I'm on tour. Working on the farm keeps me in shape."

Damn, now I'd fantasize about him tossing big bales of hay around. Ooh, or those big quads cinched around the heaving sides of a horse. Though it'd be a shame to cover them up in a pair of jeans. Maybe a kilt, like Jamie in *Outlander?* Mmm, yes. I squeezed my thighs tighter. I'd have to see to those needs first, before dinner.

"Well, if there's nothing else, I should probably, um…" I tilted my head back toward my room.

"Oh. Right. The first event tomorrow's at noon. Meet you downstairs in the lobby at eleven?"

"Sure." Though we'd already covered all that during the ride from the airport.

"G'night. Night, Bilbo." With one finger, he rubbed Bilbo Baggins on the top of the head, right between his ears, the way he loved. That put his finger teasingly close to my chest. For a second, I imagined that finger slipping to the top of my towel, dragging it down, before he pressed his sweaty body against my clean one.

Wow. I really needed to unpack that vibrator.

"Night, Niall." The towel gaped a little when I bent to pick up my to-go bag, and I didn't care. I let the door close behind me, shutting out his slack jaw and blown pupils. Two could play the teasing game.

16

NIALL

IT WAS WAY TOO EARLY when I dragged myself out of the hotel's elevator in Miami. Had I even slept since Chicago? I hadn't in Nashville. My run had relaxed me enough, I'd hoped, to write. I'd been looking forward to a hot shower and a few hours with my notebook, but then I'd had to knock on her door.

I could've passed it by. She'd probably known her dinner was there. I'd wanted to check on her. No, I wouldn't lie, not even to myself. I'd wanted to see her. Away from the stress of the crowds, I'd wanted to catalog a few more of her movements, compare them to what I'd imagined Lobelia doing.

I'd gotten a lot more than that. Two days later, it was still burned like an afterimage on my retinas. An expanse of pale skin just a few shades darker than the hotel's white towel. Droplets of water still clinging to her cheeks, her shoulders, the tops of her feet. Her dark hair hanging wet and uncombed down to her breasts, which the towel barely contained. And I'd stared at her like a creep while I muttered words like *respect* and *boundaries.* All I'd wanted to do was tug that towel off her, press her right up against the door, and kiss her until neither one of us could breathe.

I slapped my hand against my forehead to jostle out the lascivious thoughts. She was my tour partner. A newbie to the industry. It didn't matter that people did it all the time. Niall Flynn didn't do that. Not after the example my dad had set on his business trips. The road was full of opportunities, but a fling on tour wasn't what I wanted. I was holding out for the real thing. Commitment. Mutual respect. True love. Happily ever after, just like in the stories.

Fortunately, I'd channeled my sexual energy to write. I'd filled an entire notebook. Too bad I'd have to go back in and scratch out all the sexual innuendo before I sent it to Gabi.

A laugh—no, a giggle—caught my ear. I blinked. My mental image of Sam didn't square with the woman who was curled on a sofa in the hotel lobby, her dog in her lap and her phone held out in front of her, giggling.

Like I was under a compulsion spell, I drifted closer. Sam's focus was on the screen, and she didn't notice. Bilbo did, and he wiggled in her arms.

"And then I lost it," she said, closing her eyes and shaking her head. "I told him he should do fitness videos on TikTok!"

Sam listened for a second. "No, sorry, you're going to have to be satisfied with the publicity shots. He turned me down." She shrugged. "It took two rounds with my rabbit to chill out." She paused for a second and then giggled again.

I was on fire. They were going to find a pile of ash and my flannel shirt if I let myself imagine her lying on the bed, the towel flung aside, her legs spread, and—

Tour partner, Niall. I wouldn't be one of those guys who used his success to lure in a newbie. I cleared my throat.

When she looked up, her cheeks pinked. Not like the flaming red my entire face had to be, but a delicate, rose-petal pink. "Oh. Hey, Niall. Come say hi to my friend Marlee."

"What?"

She patted the sofa cushion. "I know we have to go. It'll only take a minute. She wants to meet you."

Sorcery. I sat beside her.

"Closer." She pulled out one of her earbuds, wiped it on the hem of her shirt, and then jammed it into my ear.

"...so handsome!" The pretty white woman on the screen clapped her hand over her mouth. "Sam! You didn't—Hi, Mr. Flynn. Or should I call you Niall?"

I gave her my photo-ready smile. We could be normal. I could pretend I hadn't heard Sam's side of their conversation. "Nice to meet you, Marlee. Niall is fine." This close to Sam, I could smell the rosemary in her hair. And dog breath. Bilbo licked my chin, and I stroked his silky fur. My other arm jammed awkwardly into my side. Sam had made me sit close enough that we both showed on the screen, and there wasn't room for my shoulder. I turned toward her and propped my arm along the back of the sofa. Her shoulder notched into my chest like it belonged there.

"Can you believe Sam didn't tell me she was writing a book? She was doing her Ph.D. research and interning, too. She's amazing, right?" Marlee raised her eyebrows.

I stole a glance at Sam, who pressed her lips tightly together. "Amazing." I wrote full time and hadn't produced a book as groundbreaking as hers. "Have you read it?"

"I—ah—I started it." Marlee toyed with the ends of her hair with the hand that wasn't holding her phone. "It's not what I usually read."

"You should read Niall's book," Sam said. "I'll get him to sign a copy and bring it to you when I get back."

"You've read it?" Marlee tipped her head to the side. What did that mean? Why was Marlee surprised that Sam had read my book? I turned to her, but her face had gone expressionless.

"I started it. Everybody loves it."

Oh. She hated it. My face burned again. At least I didn't have to worry about Sam recognizing herself in Lobelia. I glanced at my watch. "We need to—"

"Gotta go, Marlee. Tell Tyler I said hi." Sam smiled at the screen, but she looked pained.

"I will. Call me this weekend and tell me how it's going. That is, if you're not too busy being OTPs." Marlee pursed her lips and waggled her eyebrows. "Not on Saturday morning; that's when I go to see Dad. Nice meeting you, Niall." She waved, and the screen blanked.

Sam shoved the phone into one of the many pockets of her cargo pants and held out her hand. I dropped the earbud into it. She wiped them both again with her shirt and dropped them into a different pocket.

"OTPs?" I took Bilbo from her so she could gather her things.

She busied herself with the dog carrier. "One true pairing. Marlee's a bit of a romantic."

"She thinks you and I are—" I pointed a finger between us.

She stood and took Bilbo from me. When she brushed my hand, my skin sang. "She sees them everywhere. Legolas and Gimli. The Burger King and the Starbucks mermaid. Even Bilbo Baggins and my neighbor's Corgi. It's nothing."

"Nothing," I echoed. I was glad Marlee wasn't there in person to see the bulge in my jeans from hearing Sam talk about masturbating. But that was just a physical reaction. It didn't mean anything. Certainly not that we were meant to be together.

"Time to go, right?" Without looking at me, she turned toward the exit.

"Definitely." I wouldn't think about Sam like that anymore. I couldn't. She was my tour partner, and we'd be together for two more weeks.

She was not my OTP.

Regardless of what my body thought.

17

SAM

NEW YORK. By the time we checked into the hotel after midnight, my nerves buzzed like the server room back at the university. But the rest of my body moved like I was in a tub of homemade slime, the kind Jackson and Andrew and I used to make from Elmer's glue and Borax when Joelle was our nanny.

We'd spent the day at a fantasy convention down in Florida. Between keeping an eye out for camera phones, being hugged by strangers in spandex or faux fur, and having Niall spray my hands every few seconds with sanitizer gel while reminding me of the dangers of "con crud," my firewall was down. I felt too open, too exposed.

As I pocketed the key card, I asked the hotel clerk, "Would you ask the bellman to send my suitcase up? I need to walk my dog."

The trip from Florida had wrecked poor Bilbo Baggins. He blinked slowly up at me. But if he didn't go out now, he'd wake up at some unreasonable hour of the morning even though we didn't have to get up early for an event the next day.

"It's almost 1 a.m. You can't go out alone in New York City."

Niall must've overtaxed his voice at the convention. It was rough as gravel, and it made heat pool in my belly.

Yeah, the way he'd tried to take care of me at the convention had reminded me too much of Mother. But it had also been kind of adorable to listen to his dire warnings about bringing home too much swag. Then when he'd gotten up on stage and said brilliant things about books, I'd gotten a little warm, if you know what I mean, and it wasn't because of the Florida heat. Too bad I was too tired to do anything about it. I'd walk Bilbo Baggins and then fall face-first into clean, white sheets.

"Of course I can. I've got a guard dog right here. You'll protect me, right, Bilbo Baggins?"

He curled up on the hotel carpet.

Raising his eyebrows, Niall crossed his arms. "That dog is more cat than Cujo."

"He's just saving up his energy for all the protecting he'll be doing. Come on, Bilbo Baggins." I scooped him up and grabbed a plastic bag from his carrier.

Once we were out on the rain-slicked sidewalk, I set him down. I stretched, inhaling the scent of ozone and taxicab exhaust. The passing storm had left heavy clouds racing west to east overhead, the undersides glowing with the reflected lights of Manhattan.

Bilbo Baggins sniffed a fire hydrant. I'd be sure to take him to Central Park tomorrow—oops, later today—so he could play with other dogs. He was an extrovert, unlike me.

He stilled, cocking his head to listen to the heavy footsteps that echoed off the stone buildings behind us. His skinny legs trembled.

I knew better than to show fear on the city streets. "Focus, Bilbo Baggins. Do your business so we can go to bed." I tugged on his leash and paused at a sad-looking tree growing out of a small patch of dirt in the sidewalk. Bilbo Baggins sniffed it, trying to evaluate its worthiness for his squat. Then he raised his head, let out a single yip, and pressed his tiny body against my leg.

I glanced over my shoulder. A dark, hulking figure loitered a few yards away. I wished I'd let Marlee talk me into bringing a canister of pepper spray. "Let's go, Bilbo Baggins."

I dragged him to the next tree. The figure followed. Copper gleamed under a streetlight.

I sighed, the tension rolling off my shoulders. "Stop lurking over there," I called. "You almost scared us."

Niall approached, slowly. "You should be scared out here in the middle of the night."

As soon as he spoke, Bilbo Baggins did a full-body wag, dancing until Niall bent to scratch him between the ears.

"There are people all around." I waved at a threesome of women across the street, tottering in their high heels. "And he may look friendly now, but Bilbo Baggins is fierce when threatened."

Niall snorted. "Is that why you brought him? For protection?" How did he still smell like cypress and eucalyptus after being hugged by all those sweaty cosplayers?

"Ha-ha. I don't need protection. I couldn't leave him behind in a kennel. He belongs with me. He's my best friend."

"You mean like 'man's best friend?'"

"No." I was too tired to chuckle and tell the lie. "I mean, he's the one who's been there for me through…everything." I waved my hand in a feeble communication of the stresses of three years of graduate school, my frustrations with CASE, and dealing with Mother's expectations. Bilbo Baggins never expected anything of me other than kibble and a place at my side. And his bulging brown eyes were full of love whether I'd made a brilliant A.I. discovery or utterly failed at everything I'd tried that day. I wished I'd had him in undergraduate when things blew up with Stephen.

Bilbo Baggins had done his business, and I bent to pick it up. Niall crouched and held out his fist. Bilbo Baggins trotted up to him, sniffed his hand, and licked his knuckle. As Niall scratched him behind the ears, Bilbo Baggins wagged his tail and closed his eyes.

Damn, I wanted some of that. But aside from the hand at my back at that first signing in Chicago, Niall hadn't touched me on purpose. Not even a handshake. Weren't Midwesterners supposed to be demonstrative? He'd hugged Qiana that first night, in Columbus.

But he didn't want to touch me.

Exhaustion hit me like a crushing wave. I could've crawled onto the nearest set of steps and taken a nap right there. I tied off the bag and turned toward the hotel. "Let's go."

Niall stood and fell into step beside me. Bilbo Baggins had other ideas. Confident now with Niall as his protector, he moved at a snail's pace, sniffing at bits of trash on the sidewalk. At this rate, it was going to take us half an hour to walk the two blocks to the hotel.

"You have a dog, too, right?" I remembered the one in his author photo on the back flap of his book. "A big, dark, hairy one?"

He grinned, his teeth flashing in the streetlight. "An Irish Wolfhound. Thorin Oakenshield."

I laughed, the sound surprising the quiet street. "What a coincidence."

"Hardly," he said. "You and I are both Tolkien fans. It makes sense that we'd name our pets after our favorite characters."

"I guess so." I looked down at Bilbo Baggins in case my expression cracked. I almost always thought about Dad right before I went to bed. Remembering how I used to cuddle up against his wide chest, his black-socked feet hanging off the side of my narrow twin bed, the book in my lap. He'd sat silent, letting me struggle to pin down the words before I shouted them out in triumph. Other times, when school or Mother had been too much, he'd read them out himself, his steady, low voice weaving tales about warriors, adventurers, and a burglar.

"You all right?" Niall asked. "I thought for sure when I brought up Tolkien, you'd have something to say."

I winced, remembering that first signing when I hadn't known how to answer the question about inspiration. Since then, I'd learned to talk about Tolkien. It wasn't even a lie, really. I'd loaded *The Hobbit* and the *Lord of the Rings* series into CASE to teach it about language. Although the answer seemed to resonate with the readers, it didn't make me feel less like a fraud. "I'm just tired."

"Let's get you to bed, then." His body tensed. "Your bed, I mean. Alone. Shit," he muttered. He whistled, an eardrum-piercing sound in the quiet street. "Come on, Bilbo."

Bilbo Baggins trotted up, and we walked faster toward the hotel.

As we passed St. Patrick's Cathedral, Niall asked, "Have you been to New York before?"

"A few times." Dad used to come for work, and when a trip lined up with a school holiday, sometimes we'd all go together. After Mother had married Charles, I'd come once with them, but I'd refused their next invitation.

"Any plans while you're here? When we're not doing events?"

"Central Park. I'll take Bilbo Baggins there tomorrow."

"What about shopping? Museums? Shows?"

"Not exactly dog-friendly. Bilbo Baggins and I haven't spent a lot of quality time together this week, so I want to make it up to him."

At last, we walked through the automatic door into the light of the hotel lobby. Niall said, "I like parks, too. If you need a—a companion, let me know. I throw a good tennis ball."

The elevator door was already open, and we stepped inside. Niall hit the button for our floor. I'd stopped questioning all the neighboring rooms. It must've been a Happy Troll policy.

"Thanks for the offer. I'll consider it."

He smiled, but his eyes were glassy with fatigue. He'd been up early that morning—yesterday morning—for a phone interview.

The tour was just as hard, if not harder, on him. The expectations were higher for him than for a newbie. Plus, he was saddled with having to coach me through those miserable Q and A sessions.

The doors opened on our floor, and I pulled the key card from my pocket. "Well, good-night."

He walked with me to my door. "Just—just peek inside. Check that your bag made it up and everything's okay."

"Really?" He'd protected me since that first day in Chicago, but this was something more. "We've stayed in hotels every night this week. I'm sure it's fine."

"This is New York. Humor me." He leaned against the wall.

I opened the door. How far did this protective streak go? "Do you want to come in?"

His sleepy eyes widened. Shit! That sounded like I was inviting him in for sex. Which he'd made clear he didn't want.

"I meant to look for trolls or serial killers, whatever you think is hiding under the bed in scary New York. Not, like, a nightcap. Do people even have those anymore? Do you think this place has a minibar?"

He pushed off the wall with a huff that could've been a laugh or exasperation. "With the prices in New York, you might be safer with the trolls than the minibar." He took two steps into the room and shoved his hands into his pockets, as if to avoid touching anything in my space. The door swung shut with a thump and a click.

The room was tiny, with only enough space for a double bed, a compact bathroom, and a shallow closet. I dropped Bilbo Baggins' leash so he could sniff it out and tossed my coat on the bed. I opened the closet door. Nothing but empty hangers and one of those little safes with the keypad. I flipped on the bathroom light and even pushed back the shower curtain. Next, I checked the lock on the door to the adjoining room.

It wasn't until I turned around and saw Niall watching me that I remembered it was the door to his room. My cheeks heated. "Sorry, I—"

"It's fine. The tour is a lot of togetherness. We need boundaries."

The room was too small for boundaries. He filled it up with his big frame and his flannel and that woodsy scent he carried.

"I guess we're all clear, then," I whispered, not wanting to disturb the late-night stillness.

"Good." He scratched his chin, the sound rasping through the tiny room. The rolled-up sleeves of his plaid shirt exposed the red-gold hairs on his forearm. The flannel looked soft. So did the hair.

The next thing I knew, I was touching his arm. Just one finger dragged through the forest of springy hair from his elbow to his wrist. It was as silky as I'd imagined. The sensation traveled up my arm to warm my chest.

I froze. "Sorry, I—"

"It's okay. You can touch me."

Greedy, I slid my fingertip onto the back of his hand and traced over the bumps of his knuckles.

He turned his hand over, exposing his palm. This side of his hand was clear of freckles, but it was ringed in calluses that snagged at my fingers. When I traced a path onto the smooth skin inside his wrist, he shivered.

He unfolded his other arm and brought it up slowly. He laid his hand on my shoulder over my T-shirt, his fingers curling back along my shoulder blade. "Is this all right?"

"Yeah." If he squeezed a little harder, it might work out the knot of stress I'd carried in my shoulders since I'd seen that person dressed as The Magician at the convention.

Instead, his hand drifted across my back under my looped-up ponytail to my nape. I shivered.

"Still good?"

His hand was warm, almost hot, on my neck. He squeezed, easing the tight muscles. Prickles of relief flowed down my back. I nodded.

He slid his other hand out of mine and, with one finger, tipped up my chin. This close, the bristles on his cheeks and chin sparkled golden in the soft glow from the lamp. His lips were the soft pink of ballet slippers. I hated the class Mother forced me into but loved those shoes.

So comfortable. So plushy. So kissable.

When I pushed up on my toes, my boots creaked. Still, I wasn't tall enough to reach his mouth. His impossibly tall mouth. He'd have to bend to meet me.

When he didn't, I peeled my gaze off those satiny lips and checked out his eyes. I'd expected them to be focused on my lips. No, Niall Flynn couldn't be as transparent as the guys I'd hooked up with at the university. Instead, he stared into my eyes, emotions I couldn't read churning behind the gold-flecked green.

He dropped his hand and stepped back until his back hit the door. My chin missed the support of his finger, and my chilled neck erupted in goosebumps.

"I'll—I'll be right next door," he said.

I sagged against the wall. "Oh. Okay."

Before I even finished speaking, the door shut behind him. Bilbo Baggins snorted awake and let out a sleepy half-bark.

I blinked hard and shook my head. Bed. I was tired. That was why I'd misread the signals and tried to kiss him.

He wasn't interested. Not in me. Like all the others, he needed something from me. To perform at the book signings. Like Mother needed me to perform at her social events.

And, really, I'd been trying to get something from him, too. Scratch an itch. Safely, with no risk of catching feelings or wanting more. Because less than two weeks remained of the tour. Like this hotel room, there was no room for anything else.

I unzipped my suitcase and pulled out a pair of pajama pants. After I changed into them, I reached out to caress the adjoining door, the one that led to Niall's room. I imagined opening it to find his square frame filling it, leaning against the jamb with his eyes half-open the way they'd been before I'd touched him.

No. I flopped back on the bed. Exhaustion had lowered my

inhibitions, led me to think Niall wanted to kiss me. Of course he didn't. He was made for public consumption, basking in the camera flashes. He needed bling on his arm, not someone who wore cargo pants and shapeless T-shirts and hid behind her dog. He didn't need someone who turned her face away from photos, who preferred the solitude of a computer lab to crowded movie premieres.

Besides, I had secrets. Secrets I was in danger of revealing if I let Niall get too close. Secrets that'd be disastrous to the tour, to CASE, to my future. Opening that door was something I could never do.

I scooted under the covers, but as tired as I was, my eyes refused to close. My leg bumped against my laptop bag.

Sitting up, I reached inside it and pulled out the paperback copy of *Secrets of the Wood Elves*, the one Niall had signed for me in Chicago. I cracked it open to the first page of Chapter 2, and when the letters stopped swirling, I started to read.

18

SAM

MY FINGERS ACHED. My signature—the fake one—had turned into an unrecognizable squiggle, the S and the C the only legible letters. But I was trying. Some of these people had waited in line for over an hour. They didn't know the book had been written by an A.I. and its author was more fake than the wood-grained surface of the laminated table.

It helped that Qiana was there. She worked the bookstore's line and printed the names on a sticky note. I gave each person a quick smile, copied the name from Qiana's note, and then scrawled *Sam Case*. Ten seconds. Fifteen if the person wanted to say something like, "I loved your book" or "It's great to meet you." No selfies, please and thank you.

Niall's line moved a lot more slowly.

When my last person walked away, clutching fifteen dollars' worth of newly inscribed bound paper, Qiana sank into the hard wooden chair next to me.

"Not bad for a Sunday afternoon."

From the grin on Qiana's face, not only was it "not bad," but it was pretty good.

"Is the publisher happy with the results from the tour so far?" We needed sales data to show how successful the world's first A.I.-generated novel had been. With the data, surely Martell would approve my dissertation.

"Happy? The Troll is ecstatic. Niall's book is selling well; he'll make the lists next week. But your sales are also creeping up. You're getting great word-of-mouth."

"Getting what?"

"Word of mouth. People are telling their friends how great your book is, and they're buying it."

I made a fist and stretched out my aching fingers. Sales were what Martell wanted to prove CASE's success. Talking to all those strangers, public speaking, even my sore hands were all worth it if I'd come out the other end with my Ph.D. My heart gave a hopeful skip.

"Are you having fun on the tour?" Qiana asked, gathering up the pens scattered across the table.

"Um." I glanced at Niall, but he was busy chatting up a fan. He'd tried to pretend things between us weren't weird. His words had been the same as before: *Good morning* and *How did you sleep?* and *What did Bilbo think of the park?* But his smiles had been the camera-ready ones, and he hadn't so much as brushed my shoulder with his in the car.

Qiana chuckled. "I know, it's a hard slog, especially as tight as this one's scheduled. Have you had any time to yourself to kick back, watch Netflix, paint your nails?"

In the Jones-Hayes household, painting one's nails involved a trip to the spa and preceded the torture of a social event with scratchy lace or slippery satin. And the argument with Mother that black nail polish should be appropriate for a black-tie event, which I never won. "Bilbo Baggins and I went to the park this morning."

"Aw. Little Bilbo." Qiana stared off at the nearby display of cookbooks. "How about you come over to my apartment after?

It's not far from here. And there's an Indian takeout place next door. It's amazing."

I'd been looking forward to snuggling with Bilbo Baggins in bed back at the hotel. I wasn't looking forward to my other task: deceptive texts. I owed one to Mother to tell her the "road trip" was going well. Jackson had texted, but I hadn't read it yet. I hated lying to him the most. At least I could be honest in my text to Dr. Martell. He already knew how little I wanted to be on the tour, and he wasn't expecting me to lie and tell him I was enjoying it.

I opened my mouth to refuse her invitation—politely, of course—but under Qiana's red lipstick, her smile was irresistible. It didn't seem like a perfunctory *I-can't-figure-out-how-to-end-this-interaction* invitation but like an overture of genuine…friendship? Was Qiana serious about wanting to be my friend?

Only because she thought I was something I wasn't.

I shook my head. "No, I—"

"Come on. It'll be fun. We'll chill." And she gave me puppy-dog eyes and a pout as if she actually wanted me to come.

I needed some chill. Especially after that almost-kiss last night. Having a built-in excuse to avoid Niall would be perfect. "Okay."

Qiana clapped her hands. "Fantastic! I have a baby coral color that's too light for me but is going to look great on your nails. We can go as soon as I check in with Niall."

A woman stood next to Niall, so close she must've violated his personal germ buffer. I frowned. Sure, he hugged his fans, shook their hands, posed for pictures with them, but there was something easy between Niall and this woman. And she looked familiar. Long, dark hair curling over her shoulders. A magenta suit that somehow looked fun and casual instead of stiff and constricting. Curves for days. Her sharp brown eyes belied her bright, relaxed smile.

Qiana knew her. "Gabriela!" She walked toward her, her arms open, and hugged the woman. Niall towered over them, beaming.

A friend, then. A girlfriend? My insides prickled. Shit, no wonder he'd backed away from me last night.

"Sam. Come meet Gabi," Niall called.

My boots wanted to remain stuck to the floor, but I couldn't resist Niall's and Qiana's beckoning grins. I forced myself to smile, approach, extend my hand. "I'm Sam."

The woman grasped it, her light brown hand a contrast to my pale one. "Gabriela Padrón. I'm Niall's agent."

Judging from how close she stood to Niall, she was more than that.

"We met at that literacy fundraiser in San Francisco, but we didn't get a chance to talk." Gabriela scanned me, not head-to-toe, but picking out features to examine for a few seconds like dead butterflies on a tray. "Enjoying the tour so far?"

"It's okay. Tiring."

"Sam's been a trooper, though," Niall said. "She's great with the readers, especially kids."

Gabriela's gaze lingered over my *Neverending Story* T-shirt. Then she smiled like she knew a secret and leaned into Niall. "Not everyone gets to ride the coattails of a writer of Niall's caliber."

Niall's brow turned pink, then the color ran down his face. "Sam's book is doing great. It might be me riding her coattails." He chuckled in a way I hadn't heard him do before. As if someone was forcing him.

Qiana, bless her, said, "Sam and I are going back to my place. I assume you guys are going to hang out?"

"Yeah," Niall said, "since we're free the rest of the night."

The rest of the night? I hated how Gabriela draped herself over him. I half-expected her to rub her face on him, like a cat. Or maybe piss in a circle around him.

"Sounds good," Qiana said. "I'll pick you up tomorrow at ten."

With an easy wave, Niall turned with Gabriela and walked out of the store.

"Rawr," Qiana said. "The claws come out."

So I hadn't made it up. "What was that about?"

Qiana waved her hand. "Oh, she's just protecting her boy. Wanting to be sure the young upstart knows her place." She grinned. "Let's go. I'm starving."

Her boy?

Two hours later, Qiana handed me the bottle of coral nail polish. I frowned at it. "Do you have anything less…pink?"

Qiana grinned. "I've got lots more choices. Just a sec." She stepped through the doorway into her bedroom.

She returned a minute later with a rattling tray of colorful bottles. "We have mermaid green, gold, dark blue, purple, red. See anything you like?"

I scanned the selection and picked up the black bottle. "This one."

"A goth girl. I should've known." She pushed the pink polish into the middle of the pack and shook up a bottle of dark cherry. I mirrored her action with the bottle of black polish. She spread a sheet of newspaper over the coffee table—small but solid, and much nicer than my dumpster rescue—and uncapped the polish.

She stroked the deep red over her thumbnail. "So, tell me about yourself. I've heard all about the tour, but now I want to hear about the other twenty-some-odd years of your life."

"There's not much to tell." I shrugged like there really wasn't, like I wasn't shrink-wrapped in secrets. "I grew up in San Francisco, and now I'm a graduate student." I tried to copy Qiana's smooth strokes on my stubby nails. The shiny black against my pale skin made me smile.

"What's your family like? Big? Small?"

"Really?" I hadn't meant for the word to burst out. But I hardly ever met anyone who didn't know the Joneses. "My father was Jasper Jones. He founded a startup that was acquired by Gurusoft. My mother runs the Jones Literacy Foundation. They work mostly on the West Coast. And my brother's Jackson Jones. He founded Synergy Analytics, and he's—he was—in the tabloids a lot. You—you don't know?"

Qiana's stare was blank. "I don't really follow the tech news."

"Oh." My chest eased, like I'd taken off one of those lead vests they make you wear to take X-rays at the dentist. She didn't have a dozen preconceived notions of what a Jones should be like. "Cool. I guess we're a big family. I have two brothers and a sister. Plus some other family in the Bay Area."

"Yeah?" Qiana held out her hand, examining her glossy red nails. "You guys close?"

"I guess so? My mother hosts brunch every Sunday. But it can be a little much."

Qiana looked up from her nails and smiled. "I get that. They must be so proud of you."

Whoa. The heaviness descended again. I rubbed a spot of nail polish off my cuticle and tried to reset my face.

Qiana blew on her nails. "How long have you been writing? All your life?"

"Not so long." Something twisted inside me. It was worse than the Q and As. This time, I was lying to someone I knew. Who was trying to be my friend. "What about you? Did you always want to be a publicist?"

Qiana swiped her thumb under a fingernail. "I always wanted to write."

"Why don't you?"

She frowned. "I loved reading as a kid. I guess I never thought it was something I could do. But now I work around authors and books every day." Her frown dissolved. "It's like a dream to get paid to connect writers to readers."

I knew what it was like to be discouraged from pursuing my interests. Mother would've been so much happier if I'd done something she could understand, like finance or business. It was pure stubbornness—and Jackson's encouragement—that made me push past Mother's resistance. "But you can do whatever you set your mind to. Why don't you write a book now? You're not any older than I am."

Qiana nibbled on her red-stained lip. "Maybe. I—I've considered going back to school. For my MFA. Fine arts," she added when I stared at her blankly.

"Oh. You should. Definitely. If it'll give you the confidence to pursue your dreams." Grad school had been hard, but it was the steppingstone to my independence.

"I've been saving up for it. With the success we're projecting for your book and Niall's, the bonus pool should be good this year. Maybe next year I can afford it."

Qiana might as well have punched me in the stomach. I'd never worried about money, not even after I'd given away my trust fund. My stipend kept me in ramen and thrift-store clothing, and if I ever had an emergency, my family would swoop in and rescue me whether I wanted it or not.

Qiana didn't have that safety net.

The door rattled, and muffled voices came from behind it. "My roommates are home," Qiana said. "Want any more food before they scarf it?"

"No, thanks." I scrambled to my feet. The afternoon with Qiana had been…nice. But I couldn't face small talk with her roommates. "I should go. Thanks for letting me hang out."

"No prob. We can do it again sometime." And there was that radiant grin again.

It wasn't even a lie when I said, "I'd like that."

The door opened, and I waved and slipped out.

As I clomped down the stairs, the conversation stuck in my brain like a runtime error. *Sales. Bonus.*

Sometime soon, Heidi and Martell would disclose the full story of CASE and *Magician in the Machine.* When they'd told me about the plan, I'd focused only on that scroll just out of my grasp. I hadn't given a thought to—

I stilled, clutching the banister. When they revealed the truth, what would happen to Qiana? Would she earn her bonus and her MFA dream, even though the book turned out to be a lie?

Surely she would. Heidi had it all under control. I released my death-grip on the rail and continued down the stairs more slowly.

Lie or not, the sales were real. Growing up with an entrepreneur for a father and a CFO stepfather had taught me that people couldn't usually argue with cash.

But.

When I stopped pretending to be an author, I'd return to my world of solo programming and—I hoped—a research position at a quiet lab. Regardless of what Heidi said, the fallout from the truth would leave behind a mess someone would have to clean up.

It wouldn't be Qiana, would it? And how much would she hate me, even if it wasn't? I'd lied to her face about being an author, someone interested in books.

This friendship stuff couldn't continue. Not with Qiana. It would complicate my exit strategy.

But CASE was the machine, not me, no matter how much I tried to suppress my feelings. And the Balrog's pit in my stomach told me it was already too late to make a clean break.

19

SAM

SHUFFLING out of the elevator at the hotel, I could almost feel the weight of the fluffy, white comforter I planned to pull up over my head to block out the world. No texts. No talking. Just me and my guilt.

And Bilbo Baggins.

The little guy had napped hard after our adventure in Central Park this morning, and I hadn't wanted to drag him to another bookstore, so I'd tiptoed out alone. Though I hadn't planned to go to Qiana's after. Our blanket fort would have to wait for me to take him out to pee.

I expected Bilbo Baggins to have heard my footsteps, but there was no snuffle under the door as I slid the card into the lock. Was he still asleep? When I opened the door, I checked the bed. Only a few black hairs on the white comforter. One more frantic glance around the tiny hotel room confirmed Bilbo Baggins wasn't in it. My heart stuttered to a stop. Then it raced. Maybe he was under the bed. In the bathroom. Hiding behind a curtain? Had something happened to him? Was he wandering the streets of New

York, alone and terrified? I pursed my trembling lips and whistled.

A muffled bark answered. It sounded like it came from next door. Niall's room. How could he have gotten in there? The adjoining door had been locked when I'd left.

I unbolted and threw open the connecting door. Niall's side was already open. Did he always keep it ajar?

It didn't matter when Bilbo Baggins danced at my feet. Kneeling, I scooped him up and cuddled him over my heart, then I buried my face in his silky fur. "Bilbo Baggins, what are you doing here?"

Then I froze. Oh no. I'd barged into Niall's room, uninvited. What if he was in bed? What if he was in bed *with Gabriela?* I closed my eyes tight against Bilbo Baggins' side.

I sensed a body looming over me, and heavy steps sank, muffled, into the carpet next to where I squatted. My heartbeat slowed.

Niall's voice cascaded down from far above. "Bilbo was barking. I was afraid someone would complain and report him to the hotel staff. So we, um, liberated him."

"Liberated?" I opened my eyes. The stiff knees of Niall's jeans were two feet from my face. At least he was wearing pants.

"Yeah, um." His feet shifted. "Gabi picked the lock."

"For real, you guys should stay in hotels with better security." Gabi's voice came from the chair, not the bed. Her shoes were off, her legs curled up under her.

"We're staying in adjoining rooms for exactly that reason, Gabi," Niall said.

"What?" My fingers stilled in Bilbo Baggins' fur.

"Yeah, I—" Niall scrubbed his hand through his hair. "After that first night, in Chicago, when we had adjoining rooms, it seemed like a good idea. Safer. So I called Qiana and asked her if we could have them going forward."

"You put us in adjoining rooms?" Heat crawled from my chest up my neck.

Gabriela levered up out of the chair and stood next to Niall. "If you guys adjoin each other, that means no one else can come in that way. While you're here, I'll get some portable locks for the exterior doors from my cousin. That mutt of yours is no guard dog. He went right to Niall."

What if I'd left my laptop open? I'd been working on my dissertation earlier. He could've seen it, discovered my secret. Heidi would enforce that NDA I'd signed. Martell would kick me out of my program. No Ph.D. I'd have to move back in with Mother and Charles. The heat boiling inside me had nowhere to go, so machine-gun words shot out of my mouth. "You went into my room. You invaded my privacy."

"Whoa." Niall held up his hands like a shield. "We were trying to help."

Same as my family. I'd thought he was different. He wanted to protect me, but he gave me space when I asked for it. Not today. He'd stomped right through the boundaries he'd told me we needed.

"I don't need your help. I don't want it. I can handle myself. And my dog." Scooping up Bilbo Baggins, I stumbled to my feet and stormed back into my room, slamming both doors. I bolted the door on my side and slid the chain.

Bilbo Baggins wiggled out of my arms and leaped to the carpet. He sneezed twice.

I sank to my knees and rubbed his soft ears. "Sorry, Bilbo Baggins. You were only trying to be friendly," I whispered.

He pushed his cold nose into my palm. If Niall hadn't rescued him, the hotel manager might have come and taken him. And Bilbo Baggins probably preferred being kidnapped by Niall to being confiscated by the manager.

So why was I still so upset?

When Gabi flashed into my brain, my skin heated again. Gabi standing not six inches away from Niall today at the bookstore— definitely in the intimacy zone. Gabi's bare feet on the carpet of Niall's hotel room, her shoes piled next to Niall's. Maybe when

Gabi went up on her tiptoes in front of Niall, Niall didn't back away from her kiss.

Jealousy wasn't something I often felt, at least not of a romantic variety. Since Stephen, I never let myself care enough about my partners to feel it. But in Niall's room, it had controlled me, made me lash out.

Shit! Those prickles of jealousy meant I'd let myself care about Niall. Even though there was nothing to feel jealous of. Niall didn't like me like that. That much was clear. And he shouldn't. He had exactly the kind of life I didn't want. Public. Photographed. All I wanted was to hide away in a lab, far from the fans, the book talks, the people.

The heat washed right out of me, leaving me shivering on the carpet. My throat felt scratchy. Maybe I'd caught something at the convention or one of the signings despite Niall's compulsory hand sanitizer.

Tea. Tea would soothe my throat. Maybe there was some in the minibar.

I'd just stood when there was a knock at the door. Not the inner, adjoining door, but the outside door.

A knot tightened in my stomach. I could guess who it was.

20

NIALL

AFTER KNOCKING on Sam's door, I shoved my hands in my pockets. I wanted to rub away the clench that twisted my stomach when I remembered the look of betrayal on her face. I'd been the one to bring up boundaries last night. I'd promised her I wouldn't overstep them. I'd backed away from the kiss when all I'd wanted to do was pull her against me and take her petal-soft lips.

And then what had I done? I'd barreled right into her personal space. I had her phone number now. I could've called her to tell her the dog was barking and ask if I could get him out. But, no, I'd wanted to solve the problem for her. And maybe, in the back of my mind, I'd wanted her to have to come to my room. To come see me.

What was it about this woman that drove me from the peaks of excitement to the troughs of humiliation? I was going to get the bends from my mood swings around her.

Gabi thought I was nuts. She thought Sam had overreacted. But she didn't know what had almost happened last night. I had a lot more to apologize for than stealing her dog.

After I apologized, I needed to hightail it back to my room so I wouldn't be tempted—again—to kiss her.

But when she opened the door, her lips turned down and her eyes shimmering, I forgot every one of my good intentions.

"Did you even check the peephole?" I could've been an ax murderer, and now her door was open. Even Gabi's cousin's extra locks wouldn't protect her from her own lack of caution.

She scowled.

Back off, Niall. My gut response was exactly why I needed to apologize. I kept my voice low. No need for everyone on the floor to hear me grovel. Thank God Gabi had already caught the elevator down. "I'm sorry. I can be kind of overprotective. I'm used to taking care of my family. Not that that's an excuse. I understand you don't like it. I'll try not to do it to you again."

The line between her eyebrows smoothed out, and she blinked up at me. Did that mean I was forgiven? Or that I'd just gotten started?

I rolled my shoulders back and flexed my hands to relieve the tension. "All right?"

She wrinkled her nose, the way she did when she was thinking. "Want some tea?" She opened the door wider. Then, as I took a step forward, she half-shut it again. "Wait, is Gabriela still here? I don't want to…"

"No. She went home. She's coming to the signing tomorrow. Can I still come in?"

"Yeah." She stepped away from the door, went to the credenza under the TV, and started opening cabinets. I'd found the coffee in my room that morning, so I knew where the hotel kept it, but I remained silent. Gave her plenty of space. Let her find it on her own.

Sam's room was the same as mine, only flipped. Yet somehow it seemed smaller. Maybe it was just the crackling tension that made it feel crowded. Ignoring the unmade bed—I had to ignore the bed—I had two seating options: the desk chair or the armchair by the bed. Sam's computer bag lay on the desk, and her open laptop had a crushed-in corner. The screen was black.

Off or not, I didn't want to give her the impression I was snooping. So I crossed the room to the chair in the corner and shoved my hands into my pockets to avoid touching the rumpled white duvet.

Bilbo Baggins sat at my feet, gazing at me with adoration. When I bent to scratch him between the ears, he wiggled with full-body joy.

"Earl Grey or English Breakfast?"

I wasn't a fan of tea at all, but this was about détente. "You pick, and I'll take whatever's left. Mind if I sit here?"

"Go ahead. Do you take anything in it?"

"No, thanks." I eased into the chair. What was going on in that razor-sharp brain of hers? She was processing something. Maybe she was still stewing about how I'd broken into her room. I scrambled for something to break the tension. "C. S. Lewis said, 'You can never get a cup of tea large enough or a book long enough to suit me.' Right?" I raised my eyebrows, hoping for at least a smile.

"Tea goes cold if your mug is too big, and in my opinion, plenty of books could be shorter." She handed me the steaming mug of tea. "*Ulysses*, for example. Even the cheaters' guide was too long."

Crap. My books were too long. That was why she hadn't finished *Secrets* yet. She was bored. I wrapped my hands around the mug. The herbal scent of the tea tickled my nose. It reminded me of Mom's flower garden, which wasn't something I wanted to drink.

Standing in front of me, she blew on her tea. "I'm sorry. I shouldn't have blown up at you like that. You were trying to help. I'm just having some…feelings today. It's got to be the tour. Did your last tour make you act out of character?"

Not like this one had. Of course, my first "tour" had been me driving my car from the farm to Columbus, to Cincinnati, to Cleveland, to Indianapolis. Never farther away than Chicago, never anywhere I had to stay overnight. Happy Troll was a small publisher, and I was a debut author. There had been no three-week slogs through airports and bookstores, day after day. That had come later, as my book had crept up the charts, as it had garnered attention from bloggers, from the media, and eventually from Hollywood.

I'd never tried to kiss someone I'd met on tour or broken into their room. Not before this.

"This tour is a lot. I understand how it makes you feel off-kilter."

She touched her lips to the mug but didn't drink. "Yes. Anyway, I've been on edge and that makes me easier to set off. It's not an excuse, and I'm sorry."

"Wait. I'm the one who should be apologizing. I crossed the line."

One corner of her mouth quirked. "So did I."

Was she talking about last night? When she'd lifted on her toes and her eyelashes had fluttered down, every cell in my body had cried out to kiss her.

Fear had stopped me. I hadn't yet told her the full truth. The liberties I'd taken with her image. Lobelia. I had to tell her. Would she think I was a creep? And what would Qiana say when she found out? Toast. I'd be toast. She'd cut off the ends of her braids that matched my cover, scrub off that red nail polish, and switch to acid green for Team Sam.

Sam sat on the bed. Bilbo jumped up beside her, curled up into a circle, and let out a dramatic sigh.

She sipped her tea, grimaced, and set it on the shelf by the bed. "Gabriela's your agent. Is she also your..." She shoved her hands between her knees. "Your girlfriend?"

"No!" Had Gabi's prickly protectiveness added to Sam's stress? This was a new part of the calculus. "I mean, we dated. In college. For a couple months. After we broke up, we stayed friends. She helped me with my writing, too, and when I wrote *Secrets*, she sold the series for me. So now she's my friend and my agent. Plus"—I might as well admit another failing—"she types up my handwritten manuscripts and does all the email stuff. You can probably tell I'm not into technology."

"Oh? I hadn't noticed." Sam's pink lips curved a fraction of an inch.

I set my mug of bitterness on the credenza. The chair was so close to the bed it didn't require even a step to reach it. More like a pivot.

I pivoted.

What am I doing? My arm went around her waist like it belonged there. I froze for a second, but then her head dropped to my shoulder. She sighed, and that was all it took. I tugged her tighter and rested my chin on the top of her head.

"I like you, Niall. And it made me jealous to see her in your room."

"Wh-what?" My heart thumped as if Sally, our most ornery goat, was trying to kick through its walls.

She untucked her head and looked me in the eye. "Should I be more circumspect? Do you want me to pretend I'm not attracted to you? I could do that, but what's the point? We're on tour another couple of weeks, and then we probably won't see each other again."

"You—you just took me by surprise. No, I want you to be you. I guess I'm not used to people saying what they mean. Other than my family."

"We won't be together long enough to waste time tiptoeing around what we want to say. We should say what we mean." She stared me straight in the eye.

My stomach clenched every time she reminded me our time together was short. It meant she was right. I couldn't waste a minute with this amazing woman.

"I like you, too." Some of the silky strands of her hair had tangled with my stubble, and I smoothed them away, tracing her cheek with one finger. "Is this okay? Touching you?"

"Yeah." She lifted her chin. "I promise I'll tell you when it's not." She laid her hand over my galloping heart.

Mom always said when I was given an inch, I'd take a mile. I ran my hand from where it rested on her hip up her spine and then massaged her neck.

"How's this?"

The tension in her muscles eased. "It's great. When you touch my neck, it makes me all calm and floaty."

I filed that away. Calm and floaty sounded good, and I wanted her to feel good. I wanted to be the one who made her feel good.

With my other hand, I tipped up her chin, the way I'd done last night. I cradled her jaw in my hand. She stared at my lips, the way she'd done last night. When her tongue flicked out to wet her pillowy bottom lip, my brain gave up on rational thought. Gone was the hesitation about kissing my tour partner. About what Qiana would think. I couldn't remember a single reason why I shouldn't be on the bed in her hotel room, holding her. The only thing that existed in that moment was the desire that burned inside me, heating my skin. Desire for Sam.

I kissed her.

I had enough restraint left to make it a gentle kiss. Her lips were as soft as they looked, and I carefully kept my stubble away from her delicate skin. Still, my lips tingled where they touched hers, itching for more. Wait. Had I gone too far? I dragged my lips away and tried to corral enough air in my overtasked lungs to speak.

"Was that okay? I—I'm sorry I didn't check first. I just—"

Her lips crashed onto mine, and there was nothing gentle about our second kiss. It was hunger. Lust. Passion. I wasn't sure whose tongue dipped inside whose mouth first. Our teeth clacked together. I tugged her closer, one hand on her neck, angling her head to meet my lips, the other hand on her back, pressing her chest against mine.

Her fingers curled into my back, making sharp points of pressure through my flannel shirt. A counterpoint to the pressure building against the zipper of my jeans.

Whoa. If I didn't slow down, I'd have her flat on the bed. And I'd deserve it if Bilbo took a chunk out of my leg. Or another appendage.

Gently, slowly, I pulled back until our lips parted. I licked my throbbing lower lip. "Wow." I heaved out a breath, stirring the silky hairs that had escaped her ponytail. If we did much more of that, I was going to come in my pants like a teenager. "Maybe we should stop there for now."

"Coward." She smiled, one corner kicking up higher than the other. "My brother Jackson's favorite quote goes something like, 'If things seem under control, you're not going fast enough.' He's a big Mario Andretti fan." But she scooted a few inches away.

My heart was going like a race car's engine. We'd gone plenty fast enough for me. I needed a minute—an hour, maybe all night —to process how the kiss had changed things between us. "I'm sorry, I—"

She laid a finger over my lips. "Don't be sorry. I get it." She scooted a couple more inches away. "It's out of our systems now. We can finish out the tour like colleagues and not a pair of horny teenagers."

A chill crept into my heart. *Colleagues?*

"It's all good. We're good, right?" Her lowered eyebrows showed the vulnerability her words didn't.

"Of course we are." I could do colleagues. I just had to scrub that afternoon out of my memory so I never again thought about her kiss-swollen lips. Her dark hair mussed from my fingers. Her blown pupils edging out the violet. From kissing me.

Good luck with that, Niall.

21

SAM

OKAY, fine. You want to know the truth? I regretted it the second the words were out of my mouth.

Out of our systems. Colleagues. Bullshit.

I scrawled my fake signature across another title page and handed the book to the reader. Fake smile. "Thanks for coming."

While I waited for her to shuffle away and make room for the next person, I stole a glance at Niall. He smiled, too, but it wasn't his aw-shucks, humble-farmboy-turned-star-author grin he usually gave the readers. It was his camera-ready smile, and this time, his jaw was so tight it looked like he was trying to crack a walnut between his molars.

I'd wanted it to be true. I should've known better. Niall wasn't one of my casual flings looking to scratch an itch. It wasn't only lust that squeezed his green irises to a slim corona. His stubbled jaw had been slack with some overwhelming emotion—awe?—when he'd stared into my eyes after our kiss. It had been a lie. I'd wanted more even as I'd said it. That impressive bulge in his jeans? I'd wanted to touch it, taste it, ride it all the way to the next stop on the tour. I suspected even if he slept in my bed every night, I'd never get his careful-yet-confident touches, his worship-ful-yet-dirty stares out of my system.

So I'd thrown the power switch, hoping when we came back online we'd have forgotten all about it.

Yeah, that hadn't worked out.

"Ms. Case." The voice was horrifyingly familiar, especially with X-rated thoughts flickering through my mind. I snapped my gaze off Niall and onto my brother's saucer-sized Austin, Texas, souvenir belt buckle, then up his ZZ Top T-shirt and onto his bearded face. The corners of his mouth turned down, stern. His brown eyes glinted like smoky quartz. It was his *What the fuck, Sam?* expression.

"Jackson." He wasn't holding a book, so I grabbed one off the stack. I winced as I scribbled *To Jackson* and *Sam Case* on the page. I might as well have written *Liar*, too.

"We need to talk."

I felt, more than saw, Niall's head snap up beside me.

"You're holding up my line," I said through gritted teeth.

Jackson crossed his arms. "I can stand here all night."

"Sam, are you okay?" Niall asked, low. "Is he—"

"I'm fine," I muttered. What the hell was he doing in New York?

"Dinner. Six o'clock." Jackson named a restaurant I'd seen on the way to the bookstore. "Bring your friends." An evil smile teased at one corner of his mouth.

"Get out of my line," I growled.

He raised his eyebrows. A throat cleared behind him.

"Fine." He was going to find out eventually. "But I'm coming alone."

"Perfect." His gaze skated over to Niall and then back to my face. "See you at six." He turned and strode away.

Niall leaned toward me. "You sure you're okay? Who was that guy?"

"My bookie." I fake-smiled at the next person in line and held out my hand for her book.

Later, when the people were gone and we were packing up, Niall turned to me, red eyebrows furrowed into a V, and said, low, "Are you sure about meeting that guy tonight?"

But it wasn't low enough. Or Qiana had superhero-level hearing. "Sam's meeting a guy?" She sidled over and nudged me. "Is he cute?"

"Ew. He's my brother." I kept my face down, focused on the green Sharpie in my hand.

I didn't have to be looking at Niall to sense his stiffness. "Your brother?"

"Which brother?" Gabi glided over and perched one hip on the table. "Jackson or Andrew?"

My head shot up at that. She knew my brothers' names? "Jackson."

"The entrepreneur-slash-philanthropist. Married. Used to be a billionaire, but now that he and his wife have given so much away—mostly to organizations that support neurodivergent kids —he's simply fabulously wealthy."

My jaw dropped open. "Are you *cyberstalking* me?"

"Just trying to get to know you." Gabi's smile was dangerous. "It's not hard when your family lives in the public eye."

I was breathing, but air wasn't getting in. A weight crushed my chest, keeping it from fully expanding.

"I'm going with you." Niall pried the Sharpie out of my numb fingers and handed it to Qiana.

"If Niall's going, I'm going." Gabi stood.

"Can I come, too?" Qiana asked. "I want to meet your family."

No. No no no no no. Alarms blared and red lights flashed in my head.

"Sam, are you okay?" Niall was in my face, his hands gripping my shoulders. "You look—"

"I don't think her skin is supposed to be that color," Qiana said.

"Green. Definitely green." Gabi sounded more fascinated than worried.

"I'm fine." I drew myself up. I could do this. Let my pretend, new world of publishing crash into my real world. I could walk this tightrope without violating the NDA. "I don't need you to come."

"I'll walk you there," Niall said, releasing my shoulders at last. "Just to be sure you don't pass out on the sidewalk."

"Where are we going?" Qiana asked.

Defeated, I gave her the name of the restaurant.

"Let's go." She led us outside and turned left.

Niall walked beside me, not touching me but close enough that our arms would've brushed if he hadn't been holding himself so stiffly. Really, it was better that way. Better that he be angry with me than that he give me one of his soft looks, like the one he'd melted me with yesterday when he apologized for breaking into my room.

Gabi walked ahead of us with Qiana, but I didn't miss her narrow-eyed glances every time we paused at a crosswalk. Though more often than not, her dagger-sharp gaze landed on Niall, not me.

We arrived a few minutes before six, but Jackson was already there, lounging on a chair in the waiting area, eyes on his phone. He looked up when the February-cold air gusted in around us.

He beamed. "Samwise! You brought your friends."

"No, they're just—"

"Hi, I'm Jackson Jones." He shook hands all around, his knuckles going white when he gripped Niall's hand. "Table for five," he told the host, who whisked us away into the dark interior to a round table in a quiet corner.

I sat next to Jackson. When Niall tried to sit on my other side, Jackson shook his head. "Sit there, where I can see you, Prince Harry." He indicated the seat across from him. Gabriela and Qiana filled in the seats on either side of Niall.

Qiana gripped my hand under the table. "Something strange is going on here," she whispered. "It's straight out of *Real Housewives.*"

"Welcome to dinner with the Joneses," I muttered.

I picked up the menu and pretended to read it. "So, Jackson, what are you doing in New York? I thought you were on baby watch." Their baby was due in a couple of weeks, right around the end of the tour. It was one of the many reasons I'd tossed out for Dr. Martell about why I couldn't travel. Though when I'd told Alicia about my trip, she'd assured me she'd probably go past her due date since it was her first. I'd be back in time for the birth.

"Foundation thing today. Alicia told me I had to go. Apparently, we get ten percent more in donations when I'm there with my charming smile." He flashed it around the table, that dazzling pirate's grin.

On my other side, Qiana sighed. "Swoon."

"I'm heading home first thing tomorrow morning. I *did* text you I was coming."

I probably should've read that one. But I'd given up my texting time to make out with Niall. "So sorry we won't be repeating this family reunion," I mumbled, eyes on the menu.

The waiter came to get our drink order, recited the specials, and left.

Jackson set down his menu. "I have a piece of fan mail for you." He reached into his pocket and pulled out a regular business-sized envelope with my name scrawled across it.

Taking it from him, I lifted the flap and unfolded the piece of paper inside. It was a colored-pencil drawing of The Magician. The stiff-looking white robe gave it away. The figure had my blue eyes and dark hair, even my scattering of freckles. In sloppy print across the bottom, it read, *Dear Sam, All my friends think The Magician is sick. I think you're awesome. Love, Noah.*

I swallowed. I was the exact opposite of awesome. I'd lied to my nephew. To my brother. To everyone at that table. I set the drawing next to my empty charger.

"So, Sam, tell me about this book." Jackson's gaze was so pointed it could've plucked the truth out of my brain like a pair of tweezers.

"Um." I held up a finger and grabbed my glass of water. I guzzled it down in a way that would've shocked Mother.

"Wait." Gabi straightened. "You didn't know about your sister's book?"

"No, seems she forgot to mention it at our last family brunch."

Ice rattled against my lips, and I set the glass down. Did he remember Noah reading it at brunch last month? That even Nat had said she'd read it, and I'd said nothing?

The glitter in his eyes told me he did.

"I, ah—"

The waiter arrived with our drinks. For a wild moment, I considered knocking over Qiana's glass of red wine. Maybe I could run for it during the resulting chaos.

Before I could make a move toward her glass, she put her hand over the base. "You should read it. It's amazing. We're calling it a genre-twisting blend of literary fiction and sci-fi with urban fantasy elements. It's got edge-of-your-seat action with prose that bends language as we know it."

"To Sam, then." Jackson raised his glass of tequila. "And her literary career." He drank, and so did the others. I raised my empty water glass, and a busboy scurried over to refill it.

Relieved, I sipped my water and slumped back in my chair. He was going to let it go. I'd spill the whole secret to him—NDA or no—as soon as I got back to San Francisco. And I'd do it while he was holding his baby so he couldn't throttle me.

"Yet—" Jackson set down his glass. "I can't recall your ever having written anything before. Other than code."

That was all he had to say. That one word, *code*. He knew. He understood what I'd been working on with CASE, and he'd connected the dots. Now he was about to lift his hand from the page and show us all the whole picture.

I glanced toward Qiana's wine glass, but she'd pushed it out of my reach.

"It's the best debut novel I've ever read," Niall said, a challenge in his tone. "Pure, raw talent. I can't wait to see how her style evolves."

Jackson swung his gaze from me to Niall. "Niall Flynn." *Challenge accepted.* "I'm more of a gamer than a reader, but even I've heard of you. Didn't I see you were dating Lulu Bridges last summer? Stunning woman. Makes the cutest little squeak when she—"

I stomped his foot. My brother knew a lot of gross facts about B-list actresses.

"—laughs, I was going to say." But Jackson didn't look at me. He stared across the table at Niall, whose hands were curled into fists on either side of his charger.

The waiter, who had to have the world's worst timing—or the best—came to take our order. After she handed the menu to him, Qiana gave me a wide-eyed stare. "So much better than *Real Housewives,*" she whispered.

When the waiter left, Jackson leaned back in his chair and continued as if he hadn't been interrupted. "So, Niall, since Lulu didn't hold your interest, can I assume you're"—swirling his glass of dark tequila, he flicked his eyes to Gabi and then to me— "single?"

Niall gazed at me, uncertainty in his candlelight-darkened eyes.

"Jackson—" I had to stop him now before he launched into the what-are-your-intentions interrogation.

"I think Niall's capable of explaining those doe-eyed looks he keeps sending your way. He's a writer, after all. A master of language."

"We're colleagues." I curled my fingers around my napkin. "Friendly. That's it. You know I don't do anything more." Jackson knew why, too.

His eyes were full of that knowledge when he turned them back to me. "Sam, I—" He frowned and pulled his phone out of his back pocket. "Excuse me." Shoving away from the table, he put his phone to his ear. "Sweetheart," he murmured in the softest tone I'd ever heard him use.

Niall's face was expressionless stone. That word I'd used again —*colleagues*—lay like a dead bird in the center of the table.

I let a few seconds pass, trying to figure out what I could say to make it better, to make him not hate me, so we could rewind to our first night in New York when we'd talked and everything between us had been less fraught.

"Niall, I—" But words failed me, the way they usually did.

A heavy hand wearing a glinting wedding band landed on my shoulder. "Sam, a minute?" Jackson tilted his head toward the bar. I stood and followed.

My brother vibrated with something I'd seen often when we were growing up: a need to *move*. And *fast*. Back then, he'd hop on his bike and race away, seeking hills he could tire himself out climbing and then coast down the other side, the wind in his face.

"Alicia's gone into labor. I need to get home *now*. Fuck!" He ran his hand through his hair, the one that wasn't gripping his phone. "Why the *fuck* didn't I take the jet?"

"Wait, what? *Now*? She's not due until the end of the month."

"Tell that to the baby." He gripped my shoulders. "I took care of the tab. You guys stay and enjoy your dinner. Make my excuses. Do *not* apologize on my behalf to that—Niall. I was kidding—mostly—earlier, but still. Looks like you're playing a dangerous game. You're trampling on his livelihood *and* breaking his heart? Pretty cold, Sam."

Trampling on his—I stared down at his western boots, toe-to-toe with my combat boots. "I didn't mean to—"

"I know. Neither one of us is all that emotionally aware. In tune with feelings and shit. Just think about what you're doing, okay? And how it might affect your new friends."

I nodded. He squeezed my shoulder, and then his boots were gone, pounding the floor to get home to his loved ones as quickly as his wealth and connections could get him there.

I glanced back at the table, where Gabi and Qiana turned back to each other like they hadn't been staring at us. Niall didn't bother pretending. He held my gaze.

I couldn't. I couldn't go back there and deal with the fallout of the grenades my brother had lobbed.

"I'm sorry," I mouthed. Turning, I followed the path Jackson had taken out of the restaurant. But instead of heading home to people I loved, I found a taxi that'd take me back to the hotel. Where Bilbo Baggins didn't have any expectations of me. Where I wasn't ruining everything that was important to him.

22

NIALL

"SAM." I knocked on her door. Not loudly—it was late—but forcefully enough that she'd hear me. She couldn't be asleep. Not after that dinner. I was so wired from being on edge I might not sleep for days. Did her brother know I'd made out with his little sister the night before? He was an inch or two taller than me, not as bulky, but he'd fight like a snake, distracting me with his sharp tongue and then striking unexpectedly. I wouldn't be able to fight back, anyway; I couldn't hurt the brother of someone I was growing to care about.

What had he said to Sam to make her go pale like that? If he'd said something hurtful, I'd find him and put him on the floor, brother or not.

Bilbo snuffled at the bottom of the door. Then he yapped. Good. She'd have to come to the door.

The chain clacked. Then the bolt. Then the extra bolt from Gabi's cousin. The door cracked open to reveal a sliver of Sam: dark hair in her face, drooping eyes, pale skin, tank top and pajama pants. I blinked away from her collarbones and creamy shoulders to focus on her face.

"I had to see that you're—Are you okay?"

"Yeah, just…just tired." She opened the door wide enough for Bilbo to slip out.

When he scratched at my ankles, I bent to scoop him up. He licked my chin. "He—your brother—didn't say anything cruel, did he?"

Her eyes widened. "Jackson would never. He was fine. He had to leave. His wife is in labor."

"Oh. Wow." An image burst into my head of Sam holding a child, looking down into its big blue eyes, bouncing it a little, humming. "Can I come in?"

"No."

The answer came too fast, like she didn't need to think about it. Shit, I'd fucked everything up the other night by coming on too strong. She wanted to be colleagues. Me? I was standing in the hallway outside her room begging to be let inside. Colleagues didn't do that. Only people who cared did. And I couldn't fool myself anymore: I cared. I needed to tell her. To be honest with her. "Just to talk?"

She considered for a second. "No. I'm really tired, and we have that thing at the publisher in the morning." She held out her hands for the dog.

"Don't shut me out, Sam." It was a plea.

She stared at my middle shirt button. "It's late."

I placed the dog gently into her palms. "I'll see you in the morning, then. Want to have breakfast before?" We'd talk then.

"I don't think so, Niall. Good-night." She shut the door, and the chain jingled.

Fuck. What had I done?

THE NEXT MORNING, I paced in front of the hotel's automatic sliding doors. I almost went to the front desk half a dozen times to see that she hadn't checked out. She was five minutes late, and it was still rush hour, and…shit. I didn't give a damn if we were late. It was Sam I was worried about.

The elevator doors opened, and she sprang out with Bilbo on his leash. "Sorry. Sorry I'm late." Her eyes weren't haunted this morning; they sparkled. "I was waiting for the news. I'm an aunt! Of a newborn this time." She flipped over her phone and showed me a photo of an infant, its face scrunched up under one of those pink-and-blue hospital caps. A clear tube ran under its nostrils. "Don't worry about the oxygen. They said she's doing fine."

Grinning, she held out her arms, and I stepped into her embrace, squeezing her tightly. I inhaled her rosemary scent. Maybe we could get back to friendship, where we were before we'd kissed. Before everything had gone to shit. "Congratulations."

She tugged herself free. "It's a girl. They named her Valentine. Because, you know, it's Valentine's Day."

I'd lost track of the days. "Happy Valentine's Day." Shit! Would she think I wanted to force her into some romantic activity? "I mean, for your niece."

She scrunched up her nose. "You're right. It takes on a new meaning now. It *is* her day. And knowing my brother, he'll try to get the *Jones* added to the holiday's name. He's absolutely over the moon about her. Shit! We're running late. Sorry. Let's go. Is there a car?"

"Waiting outside." Pulling my coat more tightly around myself, I led her out the automatic door to the town car at the curb. She slid in with Bilbo, and I followed.

Sam filled the car with talk about her new niece and showed the driver and me every new picture as it came in. The baby with her mother, a beautiful blond woman. The baby with an older kid, maybe a preteen, leaning slightly away, his eyes wide, like the child was a werewolf instead of an adorably hairless human baby. Jackson, who somehow looked wired and exhausted and over-joyed at the same time. Jealousy prickled in my chest. He had everything: a successful business, a woman who loved him, a family. And he'd given me shit about my intentions toward his sister.

Well, guess what? I intended to kiss her again if she'd let me.

Sam had just ordered a bouquet of yellow roses to be sent the next day—we'd both goggled at the Valentine's Day markup—when we pulled up in front of Happy Troll's building.

As we rode the elevator up to the lowest of Happy Troll's three floors, Sam scrunched her nose. "Why are we here, anyway?"

I watched the floors light up on the screen above the door. "Meet-and-greet. I usually visit when I'm in town. To thank all the people who worked on my book. They like to see the face behind the words."

In the quiet of the elevator, I heard her swallow. I reached for her hand but stopped short, then tucked my hand inside my pants pocket. "It'll be fine. All these people support you. No hard questions today. I promise."

Her smile was weak, but she nodded.

When the door opened, Qiana was there, bouncing on her toes. "Sam!" She hugged her like she hadn't seen her less than twenty-four hours ago. "Niall! It's so exciting!"

"What's exciting?"

"Oh." Her eyes went wide, and she pulled her red lips between her teeth. "That…that you're here. Today." She whirled and headed down the hall. "Heidi's in the Commons."

Something was up. Heidi had assistants to fetch her coffee, so the most plausible reason for her to be in the common area was to make an announcement. Had the new bestseller list come out?

Was I on it? Or Sam?

I trailed Qiana, walking at Sam's side with Bilbo between us, prancing like he owned the place, into the central open area where, sure enough, the counter held an assembly of champagne flutes and an equally large number of people.

"Who are all these people?" Sam whispered.

My heart raced. "Assistant editors—they do the heavy lifting after Heidi's acquired a book. Designers create the covers and make the interior look good. Marketers and salespeople ensure all the outlets want to sell the books."

"So many people."

"Yeah." I didn't bother to tell her about finance or human resources or management who made the company work. Her wide eyes told me she was already overwhelmed.

It had to be good news, right? Fuck it. I reached down and squeezed her hand. She squeezed back.

Heidi stood at the far side of the room where she could survey everyone. "Here they are," she sang out. "The Stars of the Show!" Heidi had a flair for drama.

Sam gripped my hand harder.

"It's good news. It has to be," I whispered, as much for my benefit as for hers.

Assistants passed flutes of champagne through the crowd of people. I took one, the glass cool in my trembling fingers. Sam gripped her glass, her knuckles white.

"Everybody has one? Good, good," Heidi said. "Now, I have some Fantastic News to share. I received a call this morning from the Tower Prize committee. We have not one but Two Nominees here with us today." She paused, a grin lifting her normally serious face. "Our very own Niall Flynn and Sam Case have been nominated in the Fantasy category."

My stomach swooped. The tension drained out, leaving my bones loose and buoyant. Warmth spread through my chest. This was better than the bestseller list. A nomination for the Tower Prize, as Heidi would say, was a Very Big Deal.

Heidi paused for the applause and whoops. She cleared her throat. "Additionally, *Magician in the Machine* has been nominated for Best First Book." She lifted her glass. "Congratulations, Sam and Niall."

The space erupted again with cheers and whistles. I didn't bother trying to drink the champagne. My back was thumped— repeatedly—and after Qiana released Sam, she hugged me, hard, right below my ribs.

"Congratulations, you guys!" She beamed at us, but then her smile faltered. "Sam, aren't you excited?"

The grin melted off my face when I looked at Sam. She'd gone pale, her breath shallow and too fast. "Do you need to sit down?" Had she caught the con crud after all?

"No, I—I'm fine." Her face was hard and pale like marble. "Just surprised, is all."

I almost believed it. She wasn't familiar with the various prize nomination schedules. Last year, I'd waited by the phone on the day the nominees were announced and, when it refused to ring, lay on the couch, flattened by the pressing weight of disappointment. Today, I'd been too busy worrying about Sam to remember the nomination announcement.

But there's a difference between good-surprised and bad-surprised. I must have been glowing with the pleasure of recognition, of validation.

Sam was not.

Instead of her normal military-straight posture, her shoulders curved in. She squeezed the champagne glass, her gaze darting around the room.

Bilbo leaned against her leg and whined.

I shoved my glass of champagne into Qiana's hand. "Cover for us. We need a minute."

Wrapping an arm around Sam's waist, I guided her into Heidi's office. I eased her into one of the guest chairs and then gently pried her fingers off the stem of her champagne flute.

I laid my hand on the back of her neck the way she'd said she liked. "I'm going to let you chill out for a little while. I'll be right outside the door, so call me if you need me. I'll check on you in five minutes, okay?"

She said nothing, other than a barely perceptible nod.

I eased the door closed and then leaned against it. I crossed my arms. No one was coming in. She needed a minute with her thoughts, five minutes away from all the strangers and the noise. She'd be fine, wouldn't she?

Unless…

Just a minute ago, I'd felt vindicated, validated, on top of the world. Recognized for my work by experts in my field.

But, as usual, Sam was a step ahead of me.

Only one of us could win.

What if it was her?

What if it was me?

23

SAM

SITTING in Heidi's guest chair, I stared down at the text.

> Martell: Congratulations, Samantha! This is the
> validation we've been seeking for CASE. Soon,
> everyone will see what it can do.

Dr. Martell must've been watching for the Tower Prize announcement. I hadn't even known the prize existed until five minutes ago. According to Niall, it was a big deal in the science fiction and fantasy community.

And if *Magician* won, and then Martell and Heidi announced that an A.I. had written it, how would the community feel? All those people I'd met who'd read and loved the book. Writers like the ones on the panel at the convention. And Niall.

Niall. I twisted my trembling fingers in my lap.

The man hated technology. Who wouldn't with a father like that asshat, Paul Swift? He'd hate the idea that I'd "written" *Magician* by coding it on a computer and then making a mistake with the inputs. Jackson was right. It'd threaten his livelihood. Plus, it'd offend his artistic sensibilities to think a computer could create literature.

Clearly, he'd been hoping to be nominated. And to have that nomination spoiled by this, by CASE? He'd never forgive me. I couldn't live with that. With those kind, green eyes crystallizing, cold and hard. With the special smile he'd given me earlier when they'd announced the prize dropping into a rictus of shock and disappointment. I had to tell him.

Bilbo Baggins whined and licked my cheek.

"Don't worry, Bilbo Baggins," I whispered. "I'll fix it."

Behind me, the door opened. Perfect. I'd tell him there in the quiet office where no one would disturb us, and he could yell as loud as he wanted. I turned. "Hey, Niall—"

"Samantha." Heidi's mouth was a red slash. "What thrilling news. You must be very excited."

It wasn't excitement that swam with a pair of lead fins in my stomach. "Um. Not really? This is all kind of a lot." I stroked Bilbo Baggins' silky fur.

Heidi strode around me to sit behind her desk. I had to squint to see her features against the grayish winter glare from the window. "Qiana says you've done well on tour. The sales figures are stellar. And with the prize nomination, we expect them to increase."

"Oh. I guess that's good?"

"It's excellent. We've been very pleased with *Magician in the Machine*. And with you, Samantha." She leaned her elbows on the desk and steepled her fingers.

"Thank you." I guessed if I couldn't pretend to be a socialite, I had a future career in pretending to be an author. Mother would be so pleased. "But, if the nomination increases the sales, isn't that all we need to prove CASE's validity? We don't need the contest. Could you pull *Magician* out, quietly? I promise I wouldn't say a word."

She leaned back in her chair. "Samantha"—the only sign of her displeasure was a tightening around her mouth—"why would we want to withdraw from the contest?"

"Because the book is fake. Because it's a lie. Because you have a real author nominated." I gestured vaguely at her one bookshelf where the books were arranged by color. Maybe she had a copy of Niall's book in the greens? Or his second book in the reds? "Don't you want Niall to win?"

She waved away my words. "Niall can win next year with his next book. This is *your* time, Samantha. CASE's time. Time to prove that what you've done is special. That *you're* special. There's no downside to this. Even if *Magician* loses, it's still been nominated as one of the best half-dozen books of the year. We've proven that it's just as good as a manually written and edited book. Better than most."

"And—and if it wins?" I clutched Bilbo Baggins so hard he wheezed.

"If *Magician* wins, we've shown the world that CASE has written the superior book. And Happy Troll has the inside track on publishing more A.I.-produced books."

"But—but what about Niall and your other authors? What about your assistant editors? What about Qiana?" A starburst of pain stabbed behind my eye.

She flattened both hands on her desk. "I can repurpose the assistants to read CASE's output and find the best stories. I don't expect it to produce something as noteworthy as *Magician* every time. Well, not yet. And there will still be room for Niall and some of the other authors. Though I have to say I'm looking forward to dealing with fewer divas going forward. And their agents.

"Now, with this much less expensive and more efficient way of procuring content, we can finally push past the thin margins we've always had." She shoved against the glass surface of the desk and stood, straight and cold, in front of the gray, snowy streetscape beyond the windows. "Traditional publishing is going the way of the dinosaurs. Happy Troll is about to rise from the ashes like a phoenix."

"Wait. You're planning to use CASE to cut back on writers and editors?" All those people drinking champagne out there. How many would still be there this time next year if we could get another dozen books out of CASE? Two dozen?

Happy Troll wouldn't need my face when CASE wasn't a secret anymore. No book tour meant no Qiana.

And more books by CASE meant less room for books from Niall. Although I hadn't gotten far into *Secrets of the Wood Elves*—his writing was beautiful, but it took me so long to decipher—I'd gotten far enough to know it was a story worth telling, worth reading.

And the fact that he'd get fewer opportunities to write more and less money for each book? That was all my fault.

"Samantha, it's business." She spread her hands out to encompass the office, which I'd just realized was decorated in shades of black and gray except for the single case of books. "You come from a family of entrepreneurs. You should understand this."

Heat erupted inside me, and I stood, too. "That business affects people's careers. No. I won't do it. You have to withdraw *Magician.*"

"I have to do no such thing." Heidi eased back into her chair. "The only person who *has* to do anything is you, Samantha."

From a drawer, she pulled a stapled sheaf of papers. She turned it around to show my initials on the first page. "That's the nondisclosure agreement. If you violate it before we release you from it, we'll sue. You might think you don't have enough money for us to bother with, but I'll ensure it's a very public lawsuit."

I winced. Mother's disappointed face filled my imagination.

Then Niall's replaced it. If I told him now, maybe he could do something. Find another publisher. Focus on film rights and merchandising. Start a writers' union? He might still hate me, but at least he could have time to think, to plan.

"Let me tell Niall. I feel weird keeping this from him while we're on tour together."

She narrowed her eyes. "I understand you and he have grown very close. And Qiana calls you a friend."

I said nothing. She wouldn't use my friends against me, would she?

She would.

"No. I don't want news of this getting out until after the Tower Prize is announced. I wouldn't want the nominating committee to remove *Magician.* You've done so well already. You can keep it quiet for another week on tour. And then you can scurry back into your lab. I promise I'll give John a good report. I might even come to your hooding ceremony."

Heidi was a smart woman, and she knew my kryptonite. I'd walk across that stage, Mother and Dr. Martell would smile, and then I'd take my Ph.D. to Idaho. I hoped the university was in the middle of nowhere, where you couldn't get a cell signal. Maybe the research lab was tucked under a mountain.

Funny, it didn't seem as appealing as it used to. Hiding from my problems suddenly seemed cowardly.

And I was a coward. The lead spread upward into my chest. Heaviness—inertia—consumed me. "Okay. I won't say anything."

"I knew you'd see reason. Now, let's get back out there and continue the celebration."

24

NIALL

FOR THE SECOND time in as many days, I knocked on Sam's door, worry curling in my belly. She'd been ecstatic over her newborn niece this morning, but everything had turned at Happy Troll. Why hadn't she been as thrilled as I was about the prize nomination?

I clutched the bottle of champagne Qiana had slipped me from the celebration. A pair of the hotel's wineglasses clinked in my other hand.

Even though it was only five, Sam answered the door again in a tank top and sleep pants. The curtains of her room were pulled shut.

"Were you asleep?"

"No, working." She glanced back at her laptop, open on the desk, and leaped back into the room to slap it shut.

"Can I come in? I brought this." I waved the bottle at her.

She wrinkled her nose. "Champagne's not my thing."

"It's not?" When I stepped into the room, the door banged shut. I winced.

"It reminds me of too many stuffy parties. Like the one where I met you."

"You think I'm stuffy?" I set the glasses on the edge of the desk, far away from her delicate computer equipment.

One side of her mouth turned up. "I thought you were one of them when Gabi's photographer showed up. I'm glad I was wrong."

"I—ah." It was confession time. I couldn't keep going with Sam unless I told her the truth. "I also formed an impression. About you. Actually, it wasn't about you at all. Just your"—I waved a hand at her rumpled plaid pants and her camisole— "appearance."

"My appearance?" She crossed her arms over her chest, and one strap slipped off her shoulder.

I averted my eyes. Why was her shoulder so much sexier without that length of elastic? "How about a beer from the minibar?"

She snorted. "I checked the prices. Ten bucks for a Coors Lite? No, thanks."

"I'm buying. I think this'll go better with a little alcohol." I opened the mini fridge and pulled out a pair of bottles. I offered them to her, and she picked the pilsner. I twisted off the cap of the lager, raised it toward her in a half-toast, and took a long pull.

She found the opener on top of the fridge, popped off the top, and sipped her beer. "A dollar. That's how much that sip cost."

I frowned. "Why are you worried about money? *Magician* is selling well, according to Heidi. Plus, you're an heiress."

This time, she glugged back the beer. Her lips popped off the neck, shiny, pink, and wet. "Not anymore. I gave away my trust fund. I didn't want to be a target. A victim. Not again."

"A victim?" My heart stalled in my chest. "Were you kidnapped? Blackmailed?"

"I'd rather not talk about it." She sat on the bed next to where Bilbo was curled up. "What'll go easier with alcohol?"

I raised my eyebrows at the desk chair. After a glance at her closed laptop, she nodded. I rotated the chair to face the bed and sat in it.

"I was struggling when I met you. With my writing. I was stuck. And meeting you shook something loose in my brain."

Her lips curled up into the first smile I'd seen since she'd shown me the photos of baby Valentine this morning. "You called me your violet-eyed muse."

Warmth spread from my neck up my cheeks. "But there's more. I—I created a character. Based on you. On your appearance. And things I imagined about you."

Her eyes widened. "Things you imagined about me? Like fantasies?"

The heat spread up over my forehead. "Not sex fantasies. Just regular fantasy stuff. I imagined a wood sprite with your features. Your eyes. Your"—I swallowed—"skin. She saved Nieven from the trap he'd fallen into. And then she joined him on his adventures."

"What's her name?"

"Lobelia. Like the flower."

She scrunched her nose.

"I don't suppose you've read *Treachery* yet?" I'd seen her reading *Secrets,* but she always closed the book quickly, like she was embarrassed. I was the one who should've been embarrassed. Her debut novel was worlds above my little adventure tale. A juvenile effort next to her work of literature.

"I wanted to finish *Secrets* first." She trailed her delicate fingers through Bilbo's fur. "I love it so far, but I have a confession, too. I, ah, I'm not a fast reader. I have dyslexia. It'll take me literally forever to finish a thick book like that. I might not make it to *Treachery.*" She bit her lip.

Now some of her answers during the Q and A made sense. How she was never able to name more than a few authors who'd inspired her. How she didn't appear to have a current knowledge of popular fiction. How she'd turned green before each public reading.

"That must have been a lot to overcome. And yet you managed to get all the way through grad school."

She looked up from the dog, her smile twisted and bitter. "It's not something I've 'overcome.' It's something I deal with every day. Something that'll be with me for the rest of my life."

"I'm sorry. I didn't mean it that way." I'd wanted to express my admiration, and then I'd gone and fucked it up.

"I know." She leaned forward, laid a hand over mine. "Most people say that. Remember, I grew up with lots of advantages. Private schools. Tutors. It was easier for me than it was for some."

"I bet you still worked your ass off. The way you've done to get better at the book talks."

She bit her soft, pillowy lip. "I tried. It was never enough for my mother, though. And when she finally accepted I wasn't going to get over it, she figured she'd train me up to be a good wife to a smart man."

My blood heated. "Meaning he'd be the brains of your relationship?"

"Yeah." She traced a pattern on Bilbo's fur. He twitched in his sleep. "I wasn't very good at that, either."

I took a big swallow of beer, hoping it'd cool me off. It didn't. "But you were good at writing."

She paused. "Not really. I was good at computers, though. Somehow the code didn't swim for me the way words in books did. My brother Jackson discovered that, and he encouraged me. He was kind of a replacement dad to me after."

After she'd lost her dad. Maybe I had one of the world's shittiest dads, but at least I still had one. I wish I'd known that about Jackson before I'd been so surly with him at dinner the other night. Though I still didn't like the way he'd talked to her about her book. "But he didn't support your writing."

"He has his reasons. And they're pretty good ones." She picked at the label on her bottle.

I put my hand over hers. "Your book is amazing. Think about all the people you touched with it. The way Tolkien touched your heart." She'd said she wasn't a big reader, but the proof she liked books snored at her side.

"That was really my dad. He loved Tolkien and L'Engle. Or he loved reading them to me. When I got old enough, we'd take turns reading, and he was so patient with me. My mother would've given up. But not my dad. He didn't give up on anything."

She was silent for a minute.

"Did you want to talk about it? About him?"

"No. Not now, anyway. Maybe another time."

I understood not wanting to talk about growing up without a father. But then I had an idea. "I could read to you. If you want."

"Really? Seriously? You'd do that?" Her eyes widened. "Because I love listening to you read. At the events. I always want you to keep going."

I chuckled. "That's the point. And now, just for you, I'll keep going."

She jumped up and dug through her computer bag until she produced the book. The edges of the paperback were a little curled and worn, but the spine was still stiff.

"Come on." She tilted her head toward the bed.

Oh, fuck. I hadn't thought about that. I circled the bed on the other side, toed off my shoes, and sat gingerly on top of the covers. I stretched out my legs on the bed and leaned back against the headboard. She tucked her legs under the covers, fluffed a couple of pillows, and leaned back beside me.

A bookmark from the store in Chicago marked the middle of a scene in Chapter Three. "Should I start here?"

"Yeah, that's good."

I read my words to her. I'd written the first draft of that chapter years ago, when I was still in college. The words seemed immature, clumsy. Like I'd been back then. Nothing like Sam's elegantly nubilous prose. I'd seen a tiny sliver of her tonight, but otherwise, Sam was like her book. Beautiful. Impenetrable.

After a while, Sam's head came to rest against my shoulder,

and then it was only natural for my arm to go around her and tuck her closer to me. I tried not to think about how her dad had probably held her just like this. Not while I smelled the rosemary in her hair and while I tried to keep my eyes on the page and not on the upper swells of her breasts where they disappeared into the fabric of her camisole, the shallow valley between, the pointed nipples the thin material didn't hide.

"Why'd you stop?" She turned her face to mine and must have seen the unadulterated lust there. "Oh."

I dropped the book onto the covers. "It didn't work."

She licked her lower lip. "What didn't work?"

"Getting it out of my system. It's still in my system." Poetic, I know. But the blood had left my brain and pooled elsewhere.

"What's in your system?"

"You." I lowered my head. I wanted to crash my lips onto hers, take them, plunder them like my Viking forefathers. But I was a twenty-first-century man, and I had more restraint than that. Well, usually I did. I hesitated, an inch from her lips.

She stretched her long neck up and kissed me, her lips no longer soft but demanding, urgent. She took, and I gave. And gave and gave and gave until I was breathless. I broke the kiss and tucked her head under my chin, breathing like I'd just run up the nine flights of stairs to our floor.

She planted a kiss on my neck, and I shivered. Her lips curled against my skin. "How about now? Am I out of your system?"

Never. She'd never be out. Not as long as I could hold her in my imagination. I shook my head slowly, rubbing my nose into her silky hair.

"I think it'll take more than a few kisses, don't you?"

I nodded.

She pulled back far enough that she could look me in the eye. Her pupils had all but consumed the irises, but her expression was serious, almost fierce. "At the end of the tour, I'm going back to San Francisco. I'm finishing my degree, and then I'm going on to a postdoc position somewhere far away from everywhere. No more book tours, no more"—her breath hitched—"anything. You and I are done when the tour ends. Understand?"

She probably had to go back into her writing cave to produce another book, just like I had to return to the farm. She needed space for that.

My chest tightened. But she'd said more than that. *You and I are done.* That sounded permanent. As in, she didn't want anything permanent with me. She wasn't the first. That had been my dad. And then all the girls who thought it'd be fun to hang out with a farmboy-poet but then run at the first sign of fresh manure.

"Niall." My name on her lips halted my racing thoughts. "I like you. A lot, okay? But we have different goals. We're not going to work out long-term. But I'd like to enjoy you while I can." She shifted, and the strap of her camisole slid down again, revealing the top of her breast.

Rational thought fled. "Yes," I growled. Pushing her to her back, I kissed her shoulder where the strap had been and then trailed kisses along the upper curve of her breast. Nosing aside the fabric that barely covered her nipple, I licked it. Her skin tasted herbal, too. Earthy. Like the forest after a good rain. I sucked her nipple into my mouth and laved it.

She buried her hands in my hair and held me to her. "I'm glad we're"—she moaned—"in agreement on the plan."

I pulled up a little, stretching her nipple, and let it pop free. "The not-permanent plan."

She squirmed. "That's the one."

I tugged down the other strap. "When I'm done, you'll wish I was permanent."

"Not a chance."

But that was before I descended on her other nipple, swirling my tongue around it. My teeth. A tiny bite on the underside of her breast that made her suck in a breath. Then a harder bite right on her nipple.

She made an unintelligible sound that might've been my

name, or maybe "never," but she held my head, and I kept up the attention on her breast until she released me, her breath rasping.

I placed a gentle kiss right over her heaving sternum. "You sure about that? The nonpermanent thing?"

"Oh, big talk for a guy who thinks he hit a homerun but ended up with a double." Her lips tilted up, playful.

"Ended up? I'm thinking about stealing third." I tunneled a hand under the covers, over her pajama pants, but stopped at the waistband. I raised my eyebrows.

"Niall Flynn." She fluttered her eyelashes. "I thought you were such a nice young man with your door opening and carrying my bags and protecting me on nighttime walks."

"I don't think you want nice." I cupped her between her legs. Sure enough, the crotch was damp.

She shook her head slowly. "No. I don't."

I followed her contours with a lazy finger. She squirmed.

"What do you want, Sam?"

"I want you."

I reversed my hand, delving inside her pajama pants—she wasn't wearing panties—and finding the hot wetness inside. I swirled a finger through the peaks and valleys I'd just mapped. Then I slipped a finger inside her. She groaned and ground her hips up.

I pulled out my finger, ghosting over her clit, and showed her the wetness on my middle finger. When I popped it into my mouth and sucked, her breath caught.

"You're not a nice young man at all," she whispered.

"No. I grew up on a farm. I learned to fuck in haylofts. Sheds. Under the trees in summer. Not hotel rooms. But I'll make you feel better than any of those society guys ever could. Do you want that, Sam?"

Her eyes were dark, hooded. "I do."

I shoved the covers off her and tugged down her pajama pants. I flung them onto the floor. Her camisole still bunched at her waist, but I couldn't wait. I positioned her, knees bent and spread wide enough for my shoulders. Between her legs, she was flushed pink and swollen, her arousal dripping from her and her scent filling my nostrils. But before I dipped my head to her, I asked, "You okay with this?"

She lifted her head and tucked a pillow beneath. "Yes. Yes."

I licked her, a long swipe of the tongue from her slit all the way to her clit.

"Yes." Her voice was breathy.

I spread her with my thumbs and got familiar with her scent, her taste, what made her squirm, what made her suck in a breath and go still. Sweeping a finger through her wetness, I replaced my tongue with my finger and delved inside, thrusting in the same rhythm I was humping against the mattress. Her hips bucked. I wedged a second finger inside, and she moaned. She was tight and wet, and I wanted nothing more than to push myself inside and feel her, skin to skin. Not yet.

Still working my fingers, I trailed my tongue up along her swollen lips to her clit. I circled it with the tip of my tongue. She clenched the sheets in those delicate fingers, her knuckles going white.

I flattened my tongue and swept over it. She let out a strangled moan, like she'd been holding her breath. I licked her clit once more before I sucked it, gently, between my lips. Her legs trembled.

I checked her face. Her head was thrown back against the pillow, inky hair spilling across it. Her mouth was open, her breaths coming fast, and her eyes squeezed shut. "Look at me, Sam." I wanted those clear, intelligent eyes on me. Maybe we weren't permanent, but I was here, now. Giving her pleasure. And the caveman part of me wanted her to know it. "Watch me make you come."

Her eyes flicked open, and the way she looked down, heavy-lidded, at where I lay, prostrate, on the bed, made me feel like a servant, bowing before his queen. She was beautiful as one of the elf-queens in my books, diamond-hard and glittering. But I'd found a way to her innermost chamber, where she was naked and writhing and earthy. I was the one stretched out on my belly before her, but she'd given me the power to please her tonight.

I grazed her with my teeth, and she cried out. All it took was one more hard suck, and she bowed up, pressing hard into my face. I pistoned my fingers in and out another few seconds and then slowed as her legs went slack and splayed out to either side. I eased off her clit but kept up a series of long, lazy licks until she groaned and touched my head. Giving her one last lick, I laid my cheek on her thigh. Her eyes didn't leave mine.

"You learned to do that in a hayloft?"

I chuckled. "It wasn't exactly on the 4-H curriculum, but we'd sneak off sometimes when the meetings got dull."

"What else did you do in these very educational 4-H sessions?"

"A little veterinary science, a little cunnilingus. A few hours of soil analysis, a literal roll in the hay. We just had to be careful not to spook the animals below. Nothing worse than a braying jerk of a donkey to ruin the mood."

She smiled and twirled a lock of my hair. "I wish I'd known you then. I think you'd have been a good friend."

Her downturned lips said she'd needed a good friend or two in high school. After losing her dad, hounded by a mother with unrealistic expectations, with Jackson likely away at college, she'd have been lost and lonely. And high-school kids had a way of sniffing that out and exploiting it.

"Sorry, you're a little old for 4-H, but we can be friends now." An idea tickled at the back of my brain. I'd have to check with Mom and Grandpa first, though.

"Friends with benefits, as they say?" One corner of her mouth quirked up.

I trailed a finger up the inside of her other thigh, raising a trail of goosebumps on her skin. "My benefits are a lot cheaper than the minibar."

Bilbo, who'd evacuated the bed when it had started to shake, whined and scratched at the door.

Sam groaned. "I forgot. It's time for his last walk. Just a minute, Bilbo Baggins." She propped herself up on an elbow and tugged up her tank top.

I levered up and laid a hand on her leg, stilling her. "I'll do it. I'm still dressed." Though a walk with a hard-on would be uncomfortable at best.

Her eyes widened, like she'd just realized it. "I came all over your face, and you're still dressed?" She covered her face with her hands. "I'm, like, the worst friend-with-benefits ever."

"No." I grabbed her wrist and pulled one hand off her face. I kissed her palm. "I had a good time. And now Bilbo and I are going to have some guy-time. You relax, okay?" She needed it. And she'd needed that orgasm. The prize announcement had been a lot for her. All those people at the publisher's office. She was probably envisioning the new strangers she'd have to meet at the prize ceremony. Leaning forward, I brushed her lips with mine and then scooted off the bed.

Bilbo's leash hung over the doorknob. I clipped it to his collar and closed the door gently behind me.

25

NIALL

SAM MIGHT HAVE SAID she brought Bilbo with her because he was her best friend, but Sam wasn't Bilbo's only friend.

Bilbo was a dog-whore.

From the moment I stepped out into the lobby with him, Bilbo drew admirers like buzzards to carrion. Two old ladies in silk suits stooped on creaking knees to pat his head. Bilbo grinned the whole time.

The bellman called out, "Wait, Bilbo Baggins," and hustled over with a dog biscuit. Bilbo crunched it all over the hotel carpet and let the man scratch him behind the ears.

Outside, Bilbo trotted down the street like a don in a gangster movie, accepting accolades and treats as his due. Laptop-toting women, yoga mat–carrying women, and women with double strollers followed him and asked to pet him or take selfies with him. Bilbo would be featured in more Instagram posts that day than I was at that fantasy convention.

Not that I was jealous. Of a dog.

Did Sam attract this kind of attention when she walked him? Would the men who hung back and admired Bilbo at a distance have approached Sam if she'd been walking him? Would they have tried to get her number?

The damn dog was dangerous.

When a trio of tourists with more camera gear than Annie Leibovitz stopped us just inside the park, it gave me an idea.

I pulled out my phone to take my first-ever camera-phone picture. I'd send it to Gabi in a text message—another first.

I fumbled the phone, thumbing the screen to wake it up. Shit, it was out of batteries. Or broken.

Or…off.

I pressed the power button, and finally the screen came to life. And went through a minute's worth of electronic music and video. The thing was more trouble than it was worth. Meanwhile, I accepted one of the tourists' complicated cameras to take a group shot of them with their new best friend, who even smiled for the shot, his tongue lolling.

Ham.

My pocket buzzed. After handing the camera back to the tourist, I pulled out my phone. Gabi's name flashed on the screen.

"Hey, I was just thinking of you," I said.

"Me? The latest Tower Prize nominee is thinking of his lowly agent, typist, and erstwhile best friend?"

"Erstwhile?"

"It's one of the many words I learned transcribing your manu-scripts. It means former—"

"I know what it means. Why are you my erstwhile friend?" I found a bench in the park under a streetlamp as the sky faded from sunset pink to twilight gray. Bilbo stretched out at my feet.

"Why did I have to find out about the Tower Prize from the freaking internet? My friend Niall would've called me to share the good news, maybe even come over with a bottle of bubbly. So when I got no call, I thought, fuck, he got the shaft again. Let's see if that phony princess, Samantha, got a nod. And, lo and behold, there's both of your names on the list of nominees."

"Sorry. If I win, I'll be sure to thank you in my acceptance speech. I was distracted."

"*When* you win. Distracted by the nomination or something—someone—else?"

"Sam was a little overwhelmed by the announcement. I had to make sure she was all right."

"And?"

"She's better now." Gabi was my best friend, but I wasn't about to tell her I'd relaxed Sam by eating her out. "She's been on edge. Especially after that dinner with her brother. I'm not sure what's going on with her." She might've laid herself bare for me, but her mind was still locked up tight as the crown jewels.

"She's an enigma, all right. She's not nearly as swanky and snooty as I expected. She seemed pretty cut-up over that kid's drawing."

"Sam likes kids. She's good with them."

"She is? What a coincidence. You like kids, too. As I recall, you had a plan to fill that farmhouse with—"

"No, Gabi, we're not talking about that now."

"I'm just saying, maybe you've got more in common with Sam than you thought."

I stood and paced around the bench. "What's that supposed to mean?"

"You like her."

Bilbo barked once. I froze and looked at him. Bilbo thumped his tail. "Of course I like her."

Bilbo barked again.

"No, you like-like her. You have visions of taking her to the farm. Showing her your secret cove. A big wedding in the meadow. Popping out posh little blue-eyed babies."

"That's ridiculous." How the hell had she guessed? "Shh, Bilbo." He stopped barking, gave his rear end a quick glance over his shoulder, and spun in a circle, chasing his tail. He needed space to run, not walks on a leash.

"You haven't slept with her, have you? You know how you get

when sex is involved. There's meeting the family and trips to the farm and talk about forever—"

"No." Then, under my breath, "Not exactly."

She gave a dramatic gasp. "What the fuck does 'not exactly' mean? Was there an orgasm?"

"There may have been." How did she always drag my secrets out of me?

"Then it was sex. Watch out, Niall. The princess has secrets. Don't get emotionally invested until you know what they are."

"Everyone has secrets." Sam's dyslexia wasn't my secret to share.

"I know you like her. But she's going to shred your heart when she leaves." I knew what she was thinking, even though she'd never say it. That I was sensitive to people leaving me. Because of what my asshole of a father had done.

But Sam wasn't like him. "I'll be careful."

"Liar. Guard that soft heart of yours, Niall."

That was why we'd stayed friends after we'd broken up. The fussing. "You guard it. You had it last."

Gabi snorted. "Please. If you'd wanted me, you'd have followed me to the city. Don't try to get me off track. This is important."

"What is?"

"Niall." She stretched out my name like I was a child or a very naughty puppy. "You're both nominated for the Tower Prize. That makes you rivals."

"No!"

"No? What, is one of you going to withdraw from the contest?"

"Of course not. This is great for both of us." But...should we? What would happen if one of us won? That would mean the other lost. Would the loser be bitter about it? Would I? Should I withdraw to save myself the pain?

"Niall. Do. Not. Withdraw."

"I won't. Probably. Being nominated is an honor. It's huge for our careers. I'm sure Sam and I will be fine, whoever wins." In fact, when I got back to the hotel, I'd practice my I'm-so-thrilled-you-won smile in front of the mirror.

"This is me rolling my eyes, Niall."

Bilbo sat up and barked. I patted his head.

"I need to take Bilbo back."

"I'll see you tomorrow at the signing. Get some rest, okay?"

I tugged on Bilbo's leash to direct him back toward the hotel. "I will."

"Good. And Niall?"

"Yeah?"

"If you're nominated for a Pulitzer or a Nobel, you'll call me, yeah?"

"You got it."

Bilbo led the way back to the hotel, his tail flying behind him like a flag.

———

I RAPPED SOFTLY on Sam's door in case she'd gone to sleep. Today had been a lot for her. For us both.

But she answered, wearing sleep pants and that camisole that drove me wild. My erection, which I'd finally walked off, sprang to life again.

"Thanks for taking care of Bilbo Baggins."

She scooped him up and cradled him in her arms, asking him nonsense questions like he could answer as she walked into her room. I dropped the leash and let it trail on the carpet behind them.

She glanced over her shoulder. "You coming in?"

Without engaging my brain, my feet carried me into her room. The door banged shut behind me.

She unclipped Bilbo's leash and set him on the floor. He ran into the bathroom and noisily lapped his water.

"That dog is dangerous," I grumbled. "I can't even tell you how many people stopped us to pet him."

She laughed, too loud to be a society tinkle, but the music was still there. "He loves the attention. He'll be so sad when..." Her smile faded.

My heart sped up. "When what, Sam? When the tour's over?" Was there a chance she wouldn't be ready to let me go, either?

She grimaced. "When we leave San Francisco and go to my postdoc. It's at a tiny, selective university that does very cool things with computers, but it won't have nearly as many opportunities to make friends."

"You've chosen a small university?"

"Yeah. From Google Maps, it's mostly cornfields, a little town, and the university. Nothing else for miles."

"Sounds like where I grew up. Except for the university. You've got to go into the city for that." Fuck. I'd finally met a woman who liked wide-open spaces and small towns, and she needed a world-class university. Enchanted Forest was the most beautiful town in the world, but it wasn't known for its computing capabilities unless you counted the two ancient public workstations at the library.

"Did you like growing up there?" She rubbed one bare arm with the other hand, like she was cold.

"More than anything."

"I know I'll like the university. The key factor is that it's a thousand miles from home and two hours from the closest major airport. I'll finally get some space."

I couldn't stop the half-baked idea from spilling out of my mouth. "Hey, if you need space, we've got a couple days off coming up. I was planning to go home to Enchanted Forest and see my family."

She grinned. "I still can't believe you live in an actual town called Enchanted Forest."

I shrugged. "It deserves the name. It's the best place on earth. You could come, too. It's quiet. You'd get a break from all the people. The stress. And Bilbo could run and play as much as he wants."

At the sound of his name, Bilbo trotted out of the bathroom and wagged his tail.

"Oh. Um, I was planning to just hang out at the hotel. Get some work done." She waved at her laptop on the desk.

"Of course. No pressure. You can think about it."

"Sure."

It was a thanks-but-no-thanks *sure*. And she was probably right. Maybe it'd be better if she declined the invitation I hadn't even meant to extend. Gabi's words echoed through my head. *Meeting the family and trips to the farm and talk about forever.* Sam had assured me she wasn't a forever kind of person.

"I should go. I've got that early-morning talk show tomorrow."

"A talk show?"

"Yeah." I rubbed the back of my neck, which had gone hot. "Qiana called me this afternoon. They had a guest back out. And after the nomination, they asked me to fill the spot."

"That's wonderful, Niall. Television." She sounded sincere. Her violet eyes shone.

"This isn't going to be weird, is it? Both of us nominated for the Tower Prize?"

She paled, and that was all the answer I needed. Of course it was going to be weird.

"I don't want to think about the Tower Prize. Not tonight." She stepped up to me and put her palms on my chest. "You did such a good job of distracting me before. Want to do it again?"

She must've felt my heart racing under her hands. My breath heaving. My balls, which had been aching for an hour, since I'd buried my face in her, tingled. Of course I wanted to do it again. But I put my hands over hers and pulled them off my traitorous chest. *Guard that soft heart of yours, Niall.*

"I'm not sure that's a good idea." The words felt like glass shards in my throat.

She grinned. "Because it's Valentine's Day? I swear I'm not one of those love-obsessed people who'll cling to you like a barnacle if we have sex on February fourteenth."

"No, of course not." If I believed in Valentine's Day magic, I'd have made love to her right where we stood. If only I could get her to cling to me and not want to toss me away as soon as the tour ended.

Her playful smile faded. "Because of the prize? Because I—"

"No." I squeezed her hands. "The prize has nothing to do with us." I tried to get the words right in my head before I said them.

"Then why?"

"I'm starting to have some…feelings about you. Feelings I know you don't reciprocate. And sex is going to complicate that."

"But we already had sex."

A pain erupted over my left eyebrow. Gabi had said the same thing. "And it was fantastic. But I need to stop there. Unless you've changed your mind about ending things when the tour ends?" I hated the hopeful rise to my voice. It sounded too much like the hundred times I'd asked my father to come home.

She shook her head. Her eyes had gone dull like she'd pulled a velvet curtain down over them.

I kissed her, softly, briefly. "Good-night, Sam. And the invitation to the farm? Purely platonic. I think you could use the break."

She looked down at her bare toes.

When I kissed the top of her head, I had to hold my breath to avoid her tempting scent. I scratched Bilbo's chin and left her room, shutting the door gently behind me.

Platonic. As soon as the word was out of my mouth, it echoed with falsehood. Aside from my friends in Enchanted Forest, I'd never asked anyone there I didn't think I was in love with. The farm was too special, too close to my heart, to clutter up with acquaintances.

Sam belonged there. She'd punched her way into my heart and set up camp. And I'd let her in, dangerously close to everything I held sacred.

26

SAM

STEWING in the back seat of the town car idling in front of the television studio, I pried my fists open so I could phone a friend.

"Oh. My. God," I said as soon as Marlee answered my video call.

"What is it?" When she moved with the phone, I spotted a bare, muscled shoulder and bedsheets behind her. Bilbo Baggins, nestled close to me in the town car, cocked his head at the sound of her voice.

"Shit, I forgot about the time difference. Did I wake you up?" I put a hand over my eyes.

"My alarm would've gone off in a few minutes. Don't worry about it. And you can open your eyes. I'm wearing a nightgown. Are you okay?" She flicked on a light and sat down at her kitchen table. A coffeemaker grumbled in the background.

"I—" Suddenly, the rage that'd made me phone my friend waned to a dull pain in my lungs. "I guess I was having some feelings, and I wanted to see a friendly face."

"Feelings about…?"

I could've said anything. Travel. My Ph.D. But what came out was the truth. "About Niall."

"Your hottie tour partner?" Her eyes widened. "He *is* your OTP!"

"What? No." I fumbled my earbuds into my ears.

"But, Sam, you said you had feelings. You haven't had any feelings for anyone you've—wait! Did you guys sleep together?"

I covered my face, glad Marlee was coming through my headphones and not my phone's speaker. What we'd done on my bed hardly counted since I was the only one who'd gotten off. And then after, when I'd have returned the favor, he'd turned me down. "Sort of?"

"Sweet, sweet Stephen Hawking. And was it…?"

"Yes, of course." My cheeks burned. "Farmboy magic," I mumbled.

"Then what—?"

"Feelings suck." I lowered my voice so the driver didn't have to pretend so hard not to hear me. "He did an interview this morning on one of the talk shows, and—"

"Which one?"

I told her the name, and she glanced offscreen, typing something into a laptop. I'd felt the same way as when I'd gone into his room and Gabi was there. A roiling in my stomach and the need to strike, to incinerate the icky feeling with a punch of kinetic energy. I'd jammed the off button on the TV remote so hard it'd stuck in its slot.

I smoothed Bilbo Baggins' fur. "Anyway, the interviewer was all flirty and…and simpering, and he ate it up, and then I got heartburn and had to eat, like, a million antacids."

"Brandi Brewer. Yeah, she's pretty. But he's sleeping with *you*."

I winced, remembering how he'd turned me down the night before. "Not exactly."

"Oh. *Oh*." Her eyes went all soft and melty, like caramel. "But you want to."

"Just—just for the sex."

Marlee shook her head. "If you wanted him just for sex, you wouldn't care if he flirted with Brandi Brewer. You're in it now."

"In what now?"

"In love." And she gave an honest-to-God happy sigh. She looked up, and her fiancé, Tyler, kissed her lips. Then he shuffled out of frame.

"I can one hundred percent tell you I am not in love with Niall Flynn." Though what would it be like to have someone kiss me in the morning like that? To set a cup of coffee at my right hand? I blinked to lubricate my prickling eyes. Sure, it'd be nice. But I was good at computer science, not relationships. Stephen had proven that.

"But—"

The car door opened, and Niall slid into the car. "Sorry I'm late. I—"

The rush of warmth I felt was only happiness that I could end the conversation with Marlee, which hadn't gone the way I'd wanted at all. It wasn't because of Niall. "Hey, Marlee, I've got to go."

"Wait, no. We're not done. You've got to let yourself—"

"Talk to you later bye," I said in a rush and clicked the end button. I tried to smile at Niall, but the pomaded russet waves of his hair reminded me of how good he'd looked on camera. Next to Brandi.

"Hey, sorry." Niall's eyes drooped, and purple shadows were only half-concealed by his carelessly wiped-off makeup. "That took longer than I thought it would."

Of course it had. Because of all the flirting. I pulled out the smile I used at Mother's functions. "Don't worry about it." I grabbed a tissue from the box in the console and scrubbed at the traces of foundation on his face.

"Hey, I need some of that skin." He stilled my hand and took the tissue from me, wiping more gently than I'd done. "Is something wrong? Are you mad because I'm late?"

"No. I don't even want to do this." That day's reading was at a local university. Being one myself, I knew the students would engage in a game of one-upmanship with their difficult questions for us. I wouldn't be able to float by with my vague answers about Tolkien and L'Engle. And Niall shouldn't have to rescue me.

"Then what's wrong?"

He rubbed at his cheek, and my gaze arrowed to a spot just to the left of his mouth. "Is that lipstick?"

"What?" But he must've known what I was talking about because he wiped the spot.

"Is it yours or hers?"

"Hers?" His red eyebrows rose.

"That—that interviewer. The blonde. What's-her-name." Of course I knew her name. He'd only said it about a hundred times during their interview.

"Brandi Brewer. So you watched it."

"I had it on while I was getting dressed." I shrugged and looked out the window.

"You're not upset, are you?"

"Of course not. What do I have to be upset about? It's not like we're—Anyway, I didn't think it was professional of her to flirt with you like that."

"Flirt with me?"

I stared at the buildings we passed, but I imagined his red eyebrows raised somewhere near his hairline.

I hated myself even as I raised my voice to a nasal imitation of Brandi-Brewer-the-interviewer. "'I don't interview a lot of writers with a physique like yours. Care to share your workout routine?' 'Any chance you'll be doing a walk-on role on the show?' 'Are you seeing anyone?'" How my gut had churned when she'd asked that. Of course he'd said no. And the air kisses. Ugh.

Why was I acting like this? *Feeling* like this? I'd never been jealous. Okay, I'd been jealous of the girl Stephen had dated after me. Even though I'd known he was a snake, I'd given him my heart, and I hadn't gotten back all the pieces after he'd broken it. Which was exactly why I couldn't give any part of it to Niall. If I lost any more pieces, could it keep beating? A cold, heavy lump weighed in my belly.

"Sam." He waited until I dragged my gaze back to him. "It didn't mean anything. I didn't care about her. Not like I—" The blush started at his neck and washed all the way up to his cheeks.

The lump in my belly eased. Okay, then.

"Oh. Hey. I had an idea." His eyes sparkled. He pulled his phone from his back pocket, frowned at it, and tapped.

My phone vibrated in my hand. "You texted me?" He'd called me about logistical stuff, but he'd never texted me.

"Better than a text." He smiled, closed-mouth, like he was holding back a secret.

I glanced at the screen. A notification appeared at the top.

```
Niall Flynn has gifted you the audiobook
        Secrets of the Wood Elves.
```

"An audiobook?"

"Yeah, I thought you'd like to listen to it instead of read it. Like we did yesterday afternoon."

Yesterday afternoon's session had the bonus of an orgasm. No matter how good the professional narration was, I didn't think I'd get off from it. Still, it was nice. Thoughtful. Very Niall-like. "Thank you." I leaned over and kissed his lips, just a peck, really. I wanted to linger for more.

"You're welcome." He licked his lips. "Let me know when you're ready for the second one." His shiny lips twisted up into a flirty smile.

Warmth bloomed between my legs. *Now now now,* my body chanted.

"Okay." My voice was too high and breathy. I cleared my throat. "Sorry I was weird earlier. The tour is getting to me, I guess."

He took a deep breath. Let it out. "I don't suppose you've given any more thought to coming home with me?"

Thought? I had lots of thoughts about it. Most of them were *Danger* and *Don't be an idiot*. But he'd made it sound like nirvana, free from pressure and crowds. Beyond wifi, where I wouldn't have to answer Heidi's and Dr. Martell's irritating reminders about the NDA and about the Tower Prize being the endgame to this whole charade.

"Platonic, right? We'll just hang out and you'll show me the famous farmboy workout you talked up with Brandi?"

"Platonic. And you'll be doing it, too. Everybody works on a farm."

"I'm not scared of work." Sore muscles might get my mind off everything else.

No. I didn't belong on Niall's farm, platonic invitation or not. With the lies I'd told, I didn't deserve to be his friend. Still, I couldn't stop the words from tumbling out of my mouth. "Okay, then. I'll go."

Niall's smile was better than anything he'd given Brandi during that interview.

27

SAM

I HUGGED Bilbo Baggins tight as Niall parked the rental car in front of the two-story white farmhouse on Friday morning. It was a Hallmark movie set with its wraparound porch and rocking chairs. All it needed was a bunch of daisies growing in front. But in Ohio, February was too early for flowers.

Niall pulled the key out of the ignition. An easy smile tugged at the corners of his mouth. "Okay so far? This isn't too terrible?"

It was terrible. *I* was terrible to have let him talk me into this. Even if Niall hadn't accepted it yet, our friendship would end as soon as the tour did. Because if it didn't, the lies I'd stacked up between us would topple over and crush us both. There was no reason to get closer to him. And coming to his farm was about as close to Niall as I could get.

So I told him another lie. For someone who was an awful liar, I told them more and more easily. "It's fine. I'm good."

"Then let's go inside. We'll say hi to Mom and Grandpa, and I'll give you the grand tour."

When I opened the car door, Bilbo Baggins jumped out and ran in circles, sniffing the ground. Slinging my backpack over my shoulder, I caught the scent of menthol—not eucalyptus now, but pine—and cedar. Ohio smelled like Niall.

He came around the front of the car and slid his hand into mine. He tugged me up the front steps and through the unlocked front door.

"Mom, I'm home," he called in the old-fashioned entryway. A neat row of boots—most of them muddy—sat in a tray next to the front door. Bilbo Baggins sniffed them. "Don't bother taking your shoes off," Niall said. "We'll only be inside a minute."

The scent of baking bread wafted through the house. We passed through a doorway to the right into a bright yellow kitchen with white-painted cabinets. Niall's mother—I recognized her from Niall's book launch—wiped her hands on a faded blue gingham dish towel.

"Niall. And Sam." She held out her arms, and Niall let go of my hand to step into his mother's embrace. After a long hug, she released him and opened her arms to me. She was softer than my mother, less angled bone and more pliant muscle, and her callused hands snagged on the back of my canvas coat. Up close, she smelled of yeast and lemons. Bilbo Baggins danced below, his toenails tapping on the linoleum.

Niall's grandfather stood from where he'd been sitting at the kitchen table and hugged Niall. He held out his rough right hand to me, and I shook it. His left arm was in a cast.

"It's good to see you again, Mr. Flynn. Ms. Flynn." I tried to smile like I meant it.

His smile was more guarded, less free than Niall's mother's.

She swiped a crumb off the counter. "Please, call me Elaine. Or Laney. And my dad is Jerry. Are you two hungry?"

"No—" I began. We'd had pastries and coffee at the airport waiting for our early-morning flight.

But Niall spoke over me. "I want to take Sam on a tour of the farm. Mind if I pack us some sandwiches? I promise we'll be back for supper."

Elaine's laugh rang out through the kitchen. "If I had a dollar for every time you lost yourself in those woods and missed supper." She patted Niall's shoulder. "Today's bread is still in the oven, but I have some of yesterday's. You know where everything is." She squatted down to stroke Bilbo Baggins, who flopped to the floor and exposed his belly.

"Not a watchdog, this one," she said.

His head in the refrigerator, Niall said, "No, more like an icebreaker. That dog has friends in six cities. He's more extroverted than either of us."

Elaine grinned, and she stood, resting a hip on the counter. "Have you enjoyed the book tour so far, Sam?"

"I guess?"

She chuckled. "I can't imagine how grueling it must be. All that travel. All those people."

Niall set down an armful of items on the butcher-block island. "It's not so bad. The adulation of fans. Restaurant meals. Daily housekeeping. And a distinct lack of stall-mucking." He glanced at me. "Though Sam's a city girl. I don't think she's ever experienced the joy of a good stall-mucking."

"I've had a riding lesson or two, and my parents used to take us to a farm outside the city. I'm not afraid of your barn. Or your livestock." That farm had been one of Dad's favorite day trips. Mine, too.

Grinning, Niall piled turkey onto thick slices of bread.

"I see how it is," Jerry said. "You get here too late for morning chores, and you'll be lying around in the woods all day." He snagged a piece of turkey from the container.

Niall's smile tightened at the corners. "I promise I'll help you with the evening chores. And if you've got a list of things for me to do, I'll tackle them before we leave tomorrow."

"Nah." Jerry slapped Niall's back. "I was just jerking you around. The Turner kid's been helping us out. You enjoy the day with your lady friend." He shot me a sly glance.

Niall wrapped the sandwiches in waxed paper. "Really, I want to do chores. I promised Sam she could help, too."

Jerry's sharp gaze landed on my hands, and his weathered face wrinkled into a smirk. I curled my fingers into my palms. No, I didn't have calluses from holding a shovel or a pitchfork or whatever, but I could work. I narrowed my eyes at him.

Niall missed it all. "Ready for our tour, Sam?"

"Mind if I use your bathroom first?"

"We can hit the outhouse as the first stop on our tour."

I blinked. *Outhouse?*

"Don't tease her like that." Elaine swatted his arm. "Right this way, Sam."

Elaine led me back to the entryway and pointed to the end of the hall. "Straight ahead. It may be a bit rustic, but we do have indoor plumbing."

As I washed my hands at the vintage pink pedestal sink, I glanced into the mirror. My freckles stood out against my pale cheeks. What had I done? Getting closer to Niall would make me miss him when we went our separate ways at the end of the tour. If the truth came out before then, I'd have to watch while the sparkle left his eyes and his stare went flat and cold. It'd snap my heart in two.

And what was up with Niall's grandfather? He'd looked wary almost from the moment I'd walked in. What did he suspect?

I dried my hands on the embroidered towel and returned to the kitchen, my boots making the floorboards creak. When I stepped through the doorway, Niall whispered something to his mother, and she patted his red-stubbled cheek. A tote bag hung off one shoulder, and he had a couple blankets folded under his other arm.

"It's a good day for it. Should get up into the sixties," Elaine said. "You two have fun."

"Don't get lost. And watch out for bears," Jerry called from behind his newspaper.

"Grandpa! Don't try to scare off Sam." Niall shouldered a backpack and held out his hand to me.

"We won't really get lost, will we?" I murmured as he led me to the side door.

"Not a chance. But I used that excuse a lot when I was younger to explain why I was late."

"And the bears?"

"Not too many in these parts, and most of them are hibernating this time of year."

Bilbo Baggins leaped down the porch steps and ran ahead of us toward the woods.

"Bilbo Baggins!" I shouted. "Come back!" His yaps could wake up a bear. Or draw the attention of a hungry coyote.

"Don't worry about it. We'll follow him. And Thorin will keep him in line."

A shaggy black beast, more Chupacabra than dog, bounded toward Bilbo Baggins. He woofed once, making my dog freeze.

"He's safe, right?" It wouldn't have been the first time I'd had to rescue over-friendly Bilbo Baggins from a bigger, meaner dog. I hurried toward them.

"He's a creampuff."

Sure enough, Thorin approached Bilbo Baggins, circled him, sniffing, and then crouched, his rear end in the air. Bilbo Baggins sneezed and sat.

When Thorin leaped up and galloped toward us, Bilbo Baggins followed at a sprint.

At Niall's raised finger, Thorin pulled up short and sat, panting, his body quivering. Bilbo Baggins, after a questioning bark, slowly sank down at his side.

"Good boy." Niall closed the distance and scratched Thorin behind his short, floppy ears. "Want to pet him?"

The dog's teeth were visible as he panted, the top canines as long as the end joint of my finger. I hesitated.

"Don't you trust me?" Niall put his hands on his hips.

I trusted Niall to do a lot of things—write compelling fantasy stories, forget to turn on his phone, and kiss like it was his job— but I wasn't sure about his oversized, overcoated, over-toothed dog. But because I'd come to some sort of upside-down world where I went to the family home of a man I'd known for two weeks and spent my day off walking around a farm instead of working on my dissertation, I extended a hand. When the dog didn't snap it off, I stroked behind his ear. He closed his eyes and pushed his head against my palm.

"You're friends now. Let's go," Niall said, taking my other hand.

Cool, pine-scented air brushed against my cheeks as Niall pulled me toward the trees. We passed a few patches of snow, melting under the sunshine. The dogs zig-zagged ahead of us, sniffing out the trails of other animals.

Niall pointed at a faded red barn. The outline of the state was painted in white on one side with the word *Ohio* in script above a red and blue banner. On the front, a square was painted like a quilt in red, blue, and gold, cheery against the soft blue winter sky. "We'll go see the animals later. I want you to see the creek in the morning light."

Beyond the barn, brown fields stretched to another faraway tree line. "What do you grow here?"

"Soybeans and corn to sell. Hay for the livestock. Mom has a kitchen garden where she grows vegetables for the family. And the animals aren't pets. We sell the alpacas' wool, the goats' milk, and eggs when the chickens are laying. Sometimes we trade with the other families. The Turners keep bees for honey, and they raise hogs. We try to be self-sustaining when we can."

I almost never thought about where food came from. I'd pictured Niall as some sort of gentleman farmer from a Jane Austen movie, spending his days writing in an oak-paneled library while the farm took care of itself. Not on this farm.

"But this," he said, stepping under the canopy of the forest, "is my favorite part of the farm."

By the time we'd reached the second tree, the sounds—the distant roar of a tractor, the rumble of pickup trucks on the road at the end of the driveway, the screaming of hawks—muted. When we reached the third tree, the sunlight had faded to dusk. The sharp scent of growing things and dark decay filled my nostrils.

"Before the European settlers came, the whole area was like this—wooded. You saw how much has been cleared on the drive up from the airport."

"City, then subdivisions, then farmland. I didn't know it used to be forest."

"Only small pockets remain. We're lucky they left this." He stroked the trunk of a tree. "Come on. I'll show you the best spot."

Water burbled nearby, and Niall headed toward it. The trees leaned together and nearly touched overhead, but a few rays of sunlight penetrated the canopy to sparkle on the clear water of the shallow brook below. Rocks lined the stream bed, and a few had tumbled in from the sides to serve as natural crossings.

A Fiat-sized flat-topped boulder bent the brook around it. Niall hopped up and extended a hand to me. I gripped it and clambered up the side, my muddy boots slipping, to stand beside him. The dogs lapped from the stream below. Thorin lay down in it, cooling his belly.

"During the Ice Age, receding glaciers carved out this stream and left this boulder." He set down the bag and shook out a blanket. He sat on it and leaned back on his hands. "When I was a kid, I used to come here and imagine woolly mammoths lumbering by, back when it was all ice and snow."

I sank down beside him, imagining the giant hairy beasts. "You came here a lot?"

"Almost every day. Even in winter."

In my mind, a lanky, teenage Niall tossed pebbles into the water. "How long has your family lived here?"

"Generations. Mom moved to the city for college, where she met my dad." He stared into the water.

"When his business started to take off, he traveled more. California, mostly, but also Asia and the East Coast. He used to come back on the weekends, but then his trips got longer. Mom didn't want to raise me in California. So she moved back home to the farm." He smiled, tight. "Even when I was a toddler, I didn't like being cooped up in an apartment in the city. Anyway, his visits here got shorter and shorter. Then he married, started a new family, and stopped coming at all."

I found his hand and squeezed it. I knew what it was like to lose a father. Though I didn't know what it was like to have a bad one. "I'm sorry."

He shrugged. "He has his life; I have mine. I wish—" He shook his head. "I'm happy here." He lay on his back, folding his arms behind his head and closing his eyes against the sun.

I leaned over him, casting a shadow over his face. "I can see why. It's beautiful."

"You should see it in the—" He opened his eyes. His pupils unfurled, narrowing the green. He curled up and kissed me.

It was slow, tentative. A test. Would I back away? Would the city girl think it was weird to kiss out in the forest with the mud and the birds and the squirrels chattering overhead? This city girl didn't. When he set his cool palms on my cheeks and gently pulled me down to him, I rested on his chest and returned his soft, lazy kisses. His fingers tunneled through my hair, making my scalp tingle. Soon, the tingle spread across my skin, all the way down to my toes. The forest *was* enchanted.

The water splashed, and the breeze rustled through the boughs of the pines. Kissing Niall here, in his special place, the sun warming my back, was nothing short of perfect. Time lost its meaning. So did the space between us. We both wanted solitude, but this shared loneliness was even better than being alone.

He pulled away first. His eyes were almost black, with only the narrowest green ring, like moss on a stone. He winced. "I'm sorry, but I—I have an idea. Would you mind if I wrote it down?"

Huh. Maybe I was the only one who felt the enchantment. I shoved up on my hands. "An idea. That you got from kissing me?"

"Well—" He sat up, too. "This is the home of the wood elves.

They speak to me here. And when you're with me, they speak even louder."

I snorted. "Fine." Then something itched at my insides. "It's not bothering you that I'm here, is it?"

"No." He reached out and caressed my cheek. "You inspire me."

"Right. Lobelia." I examined the rough surface of the boulder.

He curled a finger under my chin and lifted it until I met his gaze. "No. You, Sam. Like I said in the dedication, you're my muse."

My insides warmed. His muse. I inspired him. I leaned forward and kissed him. "Okay, you write. I'll check on the boys." I slid off the rock into the mud and whistled for Bilbo Baggins.

I found plenty of sticks to throw. The dogs brought some of them back. Every once in a while, I'd peek up at Niall. Sometimes lying on his stomach, sometimes curled up with the notebook on his knees, he squinted at the page and pushed his left hand awkwardly across it.

My phone had zero bars in the forest. So I turned it off and listened to the water, the trees, the birds. Instead of checking my email, I watched the glint of sunlight on the water; the tree limbs, some bare, some evergreen, swaying; the pale yellow sun as it tracked low across the sky. I'd never been into meditation, but if I'd ever wanted to, this would be the place. The peaceful sounds encouraged an inward focus, a stillness.

Though when I focused inward, I didn't like what I saw.

Secrets.

Niall had brought me to his favorite place in the world, his hidden refuge. He was opening his life to me like a treasure box. But me? I was still locked up tight.

Would it be the worst thing if I told Niall about CASE and *Magician*, even though Heidi had told me not to? He seemed like the type to keep a confidence. Though I'd been wrong about that before. I shuddered, remembering the cold shock, like being tossed into the frigid stream, when I'd read Stephen's text demanding money for the pictures.

Worse, what would Niall say when I told him about CASE? The sparkle would disappear from his eyes, the smile from his lips. He'd hate how I'd twisted his art. How I'd lied to him from the first day of the tour. Even before that.

Wouldn't it be better to do what Heidi had told me, to keep it quiet until the tour ended and we went our separate ways?

I'd listened to enough of *Secrets of the Wood Elves* to know what ever-honest Greva would say about that. She'd call me a coward. And she'd be right. But I wasn't strong enough to look into Niall's face and tell him the truth.

"Hungry?" Niall's voice was gruff from disuse, and he cleared his throat.

"Yeah. Just a sec." I took a deep breath and shoved my dirty hands into the clear water. I'd known it'd be cold, but *shit*, it made me squeal a little and sharpened my thoughts to icy clarity. It was better to keep pretending for the short time we had left together.

I flicked the water off my reddened hands and then clambered up beside him. He'd already set out lunch on the blanket—sandwiches, apples, bottles of water, a thermos of coffee, and even a couple of homemade cookies. I tore into a sandwich and forced lightness into my tone. "Good writing?"

"Yeah." He still had a dreamy, unfocused look on his face.

"You said this is where you created the wood elves?"

He smiled, mysterious. "I'm not sure I can take credit for creating them. I always imagined there were beings out here. I guess from the fairy tales Mom used to read to me. I used to look for them. Sometimes I'd bring them a cookie or some milk. I started writing stories about their adventures, and, eventually, the stories turned into a book."

"You always write in longhand?"

"Yeah. I mail my notebooks to Gabi, and she transcribes them. She sends me printed pages back, and then I edit those. I know, I'm a Luddite." He ducked his head. "I guess it started as my little rebellion against my father. And then it just came naturally."

"I don't know how you do it. I sign books for half an hour, and my hand aches." We'd finished our sandwiches, so I lifted his left hand and gently kneaded it from the palms out to the fingertips. Slowly, the tightness eased. I squeezed and wiggled each finger. Then I worked down each finger bone to his wrist, where I made little circles.

He groaned. "Feels good."

"Before he went off to college, Jackson taught me how to massage my dad's hands. They got cramped from coding. Typing. He worked so hard."

"The foundation is named for him. He died a while ago?"

I kept my gaze on the freckled back of Niall's hand. "Yeah. When I was eleven. Heart attack."

He put his hand over mine, stilling it. "I'm sorry. Sounds like you were close."

I started again, working between his fingers. "He understood me. Kinda like Jackson but not as clueless, you know?"

He chuckled. "Your brother's a sharp man."

"About some things. Not about others. When I—" I swallowed. "I had a boyfriend who hurt me." Niall's hand curled into a fist, and I flattened it, massaging the back. "Not physically. Emotionally. I thought we were in love, but he was using me. He —ah." I cleared my throat. I hadn't told anyone this story since it'd happened. Not even Marlee or Alicia. "He blackmailed me. Used some pictures he'd taken of me—nudes—to demand money from me. He gambled. On the internet. He'd built up a ton of debt on his credit card, and his parents wouldn't pay it off. I didn't have access to my trust fund yet, and I had to ask my family. My mother gave it to him, of course. Couldn't let those pictures spoil the perfect image of the Joneses." I kneaded his hand in silence for a minute. "Ever since, Jackson hasn't trusted me to make smart decisions about guys. About anything. None of them have."

I froze. Why the hell had I told him all that? Sure, I tended to overshare when I was nervous. But I wasn't nervous. Maybe it was that forest magic that'd lulled me into it. Was there some spell I could use to rewind time and take it all back?

"What's his name?" Niall's voice was growly like Jackson's had been that night.

Where was that rewind button? He'd reacted just like my family had. "Don't worry. Jackson and my other brother, Andrew, took care of him." I kept my voice light like it was no big deal they'd broken Stephen's nose and made it so he couldn't find work from Sonoma to Los Angeles. He'd had to move to Arizona, I'd heard. People were always taking care of stuff for me. And the worst part was that I let them.

"Hey." He didn't touch my face this time, but he waited until I met his gaze. "You're fierce. Strong. Successful. You can make your own decisions."

I looked up. No one had ever said that to me. Did he really believe it? Because I wasn't sure I did.

He squeezed my hand. "You've been amazing on this tour. You're going to win the Tower Prize."

All the happy bubbles popped, and my stomach filled with concrete. "Let's not ruin today by talking about that."

"Okay." He brought my hand to his mouth and kissed it. "What do you want to talk about?"

No more sharing. He was going to tempt me to share too much. To break the NDA. To wreck this perfect moment, this perfect place he loved. No.

I forced a teasing smile onto my face. "I was promised cute farm animals."

He snorted. "I don't know about cute. But they are farm animals." He cast a glance at the sun. "We'll go see them before supper." He packed everything back into the tote bag while I folded up the blanket.

He slid from the boulder and held out his arms. I'd dismounted alone earlier, but when I dropped into his arms and landed against his hard chest, the concrete was gone, replaced by butterflies. I breathed him in, remembering the taste of his skin, the caress of his lips, and my core clenched. I lifted onto my toes to kiss him again.

Fiery sparks erupted where our lips met. They burned a trail down my spine and ignited a fire between my legs. My hands wandered from his chest and bumped down his abs to the waistband of his jeans.

"Whoa." He pulled away. "Hold that thought. Until we're somewhere warmer."

When I tugged him closer to me, the hard length of him pressed into my stomach. "I'm plenty warm," I murmured.

He rolled his eyes to the sky. "God, I—Sam." He blew out a breath. "Farm animals. Dinner. Chores. And then I'll warm you back up again."

"So traditional," I grumbled.

He kissed my forehead. "It'll be worth the wait, I promise."

He whistled for the dogs and, hand-in-hand, we retraced our steps out of the woods. When we'd cleared the trees, we veered right toward the barn and Thorin took off, easily outstripping Bilbo Baggins with his long, loping stride. Niall and I walked slowly, swinging our joined hands between us, breathing in the earthy scents of the farm, watching the sun sink toward the far tree line.

Compared to the bright sun outside, the barn was dark, and it took a moment for my eyes to adjust. While I waited for my vision to resolve, I let the smells wash over me. Sweet hay, earthy manure, and a musky animal scent.

Niall led me to some enclosures along the right side. "Goat pens. Though they're still outside. We'll bring in all the animals after supper." He turned the corner. "Alpaca stalls."

"Where are the chickens?"

"Chicken coop." He gestured beyond the other wall, toward the house.

"And where's the infamous hayloft?" I raised my eyebrows.

He walked back toward the goat pens to a solid-looking ladder I'd overlooked on our first pass. "Straight up."

I followed his pointing finger to a lofted area above, open to the interior of the barn.

I set my hands on the smooth wood of the ladder. Then I set a foot on the bottom rung.

Niall smirked. "I'll warn you, there's probably more spiders and less romance than you expect."

I tossed him a saucy grin over my shoulder as I ascended. "Spiders don't scare me. And I can bring my own romance."

He opened his mouth, but no words came out. I focused on the ladder and continued my ascent.

He was wrong about the hayloft. It looked like it'd been recently tidied with fresh hay. But when I tried to sit on it, I understood what he meant. The hay stabbed me through my cargo pants. Not romantic.

I peered over the side at Niall, who stood, looking up, his hands on his hips. "Toss up a blanket?"

He strode to where we'd dropped our things at the door and returned with a quilt. But instead of tossing it up to me, he tucked it under one arm and climbed, one-handed. The dogs watched him for a minute and then scampered off toward the alpacas' stalls.

I, on the other hand, watched his every move. His strong fingers gripping the ladder rungs. The flex of his forearm as he tugged himself up. The glint of sunlight on his fiery hair. Romance? Who needed it? I had a big, strapping farm boy who excelled at kissing me breathless. I wasn't waiting until after chores. I was going to get a good, hard fuck in a barn, and *then* Niall Flynn and his forest magic and all those ridiculous feels I'd had earlier would be out of my system.

When Niall reached the top, he handed me the blanket then heaved himself into the loft. "Not so bad up here. The Turner kid must've cleaned it out." He opened the shutters, letting the late afternoon sun stream in. "We have a few minutes. This is a good place to watch the sunset." He turned back toward me, and even silhouetted as he was by the pink rays shining through the open window, I could see his jaw drop.

I'd spread out the quilt over the thickest part of the hay and wriggled out of my coat and boots. I flung my T-shirt off to the side and unzipped my pants. I shivered when the cool air hit my skin.

"What are you doing?" His breaths were shallow and short.

"What does it look like I'm doing? I'm about to go for a roll in the hay."

"We're not seventeen. There are better places to"—he gulped —"do that."

"I told you I was bringing my own romance. If you choose not to join me, I'll take a solo roll in the hay." I kicked off my pants and inched one hand down inside my panties. I was short on laundry, so I'd worn a lacy pair I hadn't even remembered packing. His gaze followed my fingers under the lace. He licked his lips.

"We don't have time." His voice had descended into a husky whisper. "Or condoms."

With the hand that wasn't circling my entrance, I plucked my cargo pants off the hay and withdrew a condom packet from one of the many pockets. I held it up, glinting in the sunlight, and tossed it onto the blanket beside me. *See?* my smirk said.

I thrust two fingers inside myself, and then withdrew them to spread my slickness around. "Join me?"

Like a zombie, he shuffled two steps toward me. His jaw slack, his gaze tracked my hand moving under the lace. Then he shook his head. "I have a perfectly serviceable bed. Inside. Where it's warm. We can pick this up after I finish my chores."

I shook my head. "Here. Now. It's plenty warm if you keep moving." With my left hand, I drew down my bra cup and tweaked my nipple. Sensation zipped down my spine, and my back arched.

"Fuck." At his hoarse whisper, I knew I'd won. Still, I spread my legs to give him a better view.

He dropped to his knees before me and drew my panties down my legs. I kept up the movement of my hand, sliding my fingers from my entrance to my clit and back, driving myself higher. He reached behind me to unfasten my bra. I paused my masturbation for just a moment so he could pull it off me. When I was bare, touching myself, he sat back on his heels and swore under his breath.

He pushed my knees apart and bent so his breath whispered over my hand. I moaned. As much as I wanted his mouth again, I wanted something different this time. I wanted to see him, gilded by the setting sun. "No. Strip."

"Strip?" He looked down at himself like he was surprised he was still wearing clothes.

"I want to see you."

He glanced over the side of the loft at the barn door. Then, quickly, he shed his many layers: coat, flannel shirt, T-shirt, boots, jeans, and socks, until he stood before me in a pair of boxers, a bulge tenting the front. The setting sun lit up every hair on his body. He was consumed by light and flame. I licked my lips.

Something settled inside me, like a key into a lock or the last piece of a puzzle snapping into place.

No. He's not for me. But no matter how many times I said it to myself, that piece inside me, the one that felt complete now, insisted, *Mine mine mine.*

He wasn't mine. Not forever. But for today. For the next week until the tour ended. And, selfish bitch that I was, I was going to take what I wanted.

"Condom," I whispered.

When he slid down his boxers, his cock sprang free, stiff and flushed. He sank to his knees again and reached for the condom. In a moment, he was sheathed.

"Are you ready?" he whispered, low.

"God, yes." I'd been circling my clit during his unsatisfyingly businesslike striptease, and I was a silicon wafer's breadth from going off.

He positioned himself at my entrance, nudging me with the broad head of his cock. I rubbed my clit faster. With a few short pumps of his hips, he was inside, and when he slid all the way in, bumping my fingers, I went off with a wailing groan.

He covered my lips with his, consuming my sounds as my spine lit up with pleasure and my legs shook against his.

Thorin gave a deep woof, and Bilbo Baggins yapped. A second later, the door downstairs thunked open, and a gruff voice called, "Niall!"

28

NIALL

FUCK. Literally.

I was sheathed to the hilt in Sam, and she'd just gone off like a firework. She still clenched around my dick, making we want to thrust into her again and again until I came inside her. The setting sun ignited strands of her hair in fiery magenta against the umber.

"Niall!" Grandpa shouted again. I could hear the dogs, those traitors, snuffling around him.

I rested my forehead against Sam's for a second and then turned to call down to him. "Up here, Grandpa. Sam and I are… watching the sunset." I couldn't see him. I hoped to God he couldn't see my naked ass.

Under me, Sam started to shake. She was *laughing*. I glared a warning at her and put a finger over her lips.

"Your mother sent me after you. Supper's almost ready." His voice trembled a little. Was he laughing, too? I failed to see the humor in any of this.

"Be right there," I called back.

Sam shook her head under my hand and thrust her hips up into me. "Fuck," I muttered, my eyes rolling back in my head.

"What's that, son?" Grandpa said.

I put a hand on Sam's hip, holding her in place. "Nothing, Grandpa. See you soon."

At the sound of the door banging shut, I collapsed against Sam. "There went a year of my life." Reluctantly, I lifted onto my hands and started to shimmy off her.

"Don't you dare!" She gripped my ass with both hands. "I was promised a roll in the hay."

"I don't think I—"

She stopped my protest with a nip to the earlobe and her hot breath in my ear. "Fuck me, Niall. Please."

She hadn't even gotten the *Please* fully out before I slammed back into her. I'd do just about anything this woman asked me to do. I was completely gone. In love.

Did she know? Was it obvious? She'd told me she didn't want feelings. She'd also told me about that felon boyfriend of hers who'd broken her heart. About how no one trusted her. But I'd heard what she hadn't said: that Sam didn't trust herself. Could I convince her she could trust this, trust us, let herself fall this time, that I'd never hurt her?

I scanned her face. She was watching me, too. She trapped her lip between her teeth. On the next thrust, I ground against her clit, and she sucked in a breath. She wrapped one leg around my back, holding me against her. I did it again, slower this time, the push in and then the slow grind. She moaned, tilting her chin to the ceiling and exposing her long neck. I dragged my tongue along her flawless skin until I reached her shoulder. I nipped it.

"Niall," she whispered, "I'm so—"

I circled my hips and thrust again. She shattered, her torso going still and her leg trembling. When her pussy gripped me tight, I couldn't hold back. I emptied myself into the condom, my vision tunneling and my back bowing in pleasure.

"Wow," she whispered, putting her hand over my heart. She had to feel it galloping for her. "Now I see what all the fuss was about."

"Devil woman." I'd fucked in haylofts before. But I'd never been this wild, this lost in my partner. I rested my forehead against hers, trying to get my breath back under control. All I wanted was to lie there with her and watch the sun descend behind the trees, the light fade into blue, and the stars ignite. I wanted to hold her all night, caressing her smooth skin, our lips connecting and our bodies joining as we pleased.

But the winter air chilled my naked ass, and it was only going to get colder. Gripping the base of the condom, I pulled out, knotted it off, and shoved it into my jeans pocket. I found her lacy panties and reluctantly handed them to her. I wished I had time to touch, to taste every inch of her silky skin. But I'd promised to do chores, and we'd been called to supper. I winced. "We're never going to live this down."

"Don't tell me that's the first time someone's caught you up here in the hayloft." Slowly, she slid the panties up her legs.

My dick twitched. I pictured Grandpa's laughing face at the dinner table, and it sagged. I hopped into my jeans. "First time since I stopped being a teenager."

"Aw. Poor Niall." But her voice had lost its teasing tone.

I stopped, mid-bend above her bra, and looked at her. She'd curled over her knees, gripping her shins, staring at her toes.

Fuck. I was an idiot. "Sam. Sam." I dropped to my knees beside her. Ouch. I was way too old for this hayloft shit. "I loved what we just did. I love—" *Whoa, there.* "I'm sorry we don't have time to, um, afterglow. I'll make it up to you tonight. After chores. We'll go out to the meadow and look at the stars, and I'll cuddle the hell out of you. Okay?"

Biting her lip, she nodded.

I picked up her bra and held it out to her. "Suppertime and after-supper chores are nonnegotiable around here."

She cocked her head as she slid on her bra straps. "That's all it is? You're not…disappointed?"

"No, sweetheart. I could never be disappointed in you."

"Promise?" Those big, pleading eyes sucked me in.

Fuck! What had that asshole boyfriend done to her? I crashed my lips onto hers and kissed her, longer than I should have, longer than we had time for. I kissed her until we were both breathless. When we pulled apart, panting, I slid a piece of hay out of her tousled hair. "Promise."

She gave me a half-smile. "Okay, then."

We banged into the kitchen, too late, of course. Grandpa and Mom both smirked at us.

"Lost again, Niall?" Mom stood and stepped to the oven. She pulled out two foil-wrapped plates.

"Easy to lose things up there in that hayloft, eh, Niall?" Grandpa roared out a laugh.

"What he lost up there?" Sam snickered. "I don't think he's ever getting it back."

While they laughed, I turned my back to all of them and washed my hands at the sink. She was joking, but it was true. Sam had my heart now. And I'd never get it back.

29

NIALL

CHORES ON A FARM aren't like chores in a regular house. Forget to do the dishes after dinner? No big deal. Sure, they might stink up your kitchen, but no one's life or livelihood is at stake. Once, when I was seventeen, I'd been rushing through my chores, wanting to get to a high-school basketball game—my crush was on the girls' team—and I'd forgotten to latch the door to the chicken coop. A neighbor's dog had gotten in, and it looked like the aftermath from the bloody elevator in *The Shining.* Not only had I grieved for all the hens for months, but we hadn't had fresh eggs to sell until the following summer.

But as hard as I tried, my mind wasn't on my chores that night. It was on Sam. On the way her skin had gone pearlescent in the sunset. How her hair had flowed across the blanket like molten chocolate. Her eyes, betraying a hint of…something as she came. I couldn't wait to make her come again and try to decipher that secret emotion.

I counted the chickens clustered against the coop. All there. I raised the door and counted them again as they tumbled inside, ready for their nests.

I'd bring Sam with me the next day. We'd spent too much time in the hayloft and hadn't met any of the animals. She'd love the goats with their velvety ears. And running her fingers through the alpacas' rough wool. I'd introduce her to each of the quirky chickens. I imagined the delighted look on her face.

She'd be delighted, right?

Gabi certainly hadn't been. We'd made sense. We met on the college newspaper staff and bonded over fantasy literature and old movies like *Labyrinth* and *The Dark Crystal* and *Clash of the Titans*. The sex was good, and I thought we had a future together. Until I'd brought her to the farm, and two hours into her visit, one of the goats had nibbled on her expensive jacket. She'd demanded to be returned to the airport. Immediately.

Sam hadn't been like that at all. She'd traipsed through the mud and shivered, naked, in the hayloft. She'd washed dishes with Mom, and she'd asked to help feed the animals in the morning before we left. Could Sam, a city girl, be happy on the farm?

Could she be happy with me?

I hadn't felt this way about anyone since...ever. Not with Gabi. Sam had set me on fire, and I never wanted to be put out. I was completely infatuated. Obsessed.

In love.

Could she love me, too, after only two weeks together? When we had less than a week left of the tour?

We needed more time. Time together, on dates. Time apart, with air to breathe, space to reflect, outside the forced proximity of the tour.

I'd ask her if I could stay in San Francisco. Not with her, but near enough for us to see each other. Sure, it'd be more expensive and less productive than coming back to the farm as I'd planned, but thinking about the end of the tour, the end of our time together, felt like I'd swallowed one of the river boulders.

Fuck.

I was in love.

The unrequited kind.

Sam wanted a fling. A literal roll in the hay.

But it was too late to stop my fall.

When I dropped the door behind the last chicken, they squawked. I latched the door, then double-checked it, before I trudged back around the pen toward the barn. When I stepped into the bright light of the barn, Grandpa looked over his shoulder from the milking stool.

"Took you long enough."

"Sorry. I guess I was thinking."

"Woolgathering, more like." Grandpa turned back to Sally's white flank. "Thinking about your Sam."

My Sam. I wish. "Was it that obvious?"

Grandpa chuckled. "I've known you all your life, son. Your thoughts show on your face."

I ambled over to stroke Sally's long, floppy ear. "What d'you think of her? She's great, isn't she?"

Grandpa kept his gaze on the milk bucket. "Bit harder to read, that one."

"Oh?" When Grandpa was cantankerous, I had to let him spin out his words in his own time.

He picked up the pail and then nodded. I untied Sally and led her to her stall. I'd taken too long with the chickens, and Grandpa had already milked Susie.

He strained the milk into a jar and cleaned the equipment before he said the next thing. "She's hiding something. Something big, by the looks of it. She married?"

I recoiled. "She's only twenty-five. She's still in school."

"I was married, had your mom when I was twenty-five."

"No, not Sam." She wouldn't have fucked me in the hayloft if she'd been married. Or would she? I'd assumed she kept her thoughts to herself because she was an introvert, but now that Grandpa mentioned it, I remembered she hadn't told her brother about her book. Was there something she was holding back from me, too? Maybe Grandpa was right, and her silence was full of secrets like a beehive at dusk.

"Something else, then. The girl is smitten, but there's something holding her back."

"Smitten, huh?" A balloon of warmth inflated my chest.

"Son, you're beyond smitten yourself." He laid his rough hand on my shoulder. "Have a care."

I laid my own callused, ink-stained hand over Grandpa's. "I'll try. But when I'm around her, I can't help myself."

Grandpa rolled his eyes up to the rafters. "You're under her spell, eh? Like in one of your books." He smiled crookedly. "Tell me, is Nieven going to end up with Lobelia at the end of the series?"

I stared at the wide planks of the floor. "I don't know, Grandpa. You know I don't plan before I write. The story comes to me. But—"

"But?"

"I don't know how that's possible. They're friends, soul mates even, but Nieven's an elf. And Lobelia's"—I moved my palms about a foot apart—"a sprite. Tiny. And a princess. They're pretty different."

"Procreation would be a challenge, eh?"

"Yeah." My eyes burned to check out the hayloft above us. It hadn't been a problem for Sam and me. The opposite, in fact.

"We end the tour in San Francisco. I—I'm thinking about staying there. After the tour. I wrote some of my last book on the road. I can finish this one away from here." Especially with Sam as inspiration.

"Did she ask you to go to California with her?" Grandpa checked the latch on the stall.

"Not yet."

"D'you think that's what she wants?"

"She said we'll end things when the tour ends. But it's what I want." I'd ask her out on an actual date. We could go back to the beginning and build a relationship the way normal couples did.

When she was ready, she'd reveal what she was hiding.

Grandpa stopped in front of the barn door. "Careful with your feelings, son. After what happened with your dad, you can be sensitive to these things."

He was right. If I were smart, I'd let her go before I fell any further. Or the hole that had gaped in my heart when my father left would reopen.

But I wasn't smart. Not according to my father. And my heart had overpowered my brain again.

Grandpa led the way out of the barn. "Sounds like you have a week to change her mind."

I latched the barn door and double-checked it. Changing Sam's mind wouldn't be easy. I wished I could will everything to fall neatly into place the way I did in my books.

But Sam was no fairy princess. She wrote her own dialogue. And I had to let her write the next scene.

30

SAM

I SCOURED THE ROASTING PAN, watching chips of my black nail polish mix with the bits of stuck-on glaze. My nail beds were still shiny black, but the ends were almost all white. Qiana's nails were always so perfect. I needed one of her hugs. And to talk to her about Niall, to untangle my feelings about him. Or would that be weird since she was his friend, too?

I shouldn't have needed to talk to anyone about him. I knew the right thing to do. End things along with the tour like I'd planned from the beginning. I'd known not to come to Niall's secret hideaway, but I'd done it anyway. I scrubbed at another spot on the pan like it was that annoying ache that started in my heart when I thought about the end of the tour.

"You all right, Sam?" Elaine asked. "You didn't eat much at dinner, and most people can't get enough of my pot roast."

The sharp scent of yeast from the dough she kneaded curled up into my nostrils.

"It was delicious. I guess I wasn't hungry."

She gave me a sharp look. "Coming down with something? Niall is always so careful on those tours."

"I don't think so. I don't feel sick, just not hungry." I'd sat next to Niall, and when his leg brushed mine under the table, everything else, including my appetite, had fallen away.

"Might it be something more…emotional?" Elaine's eyes were brown, but they reminded me of Mother's laser gaze.

I focused on scrubbing the soapy brush over the back of the pan. "Emotional?"

Elaine scooped the lump of dough into a bowl and covered it with a towel. As she washed her hands in the sink beside me, she said, "I've seen the way you look at my son. The way he looks at you. You have feelings for each other."

She took the pan out of my hands, rinsed it, and started drying it with the towel. "By my second date with Niall's father, I couldn't eat. I couldn't sleep, either. I couldn't get enough of him." She set down the pan. "Infatuation like that isn't just for love songs."

I knew that. I'd felt infatuation for Stephen before he'd broken my heart. I couldn't eat then, either. Mother, who monitored my calorie intake almost as closely as she monitored the stock market, had said something about how angular my body had become. My feelings for Niall were unhealthy, just like with Stephen. I needed to end them.

I pulled the plug and watched the water swirl down the drain.

"Sam." The back door flung open, and Niall stepped inside, wiping his boots on the mat. "Come outside with me. You won't believe the stars."

"The stars." I couldn't help my lip curling up. "First the sunset, and now the stars?"

Niall's face reddened as he glanced at his mother. "What can I say? I want to show you all the best parts of the farm."

"It's too cold out for Sam's coat. Get her one of mine," Elaine said. "I'll find you some blankets."

I shouldn't have. But I let Niall bundle me into a traffic-cone-orange parka with his green scarf and a hand-knit wool cap, and I followed him outside. The chilly air prickled at my nose as we walked away from the lights of the house and the barn toward the woods. We stopped in the meadow where the short grass crunched under our feet. Niall spread out one blanket, and we lay down, side by side. He tucked the other blanket up over us, and I didn't feel the cold anymore.

"Warm enough?" he asked.

"Uh-huh."

"Listen," he said.

There were no car sounds: no honks, no tires on asphalt, no idling engines. No ocean sounds, either. A creak-creak sound came from the left.

Creak-creak. Creak-creak. Creak-creak.

"What's that sound? Crickets?" I spoke low, not wanting to disturb the stillness.

"No, it's too early for crickets. It's the spring peepers—little frogs, no bigger than a dime. I used to love sitting out by the pond at night listening to them. I'd imagine what they were saying."

I smiled even though Niall couldn't see it in the dark. "What did they say?"

"In my imagination, one call was higher than the rest. That was the Spring Peeper Princess. And all the rest of them offered her things: the softest lily leaf to rest on, the warmest spot in the mud at the bottom of the pond, the juiciest bug."

"And which one did she accept?"

"All of them, as was her due."

"She sounds greedy."

"They were happy to bask in her presence, honored by her notice."

Niall scooted closer, eliminating the space between us. "Now look up."

The moon was a pale sliver on the horizon. Everywhere else was stars, glittering against the inky blue-black of the sky.

I'd never seen so many.

In my ear, he whispered the names of the constellations and wove their stories together. I knew them; I'd drunk them up during the mythology unit in ninth grade. And Marlee, Tyler, and I had gone out stargazing one night at Corona Heights Park. But Niall infused them with drama, with excitement, with heartbreak.

In between stories, he twined his fingers with mine. He stroked the inside of my wrist. He kissed my ear, my neck, my temple. And I let him, squirming closer and closer until he tucked his arm around me and we were chest to chest, ignoring the stars and focused only on each other, our kisses languid, warming my skin despite the cold pressing down from the stars.

I pushed him flat on his back and propped my arms on his chest. The starlight illuminated his face.

"Your freckles." My voice surprised me with its huskiness. "They're like constellations." I traced one on his right cheek. "This one is a rectangle."

His arms came around my back. "That one's a book I'll write. For you."

"A whole book? Just for me?"

His lips curved in a smile. "Maybe a short one. A novella. All about Lobelia."

"Nieven's my favorite character. Can you make it about him?"

"Of course. Anything you want."

"This one looks like a fish."

"A fish?" He squinted one eye. "It's an airplane. For the tour. And for the trips we'll make to see each other."

My heart skipped a beat, and I pushed myself off him. "Niall, no." An ache started in my chest.

"Yes, Sam. I want to spend more time with you. I feel something…something green and growing between us. Like the roots waking up inside the ground. Like you've performed an enchantment on me. And I'm not ready to let it end next week."

For a moment, hope flamed inside the dead wood of my heart. But it sputtered and died, starved for oxygen. Niall was a poet, and I'd gotten tangled up in his words.

"You mean as your muse."

"Well, that, but more. Sam, I—I care about you. Let me care. Give us time."

"I like you. A lot." I forced the words out through the thickness in my throat. "But this—us—can't continue past the end of the tour. I'm going back to California to finish my degree. I need to finish my dissertation so I can defend it and then graduate in June."

"And then on to that postdoc." His gaze darted around my face like he was tracing constellations of his own. "What about your writing?"

"I…" What could I tell him without ruining his favorite place with the ugly facts about how I'd trampled on what he loved? Nothing. I could tell him nothing. "I'm done writing. But you," I rushed on, "you're coming back here at the end of the tour to finish the series."

"I can do that anywhere. Including San Francisco, if you'll let me."

I let myself imagine it for a second. Niall, living near enough to see him every day. Not the twenty-four-seven of the tour, but dinners together. Weekends. Working on my dissertation while he sat nearby, scribbling in his notebook. The happiness I'd felt with him all day didn't have to end.

But then he'd find out the truth. And he'd hate me. He'd despise me for dragging it out, letting him think we could ever be anything more. And no temporary happiness was worth the pain that even now clenched my heart.

"I can't."

His voice trembled. "So I'm good enough for a roll in the hay but nothing more?"

"No, Niall. I—I never dreamed the tour would be like this. You've made it magical." I never used words like *magical*, but it seemed right around Niall. "But it has to end next week. Can't we just enjoy this until then?"

His jaw hardened. "You can't stop me from trying to change your mind."

"I don't suppose I can." Though I couldn't let him.

He put one hand behind my head, and the next thing I knew, I was flat on my back, Niall looming over me. He kissed my nose, his lips warm on the cold tip. He dragged his lips down my cheek and nosed aside my scarf to place sucking kisses on my neck. Molten heat pooled between my legs.

"Anything off limits in this game?" he asked, his voice rough.

"What—game?" He'd moved to my ear, tracing the lobe in a way that made me shiver inside the down coat.

"The one where I try to convince you never to let me go."

"No. Nothing off-limits." Except my heart.

He crashed his lips onto mine angrily, pillaging, taking. When I kissed him, I forgot all the reasons I could never live with him on the farm: the lack of wifi, the distance from any university with a sizable computer science department, CASE and all the lies I'd told. Instead, I let myself roll around in the moment the way Bilbo Baggins had done in the forest.

His icy hands slid under my coat, under my T-shirt. My heated skin welcomed his touch. He wedged a knee between my legs, right where I needed him, and I rocked against him. Under the quilt, we weren't writers or programmers or frauds. We were just Sam and Niall, and while we pressed together, too many layers of fabric between us, I could almost imagine it didn't have to end.

He tugged away and cradled my face in his hands. "As much as I love nature and—and doing this with you outdoors, maybe we should go back inside."

"To your perfectly serviceable bed?"

"Where it's warm, and we don't have to worry about frostbite. Where I can see you. All of you." Niall's voice was deep. "I'll light some candles."

"I'm not afraid of your candles. Or your bed. You won't win."

"We'll see."

We returned to the house, hand in hand. We creaked up the steps, and he lit the candles like he'd promised. The flickering light outlined him in ruby and gold like one of Mother's necklaces.

His bed squeaked as I straddled him and buried my hands in the rose-gold hair on his freckled chest. As I rose and fell, riding him like the waves of the ocean. As I spiraled up again and again until I flopped against his chest, exhausted.

The bed groaned as he turned us, as he drove into me like he could break me open and spill out all my secrets. When he moved a hand between us and sparked me again, I would have told him every secret I had, if I'd had the power of speech. But the only word I could form was his name, over and over, like the creaks of the spring peepers.

Like the Spring Peeper Princess, I took everything he offered.

After, he wrapped me in his arms while we breathed together. I shut my eyes, refusing to look out the window at the new constellations that had risen to remind me that the world kept turning around us.

That we'd have to get up, say our good-byes to his family, and fly to Dallas.

That the tour would end on Thursday back home in San Francisco.

That, if I didn't stop them, Heidi and Martell would announce that CASE had written the book.

That, whether or not I managed to hide the truth, Niall could never be mine.

Fucking feelings. I hadn't wanted them. And here they were, wrapping me up like ivy around one of the trees in the forest.

When his breathing evened out, slow and deep, I untangled myself from his arms, left the candlelit enchantment of his bed, and returned to my cold, dark room. But the ache in my heart followed me.

31

NIALL

"I DON'T KNOW why we can't go to a bar like normal people." Gabi hitched up the paper bag, making the bottles clink.

"Let me carry that." I fumbled the plastic key card out of my pocket and reached for the bag.

"You get the door. And then ask your princess to come out to celebrate. Where there's music. And martinis. And hot L.A. people looking for walk-on roles. Which I can pretend I have the power to offer them."

I stopped a few feet away from the door. "I want to celebrate with Sam," I said, low so Sam wouldn't hear.

"What did Sam do to help you get this deal?" Gabi shifted the bag again, and this time I took it from her. "Fuck all, that's what. I'm your brilliant agent who nabbed it for you."

"I know you are. And I appreciate it. I appreciate you. But Sam's part of my life now." Maybe she hadn't said the words, but she'd slept in my bed every night since the farm. Well, not exactly slept. She always returned to her own bed after. She said she slept better alone. Though, from the dark circles under her eyes, she wasn't sleeping well alone, either. Regardless, it had to mean something when she looked into my eyes every night when I was inside her, when she whispered my name like a plea.

Gabi narrowed her eyes but said nothing, which surprised me more than anything she could have said.

I slid the key into the slot. Red. Again, with a jiggle. Red. Again, fast. Red.

"Dammit, Niall, just let me do it." Gabi snatched the plastic out of my hand and unlocked the door in one try.

With a sharp-eyed glance, she took in the open adjoining door. "Honey, we're home," she called out.

Bilbo sprinted out of Sam's room, barking his head off, but he stopped and sat when he saw me. I bent to scratch between his ears. "Sam?"

"I'm here." She walked through the door from her room, pulling out her wireless earbuds. "Hey, I had this idea for—" She stopped when she spotted Gabi.

I strode to her and kissed her. I could do that. In front of Gabi. I'd even done it in the bookstore after last night's signing. She'd been so relaxed and easy, a world of difference since that first awkward Q and A in Chicago.

"What's going on?" She took in Gabi and the bag I still held.

"We're celebrating. Niall said you'd rather do it here in the hotel than in a bar or restaurant."

A tiny smile teased at the corners of her lips. "What are we celebrating?"

Gabi found a trio of glasses and plunked them on the desk. She beckoned for the champagne, and I set it beside the glasses. She went to work opening the foil top. "They greenlit the second season."

"They haven't finished filming season one, have they?" Sam asked.

Gabi cranked on the cork. "No, but there's been so much excitement around the stills that they went ahead. I wish I had a third book to sell them."

It was time to show her what I'd done at the farm and in the early mornings of the last few days. I hefted the bookstore tote bag bulging with notebooks from the floor and thumped it onto the desk.

Gabi set down the bottle. "What's this?"

"Book three. I finished. Well, I finished the first draft."

"Niall!" She wrapped her arms around me. Then she swatted my arm. "Why didn't you say anything?"

"I, ah, wasn't sure how long the muse would stick around. I didn't want to jinx it."

Gabi glared at Sam for a moment, but then she returned to the bottle. She popped the cork and caught the frothy wine in a glass. She poured out the other two and handed them to us. "To Niall and his wood elves. And book three. May there be many more seasons. And action figures. And T-shirts. A line of wood elf–themed housewares. And a feature film."

We all raised our glasses and clinked. "To Niall," Sam echoed.

"I can't believe you said no to the cameo." Gabi frowned at me, the same way she'd done in the studio's conference room.

"I'm ready to wind down the public author persona. I'm going to become a hermit author like Cormac McCarthy. No more movie premieres, no more *Us Weekly*. No more paparazzi. I'm settling down." I'd never liked the celebrity author stuff, but I'd done it to make Gabi happy. To move books, to fund the farm. And, I had to admit, to show my father I was worthy of his notice. Now I resolved to do what'd make Sam happy. Fuck Paul Swift. And I'd write faster to earn enough to help out at the farm. I already had a sprout of an idea for a spin-off series. I hugged Sam's shoulders and kissed the top of her head, breathing in the herbal scent of her hair.

Gabi scowled. "More photos of you reading in public would move more wood elf merch."

"Let's focus on the books," I growled. "Not collectibles."

"And the show." Gabi raised her glass before draining it. "I'll leave you two to finish the celebration as you see fit." She raised her eyebrows at the king-size bed. Thankfully, housekeeping had straightened up the sex-tangled sheets.

"Where are you going? I thought we'd hang out, order a pizza." I'd try to coerce Sam and Gabi to at least act friendly toward each other.

"While you were shaking hands, I was making a date with one of the junior execs. You're not the only one craving companionship, you know. And if it works out"—she shrugged—"maybe *I* can get a cameo out of it."

"If you want a cameo, I'll ask the producers about it."

She smirked. "It's more fun my way." She kissed my cheek, set down her glass, and sashayed to the door. "Later, kids. I'm flying out tomorrow morning, but I'll text you from the airport, Niall. Ship me those notebooks."

"Bye, Gabriela. Have fun." Sam leaned into my shoulder.

"Bye, Gab—" The closing door cut off my words.

"So I guess it's just the two of us now." I sank onto the wide armchair and pulled Sam onto my lap. I set my half-full glass on the table.

"Yeah." She set her almost-full glass next to mine. Gabi didn't know she hated the stuff.

"I bought some white wine, too. I don't know anything about Chardonnay, but the guy at the store said it was top notch."

"Maybe later." She leaned back to look me in the eye. "I really am excited for you. Are you happy about the deal?"

"I guess? It's money I have to do hardly anything to earn. Though Gabi got me script approval this time."

"That's good, isn't it? So you have control over the adaptation?"

"Yeah." If Sam could help me figure out my email, I could do it remotely.

"Hey, I finished listening to *Secrets of the Wood Elves.* I know you know this, but it's amazing."

Warmth flickered across my skin. "You liked it? It's not as good as *Magician,* but—"

"Niall." Her touch was feather-light on my cheek, but I couldn't resist it. I looked her in the eye. "I loved it. Truly. I was just about to start *Treachery* when you walked in. It's good the third book's not ready, or I'd never finish my dissertation."

I leaned forward and kissed her, taking her lips the way I couldn't have done in front of Gabi. When we came up for air, I said, "Thank you. That means a lot coming from an author of your caliber."

A tiny line formed between her brows. "Let's not talk about *Magician in the Machine.* Tonight is all about you. And I have—I have a proposal."

I waggled my eyebrows and then kissed her neck. "A sexy proposal?"

"No." Laughing, she pushed at my chest.

Reluctantly, I released her. "What kind of proposal, then?"

"I think your wood elves would make a great video game." She held up a finger to stop my protest. "I know you're not into tech. But I am. I could help. Jackson and I used to program video games together. I could put you in contact with some programmers who'd absolutely die to bring the wood elves to life."

Gabi had mentioned gaming rights to me around the time we were making the TV deal. I'd refused then. But this was different. It was Sam.

"I don't want programmers. I want you."

"Niall, I'm a programmer."

"I only want to do it with you." Gabi wasn't the only one with negotiation skills. A deal like this would bind us together, keep her with me even after the tour ended.

"But I'm—I'm leaving. I'm doing a postdoc. And then I'll become a researcher. You need someone full-time, who can have the game ready when the show releases. Not someone who programs it in her free time."

"I'll wait. For you."

"Niall." She sighed through her nose. "You don't even know if I'm any good. Gabi would never let you make a deal like that."

"Then show me." I tightened my hold on her waist. "Show me one of your games."

She unsnapped one of the pockets of her cargo pants and then snapped it closed. "I stopped doing that when Jackson started Synergy back when I was in middle school. Those games suck."

"I like it when you suck." I nuzzled her neck again. "Show me."

"Wait, you mean the game or sucking you off?" She squirmed on my lap.

I groaned. I was already half-hard. But this was important to her. "The game. First." I nipped her earlobe and then pulled away.

"Okay. Remember, this is ten-year-old stuff. Games have come a long way since then." She slid off my lap and went into her room. She returned with her laptop. "Come on, we'll play on the bed."

"You really are trying to distract me, aren't you?" I stood and discreetly adjusted my pants.

She grinned. "I think you'd like a grown-up game more than something I programmed while I was wearing braces."

"The lady doth protest too much, methinks. Now I really want to see it."

She rolled her lip between her teeth. "Then you can show me one of your naughty 4-H games."

I sat on the bed and stretched out my legs. "Deal. But remember that none of those games were sanctioned by the national organization."

She snuggled next to me with her laptop. Bilbo jumped up and curled into her other side. "I'll keep that in mind when I send a thank-you email to the council."

32

SAM

Ninety minutes.

I checked my phone. By now, I'd gotten good at guessing how long the signing part would take from a quick estimate of the number of attendees. My last ninety minutes of breathing the same air as Niall. Of brushing his hand accidentally-on-purpose as we reached for the stack of books between us. Of sucking into my lungs that woodsy scent he carried with him everywhere.

Ninety minutes of the happiness I felt when he was near.

We stepped down from the makeshift stage to the table, our movements a well-rehearsed ballet. As I lowered myself into my chair, the one on the right so Niall and I wouldn't bump arms as we signed, I rubbed my hand against the center of my chest, right above where it twinged.

When Niall turned his head toward me, something I felt more than saw, my body ached to swivel to him. My lips twitched to curve up and exchange a smile with him the way we'd been doing for the past week. I yearned to lean into him, to let him whisper one of his encouragements into my ear.

Instead, I dropped my hand to the table and straightened.

Mother's training, such a failure for what she wanted me to be, would save me. I'd smile and chat with the readers and pretend I belonged for one more night. Then, in eighty-eight minutes, I'd escape. I'd return to the isolation of my apartment. The next day, I'd be back in my office at the university. I'd be a computer scientist again. I wouldn't have to lie anymore.

His freckled arm brushed mine. "You okay?" he whispered as the store's staff organized the readers into lines.

"Sure," I lied. It was second-nature now.

"I didn't even ask. Have you been here before? To this store?"

I rolled my shoulders. Small talk was easy. Maybe I could get through the night without a hard conversation. Maybe shutting down every one of Niall's hints really had worked, and he was ready to end things. Just like I wanted.

"I have." I glanced over the queuing readers. "It's not far from the university. Sometimes I buy books here for my nephew." I could walk to my apartment from the store. I could steep myself in the city's fog and let it steam away all the lies like wrinkles from a silk gown.

But not yet. The first person stepped up to my side of the table, and I pasted on my smile, grabbed my acid-green Sharpie, and got to work.

The crowd had started to thin when a too-familiar pair of figures stepped up to the table. "Samwise."

"Aunt Sam!" Noah slouched like he could hide his initial burst of excitement. Had I tried that hard to act aloof when I was twelve? Probably.

I stood. "Holy shit, have you grown again?" I hugged him, his twelve-year-old pride be damned.

I stood on tiptoes to kiss my brother's cheek. "What are you guys doing here?"

"We meant to be here for the start," Jackson said, ducking his head. "But there was a, ah, Valentine mishap." He scrunched his nose. "I wasn't prepared for how much fluid a baby that small can eject."

"You don't remember when I was a baby? Or Nat?"

He shrugged. "I left you guys to the nannies until you got more interesting. Though Nat still isn't interesting. Don't tell your grandmother—or your Aunt Natalie—I said that," he added for Noah's benefit.

Noah's eyebrows, the color of wet sand, scrunched down. "Aunt Sam, you didn't tell me you wrote the book."

I felt Niall's attention arrow to us. "No, Noah, I didn't. There were some reasons why I needed to keep it a secret. But I'll tell you about it as soon as I can."

"This weekend? Jay says you'll probably come over. To see the baby."

"Of course I'll come over. To see all of you." I wanted to reach out, ruffle his too-long sandy hair. But he looked like he'd block me if I reached for him. *Twelve.*

Jackson plucked the book out of Noah's hand. "Then we'll get you to sign this over the weekend." He raised his dark eyebrows at me. A threat. In exchange for a promise.

"But"—my brother looked past me—"we won't be seeing Mr. Flynn this weekend, will we?"

"No," I said, not turning to look back at him. "Niall has to go home. To write. At the farm. But you should get a copy of his book. It's the most amazing story you'll ever read. Actually, buy both. You'll want to read *Secrets* first. Then *Treachery.* He'll sign it for you. Both. He'll sign both. Right, Niall?" I didn't pause for his answer. "Noah, did you know they're making a TV show of his books? Two seasons." I named one of the actors, someone he'd know from his superhero movie obsession.

I kept my gaze locked on my brother's. *Don't say a word.*

His mouth tightened. *We'll have words this weekend.*

I gulped. Jackson didn't give a shit about my NDA.

"That's cool." Noah's eyes shone with admiration. He picked up a copy of each book on Niall's side of the table and stepped in front of him. "Would you sign these for me, please?"

"Of course. It's Noah, right? I saw your drawing, the one your —Jackson showed Sam. Your art skills are impressive."

"I like art." He shrugged. "But I like programming better. I think that's what I want to do when I grow up. Like Alicia and Jay. Like Sam."

"Sam's a good writer, too." He bent over the page to inscribe it.

"Yeah, but I didn't know until—" Noah looked up at Jackson. "Until I overheard some stuff."

Jackson scratched his beard and wouldn't meet my gaze.

"You liked her book?" Niall blew on the ink the way he always did. It made me shiver, thinking of the way he sometimes blew across my skin. He took the second volume from Noah.

"Yeah, it was kinda weird, but I liked The Magician."

"Then we'll have to work together to convince her to write another." Niall nodded at my nephew.

Noah cocked his head. They weren't related by blood, but both he and Jackson turned identical, suspicious glares on me.

Shit.

"Thanks for coming by, guys. Love you. See you this weekend. What should I bring you, Noah? Something sour? Or gummy?"

"Both." If his hands hadn't been full of books, he'd have crossed his arms. His expression and posture, even holding the books, called me *bullshitter.*

"You got it." There was a candy shop not far from the bookshop, next to the bus stop. I'd buy his silence. I wished it worked on my brother, too.

"Nice meeting you, Noah. Jackson, it was..." Niall wiped his hands on the sides of his jeans.

"A truly terrifying experience?" Jackson leaned in and spoke lower than the buzz of bookstore patrons, but I heard him. "I hope you were a perfect gentleman around my sister. Shame if something were to happen to those hands of yours." He nodded at Niall's ink-stained fingers.

"Jackson? Fuck off," I whispered.

My brother cracked his knuckles. "We'll wait for you, Sam. Give you a ride home." He put a hand on Noah's shoulder and steered him away with his book bounty.

I glanced up at the next person in line. *Almost done. Fifteen more minutes.*

When the last reader walked away, Niall stood and stretched. "How about—"

Jackson, lurking in the magazine section nearby, caught my gaze. *Ten minutes,* I mouthed at him.

But Niall had seen. "You're going home with your brother?"

"Yeah, I think it's for the best." I lined up the Sharpies on the table.

"You didn't tell him about your book. You didn't tell your nephew you were a writer. Yet you're leaving with them and not me. I've seen every part of you, Sam, and—"

A couple people glanced up from the Relationships section. I stood and grabbed his arm. "Come on." I scanned the store for a private corner. Seeing none, I beelined to the closet where we'd stowed our luggage. When he was fully inside, I closed the door and leaned on it.

"Shit, it's dark." A thin strip of light from under the door lit up his lace-up oxfords and the soles of my boots. I felt on the wall for a switch.

A click, and we blinked at each other in the dim light of a bare bulb. The string hung down between us, still swinging from Niall's pull on it.

"What the hell, Sam?"

I focused on the plaid pattern on his shirt. It was one of my favorites, gray with black stripes and narrower red stripes that matched his hair. Who was I kidding? They were all my favorites. I'd paper the walls of my under-the-mountain hideaway with the half-dozen plaid patterns of the book tour.

"My family and I are different from yours. Well, your mom and your grandpa. We aren't sharers." We had been, once. When Dad was around. After that, I'd shared most of my life, my secrets, with Jackson. Until Stephen. They weaponized anything I'd told them after that. My brother only wanted to protect me, but sometimes a girl needed to make her own mistakes.

And I'd made a big one.

Niall rubbed a hand through his auburn hair, lit up in gold by the 40-watt bulb. "I'm sorry, Sam. I don't want to get in your business, but don't you think your writing is something you should have shared with them?"

"I have my reasons." I squared my jaw and wished I were six inches taller so I didn't have to crane my neck to look at him.

"What are you keeping from me, Sam?"

For a second, I weighed my options. Tell him, take the weight off my chest. He'd give me a look of disgusted betrayal and walk out. Heidi would come down on me like a hammer with her lawyers, and I'd kiss my Ph.D. good-bye. Or keep my mouth shut. Let him think I wasn't a fraud for just a few more minutes until I could return to my lonely, Niall-free life with my future intact.

"Nothing I can tell you about." I stared at his shirt button. I'd been the one to fasten it this morning after our shower. I'd liked the idea of his going out to our last tour event in clothes I'd put on him. Like a squire armoring her knight, protecting him against all ill-wishers. Including myself.

"Can't you, Sam? We've shared so much." He clasped my hand and flipped it over. Only splotches of my black nail polish remained, centered on each fingernail, chipped and ragged at the edges. He stroked my hand, pale with blue veins crisscrossing it.

"I can't."

"What about later? Have you thought about—"

"I can't do that, either. It's like I told you—"

"This—us—ends with the tour. You can't want that, Sam. I know I don't."

Each word was a nail in my heart, piercing it. I could hardly breathe through the pain. "I've loved every minute. Well, except for the first few days. But this is the end."

"So this is good-bye? Right here, in a supply closet?" He toed a can of furniture polish, and it fell over with a clank.

When I glanced up at last, Niall's mouth pinched with pain. Probably the same pain as my own nail-studded heart. Tears prickled behind my eyes, but I sniffed them back. If I walked out of there with red eyes, Jackson would punch Niall.

His hands traced my arms up to my shoulders. He cradled my face, rubbing one callused thumb against my cheek. God, I'd miss those calluses.

"Good-bye." It was all I could push past my closed-up throat.

"Sam."

In that one, cracked-open word, I heard it. His heart was splintering, too. But it was nothing to the hurt he'd feel if I told him the truth. He didn't want to know how I'd used technology to make a mockery of everything he treasured, everything he believed in.

Better to let him believe in the fairy tale a little longer until I could put some distance between us. Gabi would find him another B-list actress faster than I could say *rebound*. He'd forget me soon enough.

"Sam, I—you don't have to respond. I know it's too soon, and you probably think I'm some lovesick Romeo. But I have to tell you how I feel." He took a breath, sucking every molecule of oxygen out of the closet. "I love you."

My nail-studded, bleeding heart jumped. "No, Niall, you—"

"Don't tell me I don't know my own feelings. I know it's fast. But I can't help the way I feel. I love you," he repeated. Like if he said it often enough it'd be true.

I opened my mouth to argue, to tell him he was wrong. That my own heart was wrong, too.

Niall's lips were on mine the next second, then one arm wrapped around me while his other hand cradled my face. I gripped the soft flannel of his shirt so hard a button pinged on the floor.

My pulse pounded in my ears. I stretched up on my toes to chase the kiss, the sensation of our lips and tongues sliding together, teeth clicking in our frenzy to come closer, to join as we had that afternoon in the hayloft and every night since, to be one. I could've lived forever in that moment, in the nubby texture of his shirt under my hands, in the warmth of his lips, in the strength of his arms around me. I never wanted to be released.

At last, the correct neuron fired, reminding me we couldn't do this. We belonged in separate parts of the country. In separate worlds. I belonged in this city, where the lie had been born, and I'd accepted it. Where I had to keep lying for another few weeks until I could escape, Ph.D. scroll in hand. He belonged out in nature, forever true and pure and honest. I lowered to my heels, Niall bending over me, nipping at my bottom lip.

I tugged free but didn't push him away. He kissed my jaw, my earlobe, the spot on my neck that made my knees liquefy. My traitorous hands gripped his shirt.

Into the shell of my ear, he whispered, "We're connected, Sam. Don't you feel it? We may come from different backgrounds, we might have different opinions about art, but our souls are alike. I feel them twisting together like two vines. We belong together. We need to give it—us—a chance to grow."

My stomach muscles tensed, probably to keep my organs from leaping out of my body. I wanted so desperately to agree with him. I did feel it: the recognition of rewatching a favorite movie, the satisfaction of scanning through an elegant section of code, the pleasant purring of the server room.

I loved him. But I wasn't cruel enough to admit it. To doom him to live in my world of lies, to be tainted by it.

I pushed him away, and he stumbled back into a metal shelf. "You don't know me."

He sucked in a breath like ripping cloth. "In three weeks, we've spent more time together than most people do in three months. I'm completely enchanted."

Heat—and not the sexy heat from a minute before, but angry heat—bubbled to my skin. "Enchanted? I'm the farthest thing from a fairy princess there is." I'd listened to *Treachery of the Wood*

Elves. I'd heard his description of Lobelia. Regal and pure and noble. Nothing like me. Nothing I could ever be.

"I need to go. Jackson's waiting."

Even in the dim light of the bulb, his freckles stood out against the paleness of his skin. His voice had glass in it. "You really want me to get on my flight tomorrow?"

I found my suitcase's handle and gripped it. "I do. Your place is at the farm. And writing in that bend in the creek."

A pause. "You're going to Vegas next month, right? For the prize ceremony."

"No, I—I can't."

"Of course you can. You deserve to win. Even if you don't win, you deserve to be there."

I didn't. I stared at the spot on his shirt where red met black.

He grasped my hand. "Go for me, then. I need you there. If neither of us wins, we can get drunk together. If I win, it won't mean the same without you."

He knew exactly which button to push. He needed me. Just for me. The way no one else ever had. I could see him once more, and then never again. Because Heidi would reveal the truth after that. Against my better judgment, the word pushed itself out. "Okay."

His next kiss wasn't hungry passion but gentle farewell, and it ripped my splintered heart open.

"I'm counting on you. I'll see you in thirty-one days."

He squeezed my hand one more time, then he pushed open the door. I blinked in the brighter light of the bookstore. He stood for a few seconds in the doorway, like he was taking a scan of me. Then his lips twisted. He pivoted and walked back toward the table.

Jackson, gripping Bilbo Baggins' carrier, speared Niall with his gaze.

I shouldered my laptop bag and rolled my suitcase toward my brother.

"Everything all right? I don't need to kick his ass, do I?" He stared at the back of Niall's head.

"No. Remember, I'm not a teenager anymore. I can handle myself."

"You just stepped out of a dark closet. With a dude." He quirked a dark eyebrow.

"Point taken." I drew myself up. "I'm fine. Speaking of teenagers, where'd Noah go?"

"Bilbo was whining. He took him outside. You sure you're okay? Your eyes are red."

I blinked like I could erase the evidence. "Can you drive me home?"

Slowly, he nodded, his gaze never leaving mine. "Remember, Samwise, I'll always be available for ass-kicking. No matter how old you get." He slipped the bag off my shoulder and slung it over his.

"I don't need that, Jackson. I'm a big girl now. I'm independent."

Just like I always wanted.

But now, my heart shredded in my chest, independence didn't seem so appealing anymore.

33

NIALL

I GLARED at the slippery tie in the mirror and tried again.

Maybe I struggled because I was left-handed. Had they given me the right-handed instructions by mistake, and I'd walked past the magical How to Tie a Bow Tie *for Lefties* instruction sheet that would have taught me how to do it on the first try? The loop slid out of my fingers, leaving me pinching empty air. I started over.

The formalwear shop in the Las Vegas hotel had overwhelmed me so I'd hardly known up from down. All those oversized photos of brides and grooms, and one of them had looked like Sam, her hair up in a messy bun, holding her bouquet in one hand and her groom in the other, laughing in an unrestrained way that Sam never did.

Sam always held something back. Especially on our texts and calls over the past month. Once, I'd fumbled the phone and hit the video chat button by mistake. It'd been the best mistake of my life because I'd gotten to see her, the dark hair falling out of her bun, her violet eyes wide and surprised to see me. Even on video, she'd carefully schooled her face, biting her lip, promising nothing.

But tonight was the Tower Prize ceremony. She'd promised to

come. And after the ceremony, I'd bring her up to my hotel room, and we'd talk. Face to face. No more deflections.

My hands trembled on the tie, but I pushed one loop through the other and slowly, carefully, tugged on the bow ends.

Fuck! It looked like a six-year-old's shoelaces after an hour on the playground. I dug my fingers into the knot to untie it.

Why had I even tried it? I had a perfectly serviceable pre-tied bow tie hanging in the closet. It'd worked for the dozen or so formal events I'd attended since *Secrets* hit the bestseller list. No one at the ceremony would even care.

Sam wouldn't. She'd seen me in flannel shirts. T-shirts. Pajama pants. And a whole lot less. But—and this was the reason I'd run downstairs, my formal shirt barely tucked into my tux pants, and plunked down an absurd amount of money on a bow tie—Sam knew the real deal, and she deserved it.

I could've let the shop assistant tie it for me. Her pink-tipped fingers looked expert at it. But the thought of someone who wasn't Sam touching me made the skin at the back of my neck itch. I'd tie the tie, and I hoped to God Sam would untie it later, sliding those delicate fingers of hers along the silk, trailing them down the placket of my shirt, loosening buttons as she went.

My dick gave a hopeful twitch, but it sagged back along my thigh when I looked at the crumpled mess of the tie. I couldn't go down there looking like this.

Who could help me? Neither Heidi nor Qiana had come to the prize ceremony. Heidi told me they had an all-hands-on-deck situation back at the office.

I eyed my phone on the bathroom counter. This was one of the times I wished I had a real father, one I could ask about things like bow ties. My father had probably tied plenty. But Sam had shown me how to block and delete his number. I was done chasing his affirmation. The people who cared about me—like Sam—supported me without the chase.

Grandpa would laugh at me. The last month at the farm, he'd relentlessly poked fun at me for mooning over Sam. For doing my chores like a zombie. For checking my phone as often as a middle-school girl. For buying a laptop. The satellite internet I'd had a technician install. Though once he'd discovered that farmers' dating site, StudFarm, he'd gone strangely quiet in his teasing.

I texted Gabi. *Know how to tie a bow tie?*

A minute later, she responded with a link. YouTube? Really? Sure, I had wifi at the farm now, but no way was I wandering off into the wilds of online video.

Heidi? Not if she was in crisis mode.

Qiana. Maybe she could take a break from whatever PR emergency and walk me through it. Having her author not look like a tatterdemalion fell into the responsibilities of a publicist, didn't it?

I hit the call button and put it on speaker.

"Hey, Niall. Getting ready for your big night? I'm so sorry I can't be there. I don't know what Heidi's big secret project is, but she's called us all in tonight. I'm just grabbing a slice before I get on the subway. But I've got my fingers crossed for you and Sam." And she squeed so loud I was glad I wasn't holding the phone to my ear.

"Minor sartorial issue here. Do you know how to tie a bow tie?"

"Niall! You finally got rid of that high-school dance pre-tied one? I'm so proud. My little one has finally grown up." She gave a big fake sniff.

I let a few seconds of silence tick by. "Are you done mocking me now? Because I'm about to hang up on you and slap on that pre-tied one."

"No! I'm just having a little fun. Sheesh. Though she's right about the growly." Qiana made a *brr* noise.

"Who's right?"

"Shit. Nobody."

"Have you been talking to Sam?"

"Of course. We're friends. We've been checking in once a week."

I opened my mouth to ask what she'd said about me, but

Qiana had already teased me about my prom-style formalwear choices. I wasn't about to give her fodder for another teenager jibe.

I checked my watch. Ten minutes until they opened the doors. I wanted to be there at the start so I'd be sure to spot Sam first. The tie. I needed to unfuck my tie.

"Qiana. You are the world's best publicist. Can you please help me tie this goddamned tie?"

"Don't worry. I've got this. My dad used to wear bow ties on Sundays. Put me on video."

I tapped the button.

Nine minutes later, a crisply tied bow tie around my neck, I raced for the elevator. For Sam. We'd talk about our future. Together.

34

SAM

MOTHER WOULD'VE DIED of embarrassment if she could've seen me.

I mean, my black gown was suitable. Mother had sent it to me herself for some Jones Foundation function a few years ago. Even my shoes were the toe-pinching, ankle-turning, heel-numbing style she approved.

It was the bag. The one that broke the line of the dress, that dug into my shoulder and left a red gouge in it, that occasionally wiggled on its own.

I couldn't come all the way out to Vegas and leave Bilbo Baggins behind.

Okay, fine. I hadn't brought him for his sake. I'd done it for mine.

I couldn't sit there and smile when they announced *Magician in the Machine* as a nominee for Best First Book. Because what I'd learned during the tour, in my time with Niall, was that books were art. And technology—my technology, CASE—had no business replacing the work of an artist like Niall. I'd wronged him and every other writer, every person in that room who loved books. Then I'd lied about it.

I swallowed around the lump in my throat.

I shouldn't have come. I should have spent tonight, like I'd spent every day and night for the past month, working on CASE 2.0, trying to get it to produce scientific papers like we'd originally intended it. Though three days ago, when I'd suggested to Dr. Martell that I rewrite my dissertation to refer only to CASE 2.0, even if it delayed my degree by another year, he'd said there was no need. And to be sure I preserved the original code.

The next day, I'd keep working to change his mind. But I'd promised that night to Niall.

It was selfish, I knew, to see him again. But as much as I'd initially resisted, as much as I'd wanted to end things neatly with the tour, I couldn't. I had to see him once more. To touch him. To steal a few more moments of happiness before I locked away all those feelings forever.

I pulled my nominee ticket from one of the outside pockets of my bag and handed it to the woman at the table outside the ballroom.

She smiled at me. "Love your dress. Table Three, right up front."

I couldn't return her smile. "Thanks."

"Would you like to check your bag?" She nodded at the booth on the other side of the ballroom door.

"No, thanks." I strode toward the door, the bag bumping against my hip.

A wall of a man in a tux stepped in front of me, arms crossed. His chest was twice as broad as me. If I'd stretched out my arms, they wouldn't have met at his back. Not that I would've dared to try it.

"Ma'am, I need to see inside your bag."

I willed Bilbo Baggins to stay still. I needed him as my excuse to leave the ceremony. As soon as the category for *Magician* was announced, I'd ensure Bilbo needed a trip outside.

"No, you don't."

His face wasn't unkind, but his jaw was firm. "I do, ma'am. Last year, one of the horror writers brought in a bucket of blood. We had to replace the carpets."

I laughed, a high, anxious trill. "No blood here. See?" I squeezed the side of the bag to show it was flexible. Bilbo Baggins let out a grunt.

The Wall's eyes narrowed.

"It's full of…feminine care products. Riding the red wave, you know. My ultra-supers don't fit into one of those tiny evening bags." I gripped the bag closer. His jaw twitched.

"Sam!"

Striding toward me, his red hair flaming over everyone else in the ballroom, was Niall.

I'd seen him in a suit before. Ten months ago at the fundraiser in San Francisco. But tonight he wore a tux. Smooth black lines over his muscular frame, shiny shoes, crisp, white shirt. And a silk bow tie snug under his chin. I could spot the sheen of it from twenty feet away. When I dared to look at his face, that wide grin and those crinkled eyes beaming straight at me, my ankles wobbled in my pinchy heels.

My black silk dress with its spaghetti straps and low draped neckline showed too much skin. Anyone would be able to see through it to my heart beating frantically as a trapped bird. Discreetly as possible, I wiped my sweaty palms on the outside of my bag.

Niall took one look at The Wall and his crossed arms. "She's a VIP. I'll be responsible if there's an issue."

I scowled at them both. "I'll be responsible. But there won't be an issue."

The Wall ignored me. "I'll find you later for the carpet-cleaning bill, Big Red."

Niall chuckled. "You got it, man."

He tucked his palm around my elbow and led me toward the

center of the room. "You're beautiful." He stooped to kiss my cheek.

I pushed away. "What the hell was that?"

"What?" His red brows drew together.

"I don't need vouching for or…or rescuing. I'm not some fairy princess."

His grip tightened on my elbow. "You should know by now my fairy princesses are the ones who do the rescuing. All I meant was that, even though you're the most radiant person in the room and you draw every eye, I'm easier to spot." He tapped the top of his head. For once, the red locks were tamed and orderly.

"Oh."

"Hey, little guy. I missed you, too."

Uh-oh. I'd been too focused on being treated like the most useless Jones to notice Bilbo Baggins' wiggling. I glanced back at The Wall, who narrowed his gaze at me. "Play it cool, Flynn. I don't think he's welcome here."

"Sorry. I got excited. I missed you—both of you—so much." His ears reddened at the tips.

I wanted to lie, but I couldn't. "I missed you, too. I listened to your audiobooks again, but it wasn't the same as hearing you read them."

He bent to whisper in my ear, "I'll read to you again tonight, after this is over. I've got a room upstairs."

I hoped he didn't see my wince. I had to walk out of there as soon as they announced his category, or I'd never have the courage to leave him. Already, his woodsy scent surrounded me, melting my bones and testing my resolve. I couldn't fall under his spell. Tonight was good-bye. As soon as I'd fulfilled my promise.

"I have to leave right after."

His smile drooped. "You can't stay and celebrate? Or commiserate?"

The words took every bit of resolve I could rally. "I can't."

"Well, I can't promise I won't try to change your mind." His lips traced the shell of my ear, paused at the lobe, and then rested for a moment on the pulse point behind my jaw. I quivered.

"Niall!" A dark-skinned woman in a colorful print dress and elaborate headscarf waved. I nudged him.

He straightened before he pasted on that camera-ready smile. "Let me introduce you to some people."

He led me to a table toward the front of the room. A card sticking out of the centerpiece identified it as Table Three. The woman who'd waved stood next to an older white woman. They both smiled at us.

"Ladies, I'd like you to meet Samantha Jones, who writes as Sam Case. Sam, this is Kate Salazar and Tamarah Starr. They're finalists in the science fiction category."

"A pleasure." The lie came out as smooth as the silk of my gown. Nothing was a pleasure anymore. I'd looked forward to one last night with Niall, but knowing it was the end brought me nothing but pain.

The older woman, Kate, said, "I loved *Magician in the Machine.* So unique, so fresh."

"Thanks," I mumbled. The lies would be over soon.

"What I want to know," Tamarah said, her floral headscarf nodding toward me, "is whether The Magician actually died at the end. Or are you planning a sequel?"

Someone had asked that at almost every stop on the tour. Qiana had coached me to be vague and leave open the possibility of a second book. But I was in the last turn of the game now. "The Magician is really dead. And I won't be writing a sequel."

"Ah." Tamarah nodded. "Brave choice."

"What are you writing next, Sam?" Kate asked.

"Nothing but my dissertation. I'm finishing up my Ph.D. in computer science."

"I'm trying to convince her to change her mind." Niall's palm on my back was just as comforting as it'd been on that first stop in Chicago, when I'd freaked out about the photos and reading in public. He'd been so kind and supportive throughout the tour. He deserved more than my betrayal. And that was why I had to break my own heart and leave him.

I bit my lip to keep my chin steady. When I'd forced my expression into a polite mask almost like Mother's, I turned to him. "You've helped me rediscover my love of reading. I'd rather read others' work than produce my own. I could never hope to create anything as beautiful as your work, Niall."

Mother's training kept me upright as the dinner began. The writers talked about their favorite science fiction and fantasy literature, and I fed the rubbery chicken to Bilbo Baggins under the table.

Every time I looked over, The Wall watched me. Was it only my bag he suspected, or did he somehow know I was a fraud? Was he waiting for the order to toss me out? A hacker among these artists, a coder among wordsmiths?

I pulled out my phone to check the time. One hour before I could go back to San Francisco. Where I belonged. Where I didn't have to pretend. I was smart. I'd figure out a way to shut down CASE. Quietly. Then I could escape to a life of solitary research. In Idaho.

Niall clasped my hand and held it steady. He murmured, so softly only I could hear, "Are you all right? You're so pale."

My promise was the only thing that kept me in that chair. "I'll be better when it's all over."

He chuckled and eased back in his chair. "I'm nervous, too. I don't want to make a weird face when they announce you as the winner. I don't think Qiana would like that kind of publicity."

"You mean a meme?"

"A what?"

"It's a funny picture with a caption. They're all over the internet. Like evil Kermit."

"Like Grumpy Cat?"

"Sort of. Anyway, you're going to win. How could anyone read your book and not think it's the best?"

He grinned at me, and it was like sunshine there in the ballroom. He leaned in and kissed my cheek. "You can stroke my ego anytime."

That wasn't all I wanted to stroke. His hand rested on my knee under the table. But touching him would only make it harder to leave. I folded my hands in my lap.

The lights dimmed, and a woman's voice rang out over the sound system. "And now it's time to announce tonight's winners. We'll start with the Best First Book category."

Tamarah leaned over. "Sam, you're nominated for this, yes? Good luck."

Time to get out of there. I bent down and lifted the strap of my bag.

"What are you doing, Sam?" Niall cocked his head. "This is your category."

"Looks like the chicken didn't agree with Bilbo Baggins. I'm going to run him outside."

"You can't go now. Leave him with me. I'll take care of him as soon as they announce the winner."

"It might be"—I grimaced—"messy. I'll go." I stood and tiptoed on aching feet toward the exit. *No worries, Mr. Wall. I'll see myself out.* Why had they seated us at the front?

I was halfway to the exit when the chatter in the ballroom dipped to an anticipatory hush. "The Best First Book award goes to"—the presenter broke the seal on the paper—"*Magician in the Machine* by Sam Case."

My muscles turned to putty. *No no no no no.*

Niall's face ducked into my line of sight. "Congratulations! I knew you'd win." He wrapped me up in his arms, and I never wanted to leave that pine-scented cocoon. "Let's get you onstage. Bilbo can wait five minutes."

The applause squeezed my eardrums and tunneled my vision. I leaned into him, shaking. How long until Heidi heard? Dr. Martell? How long did I have until they revealed the truth?

"I've got you." Niall tucked my hand inside the crook of his elbow and threaded through the other tables, all the way to the stairs leading up to the stage. I couldn't feel my fingers on the strap of my bag.

"You can do this," Niall said. "Same as the book talks we did."

I couldn't climb the stairs, much less speak in front of three hundred people.

The sooner I get up there, the sooner I can leave.

I pulled my hand out of the protection of Niall's elbow and put one spindly shoe on the lowest step. Then the other. At the top, the distance to the podium stretched into one of those mirrored hallways in a funhouse. I lurched toward it.

The presenter smiled and held out the glass trophy. "It's all right, dear. Just hold on to the podium, say, 'Thank you,' and get off. We all hate giving speeches. Almost as much as we hate listening to them."

I nodded. Something was already in my hand, and I set it on the stage to accept the heavy trophy.

Hugging that slippery glass statuette that poked me in the boob, I was powerless when my bag tipped over and Bilbo Baggins skittered across the stage, almost as desperate as I was to escape the heat of the spotlight.

I hefted the trophy onto the podium, but the damn thing slid down, down, down the slanted surface. People at the table closest to the front gasped.

I caught it just before it crashed to the floor. The sharp part at the top, one of the planet's rings, sliced into my thumb. Leaving the trophy still wobbling on the stage, I took a step toward the other side, following Bilbo Baggins. Just behind the curtain, the Wall scooped up Bilbo Baggins in one hand and held him by the scruff like a kitten. Narrowing his eyes, he nodded at me. *Finish your speech. I'll deal with you after.*

Shit. I sucked the blood off my thumb.

The part of the audience close enough to witness what had happened laughed. Whispers rippled toward the back of the room.

So much for a quiet exit.

My hands and feet had gone numb, and my blood had turned to freon, chilling me from the inside. Shuffling around the menacing trophy, I stepped to the podium. I gripped the edges with both hands and stared out over the audience.

I could tell the truth right now. I could leave the prize there, tell them I didn't deserve it. That I'd fooled them all. That I was sorry. It was so late in the game now, Heidi wouldn't bother suing me. When she heard about the win, she'd schedule the announcement.

The low lights glinted off Niall's red hair like a beacon. He grinned at me from the table.

No. I couldn't tell these strangers before I told Niall.

Say thank you and get off.

I leaned toward the microphone. "Thank you."

I bent and picked up my now-empty bag. Threading it over my shoulder, I hefted the trophy and walked back the way I'd come. The Wall met me behind the curtain. I shoved the trophy at him, and he gripped it as easily as I'd have grasped a glass of water. He held out Bilbo Baggins, and I cuddled him to my chest.

A bald man beckoned to me from offstage. I couldn't feel my feet. Or my face. Only the pounding of my pulse in my ears. *You lie, you lie, you lie.*

The man guided me to a chair in a quiet corner. "We'll take a photo later when you have more color in your face. Do you need anything? Some water? A glass of brandy?"

I held Bilbo Baggins, not caring about the fur that'd stick to my sweaty chest. My bag buzzed. And buzzed. And buzzed.

Say thank you and get off.

"No, thank you." I scanned the walls for an exit sign.

"I'll come back in a few minutes," he said.

When he left, I reached for the bag and pulled out my phone. Text after text lit up the screen. Most of them were from Qiana. Lots of congratulations. Some champagne emoticons.

Then one popped up from Heidi. I opened it.

Congratulations, Sam. I think we've achieved what we set out to do. Thanks for all you've done for Happy Troll.

I gripped the phone until the plastic case dug a furrow into my palm. That was it. The signal. I stood.

Niall bounded from the stage, gripping an even bigger glass trophy. "Sam! Are you all right? I thought you'd come back to the table. I won!" He ran his hand through his hair, mussing its formal style. "I'm sorry."

The vise around my heart eased. One good thing had happened that night. "No! Don't be sorry. I'm happy for you. You deserved it."

"Mr. Flynn." The bald man was back. "Let's get you to the photographers."

"No photos," Niall snapped. Then he blinked. "Sorry, habit. I'll be right there."

He kissed my forehead. "I'll just be a minute. Stay here. We should talk. And celebrate. You'll delay your flight, right?"

I couldn't delay. Not one minute. I had to get out of there to stop Heidi from breaking the news. She had an award-winning book. Two. So what if an A.I. had written one of them? The world didn't have to know. Martell and I could bury it in a paper in an obscure scientific journal. He'd get his accolades from the scientific community, and we'd stay off the front page of the Technology section. I'd stay off Page Six.

Still, I nodded. What was one more lie, piled on top of the mountain of them?

With a last, searching look, Niall headed off toward the cameras and lights.

My phone vibrated, and I looked down at it automatically. A news alert on my name.

Science Fiction Becomes Reality: Award-winning Book 'Magician in the Machine' Written by Artificial Intelligence.

My heart stopped. I had to try three times to get my trembling fingers to scroll to read the story.

Science fiction and fantasy publisher Happy Troll announced today that last fall's release, Magician in the Machine, *was not written by author Sam Case but was created by the artificial intelligence program CASE, designed by computer science professor Dr. John Martell and graduate student Samantha Renée Jones.*

I swiped away the story. I was too late.

I had to go.

My knees wobbly, I turned toward the nearest exit sign. Home. I'd go back to my apartment and figure out what to do next. How to bury the news about CASE while salvaging the rest of my life. Because this life—the lying, the public speaking—was over.

No relief lifted my heart. It was heavy, anchoring me to the floor backstage. Still, I had to leave. I couldn't tarnish the celebration of art with my presence. I didn't deserve Niall. I didn't deserve any of them.

Clutching Bilbo Baggins, I pushed out the stage door into the alley behind the hotel. The door shut with a clank, isolating me with the pungent smell of cooked garbage from a nearby dumpster. I turned left toward the street and its waiting line of taxis.

But when I reached the sidewalk, I found a line of people. The show at the casino next door must've ended because a mass of people with wigs of every imaginable variety—sparkly ones, feathered ones, curly ones, rainbow ones—clumped together, jostling over the cabs.

In the movies, the tearful heroine always ran right into a car. She didn't have to wait behind a group of stunning older ladies in sandals and beaded silver wigs. At least in this crowd, no one would ever spot me.

"Sam!" A familiar voice rose over the ladies' voices and clacking beads. Niall pushed through the crowd. A few formally dressed people, one with a video camera on his shoulder, followed him.

"You forgot your prize." Niall held out the glass trophy.

A bright light blinded me. The red LED of the video camera flashed on.

"Niall Flynn, a few words for *Fantasy Weekly* about your Tower

Prize win?" A black-gowned woman held out her phone. The silver wigs turned to stare.

"Just a second," Niall said. "Sam, where are you—Are you leaving?"

"Sam!" A dark-haired woman in a red dress held up her phone to snap a picture or video. "Kari Singh from *Gossip Grrlz*. Is it true? Did artificial intelligence write *Magician in the Machine?*"

I opened my mouth, but no words escaped my closed-up throat. I scanned Niall for the last time, saving his image in my memory. I'd pull it up again someday when it didn't hurt so much. Bilbo Baggins yipped inside my bag.

The blogger turned to Niall. "Niall, how do you feel about a book written by artificial intelligence?"

35

NIALL

The camera lights flashed in my eyes, capturing my perfectly meme-worthy bewildered expression. I'd been running after Sam all night, and now I'd caught up, suffocating in my monkey suit in the sweltering Nevada heat, I still lagged whatever was going on.

And I knew this person. Kari-something. She'd moved up from Sam's university to a big gossip site. She stuck her phone in my face. "It's been revealed that *Magician in the Machine* was written by a computer program. A program your girlfriend created. How does that make you feel?"

Sam seemed to shrink. All but her eyes, which had widened, the black overtaking the violet of her irises. A woman in a beaded silver wig clutched her elbow.

"I—what?" I turned to Kari. If Sam wouldn't tell me what was going on, maybe the blogger could explain.

"Dr. John Martell, a research scientist and university professor, says he and Samantha Jones created an artificial intelligence called CASE. And it wrote *Magician in the Machine*, not Sam Case. Niall, can you confirm you and Sam are dating? Do you support what your girlfriend did?"

Of course I knew Sam was a grad student in computer science, but how had a computer written *Magician?* It couldn't be true. I glanced at Sam, still frozen in place. Everything about her, from her averted gaze to the sweat that sheened her temple to her stillness, shouted *guilty*.

"Sam, is it true?" My voice was low and urgent, pleading with her to deny it.

All around us, the reporters went silent. The only sounds were the clicks of the camera shutters and the tinkle of silver beads.

Biting her lip, Sam nodded. Another wigged woman pushed in closer to Sam.

"How?"

She stared at my bow tie. "Can't we talk about this later?"

"No." She could've told me at any point over the past two months. But she hadn't.

And now she'd brought this—all these strangers—into it. Timing the announcement just as I'd won the prize I'd coveted. Just as I'd felt as if I could do anything, including winning the woman I loved.

What other proof did I need? She didn't care. She didn't love me.

My heart ossified until it was a lump of stone, smooth and unbreakable, pressing against my lungs with each breath. Cold emanated from it until even the tips of my fingers lost their warmth in the hot desert air. The glass trophy slipped in my grip. She didn't care about it, either. She scorned books, my vocation, which I'd loved before Sam.

Let it play out in public, then, like a real-life soap opera.

"How—how did you do it?"

Her gaze stuck to my bow tie. "The algorithm—CASE—used fantasy books as input. From processing those stories, it taught itself how to construct its own. It has applications to—"

"Fantasy books?" So this was what it felt like to be stabbed in the heart. "Which books?" My voice came out rough through the lump in my throat. My stomach roiled.

"All the greats—Tolkien, Butler, L'Engle"—she finally met my gaze—"and you."

The reporters started shouting, but we were in a glass dome that muffled everything outside.

Chills ran over my skin despite the Las Vegas heat. "You stole my work. Corrupted it with technology."

"I was going to tell you—"

"You lied to me—to everyone. I believed you." My voice cracked on the last sentence. Surely I'd dreamed the whole thing, from the joy of winning the prize to the nightmare playing out on the street.

"I'm sorry." She whispered too soft to hear over the crowd, but I read the words on her lips.

"Niall"—Kari Singh again—"what does your father think about A.I.-written novels?"

It was exactly the sort of thing he'd support. "I don't give a fuck," I snarled. What I cared about was how the woman I loved had snapped me in two.

I nodded at the taxi behind her. "You're leaving?"

"I think I should."

I should have known she'd leave. When things got complicated, there were two types of people. People who left—like my father—and people like Grandpa who stayed to fix things. Now I knew which type Sam was.

One of the bead-wig women scowled at me while another opened the taxi door for Sam. A third guided her inside and shut the door. Their arms crossed, the silver-wigged women formed a sparkling barrier between the taxi and the reporters and me.

I didn't stay to watch the taxi pull away. I turned on the toe of my shiny dress shoe, and, shoving through the crowd that had gathered to witness the spectacle, stalked back toward the hotel. I paused only to toss Sam's trophy into the trash.

———

I SHOVED a pillow over my face to drown out the jangling sound. My teeth buzzed.

When it didn't stop, I pushed off the pillow. I rubbed the crust from my eyes and blinked to clear them. My phone flashed and chimed at the side of the hotel bed. The one I'd fallen onto, still wearing my tuxedo pants and shoes.

I stretched out my arm to grab the phone and squinted at it with one bleary eye. Gabi. I'd ignored her calls and texts last night —everyone's, actually. I hadn't even spoken to the bartender except to tell him I was a hotel guest, I wouldn't try to drive, and to keep the whiskey coming.

"Hello?" My throat was sandpaper.

Gabi's staccato accent stabbed my eardrum. "I'm in the lobby. Tell me your room number."

"What?" Gabi was in Brooklyn, typing up my latest pages.

"Room number."

As soon as I gave it to her, the line went silent.

Wincing, I sat up. I lumbered to the bathroom, keeping my head as steady as possible to avoid further trauma to my brain full of knives.

When Gabi knocked—too loud—I opened the door, still clutching the hand towel.

"Why are you here?"

She ignored my question and pushed past me into the room. I closed the door and leaned against its cool, hard surface.

She propped a hip on the desk. "Damage control. Plus, you didn't answer your phone last night. I wanted to make sure you hadn't done anything stupid."

"Is drinking two hundred dollars' worth of whiskey stupid?"

She glanced toward the bed. "At least you didn't bring anything back with you."

I closed my eyes to block out the unopened bottle of champagne floating in lukewarm water in the ice bucket.

"I got an email from the university's lawyers on the way here." Gabi's eyes glittered. "Apparently, they were colluding with Happy Troll on this. Sam was just a front. They're offering a share of the book's royalties. In exchange for the 'borrowing' they did."

My stomach turned over. "I don't want it. I don't want anything to do with—with that."

So what if Sam was just the face the university and Heidi had used to sell the book? That face had lied to me every day for the last two months.

I wouldn't take the fucking money. Not after Sam and her professor had spat on my art, my vocation. Not even to save the farm. "Find some charity to give it to. But not the Jones Foundation."

"I thought you'd say that." She pushed off the desk and strolled over to the table. She sniffed at the bouquet of crimson roses, still fresh-looking in their vase. "We could sue them."

Vindication. I twisted the towel until the fabric strained and popped. The way Sam would squirm on the witness stand when she confessed to theft of my work.

But then I'd have to see her again. The lawyers would try to settle. They'd make me meet her across a conference table. I imagined the dramatic way I'd sit, fists clenched, face stony, while the lawyers offered deal after deal. Sam would cringe and cower.

Fuck, I didn't want that.

Even my fertile imagination couldn't dream up a scenario where I didn't crumple at her feet and forgive her. Because, despite her betrayal—goddamn foolish heart—I still loved her.

"No. No lawsuit. But after this book, we're done with Happy Troll."

"Yeah, yeah. After this win, you can write your own ticket." Uncharacteristically, she dropped her gaze to the floor. "I also got a call from your—from Paul."

"About the fucking A.I.? Of course he'll be interested in that. He'll find some way to monetize it. And I fucking hate that the word *monetize* just came out of my mouth. This—"

"He called to congratulate you on your win. He wants to see you."

"Oh." I dropped into the armchair. I reached inside myself for a reaction. Any reaction. But I was empty. It was what I'd wanted all my life: recognition from my father. I toed the Tower Prize where it stuck out from under my tux jacket.

"Do you want me to set something up?" she asked.

"No. Thanks." I didn't need his approval anymore.

Gabi stooped to pick up my tuxedo jacket from the floor, uncovering the glass trophy. She laid the jacket over the back of the desk chair and then traced her fingers over my engraved name and book title. She set it gently on the desk where it caught the light from the window and scattered rainbows across the room.

Her voice was gentle. "Congratulations, by the way."

"Thanks." The scent of the roses crawled up my nose and slid into my turbulent stomach. I jumped up and crossed to the bed, where I flopped back and covered my face with my hands. "Everything is so fucked up. I'm supposed to be on top of the world today. I got the validation I've been looking for. But it all feels so...hollow."

"Oh, honey." The bed dipped, and Gabi rubbed circles on my shoulder. "You should be proud. You worked hard for this. Sure, Sam was a phony. But that shouldn't diminish this win for you. Hydrate and pop some aspirin. Then we'll get you cleaned up and go out on the town, show them you're Niall-Fucking-Flynn, Tower Prize winner, and that bitch hasn't brought you down."

"But she has." Ignoring my pounding head, I levered up and strode to the window. I forced myself to stare out at the blinding Nevada sunlight, ratcheting my headache up to DEFCON 1.

"She destroyed me. I thought—I thought she cared about me." Before the shit hit the fan last night, I'd thought she might've loved me, if she'd only admit it. But I couldn't confess how stupid I'd been, even to my best friend. "She—she used me to build her own credibility. And that fucking computer's. I never should've trusted her." Certainly not with my heart.

"When I get back to the farm, I'm going to rip out the wifi. And you can keep that." I waved to the phone on the bed. The one I'd used to message Sam. I'd take the most pleasure in smashing my new laptop with a sledgehammer.

"I'll figure out some way to write without her. Back at the farm—"

"Niall." Gabi's voice was soft. "You can't go home. Not even to find your muse again. Certainly not to lick your wounds. You have to take advantage of this win. You're going back out on tour."

"But—but I—"

Her voice was steel again. "You know I'm right."

I did. I had to ride the wave of my success. The prize win would boost my sales, and schmoozing with readers would lift them further. With that and the prize money, I could afford to hire more help for Grandpa.

"Qiana's setting it up now," she said. "You should be ready to go in a few days."

"But what about the third book? You told me I need to rewrite the end." Did I even remember how to write without Sam? I turned my back to the window and its blinding sunshine.

One side of her mouth kicked up. "You do. It didn't resolve anything. But you'll only write crap while you feel like this. Remember all that shitty poetry you wrote after we broke up?"

"To be fair, all of my poetry is shit."

She shrugged. "In the last pages you sent me, Nieven's love song to Lobelia wasn't so bad."

"Thanks, I guess." I'd written that the night after Sam and I made love in the hayloft, after she sneaked off to her room. I'd ridden a wave of endorphins and inspiration to write into the early hours.

Now I'd have to find inspiration somewhere else. Gabi was right. Again. Feeling like I did then, I'd probably kill off Lobelia with a crossbow bolt to the chest. The readers would choke on it. Heidi would make me rewrite the whole thing.

"So. The tour?" Gabi stared me down.

I'd show the world what a real writer did. "The longer, the better."

36

SAM

THE MORNING after the prize ceremony, I stumbled, drunk with exhaustion, to the university. The expression on Niall's face just before those nice women pushed me into the cab had haunted me all night.

I'd hurt him. Qiana, too. I had to make it right. I could make Dr. Martell understand that.

I knocked before I opened the door to his corner office.

"Samantha." He stood, arms out, welcoming me like a hero returning from war.

I hung back near the door. There was an extra guest chair. And two of the chairs were occupied. But neither of the guests was Heidi. For a heart-stopping second, the man's broad shoulders and auburn hair made me think it was Niall. But this man's hair was pulled back into a low ponytail, and the hands that rested on his knees were smooth, not callused. Paul Swift turned his deep green eyes on me and gave me a slow smile.

Then I saw the last person I'd ever expected to see in Martell's office.

"Mother?"

The corners of her mouth tightened in a not-smile. "Samantha."

Shit. If I was having a hallucination, it was auditory, too.

"What are you—"

"Samantha, sit down." Martell gestured at the empty chair.

I dragged myself over and flopped into it.

"Samantha!" Mother snapped.

Automatically, I straightened my spine and folded my hands in my lap. I crossed my combat boots at the ankles.

I scanned Dr. Martell's face for a clue. "What's—"

"Samantha." He spread his hands wide. "The first literary prize earned by output of an A.I. What an achievement."

I had to stop him. Convince him to stop using CASE to hurt humans, people I cared about. "But that's—"

Martell continued as if I hadn't spoken, "I received many calls after last night's announcement, but Mr. Swift's was the most intriguing."

Paul Swift let out a bark of laughter. "I'm sure you mean the most lucrative." He turned to me, but I couldn't look at his face, so similar to Niall's and yet so much more austere. Even his smile was flinty. "I hate to admit it, but you fooled even me. When I read *Magician*, I thought someone had ghostwritten it. I had no idea it was A.I. And then, when I heard the announcement, it clicked into place. And I knew I had to have CASE."

"But—but why?" I asked. Paul Swift had made his fortune in well designed, flashy phone hardware for wealthy people and early adopters who used tech as a status symbol. Not low-tech readers like I'd met on tour.

"Did you know that 30 percent of people who have access to the internet—internationally—read books daily? Of course, that's much lower than the percentage of people who play games every day, but the gaming market is saturated. Reading, on the other hand, is virtually untapped. We're going to gamify reading. Through this." And he held up his Swiftphone.

"Gamify reading?" Was he talking about making videogames

based on books? Because that was hardly revolutionary. Even I'd had that idea, and I was no business mastermind like Paul Swift.

"With CASE, we'll have an unlimited supply of stories, customized to the user's preferences. Sci-fi, horror, thrillers, romance, mystery, whatever they want. I think, with time, we could customize it even further. Favorite types of characters or plotlines. Delivered to their devices as a serial. People will earn points and badges for reading." His eyes weren't the color of moss on a stone. They were the color of money.

"But there are thousands—millions—of authors," I said. "Your son is one of them. Couldn't you just deliver their books? Why do you need CASE?"

He waved a hand. "After the initial R&D, the long-term output and margins will be better with CASE."

Dr. Martell leaned forward. "We've proved creativity isn't a uniquely human characteristic. Sure, we've seen A.I.-generated music and visual art. But literature—people laughed at the early trials. Now we've shown its feasibility. That's an impressive accomplishment, Samantha."

I'd sat in this same chair, months ago, excited about the possibilities of CASE. But I wasn't excited now. A cold, hard ball of dread sat in my stomach. Back then, I hadn't known any writers. I hadn't given a thought to how CASE might affect them.

Martell continued, "With funding from SwifTech, we'll be able to bring on additional team members to scale up CASE quickly and to produce the type of results Paul is seeking. With multiple instances of CASE running, imagine the output. The cost savings over the traditional publishing model. The reductions in employee salaries and royalties will easily offset the cost of a CASE installation. All Paul needs is another demo to fully commit."

"And that's why I'm here," Mother said. "To protect Samantha's interests."

"My interests?" The only thing I was interested in was stopping what Paul Swift wanted to do.

"That publisher took advantage of you, Samantha. Even John did." She looked down her nose at him.

My adviser cringed. "Now, Audrey—"

"You knew about Sam's"—she flicked her eyes to Paul Swift—"struggles. And yet you asked her to sign a contract. Without consulting me or my legal team. And then you sent her off with that—that—farmer."

I untwisted my ankles and stood. "Farmers grow food for the rest of us. And Niall Flynn is the most upstanding, honest, noble person I've ever met. I love him." Though it seemed cowardly to admit it only after he was gone from my life.

"No, Samantha, you can't possibly. A writer. From the"—she pursed her lips like the word tasted bad—"Midwest. I know he's your son, Paul, but really."

Paul shrugged.

Farming and art were two things I hadn't thought about before the book tour. Now I saw the value in both. I wished Niall was there to use his words, so much better than mine, to fight the battle.

Novels written by CASE wouldn't need editors. Formatters. Expensive book tours. Publicists like Qiana. And why pay a writer like Niall when they'd already sunk costs into CASE and could get a hundred times his annual output, even if it wasn't a quarter as good? Anyone could do the math and find CASE's financials appealing. But at what cost to human creativity?

I swallowed. I couldn't do this to Niall. To Qiana. To all the people who'd toasted Niall and me with champagne in the Happy Troll offices six weeks ago.

I turned to Paul. "Niall is a writer. Don't you worry about him? About his livelihood?"

"Technology is advancing human civilization faster now than in any other period in history. If Niall can't get on board with it…" He shrugged.

"Samantha," Martell said gently, the way he'd speak to a small child, "CASE will create new jobs. Installers, programmers, maintenance workers, quality checkers. Some of the redundant workers can be retrained for these roles." He shrugged. "They said the same thing when computers came on the scene. Typists became data entry specialists. Time marches on. You, of all people, should understand that."

Paul said, "Don't you agree, Audrey?"

She'd married two men who loved books. She supported a literacy foundation. My mother had to see the situation the way I did. My hope must have shown on my face.

She blinked. "I do. Samantha, this is your creation. It could make you a very wealthy woman. I can't believe you'd consider throwing it away."

"Some things are more important than money." I lifted my chin. Niall and Qiana and all the people who'd supported me were more important than my personal comfort. Than even my future. "No."

All three of them stared at me. Martell said, "What do you mean, 'no'?"

I sucked in a breath. I missed the bookstores, their smell of fresh paper and old leather and furniture polish. My adviser's office held only a faint electrical scent, overlaid by my mother's lavender perfume. He didn't have a single book in his office.

"I won't do it. I won't work on CASE."

"Samantha, don't be ridiculous." Mother gripped the chair's armrests, her knuckles white.

Dr. Martell studied me. "Are you sure? This seems unusually rash. Consider the implications. I can't approve your dissertation without further development. Plus"—he clicked the mouse and then tapped out a series of keystrokes—"plenty of other graduate students can take this work and finish what you started."

"I have to agree," Paul said. "SwifTech's developers can't wait to get their hands on this. While I'd much prefer to have your expertise on the project, it's not necessary."

A knock came at the door, and Kyle, my officemate, popped his head in. "You needed to see me, Dr. Martell?"

Martell raised his fingers from his keyboard and stared at me. His glasses reduced his irises to ball bearings. "Do we need Kyle's assistance?"

I sank into the chair. "No. I'll do it." I didn't have to do it fast. Or well. I'd drag out the work until I could figure a way out of this mess.

"We'll review your first iteration next Friday."

Ten days from today. Well, shit.

"Good girl," Mother said. "And William Winford has been calling. I've invited him to brunch on Sunday."

"No." The word rang out like a shot in Martell's office. "I'll do this thing for him"—I nodded at my adviser—"because I have to. But I'm not meeting anyone. And I'm not coming to brunch." Somehow, I stood, despite the disappointment that weighed me down. "Not if you don't support me and what I want."

I strode to the door and put my hand on the doorknob. "Good-bye, Mother. Dr. Martell, Mr. Swift, I'll have something next Friday."

I had no idea what that something might be.

37

SAM

"DOING ALL RIGHT, SAM?"

Kyle's voice startled me out of my zombie gaze. I whipped my head to face him at his desk. Was he trying to look at my screen, or was I being paranoid? Probably paranoia, considering I'd hardly slept for the past nine nights; still, I swiveled my screen a degree or two away from him.

"Fine. Just tired, you know?" I tried to smile at him, but I couldn't feel my face. Every part of me was numb.

"CASE, right? How are those modifications going? Need any help?"

That woke me up. "No, I'm fine." Maybe he *was* spying on me. Had Martell asked him to keep an eye on me? My heart raced. Or Paul Swift? Was Kyle wearing a new pair of sneakers? Air Jordans? I sniffed. It was hard to tell over the smell of rotted baseboards and rusty metal desks, but I thought I caught the scent of new leather. I turned my screen a little more.

"Okay." He ducked his head. "I know it's a lot of pressure."

He didn't know the half of it. As furiously as I'd coded to get CASE 2.0 online, I couldn't squeeze six months of work into ten days. Martell would be livid when I had no new novels to show Paul Swift at the demo the next day. Plus, CASE 2.0 still couldn't reliably create scientific papers.

I couldn't let Paul Swift—or anyone—get their hands on CASE 1.0. Not if I wanted people like Niall and Qiana and even Heidi to keep their jobs, to keep making stories that people—kids like Hero in Chicago and those teenagers at the con in Florida who'd cosplayed Nieven and Greva—loved. Hell, books that I loved.

What if Martell followed through with his threat? I shuddered. With no Ph.D., my postdoc was vaporware. I'd have to move back home with Mother and Charles. She'd keep throwing Winfords at me. And what was worse, Kyle or the SwifTech programmers would pick up CASE 1.0 right where I'd left off.

My plan sucked, and I knew it. But there was nothing else to do. I laid my spinning head on my desk. I'd rest just for a minute, and then I'd start again.

"Sam!"

I lifted my head from my keyboard and blinked. Jackson stood in the doorway.

Jackson had never come to my office before. I rubbed my eyes. Nope, not a hallucination.

"Nice look, Samwise. I especially like the keyboard print on your cheek. You've got a little drool, right there." He pointed at the corner of his mouth, just inside the edge of his beard.

With the back of my hand, I swiped at the moisture.

"Jackson Jones?" Kyle's chair scraped back, and he bounded forward, his hand outstretched.

Jackson shook it. "That's me. You must be Kyle."

"Yeah. Kyle Anderson. Sam's officemate. It's…it's an honor to meet you at last." Kyle pumped Jackson's hand up and down.

One side of Jackson's mouth kicked up in a half-smile as he gingerly removed his hand from Kyle's. Thank God I'd never mentioned our one-night fling.

"Come on, Sam," Jackson said. "We're going to lunch."

"Lunch?"

"You know, food you eat at midday? Though it looks like you haven't had many lunches lately. Let's go, Sam. See you around, Kyle."

In the hallway, I asked, "What are you doing here?"

"I came to check on you. You didn't answer my calls or texts. Mother said you told her off?"

I jogged to keep up with his long strides. "I—yeah," I mumbled.

"Good for you. By the way, you look like shit."

"Thanks. Jerk."

"It's true. And you and I are always honest with each other."

Ouch. That one hit right between the ribs.

While we walked across campus—Jackson had a sixth sense for food trucks—I told him everything. I started with Heidi and Martell's offer, Heidi's ultimatum about the book tour. I continued through the fiasco at the prize ceremony and Martell's threat. Mom's betrayal. I'd just told him about the meeting with Paul Swift scheduled for the following day and my desperate plan to appease Martell with CASE 2.0 when we reached the tamale truck parked at the far side of campus.

"Fucking Martell," he growled. "What an asshole."

"No, he just—" He'd been a father figure to me since I'd joined the department. But in that meeting, he'd shown me where his true loyalty lay. "Yeah."

I let out a shaky breath. I'd told all the secrets I'd been holding inside for months. All that was left was a desiccated husk of skin and bones. A strong sea breeze would've blown me away like an autumn leaf. "He's got all the power. I can't get my doctorate without him. I'd have to start over somewhere else. And he'd blacklist me anyway. No other department would take me."

We reached the front of the line and placed our orders. Jackson paid, of course. I didn't have the energy—or the funds—to protest.

When the tamales were ready, we took our plates to a bench in the shade.

Jackson picked up his fork. "You still want your Ph.D.?" There was no judgment in his tone. I could've said yes or no, and he'd have given me the same steady encouragement as always.

My heart filled with concrete. "It's my ticket out, you know? I have a postdoc lined up in Idaho. It's the only way I can be free to live my life."

My brother's face crumpled. "When were you going to tell me?"

I stabbed at my tamale. Swallowed past my constricted throat. "I don't know." Probably a text as I took a bus out of town. I'd be a coward in saying my good-byes, just like with everything else in my life. "I'm not like you, Jackson. I'm not strong."

"Coming back from what Stephen did to you and then going on that book tour sounds pretty strong to me. Not to mention the amazing A.I. you created."

I snorted. "The whole novel thing? That was an accident. CASE was supposed to do something else."

He leaned back. "Sometimes the best things happen by accident. You just have to roll with it."

He wasn't talking about CASE anymore. He was talking about his own life, his company, his wife, even perfect baby Valentine was a fucking joyful accident.

But nothing accidentally wonderful had ever happened to me.

Except Niall, and I'd wrecked that. A hollow pit opened inside me, sucking even the tiny pleasure of lunch with my brother into it.

"What I did with CASE disrupted a lot of people's lives. It wasn't the good kind of accident. It was the ruin-things-for-everyone kind of accident. Like my whole fucking life."

"No." Jackson looked me dead in the eye. "You're brilliant. You did things with A.I. no one's ever done before. That book it wrote changed people's lives. Including Noah's. Do you have any idea how hard it is to get a twelve-year-old-boy to read?"

I stared at the antenna on top of the nearest building. "I guess I fooled him, too. Does he hate me now?"

"No, Sam. He sees the real you. A person who cares for people. Who's amazingly talented. Who's strong and independent. Who can"—he swallowed—"make her own decisions. You don't need letters after your name to be qualified to do that, to make a life for yourself. To tell Martell exactly where he can shove his ultimatum."

My chest swelled like I really could be brave enough to tell Martell no. Like I could walk away from the path I'd envisioned for myself since I was a teenager.

I let my gaze wander over the university campus. The buildings I loved. The students—not that I'd let any of them close—lounging in the grass, walking in pairs on the sidewalks. I'd hoped to exchange it for another university, one where no one knew or cared I was a Jones. No preconceptions. No expectations. Just me and whatever I could do with my hands and my brain. Building my own future.

The future I'd planned cracked and fell to pieces around me. I didn't belong there anymore.

"Do you still play video games?"

I blinked at Jackson's change in topic. "Yeah. When I'm not busy coding my ass off. Mostly RPGs."

"Remember how we used to design games when we were younger?"

"Uh-huh." I breathed through a painful wash of memory, of the time Niall and I had played one of our old games on the tour.

"We talked about running a game company together when we grew up."

"You also wanted to be a race car driver. But then you went into business software. Which was totally weak."

He pointed his fork skyward. "Which allowed me to play with race cars. And make a shit-ton of cash."

"Cash is weak, too." I stabbed at my tamale. It wouldn't fit in my belly with all my disappointed hopes.

"Hey, what if we tried it? I could fold you into the company as a skunkworks. A side business on the down-low. We could collaborate on designing games. Cash might be boring, but it's pretty useful for staying out of Mother's house."

I set my plate on the bench. "I—I had an idea. What about games based on books?" The idea had tickled at the back of my brain since I'd listened to Niall's first book and I hadn't wanted to leave the world of the wood elves. I'd even sketched out some ideas about a role-playing game based on the novel.

"Other companies already build games based on books. There's even a few doing those choose-your-own ending immersive books."

"Yes, but with A.I., we could take it to another level. Unscripted. Adaptive. We'd partner with the authors."

Jackson sprang up. He always thought better on his feet. "It's a great idea. License the content. Hire the authors to be story consultants. Maybe reuse some of CASE's code. Wait—you went all sad for a minute there. What's that about?"

I felt like someone had ripped out my spine, leaving me floppy like one of Bilbo Baggins' stuffies. I slumped forward, my elbows on my knees, and buried my face in my hands. One author had supported the idea; now he wanted nothing to do with me. "Niall."

"Do I need to kick his ass?" he growled. "I knew that aw-shucks farmboy shit had to be a ruse."

I raised my head. "No, if anyone needs ass-kicking, it's me. I hurt him, Jackson. I hurt a lot of people."

He leaned back on the bench and gazed out at the sunny university grounds. "Maybe working with authors would soothe your guilty conscience."

"I want to make amends."

He nodded. "That's the spirit. Take action. Once you've got your shit together, you'll be ready to go after this guy, too. Show him he was a tool for letting you go."

Fuck. Just like Mother, he'd seen the pictures from Vegas.

I found my spine again. I filled my lungs with air and let it out in a short burst. "You're right."

"That the carrot top's a tool?"

"No. About taking action." Was I brave enough to stand up to Martell? To everyone who had expectations of me? I could do it if I had help. Being independent didn't mean I had to be alone.

"Of course I'm right. I'm almost always right."

"Jackson. Listen. I need your help. With something that could be just the tiniest bit illegal."

"Yeah? Sounds like your M.O. these days."

"Shut up." I punched his shoulder. "Are you going to help me or not?"

"I'm in. What are we going to blow up?"

Oh, only my whole world.

38

SAM

"MR. JONES! YOU'RE BACK!"

Kyle. It'd be hard to do what I planned with him in our office.

This wasn't Jackson's first rodeo. "Kyle, come chat with me in the hall so we don't disturb Sam's work."

Kyle zoomed past me in a flash of new-leather scent. My ancient chair creaked when I settled into it. I was going to miss that chair.

I muted my laptop's speakers—I couldn't let Kyle hear what I was doing—and typed, *Begin goodbye routine.*

Confirming. Are you sure?

Was I sure? I was throwing away three years' worth of work. Countless nights in the office with Kyle, guzzling coffee to fuel my flying fingers. Days when I didn't see Bilbo Baggins except in the morning when I woke up and in the evening when I scurried home to walk and feed him before rushing back to campus. I'd spent my last birthday there, chasing down a bug.

Not to mention all those people who'd loved *Magician in the Machine*. Who'd come to me during book signings and said it distracted them after their wife left them, while their grandmother was in the hospital, when they had a bad day at work. Shutting down CASE would take that away from them.

But letting Paul Swift have CASE meant that books written by CASE—and, let's face it, other A.I.s to come—would be cheaper, faster. They'd squeeze out books written by people like Niall. His books had touched many people. Including me.

It was time to act like Lobelia.

Courage.

My finger didn't waver. Much. I hit the Yes button.

A progress bar appeared on the screen.

The door opened, sending my heart into my throat, but it was Jackson. He closed the door. "I sent Kyle off to get us coffee at the place on the other side of campus."

"Must be nice to be a programming legend, inspiring adulation from everyone." I opened my desk drawer, but all it contained was a few pencils and a copy of *Magician in the Machine*. I closed the drawer.

"Adulation or not, Ph.D. or not, you're a good programmer. And you're a good person. You'll land on your feet after this."

"Mother doesn't think so."

"She knows only one way for women to make their way in the world. You'll show her there's a different path." Jackson leaned over my shoulder to check the progress bar. "That's fast. It must've been a beautiful program."

"It was. CASE was my baby." An unruly, disobedient one. But mine all the same. I sniffed.

"Ah, Samwise. I'm sorry."

I touched the progress bar with one finger as it counted down CASE's final minutes. "Thanks for being here with me. You're sure you don't need to go back to work?"

"Nah. Marlee will cover for me. Family is more important."

I grimaced. "I'll try to be a better sister. Especially now that—" My throat closed, but I waved at the office. Sure, it was tiny, but it'd symbolized my independence.

"If you want to stay with us for a while until you figure things out, you're welcome."

When he found out what I'd done, Martell would cut off my funding, and I wouldn't be able to pay rent. Staying with Jackson would be better than moving back home with Mother and Charles. I tried to smile. "Thanks. Just for a few weeks, until I've saved up an apartment deposit."

"Smart negotiation tactic. Unless I pay you well, I'm stuck with another person under my roof." He groaned. "And a dog."

This time, my mouth curved all the way up. "I am Mother's daughter."

"That you are." He lifted his chin toward my laptop. "How're we doing?"

The progress bar disappeared, replaced by the button to delete the files. Permanently. "Almost done."

He leaned down and peered at the screen. "Your destruction routine has a fancy button? You must've been thinking about this for a while."

I looked away. "Just—I can't. Do it for me."

"On it." His big hand covered the mouse, and the click echoed through my small office, pricking my heart.

After I blinked away the tears, I glanced back at the screen.

CASE was gone. Three years of work disappeared into the ether.

"May it rest in peace," Jackson said. Thirty seconds of solemn silence ticked by as I remembered the long nights filled with the clicks of my keyboard, the moments of buzzy discovery, the elation of scanning a perfect bit of code.

He cleared his throat. "I imagine there are some backup tapes we need to dispose of?"

"Shit. You're right." Someone could take those backups and

resurrect CASE, same as when a freak power surge two summers ago had taken down its main server. I'd spent four hours flipping out until the IT guys had restored it from the backup.

Avoiding Martell's office, I led my brother downstairs to the basement. Jackson turned his face from the camera as I swiped my ID at the entrance to the server room.

The servers' fans roared louder than the surf at the beach during a storm. The sound was familiar, almost soothing.

"Fortunately," I shouted over the noise, "grad students' work doesn't merit offsite storage. The tapes are stored here."

Shelves full of tapes filled one wall of a small back room. Since that power surge, I knew what to look for.

"Here they are." I held up the two plastic tape enclosures with my student ID number written on them in Sharpie. The backup and its backup. "Do I take them home and burn them?"

"Take them home." Jackson snorted. "And add theft to the destruction of university property charges? No, these die here. If all goes well, it'll look like the backups disappeared by mistake.

"That is"—he stared deep into my eyes—"if you're sure you want to do this? Throw away years of your work? We could take one of these copies. In case you ever wanted to pick it up again."

It was tempting. CASE represented so much work. And I could turn parts of it into the new games Jackson and I would build together. But would I be tempted to use it all and make CASE 1.1? And what if someone found it and made their own version of CASE? Someone who hadn't learned the lessons I had?

"I learned a lot about creativity, about storytelling, on the book tour. CASE will ruin the things I love. It's better this way." Tears blurred my vision.

"Computer science is creative, too."

"I know. But it's not the same as art. And there's room in the world for both without one destroying the other."

Jackson squeezed my shoulder. "I'm sorry you had to learn that the hard way."

I sniffled.

"Do you have a degausser?" He flipped the tape cartridge over in his hands.

"A what?"

Jackson rolled his eyes. "It uses a big magnet to erase data. If you had one, it'd probably be in this room. I bet you guys have been reusing these tapes since the dawn of time. I'm doing the university a favor by taking these two out of circulation. Find me a screwdriver, a drill, and some wire."

A screwdriver lay on the desk nearby, and I handed it to him. He set to work on the tape cases. By the time I'd returned from fluttering my eyelashes at the maintenance guy to secure the drill, a coil of wire, and some wire cutters, he had the cartridges open, exposing the tape bobbins.

I winced when Jackson started up the drill to make a hole in the back side of the tape case, right in the middle of the bobbin. The roar of the servers' fans masked the noise. Mostly. I hoped no one came to investigate. An unauthorized guest destroying the university's property would be difficult to explain.

Jackson stepped onto a chair and used the wire to hang one tape cartridge from a vent in the ceiling. With a flick of his wrist, he sent the plastic tape spooling down toward the floor. I grabbed the end and yanked until gravity had done enough work to keep the tape flowing. We repeated the process with the other cartridge on another vent, and soon two fluffy piles of plastic ribbon mounded on the floor.

"Now we wait," he said. "Where are the shredders?"

"There's one in the mail room on each of the main floors."

"People are going to ask questions if we're walking around with a bale of tape. You have a backpack or computer bag?"

"Upstairs."

"Go get it."

When I emerged from the stairwell, my racing heart skipped a beat. Martell stood in the doorway of my office, hands on his hips. There was no way to sneak past him to get the bags. I'd have to play it cool.

Taking a deep breath, I walked up behind my adviser, shuffling my combat boots so he'd hear me.

"Good afternoon, Dr. Martell. Excuse me." I squeezed past him into the office and went to my desk.

"Samantha, I was looking for you. Is everything ready for the presentation tomorrow?"

"I sent you the deck this morning." It had been full of lies about the stories CASE had produced. Keeping my head down, I opened a drawer. It'd all be over soon.

"It looked good. I know you don't like public speaking, so I'll drive the presentation and the demo. I need you to be prepared to answer any technical questions. Are you ready?"

I glanced up at him quickly as I pulled out a tote bag from a conference I'd attended. I could've told him there'd be nothing to demo. But I wasn't a hundred percent confident he couldn't find a grad student to wind the tape back into its bobbin and restore CASE. Besides, being caught red-handed, and with Jackson, who wasn't supposed to be in the server room, wouldn't be good. I'd send him an email later. Cowardly, but it'd get the job done.

"Sure, I'm ready." Ready to get out of there.

He frowned. "What are you doing with that bag?"

It did look odd to walk out holding an empty bag. I scanned the office for something to stuff into it. A shriveled apple sat on the corner of Kyle's desk. I grabbed it and dropped it into the bag.

Martell frowned. "You're not going to eat that, are you?"

"No." I blinked. *Come on, neurons, don't fail me now.* "My dog likes them this way. Wouldn't want it to go to waste."

He wrinkled his nose like he could smell the rotten apple. Quickly, I unplugged my laptop and slid it into my other bag. "Good-night."

"You don't usually leave so early."

I should've been used to lying by now. "I, uh, want to get a good night's rest. You know, before the big presentation." My heart pounding, I slipped past him into the hallway.

"Did I see your brother's car in the lot?"

Damn, damn, damn Jackson and his fancy car. "No, must've been someone else."

"What are the odds? I don't know of anyone at the university who drives a yellow Lamborghini."

"Hmm. Could be a loaner, I guess. See you tomorrow, Dr. Martell." Tossing my hand in a half-wave, I speed-walked to the exit. I yanked open the door and raced downstairs.

In the tape room, the cartridges continued to spool from the ceiling. Jackson leaned on the desk, fiddling with his phone.

I tugged on a strand of tape. "We need to go faster. I ran into Martell upstairs."

Jackson pocketed his phone and pulled on the other tape. "He suspects?"

"Didn't help that you drove your look-at-me-yellow car and parked it outside. I thought you gave up on the sportscars when little Valentine was born."

"I got it out of storage since it's such a nice day. How much trouble will you be in when Martell finds out?"

"Technically"—I grimaced—"CASE belongs to the university. And we're supposed to present it to Paul Swift tomorrow. So… kind of a lot?" I yanked harder. A thin ring of tape clung to the bobbin.

He didn't blink. "Could be worse. Probably just the campus police, then."

"Seriously?" I'd never even had a parking ticket. "Let's hurry."

The tape cartridge closer to Jackson clattered to the floor. "I win!" He raised his fists in the air.

I shoved the tote bag at him. "Watch out. There's a mushy apple in the bottom."

"Ew." He set the spongy fruit on the desk and then stuffed the wad of tape into the bag.

No, we didn't look suspicious at all, walking out of the server room with our bulging bags. I scurried up to the main floor and located the mail room and its industrial shredder.

When Jackson shoved the wads of tape into the opening, the machine chugged to life and started grinding. I breathed out a sigh. The shredding went much faster than the unspooling.

When Jackson finished his tape, I started mine. I kept one hand over my racing heart, pressing it back into my chest, while I used the other to feed the tape into the shredder. We'd be done in a couple of minutes, and then we'd peel off in Jackson's Lamborghini in a yellow blur.

"Samantha. What are you doing?" Martell's voice made me jump.

I turned the bag upside down over the mouth of the shredder to send the last of the tape through.

"That's not—that's not CASE." He held the wrinkled apple in one hand. His other hand covered his belly, which probably felt as queasy as mine.

I sympathized with him. Really, I did. He'd been kind to me, almost fatherly, since I'd come to the department. I'd done everything he'd asked, and it was probably a shock to find his meek little grad student destroying three years' worth of work and funding. Plus the seed money, the accolades, the papers he could have published.

"I'm sorry, Dr. Martell. I learned a lot on that tour, and now I know CASE isn't a good thing for books. Not the way I designed it."

"CASE didn't belong to you. It belonged to the university." He flung the apple into the trash as an exclamation point.

I sucked in a breath. He'd never raised his voice with me before.

Jackson stepped away from the wall, his palms held out in front of him. "Look, Dr. Martell. We'll pay whatever restitution is necessary to make you whole—"

"Jackson." I moved between him and my adviser. "This is my fight."

He nodded and stepped back, folding his arms and glaring at Martell.

"Dr. Martell, I can't keep going with CASE. It's a bad thing for too many people. It'll damage human creativity. And that's important."

"So is science. And business!"

"They're all important. But none is more important than the others."

His face went red, then purple. "I'm calling campus security. This is theft. Destruction of university property. Your mother will be so disappointed." He picked up the handset hanging on the wall.

Talking back to her was one thing. Being arrested? "Disappointed" was only the beginning.

"Better to go along for now," Jackson muttered. "I have experience in these, ah, situations."

"How many times were you arrested by campus police?"

His gaze arrowed to the ceiling. "Actually arrested or just…the subject of discussion?"

"Really?"

"Nine," he said.

"Was that arrests or discussions?"

He opened his mouth to respond, but Martell slammed the handset back onto its cradle. "They'll be here shortly."

Jackson let out a fake sigh. "This would've gone so much better for you if you hadn't done that. You'd never have had to apply for funding again."

Martell stilled.

"But now that Samantha's little error in judgment is going to be made public, I'm afraid the Joneses are going to have to flex some muscle."

Jackson's evil smile said he'd enjoy flexing his muscles.

But as I sat beside him in the back seat of the university police car that looked almost exactly like an actual police car with its flashing red and blue lights, and with the officer on his phone with someone who sounded suspiciously like the San Francisco police department, Jackson didn't look like he was enjoying the fallout of our adventure.

I'd been trying to destroy only my own future, but somehow I'd also managed to ruin Martell's dreams and make my brother an accomplice to my first-ever criminal activity.

Fantastic.

$$39$$

NIALL

I SLOSHED through the revolving door and paused to wring out my shirt tail on the hotel lobby's carpet. A sneeze exploded out of me. Great. Some bug had finally gotten through my barriers of handwashing and sanitizer, like the pounding Seattle rain through my water-resistant jacket.

"You said Seattle wasn't rainy in May," I grumbled, peeling off the fair-weather jacket. I grimaced. I'd just blamed the weather on Gabi. What was next, homelessness and climate change?

Gabi gritted her teeth. "Let's check in, then we can warm up the way the locals do, with a nice, hot cup of coffee."

"What are you, Mary Poppins?" I snarled. I didn't want coffee. I wanted a shower, dry clothes, and a warm bed. And for my heart to stop aching. I definitely didn't want Gabi, with her false cheer and concerned looks. "I don't need a nanny, you know."

She scanned me from the damp hair dripping in my eyes to my wrinkled plaid shirt to my squishy lace-ups, and when she met my gaze again, a chill ran through me. "A babysitter is exactly what you need. You're stuck with me until you can admit how messed-up you are."

"Me, messed up?" I plodded past her, dragging my rain-spattered suitcase to the end of the line at the hotel desk. "I'm a fucking Tower Prize winner on his goddamned victory tour."

"She's not worth it." Gabi's hair was already puffing up as it dried. "She's not worth your misery."

I lurched forward in the line. "I'm not miserable. Can't you tell I'm angry?"

One corner of her mouth turned up. "Is that what this is? The moping around, the hiding in your hotel room at night, the sighs whenever we pass a copy of *Magician in the Machine?*"

"I don't do that," I snapped. I hadn't felt particularly sociable after all the book events. But I didn't sigh when I saw her book— that *computer's* book. That made my blood boil.

Gabi glanced at the top of my head. "You're steaming."

"I'm soaked. And it's warm in here." I tugged at my collar.

"Did you know *Magician in the Machine* finally made the best-seller list this week? Seems people want to read a book written by a computer. That or they want to see what all the fuss is about."

"Great. That's fucking fantastic. Why am I even bothering to write a third book? Might as well just ask S—that machine to—to spit one out for me."

"Might as well," Gabi said, her tone infuriatingly mild. "Hey, the university in San Francisco asked if we could swing by there for a talk. The one where you spoke last summer."

It was like plunging into the ice-cold pool at the quarry. I shivered in my damp clothes. "A talk? In San Francisco? At the university that funded that—that monstrosity? Where S-Sam is?"

"Day after tomorrow. No big deal, right? We'll take their olive branch and show them who owns literary San Francisco. Hint: not them. Not her. Am I right?"

She might not even be there. She might be in New York, hooking up her A.I. at the publishers' offices. Replacing me and every other artist who hoped to publish a book. I spoke with more confidence than I felt. "Right."

"So I'll tell them yes?"

"Yeah, why not?" That skip in my heartbeat was excitement about the opportunity to sell more books. Or a heart palpitation from the potentially deadly illness I'd caught. Not nervousness about seeing Sam again. And certainly not hope.

After we checked in, we rode up together in the elevator. When Gabi stopped at her door, she pulled a phone out of her purse.

"Want to call home tonight?"

At the start of the new tour, I'd stayed up all night, cradling the phone and obsessively reading every news article I could find on Sam. And then I'd pulled up my texts. I'd read the last one from Sam so many times I'd memorized it:

> Sam: I can't tell you how much I regret what I did
> with CASE. Can you forgive me?

After dragging through the following day's events with icy anger knifing through my belly, I'd asked Gabi to hold on to the phone for me. Indefinitely.

As much as I could've used comfort from Mom or Grandpa, I couldn't trust myself with the technology. Not when we'd be in her hometown in two days.

"No, I'm good."

"Want to meet me in fifteen for that cup of coffee?"

"No, I—I think I'll order room service and stay in. I'm going to try to write."

Gabi stared at me, unbelieving. I'd been too afraid to tell her. Afraid of jinxing it. Maybe I no longer relied on a muse, but I hadn't given up every superstition I held about my writing.

For a week after I'd learned the truth about Sam, I'd moped. My so-called muse had turned out to be anathema to everything I loved, everything I stood for. Everything I *was*. Intentionally or not, what she'd created had the potential to destroy it all. To destroy me. All my friends in publishing. The farm, Grandpa, and Mom, too. Not all at once, but in a smaller advance here, fewer copies sold there. Until we gave up.

Then, when I'd seen that press conference with Heidi standing beside Sam's graduate adviser, rage rose hot inside me and flamed out to the tips of my hair. Heidi should've been on my side, not that computer scientist's. Not Sam's.

I'd been in Phoenix. Drinking a beer at the bar in the middle of the afternoon, steaming not because of the desert heat but because of Sam. And I'd decided I didn't need a fucking muse. I didn't need to wait for my fingers to tingle. I needed discipline. That's what my father had needed to turn an idea into a global business. What Sam had used to produce that A.I., CASE. No one ever complained about programmer's block. And wasn't my job just as real, just as valid as hers, despite what she thought?

I'd stomped upstairs to my room, dug out a notebook from the bottom of my satchel, sat at the desk with my back to the sunny window, and wrote. I didn't bother to question the quality; it was words on the page, something to start with. Eventually I'd be brave enough to hand the pages to Gabi and find out if the new ending to *Battle of the Wood Elves* was uninspired garbage or the start of something good.

Gabi shrugged and slid her keycard into the slot. "Suit yourself. I'll be in the restaurant downstairs if you change your mind."

"Thanks, Gabi." I did need her. And I was glad she knew it.

When I opened the door to my room at the end of the hall—after only two tries to get the key to work—I gazed out the window through the clouds and the misting rain to the glow of the Space Needle. The light on the antenna flashed slowly.

If she were there, would she gasp at the view? Would she sit beside me on the sofa, holding my hand and watching that light blink?

Sam.

Sam.

Sam.

Each flash was a turn of the screw inside me, tightening my chest.

I shook my head. Ridiculous. Sam was on her way, Ph.D. in hand, to that postdoc in the middle of nowhere, far from the consequences of what she'd done. Far away from me.

I dropped my suitcase at the door and pulled a notebook from my satchel. I wheeled the chair to the other side of the desk so my back faced the window. I flipped the notebook upside down and began to write.

40

SAM

"OOH, SAM. THESE ARE FUN."

Marlee stood at my dresser, holding the black lace panties I'd last worn in Niall's hayloft. When we'd…

"Toss them." I pointed at the garbage bag in the middle of my bedroom. "And stay out of my underwear drawer."

She dropped them into the moving box she was filling and scooped the remaining contents—mostly cotton panties with the elastic escaping at the leg holes—into the garbage bag. "I'm out of it. We're almost done, right? Tyler and Andrew should be here in about an hour to pick up your stuff."

"All that's left is the bathroom and this." I yanked open my nightstand drawer. When I saw what was inside, I flopped onto the bare mattress.

"What is it?" Marlee flitted to my side. "Oh."

I'd never gotten beyond the first few chapters in the hardcover books, but I listened to them almost every night. And sometimes —I wasn't proud of it, okay?—I opened the books to the title pages with his signature. He pressed hard with his pen, and on the copy of *Treachery of the Wood Elves,* I imagined I could feel the groove where the nib had creased the paper.

Marlee sank onto the mattress next to me. "You still love him."

"No, I—" She'd never let me hear the end of it. "I don't."

"Sam." She rubbed a circle on my back. "You're a terrible liar."

Bilbo Baggins trotted out from his hiding place under my desk, hopped up onto the bed, and snuggled against my hip.

I rubbed at my eye. "It's dusty in here."

"Sam. Have you reached out? Asked him to forgive you?"

I sniffed and blanked my expression. "Of course I did."

"And?"

"And nothing. He doesn't want to hear from me ever again."

She hugged me and rested her chin on my shoulder. "When I fucked things up with Tyler—remember that? When he went to Texas and got a new job? I called. I texted. I even sang a song on his voice mail. I was completely ridiculous. But it worked in the end. You should try again."

I thought back to last December when Tyler had come back from Texas. "He forgave you in person at the holiday party."

"Yeah. I guess my song didn't work all that well. Maybe don't try that. What worked was looking him in the eye and asking him to forgive me." She squeezed my shoulders. "Think about it. I'm going to pack up the bathroom while you finish up here, okay?"

"Okay." How could I ask Niall to forgive me in person? According to Jackson's lawyers, I couldn't leave the state.

I knew one person who'd know if he was coming to California. And I needed her forgiveness, too.

I pulled my phone out of my cargo pants pocket and scrolled through the missed calls until I found Qiana's name. I pressed Call.

41

SAM

ONE GOOD THING about moving in with your brother and sister-in-law is the access to disguises. Which I needed if I was going to stroll onto a campus where I'd been banned. For life.

Alicia had loaned me a pair of jeans. I had to cuff them at the bottom—curse her unnaturally long legs—and I missed the convenient pockets of my cargo pants. But not having a lot of items in your pockets is a good thing when you're arrested, right?

Noah had let me borrow a gray zip-up hoodie that'd make me look like every other student on campus.

Jackson wasn't there. In fact, he'd been away for about a week dealing with a disaster his best friend, Cooper, had caused. Which was odd because Jackson was usually the screw-up, not Cooper. Most of the time, Cooper had to swoop in to save my brother. Regardless, Alicia gave me one of Jackson's ball caps with some sports team's logo.

I tugged my ponytail through the gap in the back. "How do I look?"

"Like someone who goes to my school," Noah said from the back seat of their giant SUV.

"Like you're about to rob a bank," Alicia said. "All you need is a pair of oversized sunglasses. I don't understand why you had to change up your look."

My rule-following sister-in-law was already pissed about the trouble I'd gotten her husband into, so I'd neglected to tell her I was about to sneak back onto campus. I stared at the console and mumbled, "I thought I needed a change."

"You don't need to change. He loves you just as you are or not at all. And don't try what your brother did. No grand gestures. Just talk to him. Tell him you're sorry. Tell him you love him."

Romance-obsessed Marlee had texted me a list of grand gesture ideas the day she'd helped me move. "Marlee wants me to wait for him outside his hotel. With a mariachi band. Or possibly a marching band? Autocorrect might've garbled it."

Alicia tugged my hat up out of my eyes. "If you wanted to use your programming powers for good, you'd make an autocorrect that suggests things people actually want to say. But you're not really hiring a band, are you? You're just meeting him for coffee." She pointed out the window at the café. Beyond the opposite window, across the street, was the university's main entrance.

"Right."

I'd called Qiana to grovel for forgiveness. She hadn't been as angry as I'd thought she would. Though she'd made me promise to visit her as soon as I could leave the state. She still had her job, and she'd told me about Niall's book talk at the university.

I planned to find him there. When we'd toured together, he'd always talked with a few readers after. And I couldn't let the tiny complication of my lifetime campus ban get in the way of that, could I?

"Good luck," Alicia said. "I know he'll listen."

I caught Noah's scowl in the rearview mirror. "I don't know why you have to talk to him. He's being a jerk by not answering your texts."

I turned in the seat to face him. "When you've done something bad and hurt someone, you have to ask for forgiveness. And then it's up to them to choose to forgive you. So I have to ask. Like I asked you to forgive me for not telling you about the book."

Noah traced a frayed spot on his jeans.

"You'll call if you need a ride home, right?" Alicia asked.

"I'll get a bus back. Don't worry about it."

"Sam." Alicia flattened her lips. "The only place Valentine will sleep is the car. I spend my life in this tank your brother insisted we buy. I'll pick you up, okay?"

"Okay. Thanks." I reached into the backseat for a fist-bump with Noah, and then I gently caressed Valentine's little fingers, snug inside her car seat. She smacked her pink lips in her sleep.

I slid from the too-tall SUV to the sidewalk and waved them away. After they turned the corner, I crossed the street to the university. I tugged my cap down low over my eyes, pulled up the hood over it, and, head down, trudged to the library.

The people ambling toward the building weren't scruffy students like me. They were older, possibly faculty members or university donors. The men wore suits or sport coats, and the women wore dresses. Not a pair of jeans like mine in sight. And no hoodies. Shit, I should've asked Qiana about the dress code.

A couple of university police stood just inside the library doors. They briefly scanned me as I walked inside, and I felt their gazes on me as I merged with the stream of people headed toward the auditorium. I sped up to walk behind an older couple, trying to look like the kid they'd dragged along to get some culture.

Fortunately, no one questioned me as I slid into a seat in the middle of the auditorium.

My heart skipped a beat when I spotted Niall's russet hair at the front of the room. He bent over, listening to a shorter, dark-haired woman. *Shit!* He'd brought Gabriela. She'd never let me within six feet of him. How the hell was I going to talk to him?

The lights dimmed, and the doors shut behind me. I considered making a run for it and trying Marlee's mariachi band idea back at his hotel. But just inside the door stood one of the university police officers. He hadn't spotted me yet. I slouched in my seat, sweating in Noah's hoodie, trapped like one of the rats in the biology laboratory next door.

The lights at the front brightened on Niall, sparking his hair in bronze and copper and gold. His freckles looked pale in the harsh light, like he hadn't been out in the sun for a while. Had he been home to the farm at all, or had he been stuck inside in events like this one? Had he told his grandfather and mother what I'd done? The cold pit in my stomach deepened. I'd hated lying to them when I was there. Now they knew I'd lied. They'd been so kind, so trusting, so welcoming. And I'd hurt the person they loved most.

I'll admit it: I didn't hear much of what Niall said during his talk. In the anonymous darkness, I watched him like a creeper, wishing I hadn't ruined things between us. I wanted to wish I'd kept things strictly professional between us, that I'd never kissed him, never slept with him, hadn't gone to his farm and seen his secret writing spot in the forest.

But then I'd have never known the taste of him, the feel of his callused fingers on my skin. The brightness that lit up my darkness like a Christmas light display. Like fireworks over the bay. I'd treasure those memories, like Gollum treasured the Ring, clutching them close to my chest as long as I lived.

But unless I apologized for what I'd done, tried to make it right, there'd always be a dull spot of regret alongside those sparkling memories.

He didn't speak long enough for me to figure out a plan to sweet-talk Gabriela so I could apologize to him and then get past the security guard to escape. The lights came up and the question-and-answer session began.

The rear door beckoned in my peripheral vision. But now the officer had a partner. They guarded the exit, arms crossed. Were they watching me? I scrunched lower in my seat and slipped off the ball cap. It stuck out in the sea of suits.

"Samantha Jones" rang through the auditorium. I snapped up

my head. It was that blogger again, Kari Singh, and she had a microphone.

"—a student at this university. What are your thoughts about artificial intelligence?"

Niall's chest rose and fell the way it did when he'd been asked an unwelcome question. In the front row, Gabi turned and hit Kari with a murderous glare.

Niall cleared his throat. "Artificial intelligence has many uses, as my former tour partner would point out. Handwriting and speech recognition, for example. My agent, Gabriela Padrón, would love it if I'd adopt a handwriting recognition program and stop using her as a transcriptionist." He paused for the audience's chuckle.

"A.I. has the potential to benefit humankind in significant ways. However, as a creative, I have to admit I'm wary of A.I.s like CASE. Although, like many of you, I enjoyed reading *Magician in the Machine* and appreciated its unique use of language, its intriguing and unexpected plot twists, I think A.I.s that replicate human creativity have the potential to reduce or eliminate it. This is just my opinion, and I'd welcome a discussion on the topic between creatives like myself and programmers like Ms.—Dr. Jones and Dr. Martell." He smiled, but his eyes were sad.

I didn't realize I'd stood until the woman in the aisle nudged me with the microphone.

My heart pounded, and I couldn't draw in a full breath as all eyes in the room turned toward me. Niall didn't smile, didn't show any other sign of recognition.

"F-for-forgiveness." Shit, where was I going with that? I sucked in a deep breath and willed my mouth and brain to stop fighting for control. "How do you feel about forgiveness?"

He frowned, and every hope that'd risen from the chasm in my chest withered and died. "Do you mean as a theme in my work?"

"Um. Sure." The woman held out her hand for the microphone. I gripped it harder.

Down at the front of the room, Niall turned and strode a few steps to his left as if he were including the audience in his response. "As most of you know, redemption—which, I feel, is related to forgiveness, a way to forgive oneself through atonement for one's wrongs—is present in the first two books of the series. In *Secrets of the Wood Elves*, Nieven discovers he's the son of a distant king. He sets out on his journey to reunite with his father. Spoiler alert"—Niall grinned, feral and dangerous—"he discovers at the end of the first novel that his father's land vastly differs from the one in which Nieven was raised. Full of danger. Corruption. Treachery. Thus, the title of the second book. But Nieven, being a good little wood elf, thinks he can turn him. Another spoiler—sorry—he can't. And now the story is set for a battle between them. You'll have to wait for the third volume to see the outcome. To see if Nieven's father can be redeemed. To see if Nieven can redeem himself for the danger he's brought to his friends by leading them to the evil kingdom." Niall spread his hands in false apology, and several people in the audience groaned.

"But—" My voice rang through the auditorium, surprising even me. "Can Nieven forgive Lobelia?"

Murmurs rose from the people around me. In *Treachery of the Wood Elves*, Lobelia was a helper, a friend to Nieven. She'd done nothing that required forgiveness.

"Ah." Niall's eyes glittered across the auditorium. "I see you've anticipated me. Here's another spoiler, a small one. In the third book, *Battle of the Wood Elves*, Nieven learns Lobelia's dark secret. You'll have to wait for next summer to find out what that secret is and whether Nieven can forgive her."

The woman in the aisle wrenched the microphone from my grasp and skipped down a few rows to hand it to the next person. I sank into my seat, not caring about the next question or about the campus police who'd surely recognized me by now.

He'd given Lobelia a dark secret. Of course that meant Niall couldn't forgive me. Just like he'd written his father into the story as a villain, he'd written me in, too. As a betrayer.

Wetness on my cheek. No. I wasn't going to cry. Not here. Maybe later in my room at Jackson and Alicia's. I scrubbed away the drop with the sleeve of Noah's hoodie and tugged the hood over my hair. Between the heads of the people in front of me, I gazed at Niall, and my heart crumbled to dust.

I owed him an apology. Maybe I could figure out some way to atone, too, and finally redeem myself. If I got out of there, I swore to whatever powers ruled the library, I'd go to his hotel. Forget the band, marching or otherwise. I'd apologize. And then, I'd give my entire first paycheck to the foundation. Anonymously. No, in Niall's name. It wasn't nearly enough, but it was a start.

But first, I had to get out of there. I couldn't apologize from the campus police's holding room.

While the questions continued, I plotted my getaway. A door about halfway down wasn't guarded. It could've been a closet. Or a passage to the next room, an escape. I'd wait until the end, and when everyone stood, I'd make my way to that side door. I'd slip through it. If it was a closet, I'd wait there until everyone had gone. If it led somewhere else, I'd follow it like Bilbo Baggins in the mountain tunnels. In fact, if I could inch in front of the people to my right and sneak over there—

People around me stood. It was my chance. I shuffled to the end of the row, and then I turned against the traffic to head down toward the front to the side door. It was just twenty feet ahead, but the readers moving toward the rear exit stalled my progress. "Excuse me," I muttered. "Sorry." Slowly, I inched toward the door.

At last, I stood in front of it. I grasped the steel knob. I twisted it left. No give. Right. Nothing. I pushed. It didn't budge. I twisted and pulled it toward me. No. It was locked. I turned the handle, jiggling it. Please please please *please*. Nothing. I glanced up toward the main door. The first police officer was still there, nodding at everyone as they exited. Where was the other one?

I spotted him, making his way down the main aisle. He caught my gaze. *Shit!* He was one of the university police who'd picked up Jackson and me from the computer science building. He'd detained us for over an hour in their holding cell that smelled like vodka and bleach. His grim stare told me he recognized me, too.

He made faster progress than I did. People parted for him in a way they didn't for me. He was a few rows up, and then he could cut through the empty row of seats to nab me.

I glanced down at the front. There was another door down there. And that one had a red exit sign. It wouldn't be locked. I'd have to pass Niall and Gabi to get through it. Maybe one of the people lined up would distract them with a question.

My back pressed against the wall, I shimmied down toward the front. Across the rows of seats, the officer did, too, his eyes narrowed at me each time I dared to look at him. No matter what she'd said, Alicia would not be happy to pick me up from the campus police station.

I sped up, shoving against the people who blocked my escape. "Sorry. Sorry. Are you okay? Sorry." But they kept coming, and that red exit sign didn't seem to get any closer.

At last, the bodies in front of me thinned, and I had a clear view of the door. The red EXIT above it was the most beautiful thing I'd ever seen. That is, until a pair of green eyes, shot through with gold, caught mine.

"Sam?"

"Niall." All my forward momentum dissipated.

"Ms. Jones." A steely hand clamped around my biceps.

The police officer. He'd haul me to that holding cell again. I'd have to call Jackson's outrageously expensive-looking lawyer. Or —I shuddered—Mother. And by the time we sorted it all out, I'd have one of those ankle-cuff monitors and Niall would be gone.

No. Not until I'd done what I'd come to do. I was done running. It was time to face my problems.

I tugged against the officer's iron grip. "Niall, I'm sorry."

42

NIALL

"NIALL, I'M SORRY."

Those big eyes of hers pleaded while the guard held her in a punishing grip. I knew exactly how easily her fair skin bruised, having left a few marks of my own on her thighs when she'd begged me, "Harder." I shook off the memory. That grip was going to leave a bruise on her arm.

"Hey," I said. "Ease up. What's going on?"

"Sorry, Mr. Flynn." The cop hardly moved as Sam tried to jerk her arm away. "We'll escort her out."

"Why?" Sam belonged there more than I did. Though she wasn't displaying her student ID. "Is there an issue with her identification?"

"She's not supposed to be here at all."

I'd practically dared her to come see me by showing up at her university. Why shouldn't she be there?

"Sam, what's he talking about?"

She growled and gave another futile tug of her arm. "I'm kind of banned from campus. But that's not what's important. What's important is that I'm sorry. I'm sorry I wasn't truthful when we

started the tour. And then I should've told you when we got…
closer." She shot a glance at Gabi, who had her arms crossed, her
hip cocked, and her eyebrows up at her hairline.

"I'm sorry that what I did with CASE hurt you. That I made it
seem like I didn't value your work. Your career. Because I do.
Your books are amazing, and I don't want you to stop writing.
Ever."

She was saying all the right things, and my ego was purring
like a cat. But—"Back up a second. Why are you banned from
campus?"

The cop broke in. "Unauthorized access to private property.
Theft and destruction of university property." He tugged her arm,
and she winced.

"Hey now." Gabi stepped up, arms on her hips. "You don't
need to use that much force."

"She destroyed over two million dollars' worth of intellectual
property."

Gabi's eyes widened, then narrowed. "She's also got a rich
family with a posse of fancy lawyers. I've got a phone camera,
and I'm about to start taking video." She pulled out her phone.

For once, I was thankful for technology. The cop's grip eased.
"I'm leaving campus now," I said, hands up in an *easy-there*
gesture. "I'll escort Dr. Jones off campus. No reason to make more
of a scene in front of all these donors."

As if he hadn't noticed the stares of the people all around us,
the cop looked around and dropped Sam's arm. "We'll just ensure
she leaves university property."

"Fine." I shouldered my satchel. "You okay?"

She rubbed her arm. "I'm good. But you can't call me Dr.
Jones."

Was I ready to bridge the distance and call her Sam? I'd have
to forget all the times I'd gasped her name while we'd made love.

Gabi led us through the exit, down a hallway, and through a
rear door that opened to the outside. It was May, and a cold
breeze slapped my cheeks, reminding me I couldn't fall under her

spell. I couldn't slip my arms around her and get lost in her herbal scent, in the comfort of her body. Not until we'd talked.

As we strode toward the parking lot, I bent toward Sam. "Theft and destruction of university property? What's that cop talking about?"

"I—Dr. Martell got an investment offer. From…from your father. He wanted us to add on more features, more genres. Deliver customized stories to people's phones. And they would've built more CASEs. To sell to publishers. They would've flooded the market with cheap product, and I was worried about what would happen to you and your books. I—I couldn't let them."

I stopped walking. Goosebumps rose on my skin, and not from the evening breeze. "Sam, what'd you do?"

She stared off into the middle distance. Or maybe she was looking toward the computer science building. "I erased the program. And shredded the backups. Jackson and I did. Dr. Martell was not pleased."

You can't call me Dr. Jones. No. "You don't mean he took away your doctorate?"

"He'd never signed off on my dissertation. And now he never will. I'm out of the program."

"But what will you do now?" It was the only thing she'd wanted. My heart cracked for her shattered dreams.

She smiled at me crookedly. "I've still got my programming skills. Connections. I'm starting work at Jackson's company Monday. We had an idea for a…a piece of software." She faltered and stopped.

I glanced back at the police officers, who continued to advance. I slung an arm around her shoulders and propelled her toward the rental car.

"It's book-related software." She spoke quickly, excitedly. "We'd like to partner with some authors and build roleplaying games based on their books. Using artificial intelligence to make the character interactions in the game more realistic. It's not the same as CASE. We'll be starting from scratch. That is, if any authors are interested in working with us. With me."

Gabi had been walking a few steps ahead of us, but she stopped and turned. "I know some writers who'd be interested. If the money's good." She cocked her hip and crossed her arms in a power stance.

"Um, you'll have to talk to Jackson about the money. I'm just the programmer. But I'm sure it'd be fair."

Gabi raised an eyebrow the way she did when she thought she could increase the size of the pie or whatever negotiating bullshit. "Maybe you need a consultant to help you develop the profit-sharing model."

One corner of Sam's mouth lifted into an almost-smile. She unlocked her phone and handed it to Gabi. "Put your details in there, and we'll call you next week."

Gabi grinned. "I think this is the beginning of a beautiful friendship." She typed in her details and handed the phone back. "If it's okay with you, Niall," she said, "I'll call a car. Do a little sightseeing. You'll take Sam home, right?" She tossed me the keys to the rental.

"Is that okay with you, Sam?" I still had my arm around her, but I almost staggered back when she hit me with the full force of those violet eyes.

"Yeah."

"Be good, kids. Have a nice night, officers." Gabi walked to the corner just outside the parking lot, eyes on her phone and fingers flying.

I clicked the locks on the car and opened the passenger door for Sam. The cops watched from twenty feet away as I rounded the hood and got into the driver's seat. I pushed it all the way back and clipped my seatbelt.

I started the car. "You live around here, right?"

"Not anymore. I moved in with Jackson. Until I can save up enough for my own place." She looked out the window and rubbed her nose on her sleeve.

"Is Bilbo okay?" My heart froze. If she'd put him in a shelter, we were driving there right then. I'd be the diva dragging a purse pooch around on a book tour if I had to.

"He's fine. Jackson and Alicia have a cat who's not too much bigger than him, and they get along okay. I didn't bring him tonight. I didn't want him to—in case I got detained again."

"Sam." I reached for her hand and held it. She'd risked jail to come see me, to apologize. That had to mean something. Redemption.

A tap came at my window. The cop again. He tilted his head toward the parking lot's exit. I nodded. As soon as he backed away, I used my left hand awkwardly to put the car in reverse. I wasn't about to let go of Sam. Not after what she'd sacrificed for me.

Carefully, I steered the car to the exit and made a right turn, not caring if it was the correct direction.

A few blocks away, I pulled into the parking lot of a strip mall. "We're off campus now, right?"

"Yeah. Real police patrol this area."

"You aren't in trouble with the real police, are you?"

"Technically, I just violated a restraining order. So maybe?"

I leaned back in my seat and raised my eyes to the roof. "Why'd you destroy it, Sam?"

"Why?" She frowned. "For lots of reasons. For Qiana and the other people at Happy Troll. For Tamarah Starr and Kate Salazar and every other writer in that room at the prize ceremony. For the readers. For human creativity and art. But mostly for you, Niall. I want to read the end of the story."

"I want to read it, too." I didn't mean only the story of the wood elves. I lifted her hand to my lips and kissed her knuckles.

"Can you forgive me? You can think about it. You don't have to tell me today."

Warmth like molten gold rushed through my veins. "I already did. Thank you for making it right. Not many of those people you did it for will understand everything you gave up. But I do."

Her lips wobbled. "Thank you," she whispered.

"I'd like to start over if we can. No lies. Just truth from here on out."

"Start over?" She wrinkled her nose. "Like, from the beginning? Like, hi, I'm Samantha Jones, but you can call me Sam, and I'm a computer programmer living and working with my brother?"

I rubbed a hand over the back of my neck. "Maybe not that far back."

"Oh?" We were still holding hands, and she stroked her thumb across my knuckles. "What about as far back as when I said I liked you? We were friends then, I think. And I kissed you."

I leaned over the center console, and she met my lips gently, tentatively. But just as I angled my head to deepen the kiss, she pulled back.

"If we're only being truthful from now on, I have to tell you, all this starting over stuff?" She waved her right hand between us. "It's kind of silly because I already love you. And even if we back up and get to know each other as friends first, I'll still already love you."

The cold place in my chest warmed. "I love you, too. I didn't want to, not when I was so angry. But I do." Maybe I didn't want to go back at all. Maybe I only wanted to go forward, like Nieven always did. "I missed you. The tour wasn't the same. Would you consider joining me for the next part?"

"Ah." She grimaced. "Not only am I starting a new job, which I need to, you know, eat and stuff, but also, I'm not allowed to leave the state."

A chuckle rose out of my belly. "I see."

She rubbed circles on the back of my hand. "Just until Jackson's lawyers do their magic. They've gotten him out of worse stuff."

"Worse stuff?" What the hell had he done?

"There could be a big donation to the university involved. It helps when your brother's fabulously wealthy."

"I don't want to talk about him now. I want to talk about us."

"Sorry, I—you know."

"I know. It's one of the things I love about you, Sam."

I was glad we were parked because I'd have put us in a ditch if she'd hit me with her wide-eyed gaze while I was driving.

"I can't believe you still—" She bit her trembling lip.

"Sam. Sam." I cradled her cheek in my palm. "I love every part of you. Because that's what makes you...you. I love your big brain, especially when it gets away from you and you say more than you should."

"And I love your big heart." She put her hand over the center of my chest, and I clasped it. "Especially when it makes you want to take care of everyone you love."

"I want to take care of you, Sam. I wish..." I stopped. Sam could take care of herself.

"I know you need to do this," I said. "To use your brain and your skills to create a new life for yourself."

"A life for us," she said. "It's the two of us now."

Warmth filled my chest. Two hours ago, I'd never imagined I could be so happy. "We should go somewhere more comfortable than this rental car to talk through how this is going to work."

Her smile turned wicked. "I think we know exactly how this works. We got pretty good at it on tour." She slid her hand down and traced the waistband of my khakis.

My abs contracted, and my dick hardened. "Maybe we should, ah, dispel the sexual tension before we talk."

"I think that's a brilliant idea." She leaned in and kissed the side of my neck. "Our minds will be clearer."

I hoped so. Right then, my brain was too hazy to remember the way to the hotel. I had to rely on Sam's map app to guide us there.

Technology wasn't always a bad thing.

———

HOURS later in my hotel room, I jerked awake when Sam murmured, "Niall?" Her hair tickled my chin as she raised her head from my chest, which she'd been using as a pillow.

"Yeah?" The lamp was still on, and the light glinted off her dark hair when I brushed it out of her face. She wasn't leaving, was she? Not now, not when we'd finally been honest with each other.

"Do you think we could go back to the farm?" She scrunched her nose. "Or do your mother and grandfather hate me now?"

My racing heartbeat slowed. "They don't hate you. They'll be thrilled for us. They know I've been miserable without you. You really liked the farm?"

"Of course I did. It's part of you. When we were there, it was like you clicked into place."

"Sam." I gathered her to me, tucking her head under my chin. "You're the one who clicked into place in my life. When you were gone, a part of me went missing. I know it won't be simple to figure out how to be together, but we'll do it."

She hugged me tight. "Nothing about us is simple. Except this: I love you, and nothing, not even a lifetime ban from campus, is going to keep us apart."

"Not even the crappy cell service at the farm?"

"Nope. A little peace and quiet sounds perfect. As long as you're with me."

"Always." I stroked her hair. "Always."

EPILOGUE
TWO WEEKS LATER

SAM

WHEN THE ELEVATOR doors slid open on the sixth floor of the Synergy building, the energy was different. Wrong. It buzzed with anger like the fluorescents in the campus police station's holding cell. I shuddered at the memory.

Jackson's door was open, and Marlee and Tyler whispered at her desk in front of it.

"Hey, guys, what's up?"

Marlee jumped, her eyes wide. "Sam! What are you doing up here?"

"Meeting with Jackson. Is he ready?"

"Oh, ah"—she exchanged a look with Tyler and then flicked her gaze down the hall toward Cooper's office—"yeah, I think you're going to have to postpone that."

"Why? Did my brother flake again?" Last week, he'd forgotten about a meeting with me and hadn't come back from lunch with Alicia. When I'd ribbed him about it later, after dinner, he'd grumbled about not having any privacy in his own home anymore. Fair, since I was still living with him. But I'd been sure to take

Noah to the planetarium all day on Saturday and then to a sci-fi movie that night.

Tyler crossed his arms. "Jackson doesn't flake. He just has other priorities."

Marlee laid a gentling hand on Tyler's arm. "It's not your brother's fault. This time, it's Cooper." Her voice went low, and she twisted her lips.

"Cooper? I've never known him to—wait. He's back?" Cooper, who usually helped Jackson unfuck whatever he'd fucked up, had been AWOL since I'd come to work at Synergy two weeks ago.

"Yeah, and he really brought the drama this time. Wait until you hear what he and Ben—"

My phone buzzed in my hand, and I held up a finger. I had to be sure it wasn't the hapless intern Jackson had hired to help me. He needed more care and feeding than Bilbo Baggins.

"Hello?"

"Ms. Jones, it's José at security. You have a visitor. A Mr. Flynn."

"Niall's here? But he's in…" Where was Niall supposed to be? St. Louis? Kansas City? Somewhere in the middle of the country.

"He's asking to see you. Should I send him up?"

"Hell, yes! I mean, yes, please. I'm on six." My finger shook over the red button. Niall was in San Francisco? I wasn't ready. I ran my fingers through my hair, but they snagged in my loose bun. Shit! I pulled it out and finger-combed my hair.

A smile teased at Marlee's lips. "Look at you. Ms. I-don't-want-a-man is nervous because her boyfriend shows up to sweep her off her feet." She leaned into Tyler, and he put his arm around her.

"Don't be smug. Do I look okay?" I smoothed down my Flash Gordon T-shirt.

"You look great," Tyler said. A dimple creased his cheek. I could always count on Tyler to say the right thing.

"Gorgeous." Marlee flicked my hair in front of my shoulder.

"Though someday, I'm going to convince you to rethink those cargo pants."

"You'll rip my cargo pants off my cold, dead—" Behind me, the elevator pinged, and I whirled to find my redheaded Viking stepping out of the metal doors. "Niall!"

In four strides of his long legs, he'd wrapped me in his arms. I breathed in his piney scent. *Home.* I might've wrecked my own dreams and ended up as a midlevel programmer in my brother's high-tech building with underpowered servers, but now that Niall was there, I was exactly where I belonged.

"Sam," he whispered into my ear. His lips tickled my neck, and I shivered.

"You're supposed to be in—"

He kissed me, and the firm slide of his lips made me forget what I was saying. "I couldn't wait," he murmured.

"Hey, Niall," Marlee said. "It's nice to meet you in person."

Reluctantly, I released him. Social niceties sucked. "Niall, this is my friend, Marlee. You guys met on a video call while we were on—while we were traveling." I didn't love remembering all the lies I'd told while we were on tour together. "And her fiancé, Tyler, who's also my friend."

Niall shook hands with them both. "I've heard a lot about you two."

"He wants to know about my life and stuff." I wrinkled my nose. On our nightly phone calls, I just wanted to get to the phone sex, but Niall actually wanted to talk. Which was fair, I guessed, since I hadn't told him much about my life while we'd been together on tour.

"That's so sweet!" Marlee's voice went into that high register it did when she talked about romance.

I rolled my eyes. "There's nothing sweet about what I want to do to my boyfriend after two weeks apart." I let my hand trail from his back down to the taut curve of his ass, and I squeezed it like a ripe orange. He shifted me in front of him, and the ridge of his erection poked my hip. My brain fuzzed. I needed to get my hands on him. Pronto.

"Is there, like, an empty conference room or supply closet around here?" I pressed back against him.

Marlee flashed me an obnoxious grin. "Jackson's in Cooper's office, so you can go in there." She pointed at Jackson's office.

"See you later, Sam." Tyler's voice floated in just before my brother's office door slammed behind us.

Jackson's desk was in its usual disastrous state, strewn with hardware and papers. I tugged Niall toward the seating area. The sofa was small, but it would serve my purpose. Namely, my getting-into-Niall's-pants purpose.

"Wait." Our joined hands yanked me to a stop. Niall's mass meant he had a lot of inertia when he wanted it.

"Wait? Why?" There was a desperate ring to my tone, but I didn't care. "It's been *two weeks.*"

"I know, sweetheart. I was so desperate to get my hands on you that I flew here from Omaha for a night."

Omaha, right. "How was the book talk? Did anyone slip you her number?"

The color at the tops of his cheeks told me someone had. But it didn't matter. Niall Flynn was all mine, regardless of how many miles separated us. I didn't have to be jealous ever again.

"I've got to be in Denver tomorrow morning. But I wanted to spend tonight with you."

My chest warmed. "I like the sound of that. And we're still meeting at the farm in two weeks?"

He wrapped his arms around me. "Of course. The wifi's good, according to Grandpa. You'll be able to work as much as you need to."

"And you'll be writing. You'll read the new words to me at night?"

"Among other things." He nuzzled my neck, and need pooled in my core.

I tugged at the top button of his flannel shirt. "Show me these other things."

He stilled my hands. "Isn't there somewhere with a little more privacy? I, ah, feel like we have an audience." He nodded toward the glass wall. Marlee's and Tyler's shadows darkened the closed blinds.

"Jackson's place is too far. Besides, Alicia works there during the day. But"—the brain flash hit me like a sledgehammer—"my brother has the most amazing executive washroom."

I led him to it and opened the door with a flourish.

Niall squinted at it, hesitating at the doorway. "Amazing? This isn't any bigger than my closet at home. And the farmhouse's closets were built back when people had two, maybe three changes of clothes."

I peered into the four-by-six space. "What's amazing about it is that it has a flat surface. And a door. Now get inside so I can fuck you."

"Such a poet." He chuckled. But he backed in, tucked me into his chest, and toed the door closed.

"I'm the programmer, remember? You're the poet. Ravish me with some words."

And you bet your ass, he did. And the best part? Words were only the second-best thing that tongue of his was good for.

Thank you so much for reading *Trip Me Up!* Please consider posting a review on your favorite retailer, BookBub, or Goodreads. Reviews help other readers find new authors like me.

Want to see how Sam and Niall figure out their lives together? Join my newsletter at michellemccraw.com/Trip or use your phone's camera to take a picture of the QR code below to download a bonus epilogue!

The next book in the series, *Boss Me,* is a juicy, forbidden vacation romance between Cooper Fallon and his assistant. (Gasp!) Read on for a sneak peek of this return to Synergy.

BOSS ME (SYNERGY BOOK 4)
CHAPTER 1

BEN

TROUBLE CAME in the shape of a pair of broad shoulders.

Even hunched forward, bracketing his drooping head, they were wide and muscled, his biceps barely contained in a paper-thin vintage Rolling Stones T-shirt tucked at his narrow waist into a pair of jeans. His ridiculous Austin, Texas, belt buckle was as big as my hand.

When I hung out with the other admins at coffee breaks, they swooned over Jackson Jones's rakish good looks and flirtatious personality.

Not me. I left that for my boss.

Wait, sorry, did I say that? Regardless, I knew Jackson Jones was trouble.

He scuffed to my desk and turned a pair of bloodshot eyes on me. "He in?"

God, I wished he wasn't. Or that I could lie and save my boss from whatever fresh hell Jackson was about to drag him into.

"Something I can help you with?" I stood and smoothed down my navy merino wool sweater. I wasn't a tall man, but standing, I didn't have to crane my neck up at Jackson.

He chuckled. "Not unless you've got a miracle cure for whatever baby bug took down my kid, my wife, and the nanny."

"Sorry, I'm fresh out—oh. You're supposed to go to Boston today."

"Yeah. About that…"

I winced. My boss had just gotten back from a trip to Asia the week before. He hadn't had time to recover from the jet lag. And Jackson was about to ask him to get back on a plane to fly across the country and screw up his body clock again.

But Jackson thought Cooper Fallon was Superman, that he could do it all—his own job as the Chief Operating Officer and Jackson's job, too.

It didn't help that Cooper did nothing to dispel that notion. When Jackson asked him to jump, he asked how high. According to the executive assistant who supported Synergy's board, who'd been there almost since the beginning, it had been their dynamic since they'd founded the company over a dozen years before. They were partners, but it was nothing like 50-50. More like 80-20. And Cooper always ended up on the wrong end of that ratio.

"So can I go in?"

I hadn't realized I'd moved in front of the glass door to Cooper's office, blocking his partner from entry. I wished I could tell him no to protect Cooper from Jackson and from his own overcommitment, but Cooper didn't want to be protected from Jackson.

Even though he needed it.

Deliberately, I lowered my shoulders from where they'd crept up by my ears. I turned and rapped on the door before I pushed it open and stuck my head into the opening. "Mr. Fallon?"

When he turned from his monitor, the blue light lit his face, turning his normally golden tan skin greenish pale. His eyes were red, too. Not as bad as Jackson's, but I could tell he'd spent too much time staring at spreadsheets. He lifted a hand to the juncture of his neck and shoulder and kneaded the muscle there. I wished I could do that for him, but that would've violated our unspoken no-touching rule.

"Ben, how many times have I asked you to call me Cooper?"

I let one side of my mouth curl up. "About once a day since I started working here six months ago, Mr. Fallon."

"So approximately one hundred twenty times. And how many more times do I need to tell you before you listen?"

The snap in his tone might have scared someone else. Cooper Fallon was famous for his relentless drive and his quick temper. I knew he'd never follow up that bark with a proper bite. Maybe with an executive like Jackson, but not for someone at my level. I'd watched him, probably more than was healthy, and I knew from many hours of careful observation that even though his tone was sharp, he usually kept a leash on the fury that flashed in his blue eyes.

"Oh, I listen," I said.

Behind me, Jackson cleared his throat, and the smile melted off my face. "Jackson is here to see you. Do you have a minute?" *Please say no.*

He ran a hand through his sunkissed hair and stood, his six-foot-four frame unfolding with athletic elegance. "Send him in."

I held in a sigh and pressed the door all the way open, stepping into the office, and said more formally than I needed to, "He can see you now."

Jackson shuffled past me. "Hey, Coop."

Cooper strode around his desk and clapped Jackson's shoulder. They were about the same height, two gorgeous physical specimens, but only one of them turned me inside out whenever I was in his presence.

I stayed there, pressed against the door. "Can I get you anything? Coffee? A sandwich?" Had Cooper eaten lunch? I'd gone to the cafeteria with Jackson's assistant, Marlee, but I wasn't sure if Cooper had left his desk.

"Would you get me a coffee, please?" Jackson asked.

"Sure. How about a green smoothie, Mr. Fallon?" He'd need

the antioxidants to keep up his strength if he was going back out on the road.

His gaze flicked to me, and heat washed over my skin. But his words were crisp with frost. "Yes, please. Thank you."

And then, as much as I hated to do it, I walked out of his office and closed the door on Jackson Jones and Cooper Fallon.

———

I RUBBED at my throbbing temple and edged forward in line for the coffee kiosk in Synergy's soaring lobby. My gaze trailed up the glass elevator shaft to the sixth floor.

If I was any judge of the tightening around Cooper's eyes, he was suffering through his own headache. Not that he'd ever admit to being human enough to experience pain. Maybe I could slip him a pain reliever along with the revolting green smoothie.

Smoothies: my small but important contribution to the company. Cooper drank at least one a day. It was quick, efficient fuel for his duties as Chief Operating Officer of Synergy Analytics. Cooper kept Synergy running, and by fetching his smoothies, I did my part.

I scrubbed my hand over my face and stared out across the lobby. Who was I kidding? I didn't do it for Synergy. I did it for him.

I did it for the flare in those cool blue eyes when I handed the cup to him and said, "Your smoothie, Mr. Fallon."

I did it because of the infatuation that fluttered in my stomach the moment I shook his hand on my first day on the job six months ago. And as we'd worked together, as I'd gotten to know the driven executive who'd do anything for his partner and best friend, who'd grown the company from a business plan he'd written in a spiral notebook in their dorm room, who supported foundations that helped at-risk kids, those flutters moved right into my heart and never left.

My sister, Mimi, said I lived with my heart on the outside, and I'd fall for anyone who gave me a hint of returning my attraction.

Not true.

Cooper Fallon had given me no hints. He was always cool and polite. He said, "Thank you, Ben," at the end of each day. He'd given me an expensive but impersonal cheese basket for the holidays. He asked me about school sometimes, but he probably had to since the company was paying my tuition.

Yet I gobbled up those flares of heat when I handed over his smoothies.

A woman took her coffee and strode away from the kiosk, and I stepped forward, still two people from the front of the line. I checked my phone. Ten minutes since I'd left Cooper alone with Jackson.

Why had I tried to save time by coming downstairs to the kiosk? The place down the street knew our order. But I'd wanted to stay close enough to rescue Cooper if he needed it. Ha. Cooper Fallon would never admit he needed rescuing. Or a goddamned break from saving the world. I inched forward in line and tapped the toe of my chukka boot against the floor to relieve the nervous energy that made me want to shake someone.

Jackson, who was supposed to be Cooper's best friend, pulled this shit all the damn time. There was always a reason he couldn't take a trip or present to the board.

When I was first hired, Cooper handled it, no problem. But since Jackson's baby was born in February, Cooper seemed paler somehow. Not just his skin, but the whole of him. Like some of his actual life essence had been sucked out of him by that machine in *The Princess Bride*. His movements were smaller. His smile—rare at the best of times—was nonexistent now. Even that famous Fallon temper had cooled, like nothing was worth getting upset over anymore.

Maybe it was just a seasonal thing, and Cooper would spring back to life when the days got longer and brighter in the summer.

But I had a feeling it wasn't. It was a Jackson Jones thing. I dug a knuckle into my temple. Fucking Jackson Jones and his bullshit.

"Hey, Ben." The barista's voice snapped me back to reality. Finally, I was at the front of the line.

"Hey." I didn't come to the kiosk often, but I guessed the barista made it his job to know everyone's name.

"It's Kris." He winked at me, his dark hair flopping over one eye.

"Oh, right, I knew that. Sorry, Kris." Did I know that? "Do you have blueberries?"

Kris blinked. "Um, sure."

"Can you add a handful of them to a kale smoothie, please?" I checked my phone. Fifteen minutes, and no SOS text. That had to be a good sign. "And can I also get a black coffee and a skinny latte? Plus a caramel macchiato for Marlee. Please."

"Got it." He scooped fresh grounds into a French press. "You don't come here that often. Not as often as I'd like."

I flicked my gaze from his hands, which I'd been mentally urging to move faster, to his face. He had a Harry Styles look going with that floppy hair and those to-die-for cheekbones. Totally my type.

Except he wasn't. Not anymore. My type, apparently, was emotionally unavailable, blue-eyed billionaires. Fuck. My. Life.

My phone buzzed in my hand.

Marlee: 911. Need you NOW.

"Shit, sorry, 86 all that." I shot Kris a quick smile. The corners of his mouth turned down just before I sprinted across the lobby to the elevator bank. I pounded the button and whirled to scan the elevator doors behind me. *Open, open, open.* I hopped on my toes like that would make the elevator come faster.

At last, a door pinged, and I rushed to stand in front of it. The elevator was full, and it took every ounce of self-control I had not to shove past my fellow employees and then push them out.

When the car finally emptied, I darted inside and pushed the button for the sixth floor, then I slammed my palm over the close-door button. It wasn't the first time I'd had to rush back to my desk for my demanding boss. But I had a bad feeling today. Goddamn Jackson Jones.

I watched the floors light on the screen above the door and breathed deep. Maybe I was being unfair to Jackson. Marlee liked him. Everyone liked him. Including Cooper. In fact—

I rubbed my hand over the too-familiar burn in my belly. I needed to stop caring about Cooper. Like most people I'd fallen for, he was out of my league. Besides, his heart was otherwise engaged, and the sooner I got over my ridiculous crush, the better.

At last, the doors opened on the sixth floor, and I stepped out, my heart in my throat.

Raised voices assaulted the usual calm of the executive floor. They were coming from Cooper's office. A crowd of people gathered near the door.

Marlee trotted toward me on her pink kitten heels. Wringing her hands, she whispered, "Great galloping Galileo, Ben. They're fighting. Like, actually yelling at each other, and they wouldn't answer when I knocked. You've got to go in there and make them stop. Everyone's staring."

"Is Weston in there?" The CEO was Jackson's archnemesis, and neither man pulled any punches when they disagreed.

"No, just Jackson and Cooper. But I'm sure someone will tell Weston."

The tension in my chest eased. Jackson and Cooper got loud sometimes, but it never lasted long. At least the CEO wasn't witnessing it firsthand. Cooper could explain it away later. He had a magic touch with his boss.

I needed to capture some of that boss-magic for myself. "Back to work, everyone. Nothing to see here," I announced as I made my way to Cooper's office. Some people returned to their desks. Weston's assistant, Julie, more brazen, lingered nearby.

I raised an eyebrow, and slowly, she turned and plodded back to her desk. She didn't sit behind it but stood, staring, ready to witness whatever would erupt when I opened the door.

I knocked, but they were yelling too loudly to hear anything. I pushed the handle, but it didn't budge. Why was it locked?

Reluctantly, I flicked my badge in front of the sensor. It was keyed to only Cooper's ID, Jackson's, and mine. The light turned green. I sucked in a deep breath, pushed the handle down, and opened the door.

Cooper, his face red and his eyes bulging, roared, "I'm not putting up with your bullshit anymore!" He slammed his hand onto his desk.

It all happened so fast. When I replayed the scene later in my mind, I thought I remembered hearing a ping as if that big, ugly ring Cooper always wore had hit the glass top that protected the wood.

Regardless of what caused it, there was a crackle like fireworks popping and then silence. After a second, a shard of glass tumbled off the edge and jabbed into the thick carpet. A few smaller pieces followed it. Cooper stared at the surface of his desk. Then he looked up and scanned his best friend from head to toe.

Jealousy ignited in my gut. Why, even when Jackson was dumping his responsibilities on Cooper, was Cooper's first instinct to protect Jackson? What I wouldn't give to have that concern, that care, directed at me.

Shit, this was no time for me to moon over my boss. I had to do something to fix this. But my feet stuck to the floor. I was intimately familiar with his temper, but as far as I knew, he'd never hit anything.

"Coop—you all right?" Jackson's voice was funeral-quiet. It was the first time I'd seen him motionless.

"I—I'm sorry, Jay. It was an..."

I wanted to run to him, check that he wasn't hurt, but the

tension in the room was solid enough to keep me rooted at the door. I closed it behind me. "Everything okay in here?"

Clearly it wasn't. The top of Cooper's desk sparkled with shattered glass. His face was as white as the papers stacked neatly in his outbox. When a drop of blood plopped onto the desk, he raised his hand and gazed at it like he wasn't sure it belonged to him.

"Sh—I mean, here. Let me help." My feet unstuck from the carpet, and the next second, I stood beside my boss. His palm was crisscrossed with cuts, blood welling in each one.

I dug in my front pocket for my handkerchief and shook out the creases. I hesitated for a moment—that no-touching rule—but this was an emergency. He'd hate it if I had to disrupt his work to remove a bloodstained rug.

I folded the handkerchief in thirds and gently pressed it against his palm. His jaw tightened.

"Does it hurt?" The cuts didn't look deep, but I hadn't gotten a good look at them.

"No." The word held none of his usual crispness. Was he in shock?

"Sit down." With the hand I wasn't using to apply pressure to his wound, I reached up and pushed on his shoulder until he folded into his chair.

Finally, I looked at Jackson, whose mouth still hung open, staring at his friend. "What happened?" My tone wasn't as respectful as it should've been around the company's cofounder, but anything involving blood was extenuating circumstances.

Jackson leaped toward the desk and scooped the shards of shattered glass into a pile. "Cooper was making a point a little too forcefully. I guess he should've sprung for the tempered glass."

Fuck, if he kept doing that, I was going to have two bleeders on my hands. "Jackson, stop. I'll get maintenance up here—"

"Dammit!" When Jackson stuck his thumb in his mouth, his elbow caught the conch shell on Cooper's desk. The one I'd dusted once a week, each time wondering why he kept that one decorative item on his desk. I didn't have to wonder anymore. It tumbled off the desk, bounced once on the carpet, and shattered when it smashed on the wood floor.

The silence after was even louder than when Cooper broke his desk.

"Sorry, Coop, I—"

Pain flashed across Cooper's face. It was the same look he'd gotten the day Jackson wore his baby to the office in one of those backward backpacks. "Forget about it. I—I need to go."

"Now?" I lifted a corner of my handkerchief. The bleeding had slowed. "You can't go to a meeting like this." Only Cooper Fallon would continue his workday like nothing had happened after he'd sliced himself open. I wrapped the ends of the cloth around the back of his hand and tied them into a knot over his palm.

"People are used to me showing up as a hot mess. Not you." Jackson raked his hand through his dark hair. "Listen to Ben. Sit and rest a minute. I've got some whiskey in my office. We can—"

As soon as my fingers left the knot on the handkerchief, Cooper ripped his hand away. His blue eyes weren't as icy as usual when he turned them on me. Probably because of the blood loss.

"I need—out." He rose and stepped around me on his way to the door. His hand on the latch, he turned back.

Thank God, he was going to sit down and be reasonable. I took a half step toward him in case he wobbled on his way back to the chair.

But he stayed there, gripping the handle. "Ben, let the New England Entrepreneurs' Society know I'll be taking Jackson's place as the keynote speaker. And switch his hotel reservation to me."

Jackson popped his thumb out of his mouth. "Coop, you don't have to do that."

Cooper gave his best friend a wry smile. "Isn't that exactly what you were telling me I had to do before—before this?" He waved his handkerchief-wrapped hand at the mess in his office.

"But—"

He held out his palm. It trembled. He must have been exerting an enormous amount of control over himself. "Move all my meetings to next week."

What the absolute fuck was happening? "Yes, Mr. Fallon."

He opened the door and walked out, closing it gently behind him. No gym bag, no coat, no laptop. Was he staying in the building? Did he have a secret, primal-scream room downstairs?

"It's okay." Jackson hung his head. "You can say it. I'm the worst friend ever."

I couldn't help it. I smiled at the jerk. He was irritatingly adorable. "You totally are. But he loves you anyway."

He whipped his head up and grinned. "He does, doesn't he? I'm the luckiest guy in San Francisco."

My smile melted off my face. He fucking was. What I wouldn't give to be on the receiving end of one percent of that love. Jackson was too full of himself to notice, but I'd seen it from my first days at the company. Cooper was pining for his best friend. His obliviously straight best friend.

"You should get out of here," I said, my tone flat. "I'll call maintenance to clean this up."

"Thanks, Ben. I'll give Coop an hour or so to stew, and then I'll talk to him."

If I knew my boss, he needed more than an hour. And I guessed he'd get it on his last-minute trip to Boston. Which I now had to schedule.

Fucking hell.

I'd figure out a way to check on him, even in Boston. Because maybe Jackson Jones didn't give a shit about how much he'd fucked up Cooper's life, but I did.

————

Boss Me is available in paperback from your favorite retailer.

ACKNOWLEDGMENTS

Writing is hard, y'all. And this book was especially difficult for me to write.

Just about every writer I know has helped me with this one. Thanks to Bec, Bella, Lauren, Marit, and Yaffa, who read it when it was truly terrible and so kindly helped me make it better. I owe you all a case of eye bleach.

Thank you to Maureen Moretti, who saw the story's massive flaws but also the nuggets hidden inside.

Thanks Rhonda, Lauren K., and Carla, who convinced me I shouldn't throw this book away.

And thanks to my Contemporary Romance Writers group who write with me every week, especially Melanie, who boosts me and holds me accountable daily. Thanks also to Ainsley St. Claire for your steady encouragement.

I owe every one of you a drink someday when we can get together in person again.

CREDITS

Editing

Angela James

Proofreading

April Bennett, The Editing Soprano

Cover Design

Qamber Designs

ABOUT MICHELLE

Michelle McCraw loves reading kissing books and working in tech. One day, she decided to combine her two interests, and now she writes steamy, nerdy contemporary romance that just might make you laugh. Her books feature characters who unashamedly love science, engineering, and technology.

A native Texan, Michelle has shoveled snow during nor'easters and knows the proper response when someone yells, "O-H." She now calls Georgia home, where she doesn't miss snow AT ALL. She enjoys reading, travel, drinking bourbon, and spoiling her extraordinarily ill-behaved but adorable dogs. She has been a finalist in the RWA Vivian Contest, the Contemporary Romance Writers' Stiletto Contest, and the Windy City Romance Writers' Four Seasons Contest.

For updates about upcoming books and more free reads—plus guaranteed puppy pics—subscribe to Michelle's newsletter at michellemccraw.com. You can also follow the author on Facebook and Instagram.

facebook.com/MichelleMcCrawAuthor

instagram.com/MMOWriter

amazon.com/author/michellemccraw

goodreads.com/MichelleMcCraw

bookbub.com/authors/michelle-mccraw

when he rolls with it. But when their fake romance becomes real, will buttoned-up Mimi let down her guard for love?

"I absolutely love this twist on the grumpy sunshine trope." (5-star review)

Tempt Me

When a gaffe caught on camera threatens her company, a no-nonsense tech CEO calls on her bestie's little sister for help. But falling for her sunshiny public relations assistant could get her into even more hot water.

"THIS WAS FUN!!" (5-star review)

Fashion and Passion

After a disastrous self-help seminar, Carly finds friendship, empowerment, and maybe love with a younger admirer. Get swept away by sparkling banter, new besties, and spicy seduction, perfect for a bubbly escape.

Frenemies and Lovers

When Carly needs a date to her ex's wedding, she agrees to a deal with Andrew, a devilishly handsome younger man. Her frenemy's son. Who happens to be her one-night stand. What could go wrong? Who says you can't be fabulous over forty?

"Total catnip" (5-star review)

Books and Hookups

Writer Lucie's life is looking up: she has a new book deal, fabulous friends, and a bar where everyone knows her name. The last thing she needs is a surprise (geriatric?) pregnancy with her much-younger neighbor.

Conspiracies and Chemistry

Secretive billionaire Tessa seeks redemption from the biggest mistake of her life by betting it all on a groundbreaking biotechnology company, which happens to be run by her younger nemesis. And who knew lab coats were so sexy?

www.ingramcontent.com/pod-product-compliance
Lightning Source LLC
Chambersburg PA
CBHW051207190726
48288CB00006B/1849